DOC SAVAGE

The Wild Adventures of Doc Savage

Please visit www.adventuresinbronze.com for
more information on titles you may have missed.

Also from Altus Press

The Wild Adventures of Tarzan

RETURN TO PAL-UL-DON

DOC SAVAGE

GLARE OF THE GORGON

A DOC SAVAGE ADVENTURE

BY WILL MURRAY & LESTER DENT
WRITING AS KENNETH ROBESON

COVER BY JOE DeVITO

ALTUS PRESS • 2016

First Edition — May 2016

DESIGNED BY

Matthew Moring/Altus Press

SPECIAL THANKS TO

James Bama, Jerry Birenz, Gary A. Buckingham, Condé Nast, Jeff Deischer, Norma Dent, Dafydd Neal Dyar, Elizabeth Engel, Steve Holland, Henry Lopez, Dave McDonnell, Matthew Moring, Ray Riethmeier, Art Sippo, Doug Ellis, Howard Wright, The State Historical Society of Missouri, and last but not least, the Heirs of Norma Dent—James Valbracht, John Valbracht, Wayne Valbracht, Shirley Dungan and Doris Leimkuehler.

COVER ILLUSTRATION COMMISSIONED BY

Dave Smith

Like us on Facebook: "The Wild Adventures of Doc Savage"

Printed in the United States of America

Set in Caslon.

For Harold A. Davis,

Who came close to writing a version
of this story back in 1936....

Glare of the Gorgon

Chapter I

SHADOW OF THE GORGON

THE INDIVIDUAL WHO stepped off the Twentieth Century Limited and into the noisy din of Grand Central Terminal was trying to look inconspicuous.

He was doing a poor job of it. For one thing, he was bundled up in an ulster overcoat and gloves despite the mildness of the afternoon. His hat sat low on his broad skull and was squashed down hard, making him slightly lop-eared. This squashed effect was to conceal the man's hair, which was a flaming red. The snap brim was also pulled low, throwing his features into shifting shadow.

Conceivably, there existed men in the world whose hair was redder than the man who pushed his way through the disembarking throng with the impatient air of one who was in a brisk rush. But they would be hard to find. For the traveler was no mere carrot top. His hair—as much as was visible at the back of his head between hat and upturned collar—burned like coppery fire. It was vivid.

No doubt the passing years would dim that fiery luster if the man lived into old age. But he was not destined to live. Not for very long.

Taking the passenger-choked stairs upward, the remarkable redhead glanced about often, looking over his shoulder from time to time. Not frequently enough to be obvious that he was seeking to determine if he were being shadowed. But that was what he was doing. The casual way he went about it made it look as if he was marveling at the magnificent modern cathedral that was Grand Central Station.

The man appeared to be under thirty years of age. What could be seen of his face showed that it was clean-shaven, indicating that he had availed himself of a barber aboard the overnight train. His eyes were a somber and serious blue.

Exiting the station, he found a taxicab and flung his only article of luggage—a Gladstone bag—into the back and then threw his athletic form in after it.

Clapping the door shut, the redhead rapped out his destination to the driver.

"Hotel Paramount."

The driver was one of those who was good at recognizing accents.

"From Chicago?" he asked.

"Born on the West Side."

"Got a cousin in Cicero. Sit tight. I'll get you to your hotel in a jiffy."

With a whine of machinery, the cab pulled into afternoon traffic.

"You'll want to shuck the overcoat, buddy," suggested the driver. "It's not as cold here as it's been back in the Windy City."

Gaze shifting from window to window, the red-haired passenger seemed not to hear.

Piloting his hack, the driver surreptitiously observed his lost-in-thought fare. Studying passing scenery was typical of tourists new to Manhattan. But when the man twice flopped about in his seat to stare out the back window, the savvy cabbie understood that his passenger was watching to see if he was being followed.

The heavy ulster, upturned collar and downturned hat brim took on added significance. But the driver said nothing. It was not his business. Wrenching his curious eyes from the rear-vision mirror, he turned his full attention to navigating downtown traffic.

From time to time, he, too, looked about to see if they were being followed. He did not think so. So the hackman put that matter out of his mind.

Before long, the driver pulled in front of the Hotel Paramount, a bustling establishment catering to business travelers.

Eyeing his taximeter, the driver turned and said, "That'll be one-fifty. And if it will ease your mind any, we weren't followed here."

In the act of producing his wallet, the passenger started.

"Was I that obvious?" he croaked.

"Nah, you weren't. But I got eyes, and you look worried as hell."

Handing over two greenbacks, the passenger said curtly, "Keep the change."

"Don't mind if I do," grinned the cabbie. "Enjoy your stay."

Slamming the car door behind him, the passenger disappeared into the hotel lobby without another word. The hackman flung his steed back into traffic and put the worried man out of his mind. If he had known what was to soon befall his close-mouthed fare, he would have doubled back and flung him bodily into the back seat and conveyed the redhead back to Grand Central, there to personally place him on the next train back to Chicago.

But the red-haired young man was destined never to see the Windy City again.

STRIDING up to the front desk, the redhead accosted a thin-featured clerk and announced himself. "Dobe Castle. I wired ahead for a room."

The clerk consulted a book. Only after finding the name did he offer his welcoming smile.

"Yes, Mr. Castle. Please sign in."

While the new arrival was signing the guest book, the clerk turned to the rabbit warren of cubbyholes where messages reposed until called for. Fishing around, he produced an envelope and laid it and a heavy brass room key on the counter as the guest was returning the fountain pen to its onyx holder.

"What's this?" grunted the man who had signed his name, Dobe Castle.

People new to the big city were often ignorant of its modern ways. The clerk made a mistake; he thought the man was referring to the big brass key. He was not.

"It's your room key, sir."

"I don't mean that. What's this envelope?"

Blinking at the redhead's apparent mental thickness, the clerk patiently explained. "It is the custom of this hotel to accept messages for expected guests." He attempted not to sound condescending, and ended up coming across as annoyingly supercilious.

"I told no one that I was registering here," he snapped impatiently. "As a matter of fact, I wired my reservation from the train en route."

"The message is for Mr. Castle. That is you, is it not?"

As it later turned out, the name was an assumed one.

"Yes, of course," replied the spurious Mr. Castle, taking key and envelope and stalking off to the elevator, broad shoulders hunched belligerently.

The elevator operator eyed his solitary passenger as he whisked him upward. There were several good reasons for this study. The first was the man's heavy attire, and the fact that he continued to wear his hat indoors. The last was the brightness of the man's hair. It was strikingly, memorably red.

Noticing the other's eyes on him, the passenger grunted. "Do I fascinate you, or something?"

"No, sir," returned the elevator boy. "I just never seen hair so red."

"I've been hearing that refrain all my life," grunted the redhead without pleasure.

The lift found the fifth floor and the operator threw the door open, whereupon the redhead stepped off in search of his room.

Finding it, he worked the lock with the brass key, and entered. The room was clean and presentable, not much more. Bright sunlight streaming through the high window made the bed-clothes look newer than they actually were.

Tossing the Gladstone onto the bed, the supposed Dobe Castle stared at the envelope as if afraid to open it. When he did, he ripped the thing open at one end and shook out the message.

It was handwritten on hotel stationery. It said, "Call me. Urgent."

The note was unsigned.

The hotel guest sat down and extracted a package of cigarettes. Lighting one slowly, he smoked in silence. Only after the cigarette had burned down to a nub did he pick up the telephone handset.

A pleasant female voice said, "Hotel operator."

"This is Mr. Castle in Room Fifty-five," he said gruffly. "I wish to place a long distance call to Chicago. Person to Person to Miss Janet Falcon."

"Go ahead with the number, please."

The number was given and the wait was not long.

"Your party is on the line. Go ahead."

An anxious female voice asked, "Ned?"

"Listen closely, Janet. I just checked into the Hotel Paramount. There was a message waiting for me. It was unsigned, but it instructed me to call you."

"Oh, Ned. I sent no message. You didn't tell me where you would be staying."

"Exactly," the redhead bit out. "I made my decision on the train and wired ahead, thinking this precaution would protect me."

"Oh! That can only mean—"

"—that someone on the train eavesdropped on me. Someone in the know."

"Ned, they know where you are staying!"

"And if they know that, they may know that I've come to town to enlist—him!"

The woman's voice grew pleading. "You mustn't delay. You must reach Doc Savage. Tell him everything! But get him to come to Chicago."

"If I have to knock Doc Savage out and carry him piggyback, I'll get him to Chicago," he grated out. "Count on that."

"Ned, you can't remain in that hotel! It's not safe!"

"Don't I know it? Listen, we'd better not stay on the line. Someone may be listening in. I'll call you when I have Mr. Savage's answer."

"If anyone can untangle this frightful mess, he can," the woman said. "Please be careful, Ned. Please come home safely." Her voice was sobbing now.

"I will, Janet. I promise."

Hanging up, the hotel guest sank into a chair and broke out another cigarette. He smoked furiously, lighting a fresh cigarette by applying the glowing tip of the one about to expire to its replacement.

Sunlight filling the room made the crisp hair atop his head resemble a steady bonfire. Catching sight of his crowning glory in a decorative wall mirror, the redhead frowned deeply.

"I've got to do something about this red flag I'm carrying around," he bit out, the harsh words mingling with a long plume of tobacco smoke.

Reaching for his hat, the fire-haired one stood up to go.

In that moment, he froze.

For in the room, a nasty sound erupted.

At first, it did not seem like a human voice. A beast might have made the utterance.

Growling, the abrupt noise changed into a low, sibilant hiss. The hiss multiplied, becoming a frightful nest of noise, as of snakes fighting.

The awful sound seemed to untangle itself, and out of that miscellaneous agglomeration of nasal noises words began to form.

"Ned... Gamble...."

There seemed no source for the uncanny sound. No person or being who gave it voice.

"Ned... Gamble... your cause is known... your intentions clear. We hear you. We see you. You cannot escape us...."

"Who is speaking?" demanded the one so addressed.

"You will never reach Doc Savage, Ned Gamble...."

The weird voice wavered, became distorted. It possessed a peculiar quality that made it impossible to determine if a man or woman was speaking. Too, it evinced a disembodied quality, as if the vocalizations were emanating from a different sphere than mundane earth.

"Won't I?" Cigarette smoke squirted out with those challenging words. "You don't scare me, whoever you are."

Flinging himself to the closet door, the man addressed as Ned Gamble threw it open. It proved to be empty.

There was a midget radio on the dresser. Thinking the voice might somehow be piped in through that receiver, Gamble tried turning it off. But it was already off. Angrily, he yanked on the power cord. A blue spark spat as the plug jumped loose from the wall socket.

The voice continued, unaffected.

"Return to Chicago, Gamble. Return at once!"

"Never!"

Eyes skating about the hotel room, Ned Gamble sought the source of that warning voice.

The inner hotel room door bulged at its upper half. Gamble remembered that the other side had an identical bulge. These were the two halves of a modern convenience for busy travelers. Hatches. Each hatch was hinged. By this means a guest could place his suit coat in the inner side for retrieval by a bellhop, who could open the outer hatch from the corridor, taking the article of clothing to be laundered overnight and returning it unobtrusively by morning.

Springing the inner hatch with his fingers, Gamble discovered only frustrating emptiness within.

"Our eyes are upon you, Ned Gamble," the ugly voice continued. *"Go home. Go home and live. Remain here and die a petrifying death...."*

"I'll show you!" raged Ned Gamble. "Try and stop me."

Grabbing his hat, Gamble flung for the door, blowing defiant cigarette smoke after him. The smoke scooted across the room and seemed to produce a strange phenomenon.

The threatening voice was still speaking sibilantly.

"Seek not Doc Savage...."

The swirling cloud seemed to strike the unseen author of the warning. For the voice wavered weirdly, falling apart as if the spurt of smoke interfered with the disembodied one.

But Ned Gamble did not hear that. The slamming of the door behind him masked the inexplicable reaction.

NED GAMBLE eschewed the elevator and took the stairs to the lobby. There was a barber shop tucked in one corner, reachable directly by a glass door. He ducked in, threw his hat onto a wall peg and asked the idle barber, "How sharp is that razor?"

"Razor sharp," the other replied, at a loss for a more clever response.

Flouncing into the chair, Gamble pointed at the forest fire atop his head and instructed, "Get rid of this!"

The barber blinked. "This what?" he gulped.

"This crop of flamingo feathers that makes folks stare at me."

"You want me to cut your hair off?"

"No time for that," snapped Ned Gamble. "Shave it clean."

The barber had cut hair for a dozen years. He had seen some impressive heads of hair. This redhead was a wonder.

"Are—are you sure?"

"As sure as I hope to live to be a hundred."

As predictions went, it was to prove unfortunate. But neither man knew that.

Gulping, the barber began rooting among his professional implements for the correct tools with which to attack the magnificent thatch of adornment.

He commenced operations with a pair of electric clippers. In short order, the floor was littered by strikingly red curls.

In the chair, Ned Gamble smoked furiously. A hand mirror appeared before his face and the barber was asking, "How is that?"

"Shave it clean," Gamble growled. "Down to the bone if you can."

"You're the boss, boss."

Pouring hot water into the shaving-cream cup, the barber whipped up a fresh batch and applied the warm lather liberally. Giving his best straight razor a brisk stropping, he carefully scraped his peculiar customer's scalp clean, starting over the right ear.

The task was soon completed. Ned Gamble eyed his own reflection approvingly. Denuded of hair, his face looked broader, more rugged, as if belonging to a dock worker.

"My sainted mother wouldn't know me," he murmured. "What's the charge?"

The barber had no idea. He had never before been asked to scalp a customer. After some consideration, he said, "Shave and a haircut, one dollar."

Despite the fact that the price quoted was twice the going rate, he received two. The newly bald customer struggled into his ulster, his cigarette shedding hot ash. He was soon gone.

After the customer departed, the barber dropped into the vacated chair and marveled at the procession of humanity which passes through New York City.

"Takes all kinds, I guess…."

Then his dazed eyes alighted on the man's hat, still adorning a wall peg.

Thinking that the now-bald customer would need his hat more than ever, the conscientious barber grabbed it off the peg and ran after him.

The man had taken the passage back to the lobby of the Hotel Paramount.

But there was no sign of him there. Nor had the elevator starter sent him up, questioning swiftly disclosed.

"But I know the guest who wore that hat," the starter countered. "Had flaming red hair."

"Not anymore!" crowed the other.

The barber doubled back to the front desk and presented his problem.

The desk clerk recognized the fedora immediately.

"That would belong to Mr. Castle." He hit the desk bell, saying, "I will have the bell captain bring it to his room."

"Nix! Dibs on the tip."

The clerk sighed. "Very well. Take it up to Room Fifty-five. But a bellhop must accompany you."

"Thanks!"

A quick elevator ascent later, the barber was strolling down the corridor to Room Fifty-five, followed by a puzzled bellhop. Reaching the panel, he knocked.

A gruff voice replied, "Who is it?"

"Barber, sir. You left your hat behind."

"Keep it!"

"I can't do that," stammered the barber, sensing his tip going up in smoke.

"Then stick it in the clothes hatch. I'm busy."

Reluctantly, the disappointed barber did as he was told. Feeling for the catch, he sprang the bulging door open and made ready to place the hat inside.

The barber never completed the action.

The act of opening the hatch produced a result similar to Pandora opening her ill-omened box of troubles.

First, there was a greenish glare, followed by clouds of viscous smoke. These struck the unfortunate barber full in the face, blinding him.

Staggering back, the man let out a yell of baffled astonishment. Still clutching the fedora, he employed it to fan the smoke away from his face. The stuff spread, thinning, but the barber could not see that. The green flash had seared his eyeballs and he could see nothing.

Stumbling about, he discovered a wall, and used it for support.

"Help, oh help me!" he groaned.

THESE cries penetrated to Ned Gamble's room, where he was gathering up his things and depositing them into his open Gladstone.

Going to the door, he called through the panel, "What's the trouble out there?"

The answering voice came distinctly. "I—I can't see!"

"See what?"

The voice replied, but the words came haltingly, disjointed and slurring.

"Speak up!" Gamble shouted.

The thud of a falling body came unmistakably.

Ned Gamble hesitated, uncertain if it was safe to open the door.

Instead, he flung open the door-hatch, saw that its opposite hung open, and peered out through the open gap.

Gamble saw no one, for the stricken barber had fallen to the floor. At the end of the hall, the fire door was closing on the fleeing bellhop, but Gamble did not know that.

Across the corridor, the cream-colored wall had acquired a livid greenish-yellow splotch.

It appeared to be a shadow. The shadow had a shapeless quality, as if the person casting it were attired in sackcloth. But it was the fixed head that made Ned Gamble's eyes fly wide.

The outline was overlarge, and tangled, as if a nest of serpents were at war with one another. Forked tongues protruded. Fangs bared. But the serpentine mass did not move. It was as if the vivid yellow-green shadow was being cast by a hideous being lying in wait.

Ned Gamble exploded, "Hell's bells!"

Clapping the hatch shut, he grabbed up his bag, shoved open the window and took his departure.

The sounds of his stamping feet negotiating the fire escape rattled for a bit, then were heard no more....

Chapter II

FAINTING SPELL

THE DESK CLERK presiding over a rather down-at-the-heels lodging house situated near the Bowery looked up from reading a tabloid newspaper and scrutinized the individual who pushed in through the front door.

This individual was a man. Hatless, his completely bald head gleamed in the weak ceiling lights.

He strode up purposefully, and barked, "Need a room for the night."

The man's manner was so forceful that the clerk was momentarily taken aback. The individual's clothes were tasteful and well-kept.

"That will be two-fifty. In advance," the clerk told him, pushing the register book around.

Bending, the striking individual quickly signed his name.

Already suspicious, the desk clerk gave the register book a twirl, and eyed the name inscribed in moist ink. His suspicions became even more aroused. For the name the new guest had written was Harry Baldwin.

Narrowing eyes jumping to the man's open face, the desk clerk studied the crown of the guest's head.

Bald men have at least a fringe of hair around their ears, or some other indication that they once possessed a full head of hair. This man did not. His skull was absolutely nude in that regard. An egg might conceivably display more fuzz.

Many who sought refuge in this Bowery establishment lived on the shady side of the law. The clerk momentarily categorized the bald guest among that shifty legion.

"In town for long?" asked the clerk, handing over a brass room key stamped 205.

"Staying the night," the other said gruffly. "That's all."

"Travel far?" the clerk pressed.

The man shrugged. "Cincinnati."

The clerk did not think the guest's accent smacked of Ohio. But he avoided saying so.

"Your room is two flights up. We don't have a bellhop, but I see you don't carry much in the way of baggage."

"Thanks," said the guest calling himself Harry Baldwin. His Gladstone bag swinging in his left hand, he made a beeline for the stairs, and melted up them briskly.

There was a girl at the hotel's tiny switchboard, and the clerk bustled over to the corner cubbyhole where she worked.

"Hey, Mabel," he said. "New guest in Room 205. Says his name is Harry Baldwin. But I don't believe it."

"Sounds like a perfectly reasonable name to me," returned Mabel, in between methodically masticating a wad of chewing gum.

"This Harry Baldwin," returned the clerk, "is as bald as an egg."

"Coincidences happen," murmured the telephone girl.

"Not in this part of town. I want you to listen in on any calls he makes. Write anything down that sounds suspicious."

The telephone girl's eyes widened slightly. "You think he's on the lam?"

"This guest doesn't add up in my book," snapped the clerk, taking his departure.

"Okey-dokey," said the telephone girl, settling down to wait. She picked up a love story magazine with which to idle away the dull afternoon hours.

The telephone girl had not long to wait. The guest in room number 205 picked up the receiver in his room, opening the connection.

"Hotel operator," the girl said crisply.

"I wish to place a call to a private party in the city. His number is Empire 1-7900."

"Hold the line while I connect you to Central."

"Operator," said a feminine voice at the central telephone exchange.

"Party wishes to speak to the person residing at Empire 1-7900," the telephone girl requested.

"One moment, please," called the voice of the central exchange operator, who sounded like the telephone girl's twin sister, such was the uniformly professional manner of the women who worked modern switchboards.

Although eavesdropping was frowned upon in most hotels, this was the Bowery. After the connection was made, the switchboard operator remained on the line.

The phone rang twice. A remarkable voice answered, saying, "Doc Savage speaking."

The telephone girl's fingers flew to her carmine mouth, and repressed a gasp of amazement. The name was one she knew well. Doc Savage was an individual to be reckoned with, not just in midtown Manhattan, but throughout the world.

Doc Savage was famous the way kings and heads of state are famous. He was a man of astonishing accomplishments. Although he had been operating publicly for only a few short years, he had already stopped two revolutions, invented a new surgical procedure for brain surgery, designed aircraft that were five years ahead of anything with wings, and performed feats of strength and daring that may well be remembered one hundred years from today.

"Mr. Savage. Ned Gamble from Chicago. I wired you from my train."

"Your message was received," said Doc Savage. "But you neglected to state the nature of your problem."

The voice spoke matter-of-factly, but there was an arresting quality to it, a timbre that made the nerves shiver. It was as if the speaker was vaguely more than human.

"Listen, I hoped to come see you in the morning," continued Gamble, "but since sending that telegram, my situation has become desperate."

"Go on," invited the striking voice of Doc Savage.

"I checked into a certain hotel, and a peculiar thing happened. A disembodied voice threatened me, so I checked out fast to shake whoever had followed me here."

Interest flavored the bronze man's voice. "Followed by whom?" he inquired.

"I—I would rather not say over the telephone. But I must meet with you as soon as possible. I fear for my life. Evidently, the precautions I took before I left Chicago were insufficient."

"How soon can you get here?" asked Doc Savage.

"As soon as I can hail a taxicab."

"We will be waiting for your arrival."

"Thanks," said Gamble shakily. "A terrible thing is in the wind, and I believe you are the only man to stop it."

With that, Ned Gamble hung up the phone. The line went dead.

The telephone girl flung off her headset, and rushed out to the front desk, squealing excitedly. She loved to trade gossip with the front desk clerk, just as much as he enjoyed receiving it.

"You won't believe this!" she said breathlessly. "His real name is Ned Gamble. He's from Chicago."

"I knew he was a phony!" exploded the clerk. "What else did you learn?"

"You'll never guess who he rang up." The clerk looked expectantly. The girl chewed her gum, shifting it to the other side of her mouth, enjoying the interval of expectation.

"No less than *Doc Savage* himself!" she squealed.

The clerk whistled, the whistle misfired several times as if he couldn't quite control it. That was how greatly astonished it was.

"Doc Savage, the Man of Bronze!" he breathed. "He can't be a friend of Doc Savage's, not staying in a fleabag dump like this one. He must be in trouble."

"Oh, he is," chirped the girl. "He told Doc Savage it was life or death. He's on his way over there now."

The clerk struggled with the excitement that was firing his eyes. "They say if you have trouble that no one else can handle, Doc Savage is the gent to see."

"It was Doc Savage who solved that wave of mysterious pop-eyed killings last month.* And before that, he and his men brought that missing aviator everyone thought was dead back to civilization."**

The clerk nodded soberly. "Doc Savage is big stuff. They don't come any bigger."

A dreamy look came into the telephone girl's eyes. "I saw him once. Doc Savage stood almost seven feet tall. And so bronze he didn't even look human. And those eyes! It was as if they were solid gold. Can you imagine that? He's one of the richest men in the world and his eyes are solid gold."

Snapping out of his spell, the desk clerk suddenly got back to business.

"They are not really gold, Mabel," he scolded her. "They just seem that way."

"Well, they looked golden to me," pouted Mabel.

Their gossipy conference was broken by the rattle of footsteps tramping down the main stairwell.

"Get back on duty!" the clerk said quickly. "Here he comes."

The supposed Harry Baldwin dropped into the lobby, and bolted through without looking right or left. At the sidewalk

---

* *The Annihilist*

** *Python Isle*

curbing, he hailed a cab, there being no doorman to perform that civilized function.

A yellow cab soon pulled over, and admitted him.

The machine whisked the bald man away. Staring through the glass front door, the desk clerk's eyes followed the departing hack as it disappeared into traffic.

"What I wouldn't give to be a fly on the wall when that fellow sits down with Doc Savage!"

With that, the desk clerk returned to his boring and humdrum job, wondering if he would ever learn the truth about his new guest. He had no inkling what was coming. No one did.

THE ADDRESS that Ned Gamble gave his driver was undoubtedly the most famous in New York City. It was a skyscraper, the tallest in the metropolis, a modern marvel of limestone and steel that shot up one hundred stories over midtown Manhattan.

Only a few years old, the structure had already become a symbol of the great city and its engineering accomplishments. But the imposing edifice possessed another distinction. For several years now, it had served as the headquarters of Doc Savage.

As the cab conveyed Ned Gamble through noisy concrete canyons, the gleaming spire came into view in the afternoon sunlight.

Most tourists are struck dumb by its sheer magnificence. Not Ned Gamble. To him, the building was more like a beacon of hope. As the cab rolled northward, he could not take his eyes off it.

The taxi driver seemed unimpressed by his destination, which was a great office building housing numerous enterprises, not only Doc Savage. Many visited it every day, for business as well as sightseeing.

When the cab deposited him at his destination, Ned Gamble paid off the driver and alighted.

A newsboy was hawking the afternoon editions at the curb.

"Extry! Read all about it! Prominent Chicago inventor struck down!"

Hearing this, Gamble broke stride, and went over to the newsboy.

"Let me have one, son," he said, slipping the boy a dime.

There he stood rooted, reading the headline, and the columns of type that followed. His features gathered into a worried knot that pulled his forehead into wrinkles of corrugation, tightening his hairless scalp.

Tucking the paper under one arm, Gamble fished out a pack of cigarettes, shook it until a single tube of paper stuck up. He took this between severe lips.

His serious blue eyes looked worried, stricken.

Sets of revolving doors stood in front of the great skyscraper and many persons were coming and going, so the turnstiles of brass and glass were constantly in motion.

Eyes narrowed, lost in thought, Ned Gamble made for one of the turnstiles.

Evidently, another person had the same idea. Both endeavored to enter simultaneously.

They became jammed up with one another, and Gamble lost his cigarette.

"Pardon me!" the other man said hastily.

Gamble backed out, and tried to see where his cigarette had gone.

"Looking for this?" the other inquired in a friendly manner.

To Ned's mild surprise, the man he had bumped into was holding an unlit cigarette. The other wore a battered Trilby hat of olive green hue.

"It practically fell into my open hand," the fellow explained.

Accepting this, Gamble gruffed out a curt, "Thank you."

Both men held back, expecting the other to go first.

Finally, the other man gestured magnanimously and said, "You first, pal."

Nodding his bald head silently, Ned Gamble inserted himself into the wedge of glass and pushed his way into the lobby.

So intent was he on his business, that the bald man failed to notice that the man in the Trilby hat had not followed him inside. Instead, the other walked around the corner, for the great building had more than one entrance, and entered surreptitiously. He was grinning, as if he had put something over on someone. It was not a pleasant grin. In fact, it was rather crooked.

Had Ned Gamble observed that grin, he might have become suspicious and thrown his cigarette away.

The lobby was a modernistic marvel of marble and chromium. Church services could have been held in it, the place was so spacious.

Ned Gamble had no time to absorb the impressive architecture. Spying a bank of elevators, he made for the handiest cage.

The elevator starter directed him to a cage that was just settling onto the lobby level.

"This way, sir. Next car up."

The door stood open and Gamble stepped on board. The uniformed operator asked, "Which floor?"

"Eighty-six."

The elevator operator no doubt took many persons up to the eighty-sixth floor, but even so, he looked silently impressed.

"That's Doc Savage's floor. Is that who you're going to see?"

"What business is it of yours?" returned Ned tartly.

"I'm paid to ask questions. Doc Savage doesn't see just anybody."

"I have an appointment with Mr. Savage, I will have you know."

The firmness of Ned Gamble's voice was enough to satisfy the fellow, who rotated the control causing the cage to commence lifting.

Fumbling into his pockets for a cigarette lighter, Gamble prepared to light the recovered cigarette.

"Very sorry, sir," the elevator boy interrupted. "No smoking allowed in the cars."

Frowning, Ned stuffed the lighter back into his pocket and, holding the unlit cigarette, patiently waited for the elevator to cease its prolonged climb.

Eighty-six floors up, the cage eased to a halt, the door rolled open, and the operator announced, "This is your floor. Good luck."

Stepping off into a sumptuously furnished corridor, Gamble looked up and down until he saw a plain bronze door with a name upon it:

CLARK SAVAGE, JR.

The raised legend was in darker bronze, the letters modest.

The waxed marble floor felt reassuringly substantial under his feet as he strolled toward the impressive panel.

As he walked, Ned fiddled with his cigarette as if uncertain whether to light it or not. Nervousness took hold. Taking out his lighter, he snapped the flint wheel, and applied the tiny flame to the cigarette's end.

It was burning red hot by the time he reached the door.

There was a push-button next to the door and Gamble depressed it.

As he waited, he took rapid puffs of the cigarette, exhaling clouds of roiling smoke.

Under one arm, Ned still toted the folded newspaper that had so agitated him.

When the door opened, a waspish man in elegant attire showed his sharp-featured face and asked, "Good day. What is your business here?"

Taking the cigarette out of his mouth, the visitor spoke up.

"My name is—"

"Yes?"

The visitor appeared to hesitate, his eyes blinking rapidly.

A vagueness came into his serious blue orbs. They shifted around, as if he was looking for something he had misplaced.

"What is it, my good fellow?" pressed the waspish man.

"I—" Ned said falteringly.

Seeing that the man appeared distressed, the well-dressed fellow threw the door open wide and invited, "Why don't you step in?"

Ned Gamble seemed not to understand the invitation. His eyes lost focus, and his head began to move back and forth as if he were no longer certain of his surroundings.

Suddenly, he dropped his cigarette and clapped his hands over his ears as if to block out an unpleasant sound.

"What is wrong?" snapped the other.

"Ringing," Gamble said vaguely.

Whatever was wrong with the caller, alarm began to register on his features. One hand fumbled about in an aimless way.

Suddenly, Gamble lifted the folded newspaper and began stabbing the front page with a forefinger that seemed clumsy and uncertain.

Eyes rolling up in the back of his head, he keeled over.

No outward alarm roosted on the face of the sharp-featured man, who nevertheless began walking rapidly backward, then turned and found a button on an ornate table that sat by two high windows.

Employing a dark cane, he depressed this. From the ceiling dropped a great curtain of glass, so transparent it could only be detected by reflections of the ceiling lights.

The great pane came to rest on the rug, bisecting the reception room.

Stabbing another button on the great desk, the man called sharply, "Doc! Your visitor just arrived. But the chap appears to have fainted."

The remarkable voice of Doc Savage said, "Take all precautions. I will be there directly."

"Precautions already taken," returned the well-dressed man, snapping another switch, which caused fans in the ceiling to commence revolving.

Chapter III

THE GIANT IN BRONZE

THE TELEPHONE SWITCHBOARD girl at the disreputable Bowery rooming house had insisted that Doc Savage stood seven feet tall.

The big bronze man who stepped into the reception room from an adjoining chamber was not seven feet tall, but he gave that distinct impression.

Framed in the doorway, his head nearly grazed the transom. When he stepped away, Doc seemed to dwindle slightly, and assume the proportions of an ordinary man, not a veritable giant.

His stature was not the only thing about the bronze giant that was rather impressive. Doc Savage seemed to be molded out of some substance that possessed the hardness of bronze, combined with the flexibility of human flesh.

Innumerable tropical suns had baked his skin to the semblance of metal. His hair, lying like a metallic skullcap atop his fine-featured head, was a shade darker than that of his skin. Tendons on the back of his hands bespoke of tremendous physical development.

The bronze giant's eyes were arresting also. They seemed alive in an uncanny way that was difficult to describe. Like pools of flake-gold, they were. Vital, continually in motion, the restless golden flakes seemed stirred by inner winds, glittering hypnotically.

Striding over to the well-dressed man at the massive inlaid table that evidently served as a desk, Doc directed, "Ham, what did you observe?"

"Ham" replied, "The caller appeared perfectly ordinary until I asked his name. He began to tell me, then appeared to grow confused. His confusion turned into agitation, as if he had momentarily forgotten his own name. I asked him what was the matter, but the poor chap couldn't seem to articulate anything understandable. In his distress, he showed me an afternoon newspaper and began stabbing at the front page. That was when he collapsed. There seemed to be no reason for this, but I took the usual precautions. I shut the door and engaged the bulletproof sheet of glass which separates this portion of the reception room from the corridor door."

"You did the right thing," replied Doc. "What else did you observe?"

"Only that he was smoking a cigarette."

Doc nodded. He stabbed various inlays carved into the tabletop—in reality electrical push-buttons, and the overhead fans ceased whirring.

At the press of another button, the great sheet of bulletproof glass began toiling upward, to disappear into a cleverly concealed recess in the ceiling.

By this time, Doc Savage had donned a gas mask taken from a metal cabinet, after passing a second mask to Ham, who drew on the contrivance.

After taking that precaution, the big bronze man touched an inlay, and a telephoto device displayed the corridor on a frosted panel set flush onto the tabletop. The device was designed to show who might be standing outside the door. The screen displayed no one. The angle of the contrivance did not pick up on the visitor who had fallen to the hallway floor.

A tendril of smoke was wafting into view, indicating that the caller's cigarette continued to burn.

Together, Doc and Ham advanced on the closed door.

"I did not like to leave a stricken man lying out in the corridor like that," Ham said through his protective mask.

"One can never tell in what form death might arrive," cautioned Doc.

"Especially in our business," agreed Ham. With those words, he gripped his slim black cane. Separating handle from barrel revealed a slim rapier of immaculate steel.

Doc grasped the doorknob and prepared to fling the panel open.

That instant there came a mushy sound that was difficult to describe. Outlined by the well-fitting door appeared a brief flash of vivid green.

Ham blurted, "Grenade!"

If it was a grenade, the thing produced very little in the way of violent reaction. The portal remained firmly on its hinges.

Doc Savage held back. It was rare that the big bronze fellow ever hesitated, but neither was he rash when confronting an unknown danger.

Instead of passing through the door, the bronze giant reversed direction and made for the adjoining room. This proved to be a great scientific library crammed with shelved tomes. He moved through the profusion of bookcases until he came to a wall where one bookcase loomed narrow and tall.

Feeling for a concealed catch, Doc pulled this open, disclosing the secret passage into the outside hallway.

Moving cautiously, Doc stepped out into the corridor and looked in the direction of the reception room door bearing his name. He saw the figure lying on the floor, smoke curling from a hot spot on the folded newspaper beside him, where the dropped cigarette had fallen.

Up the hallway, an elevator door was closing.

"Someone was in the hall!" barked Ham.

DOC SAVAGE was already moving. A bronze flash, he raced for the sliding door, and almost made it.

The door closed, and the elevator sank, according to the arrow on the wall indicator above the door.

Changing direction abruptly, the bronze man went to another elevator, this one a specially designed super-speed lift that was not available for public use. He stepped aboard it, ran the door closed, and sent the cage rushing downward.

This lift was designed for emergency use, among other things, and Doc's feet all but left the floor with the momentum of its falling. There was no operator. The mechanism was entirely automatic.

When the cage reached the ground floor, Doc had to brace himself lest he crash to his knees. Opening the door, he stepped out into the lobby, knowing that the speed lift would have beaten the ordinary elevator to the ground by a fair amount.

Reaching the appropriate spot, the bronze man stationed himself before the shaft door, watching the arrow indicator reel off the floors as the cage sought the ground. The elevator did not stop along the way, indicating that it did not discharge any passengers on its way down.

When the cage finally came to a rest, the door opened. The elevator boy looked out and saw Doc Savage standing there. "Mr. Savage!"

Doc demanded, "Did you discharge a passenger on the way down, Jimmy?"

"No, sir, I didn't."

"Did you take one down from the eighty-sixth floor?"

"No, but I received a call to go to eighty-six to pick up a passenger. But no one was there when I arrived. So I ran her back down."

Jimmy the elevator boy had been an employee of the building for several years, and his reputation was above reproach. So Doc did not bother to question him any further. Instead, the bronze man returned to the super-speed lift, sending it whining back to the eighty-sixth floor.

Arriving there, he found Ham Brooks staring at a section of the corridor wall. Ham was one of Doc Savage's aides, an attorney of considerable accomplishments and one of Harvard Law School's most distinguished graduates. The wasp-waisted barrister was sharp of mind, feature and dress—often voted the best-dressed man in New York.

Ham said tightly, "Doc, you must take a look at this."

The bronze man advanced, and when he spied the greenish-yellow blotch on the wall, a strange sound escaped his parted lips.

It was a trilling, tuneless, yet definitely melodious, a sound which ran up and down the musical scale, pursuing no tune, and seeming to come from no particular spot. There was no easy way to categorize it. A searching wind slipping serpentine over shifting sand dunes could conceivably produce such a susurration. A chorus of otherworldly avians calling from some distant beyond might also have voiced it.

This was Doc's strange trilling, which only came when prompted by some unusual emotion. Here, a vague bafflement had brought it into existence, and the uncanny vocalization soon ebbed away to a nebulous nothing.

It looked as if a shadow had been cast upon the wall. But the shadow did not move. It was fixed. The shadow was no patch of grayness, but rather stood out an extremely bilious yellow-green, a hue that brought to mind a splash of vomit.

The figure depicted was on the shapeless side. Portions of the outline suggested a human being attired in a sack dress. The head of the thing, however, did not.

For it was a complicated mass of twisting forms.

Careful study caused both men to recognize the image depicted.

Ham remarked, "Jove! If I did not know better, I would venture to say that this outline was that of the Medusa."

Doc said grimly, "It is exactly that, Ham. The outline suggests a snake-headed figure attired in a robed garment."

Turning, Doc went over to the unfortunate caller sprawled before his door, knelt, and saw that Ham had already extinguished the cigarette, no doubt with his foot. Thus, no more smoke was wafting. The scorch mark in the fallen newspaper was relatively small.

Turning the man over, Doc studied his open-featured face, noted the absence of a hat and felt of the man's scalp. It was unusually smooth to the touch.

"This man has had his head shaved within the last few hours," he pronounced.

"Why would anyone do that?" wondered Ham, wringing his cane with both hands.

"No doubt to disguise himself from being followed," said Doc, lifting one of the man's coat sleeves to reveal unusually bright red hair.

Going through the man's pockets, the bronze man discovered a billfold, opened it up and picked through the papers he found within. There was a driver's license made out to Ned Gamble of Chicago, Illinois. A round-trip train ticket between Chicago and New York bearing a recent purchase date. Also, two brass hotel keys, along with receipts from two different hotels, both dated this afternoon.

Showing these to Ham, Doc said, "This man arrived on the Twentieth Century Limited and registered at separate hotels only an hour or so apart."

Ham nodded. "Switched hotels. Evidently, he knew he was being followed—or suspected as much. Did you find the man who escaped in the elevator?"

"No one escaped in the elevator," returned the bronze man. "The cage was empty except for Jimmy, who took no one up or down."

Ham twirled his cane thoughtfully. "Then where could the fleeing man have gone?"

"We can neither assume there was anyone else present, nor that there was not," commented Doc Savage, standing up.

He began to reconnoiter the corridor, looking for any signs of a lurker.

His investigations brought about nothing, for the eighty-sixth floor was entirely occupied by his own suite of offices. Going to a set of circular stairs, Doc climbed into the observation tower itself, but found no one hiding up there.

"If no one followed this man up," mused Ham, "then who or what struck him down? And what made that devilish green glow?"

"Those questions remain to be answered," said Doc Savage, returning to the body and taking it up in his great corded arms. The prodigious strength of the bronze giant became evident in the easy manner in which he toted the stricken Ned Gamble, who weighed approximately one hundred and seventy pounds.

They entered the reception room, passed through the great library, and into a scientific laboratory so large it seemed as if it filled the greatest portion of the eighty-sixth floor.

Laying the man on an examination table, Doc began checking vital signs. He found none. Nor did he expect to.

"Dead?" asked Ham.

Doc nodded. "This man is deceased."

Doc Savage was renowned for his scientific wizardry and his deep fund of learning. But the greatest of the bronze man's myriad accomplishments was as a physician and surgeon. Hence his nickname. He now began a thorough examination of the dead victim, attempting to ascertain the cause of his unexplained demise.

Much of this initially was routine.

While he worked, Ham fretted. "If I remember my Greek mythology, the Medusa was a fearful woman possessing living snakes for locks, whose fierce gaze was reputed to petrify a man in his tracks."

"This man was dropped in his tracks, but he has not been petrified," remarked Doc.

Lapsing into silence, the big bronze man continued his examination, and discovered nothing to explain the visitor's inexplicable expiration.

Moving a great fluoroscope into position, Doc arranged the movable screen so that it hovered over the dead body. Switching on the device, the bronze man studied the greenish image thus displayed.

His trilling came again; this time it sounded weird in the extreme.

Drawing closer, Ham asked anxiously, "What is it?"

"Take a look."

The dapper lawyer did. He perceived the shadowy internal organs, but nothing untoward leaped out at him immediately.

"Examine the head," directed Doc.

Once Ham saw what the bronze man was indicating, his eyes grew worried and his mouth tightened.

"What is that mass in his skull?"

"It would appear to be in the man's brain," said Doc.

"And why is it so dark, like a stone?"

Instead of replying, the bronze man went to a tray of instruments, and lifted a surgical scalpel.

He employed this to lift, first one, then the other of the man's eyelids, and showed that the glassy orbs had retreated into his skull, giving him something of the aspect of a death's head still clothed in flesh, his smooth, hairless crown aiding in that resemblance greatly.

"Ghoulish touch," murmured Ham. "But I fail to understand its significance."

Then Doc Savage inserted the scalpel into one of the man's nostrils, plunging it in deeply and working it around like a dentist probing a tooth cavity.

Ham Brooks winced as an unpleasant grating was produced.

"Good Grief! What is making that sound?"

"It is possible to insert a scalpel into a man's nostrils and penetrate to the brain," said Doc. "Certain difficult brain surgeries are performed via this method, inasmuch as it is the only method of reaching the lower brain. The scalpel is grating against his frontal lobe."

Ham looked flummoxed.

"This fellow's brain," explained the bronze man, "has seemingly turned to stone."

Chapter IV

VOICE OF MEDUSA

HAM BROOKS WAS one of the most astute attorneys practicing modern law, and had won several landmark arguments before the Supreme Court. During the late world war, he had been a brigadier general, and his lightning wits preserved entire regiments from destruction. To say that he was quick-witted was to understate the matter.

When the dapper lawyer heard Doc Savage's diagnosis, he became momentarily tongue-tied.

Ham still clutched his sword cane in one hand, and now he gripped it in both fists. He worried the thing, swapping it around, and acting like a befuddled elder gentleman, which he was most assuredly not, despite his carefully cut prematurely white hair.

Finally, the awestruck attorney got his tongue and his vocal chords untangled.

"But, how is that possible?" he blurted out. "This man was conversing with me only minutes ago."

Doc Savage shook his head slowly. "It is baffling. The human brain is made of soft matter. In death it would typically liquefy, not harden. Yet the brain of this man appears to have achieved a consistency approximating granite."

Placing one bronze hand at the back of the man's head, Doc Savage lifted Ned Gamble's bald skull experimentally.

"This man's head weighs more than the volume of his brain should permit," stated Doc. "This adds to the evidence of my nasal probe."

"I fail to comprehend this," murmured Ham. "It smacks of the supernatural."

"Taken with the silhouette of Medusa outside on our corridor wall," said Doc slowly, "your conjecture is not without foundation."

"But Medusa was a mythological creature—wholly imaginary. Was she not?"

Doc returned Ned Gamble's head to its resting place. "Where is the newspaper he carried?"

The dapper attorney had laid it on a telephone stand. Now he retrieved it.

Doc Savage took the sheet, unfolded it, and read the headline.

PROMINENT INVENTOR SUCCUMBS
TO MYSTERY MALADY

The news article was lengthy, but much of it was in the manner of an obituary. It told how Myer Sim had been struck down in his own home on the eve of attending a scientific conference in Chicago. Prior to this, Mr. Sim had intimated he was going to make an important announcement that would rock the medical world.

However, before he could attend, Sim was found slumped down on the desk of his home office in a suburb of Chicago.

A maid had heard him uttering sounds of distress, and when she went to check on him, Myer Sim was unable to speak intelligibly.

All that could be gleaned was that just before he expired, Sim appeared to be complaining of a ringing in his ears.

The rest of the article recounted how local doctors were flummoxed by the cause of death, and that an autopsy had been scheduled.

Ham had been reading over Doc Savage's shoulder—or rather around it since the big bronze man towered over the elegant attorney by quite a bit.

"Doc!" he exclaimed. "Our visitor said something about a ringing before he succumbed. And his hands were going to his ears in a baffled way."

Doc considered this. At length, he said, "If Ned Gamble's brain was hardening while he was speaking to you, he might experience symptoms of tinnitus. Certainly, his brain would cease to function normally, and his articulation would also suffer."

Ham began to pace in an agitated fashion. His sword cane commenced to twirl in his hand, making him look a bit like a drum majorette who was attired in diplomat garb.

"That could only mean that whatever force was acting upon him was doing so invisibly, and with great rapidity," he declared.

"So it would seem," replied Doc, putting the newspaper down and striding over to the telephone stand. "Long Tom is attending that conference, which starts today. I will endeavor to reach him. He may be able to assist us in this matter."

Ham nodded. "Then there is no question in your mind that these two deaths are related?"

"None at all," said the bronze man grimly, picking up the telephone.

In short order, Doc got the hotel in which the conference was taking place.

"This is Doc Savage speaking. It is imperative that I reach my associate, Thomas J. Roberts, who is attending the present conference."

The speed with which Long Tom's voice came on the line was a testament to the power of Doc Savage. Every bellhop in the establishment must have fanned out to seek Roberts.

"Long Tom speaking," said a querulous voice.

"Long Tom, have you heard the news about Myer Sim?"

"Yes, it's cast a pall over the conference. He was scheduled to give a presentation of a new invention of his."

"What is known of this invention?"

"Nothing at all," replied Long Tom. "It's a secret."

"A man named Ned Gamble trained in from Chicago this afternoon, Long Tom," continued Doc. "He telegraphed ahead to say that there was an urgent matter he wished to lay before me. But when Gamble arrived for his appointment, he literally dropped dead. A brief examination seems to indicate his brain had petrified in some inexplicable manner."

Long Tom's explosive grunt might have been a curse.

"What do you make of it, Doc?"

"It is too soon to say, and there is more to the mystery. Ham and I are going to investigate Ned Gamble's activities today. Look into the matter on your end. Talk to whomever you can find who is associated with the man. We will be in touch."

"Right!" said Long Tom, terminating the connection.

Doc Savage turned to face Ham Brooks. "We will collect Monk on the way."

Ham frowned. "Is that really necessary?"

"We have a great deal of ground to cover," reminded Doc. "Monk will be of considerable help, especially if this mystery has a chemical origin."

With that, the two men went out to the reception room where Ham collected a light overcoat and Homburg hat.

They took the speed elevator to the sub-basement garage where Doc selected a roadster capable of winnowing its way through rush-hour traffic, for the day was growing late.

The roadster came to life with hardly a sound, and Doc piloted it up a ramp that put them out into traffic. The garage door opened in response to a radio signal from the machine after Doc touched a button on the dash.

On the ride over, Ham fretted, "I sincerely hope Monk does not bring his pet pig along. The last time I shared an automobile with that infernal pest, he continually untied my shoe-laces with his teeth. I am quite certain that that misbegotten man-ape taught him to do that very thing."

Doc said quietly, "It would be best if Monk left the pig behind, for we may be striding into considerable danger."

Instead of expressing concern, Ham's dark eyes began to glow. It was for the love of danger and adventure that the Man of Bronze and his aides had first banded together to do the work that they pursued.

The remarkable group assembled by Doc Savage at the start of his career was unique. Doc Savage himself had been trained for his work. Some youth are trained to be engineers, doctors, lawyers, for the ministry. Doc had been trained to right wrongs, an ultramodern Sir Galahad, without the romantic aspects. Doc was quite hard-headed about it.

But his five assistants had not been trained in any such specialized fashion. Yet each of them had a profession, and in that line, were tops. Monk, the chemist, and Ham, the lawyer, for instance, were peaks in their lines. Long Tom was one of the foremost electrical engineers alive.

Doc soon parked the machine in front of a skyscraper in the Wall Street sector of town, in lower Manhattan. Here Monk Mayfair maintained a penthouse that had cost a small fortune.

As the elegant barrister stepped from the vehicle, Doc instructed, "Stress that Monk not bring Habeas along, due to the risk."

"Best news I have heard all day!" enthused Ham, who ducked into the lobby, and used the house phone to summon the famous chemist.

A squeaky voice came over the wire, demanding, "Who is it?"

"Your nemesis," said Ham waspishly. "Doc is parked outside. A mystery has landed on our doorstep. Doc says you may come along, but you must leave that infernal insect behind."

"You're makin' that part up, ain't you?"

"I am not!" snapped Ham. "Two men are dead, and even Doc Savage cannot figure out why."

Reluctantly, the squeaky voice said, "I'll be right down."

When Monk Mayfair stepped off the elevator, Ham saw to his immense relief that he was alone.

"Hurry, you bandy-legged baboon," Ham scolded. "There is much to do."

"Hold your horses!" Monk growled. "You clothes horse."

Born Andrew Blodgett Mayfair, Monk had acquired his nickname honestly. He was a fearsome individual, possessing the general build of a bull gorilla and weighing approximately two hundred and sixty pounds, none of it fat. His wide face was fiercely lined, and there appeared to be a bullet hole in one ear lobe. Gray scars marred his simian countenance.

Despite looking as if he was born with a deficiency of gray matter, Monk was one of the world's leading industrial chemists. Like Ham and the absent members of Doc Savage's group of adventurers, the apish chemist had gotten together with the bronze man during the Great War. After the fracas had concluded, the five had banded together to join Doc Savage in his life ideal—that of aiding those in distress for no greater reward than the enjoyment of dealing in danger in the pursuit of justice.

The other two Doc Savage associates, an archeologist and a civil engineer, were presently unavailable, pursuing their vocations.

Ham and Monk quarreled on their way to the roadster, owing to a feud that had originated during their wartime service and never settled down. In truth, they were close friends who enjoyed expressing their mutual antagonism.

Ham got in front, Monk taking the back seat. Doc piloted the roadster back into traffic.

Quickly, Doc Savage filled Monk in, concluding, "Prior to his death, Ned Gamble was last seen at a Bowery lodging house. That is where we will begin our investigation."

"Sounds Jake to me," said Monk, splitting his head almost in two with an anticipatory grin.

Ham inserted acidly, "There is nothing Jake about this. It is horrible. The image of the Medusa has been seared into my brain."

Monk's tiny brow furrowed. "Medusa," he muttered. "Wasn't that the dame who could turn a man into stone just by lookin' at him?"

"The very same," retorted Ham. "Her head was said to be a nest of vipers, and the silhouette on our wall appeared to show exactly that."

Monk seemed to shake off a wracking shudder. "Sounds like somebody even I wouldn't wanna meet in a dark alley. You say the imprint on the wall was green?"

Ham nodded. "A particularly repellent shade of greenish-yellow, rather like a tropical snake. It was as if she left her shadow behind her. It was somehow burned into the wall."

Doc Savage did not contribute to this exchange, keeping his attention upon the traffic, which was becoming heavy.

SOON, they drew up before the Grand Bowery Inn, and pushed into what passed for a lobby, and out of a chilly breeze.

The temperature had been mild for an Autumn day, but now the air was cooling dramatically as evening approached.

"I wish this infernal weather would make up its mind," fumed Ham. "I cannot tell whether to dress for Fall or Winter."

Doc Savage walked up to the front desk and accosted the clerk, who recognized him immediately.

"Mr. Savage!" he gulped. "What brings you to my modest establishment?"

The bronze man possessed special credentials given him by the New York Police Department. These were obviously not necessary under the circumstances, so great was his fame. But Doc produced them anyway.

"Consider this an official police investigation," Doc Savage imparted. "We are looking into the behavior of a recent guest of yours. His name is Ned Gamble, and he was completely hairless."

The clerk nodded eagerly. "I figured that was why you came. Earlier, a very bald man registered under the name of Harry Baldwin. The moniker made me suspicious, since we sometimes get unsavory characters registering here. So I had my switchboard girl listen in to his telephone." The clerk cleared his throat uncomfortably. "He made only one call, and that was to your offices. That was how we knew his real name."

Doc Savage asked, "Did Gamble have any visitors?"

"Oh, not at all. In fact, he was with us less than an hour. He simply registered, made the call and left in a violent rush. That was the last we saw of him."

"That is the last you will see of him," stated Doc. "For the man has expired."

The desk clerk paled slightly. "I knew something bad was in the wind. When you've been in this business long as I have, you can spot trouble in the faces of new guests."

Doc said, "Show me to his room."

The desk clerk was only too happy to oblige, and he was soon inserting the master key to Room 205.

The room looked as if it was not occupied. But on the closet floor reposed a Gladstone bag.

Setting this onto a bureau dresser drawer, Doc Savage opened the bag, and began going through the contents—the desk clerk, along with Monk and Ham, watching with great interest.

A preponderance of articles proved to be the kind of clothing a man would carry if he was taking a short trip. There was an extra pair of trousers, two extra shirts and underwear. Nothing else.

Sunlight streaming in through the windows showed that the bag was now empty.

"Dead end," mumbled Monk.

While Doc Savage was replacing the contents into the Gladstone, he remarked, "We will confiscate this for the time being."

"Of course, Mr. Savage," the clerk returned.

As they were preparing to depart the room, a voice spoke up.

The voice had many peculiar qualities, not the least of which was a kind of distortion which concealed its exact source.

"Doc Savage! This is no concern of yours! Abandon all investigation. The eyes of Medusa are upon you. If they begin glowing green, the fate of Ned Gamble will be your own."

"Blazes!" yelled Monk, bullet head jerking about. "Who's that talkin'?"

The desk clerk froze, while Monk, Ham and Doc fanned out through the room, investigating the closet, looking under the bed, even opening drawers, although no possible person could be concealed therein.

The uncanny voice continued undisturbed.

"You have beheld the shed skin of our shadow, which we left behind as a warning to you all. Do not risk our petrifying gaze! This is a warning from beyond."

"Blast it!" Ham complained. "The voice does not seem to be coming from any place that I can locate."

Doc Savage gestured for silence, his head swiveling this way and that. His hearing had been trained to an extreme, and he was using his aural organs to hunt the sound to its origin.

But the voice did not come again. Satisfied that there was no other person or mechanical device capable of reproducing a human voice in the room, the bronze man went to the window, threw up the sash, and thrust his head out.

The fire escape latticework was unoccupied. There was no one standing below. The bronze man twisted, craning his head around, until he was looking up.

There did not seem to be any open windows above. Nevertheless, Doc Savage suddenly shifted until he was sitting on the windowsill, his upper body perched entirely outside the building.

The hotel was faced with brick, and Doc's strong fingers found the crevices where the mortar held the bricks in place.

To the astonishment of no one except the desk clerk, Doc Savage was suddenly walking up the side of the building, using nothing more than the tips of his metallic fingers and the reinforced toes of his shoes to climb the building façade.

In this way, he soon reached the roof, climbed over the coping, and stood up.

Eerie golden eyes ranged the adjoining buildings, some of which were hotels and flophouses in the same class as this particular one. Doc seemed to be paying particular attention to the windows of adjoining structures, but after several minutes of intense study—which included removing a small, collapsable telescope from an inner pocket for closer scrutiny—seemed to arrive at no satisfactory conclusion.

It was easier, not to mention safer, to return to the second floor via the roof skylight hatch, and interior fire stairs, so Doc Savage did that.

Stepping back into the hotel room, the bronze giant said, "No source for the weird voice seems apparent." There was no disappointment in his tone, for the bronze man usually maintained a stoic impassivity. "We will go now."

Returning to the lobby, they thanked the desk clerk for his cooperation and reclaimed their roadster. It was soon darting through traffic.

Monk Mayfair and Ham Brooks appeared to have been struck dumb by the weird voice emanating from no apparent author.

Finally, Ham ventured, "That voice appeared womanly."

To which Monk replied, "Sounded like a man to me."

They began arguing the point, getting nowhere, but apparently enjoying themselves.

When the party reached the Hotel Paramount, they discovered several prowl cars standing in front of the building.

Police officers in blue also stood about, their expressions tight.

"Something's sure up," squeaked Monk.

Chapter V

SKULLBONE SURPRISE

WHEN DOC SAVAGE emerged from the roadster, the congregation of police officers took notice. They all but snapped to attention.

One, a sergeant, approached respectfully, saying, "Mr. Savage. Are you here to see about the dead one?"

"Which dead one?" returned Doc unemotionally.

"Why, that stiff that was found on the fifth floor. Haven't you heard?"

"We are here on another matter," said Doc circumspectly. "But it may be they are related. Please explain."

"The hotel detective called it in," offered the sergeant. "It seems a man registered in a room, and began behaving peculiarly."

"How so?"

"Not long after he took his room, he went down to the barber shop here, and had his head shaved completely bald. Can you imagine that? He returned to his room, but forgot his hat. The barber in question and a bellhop carried it up to his room, but the hop came down alone, shaken up and not making much sense. The barber was found dead in the hallway. When they entered the room, they found it empty, the window open. Looks like the guest took a run-out powder down the fire escape. Guy's name was Dobe Castle—"

"An alias," supplied Doc. "Ned Gamble was his actual name."

"So you do know something about this?" stated the sergeant.

"Take me to the investigating detective," Doc requested.

They had passed into the lobby, where the beleaguered hotel desk clerk was fending off questions.

"I have no idea about the man's business. I've told you all that I know." He looked stricken. And with good reason. The reputation of this hotel was impeccable. A death, possibly a murder, would be a black mark against the establishment.

Doc Savage inserted himself into the questioning.

"I would like to hear this man's story from the beginning," he asked.

The desk clerk looked as if he had been telling the story over and over again to successive parties. He backed up, took a deep breath, and commenced his story from the top. Obviously, he recognized the Man of Bronze.

"The guest in question checked in under the name of Dobe Castle, and he had the brightest red hair you could ever see in all of your life. When I handed him his key, I also gave Castle a message. He all but refused it. After accepting it, he went up to his room and made a telephone call."

"To whom?" inquired Doc.

"A party in Chicago."

"We're looking into that right now, Mr. Savage," inserted the detective in charge, an inspector. Doc knew him. His name was Clarence Humbolt, better known as "Hardboiled" Humbolt. He was the inspector in charge of Manhattan. Presently, the two were on excellent terms. It had not always been this way.*

"Go on," prompted the bronze man.

"After Castle made the call, he came down to the barber shop and made an unusual request. He had his head completely shaved. Then he ran back up to his room."

"I understand that he left his hat behind," prompted Doc.

"That's right. According to the bellhop, when they tried to return it to him, Mr. Castle didn't seem to want it anymore."

---

* *The Annihilist*

"That's the funny part—except it ain't funny," interjected Humbolt. "In this changeable weather, you'd think a bald guy would need a hat even more than he had previously."

"Not if you wanted to throw someone off your trail," supplied Doc.

The inspector's eyes grew wise. "You think he was being followed?"

"Unquestionably," said Doc. "After he departed this establishment, he secured a room at a Bowery flophouse, under another alias. He was there just long enough to call my office, and arrange an appointment. When Ned Gamble showed up at my door, he expired without explanation."

"Expired! Don't you mean dropped dead?"

"Exactly that."

"Well, what struck him down?"

"That remains to be seen," said Doc, not volunteering his discovery that the man's brain had somehow been petrified.

Inspector Humbolt began worrying the nape of his neck with blunt fingers.

"If that don't beat everything. Sounds like what happened upstairs."

"Take me there," requested Doc.

They all went up in a crowded elevator. Upon alighting, the first thing Doc Savage and his men noticed was the yellow-green splotch emblazoned on the hallway wall.

They studied it. It was similar to the silhouette that had appeared on Doc's corridor wall in the aftermath of Ned Gamble's uncanny demise. The pose was different, but there was no mistaking the horrible head of hair that was composed of sinuous vipers.

"We don't know what that is," supplied Humbolt. "When the body was discovered, this blot was first noticed. Looks like nothing I've ever seen before."

Doc Savage did not enlighten the inspector. He saw no point in it.

They went to the room, whose door hung open, the two sides of the closed laundry door-hatch also open wide, permitting the room's interior to be seen from the hallway when the portal was shut.

The inspector resumed his account, saying, "According to the bellhop, the guest refused to open his door. Didn't seem to want his hat, but told them to leave it in the clothes hatch. When the hatch was opened, there was a bright green light and a whole lotta smoke. You can't smell anything now, but the poor barber staggered back and practically died on the spot. The hop fled to the lobby, spilled his story, and that's when we were called."

Hardboiled concluded, "We found the inner and outer hatches open, but the guest had vanished. The window was open, so it wasn't hard to see how he eeled away."

Doc stepped in the room, looked around, and said to no one in particular, "It would seem that Gamble opened the hatch to observe the commotion on the other side of the door."

Hardboiled grunted. "We kind of figured he opened the hatch to retrieve his hat."

Doc shook his head slightly. "Ned Gamble was not interested in his hat. Otherwise, he would have opened the door and accepted it. He wanted the person who was following him to be thrown off the trail by his lack of hair, hat and distinctive overcoat."

The bronze man then pointed to the discarded ulster lying on the bed, adding quietly, "Gamble believed that his overcoat and bright red hair made him conspicuous to any trailer. So he dispensed with those items, had his head shaved, and changed hotels."

"Gamble figured he was followed to this establishment?"

"That appears to be his assumption," said Doc, looking around.

Without asking for permission, the bronze man began to go through the closet and the bureau, but found nothing. Ned

Gamble had not occupied this room long enough to leave articles lying about.

In a wastebasket, however, was a discarded newspaper. Doc extracted this and unfolded it.

The paper was the *Chicago Tribunal.* An Extra edition, dated the previous day. The sensational headline told of the sudden death of scientist Myer Sim only hours before. There was hardly any detail.

Doc committed the story to memory and dropped the paper into the wastebasket as if it held no significance to him.

"Let me talk to the bellhop," he requested.

THE FELLOW was a nervous wreck when confronted, but he told his story as best he could. He contributed nothing new to their understanding.

"Describe the flash of light," prompted Doc.

"It was green as all get-out, and it practically blinded me. I thought it was a bomb, so I lit out of there."

"What did you smell, if anything?" asked Doc.

"I didn't stick around long enough to sniff. I dived through the fire door and practically somersaulted down the stairs. It wasn't until I reached the lobby that I saw that I wasn't injured."

Doc Savage turned to Monk and said, "Monk, take samples from the hatch and the silhouette on the wall."

"Gotcha, Doc," Monk had toted with him a metal case that comprised his compact chemical laboratory. Setting this on the corridor table, he began taking out various items, which he used to scour the inside hatch doors for chemical residue. He did not test these. When he was done, the simian chemist did the same with the silhouette on the wall.

Monk had not seen the silhouette at Doc Savage's headquarters, and so took a few moments to study the image. As a chemist, he could study shades of color and deduce underlying chemical constituents. Here, the greenish-yellow splotch seemed to baffle him. His homely features gathered up in a puckered puzzlement.

Muttering under his breath, Monk took a ball of cotton and attempted to swab up a specimen of whatever had created the yellow-green shadow.

"I'll be daggone," he said suddenly.

Ham Brooks, who had been watching everything with deep suspicion in his eyes, turned and demanded, "What is wrong now?"

Monk nodded, "I thought this was painted on somehow, but it's not coming off. I don't get it."

Ham stepped up, and laid a well-manicured finger against the greenish-yellow outline, rubbed vigorously, and examined the tip of the same finger. It came away clean.

"It is not a residue, that is plain to see," he suggested.

"That's what I just said," retorted Monk.

Doc Savage paid no attention to this exchange, but had resumed speaking to the inspector in charge.

"Where is the body of the barber?"

"Where else?" grunted Hardboiled Humbolt. "City morgue. Want to take a gander at him?"

"At once," said Doc.

Looking baffled, Monk wondered, "What should I do with this? Rip out a hunk of the plaster?"

"Not necessary at this time," said Doc. "We will return if need be."

Taking their departure, they followed Inspector Humbolt to the city morgue and were soon standing around a body in an autopsy room. Chemical smell was not pleasant, but they had all visited morgues before. So they were used to it.

The Medical Examiner was saying to Doc Savage, "I've just begun to examine this man, and have as yet to make any determination."

Doc Savage volunteered no information but said, "I would simply like to observe you."

Shrugging, the M.E. resumed his autopsy.

He opened up the chest with a bone saw, used a stainless steel device to crack apart the chest cavity, exposing the internal organs.

After he did so, the medical man began to recite his observations. "Heart seems sound, major organs appear to be undiseased."

Ham Brooks decided he did not need to pay close attention to this grisly operation, and tried to pick a fight with Monk Mayfair.

"It is a relief not to have to watch where I step," the elegant attorney remarked. "Traveling with a wild pig distresses me no end." Casting an accusatory eye in Monk's direction, he added, "If only Doc would consent to leave you behind, I would be ecstatic."

The hairy chemist was not having any. He was fascinated by the exposed organs of the deceased barber.

Ham fell to examining his nails, especially the tip of the finger that had lifted up no residue. He found nothing of interest there.

"The lungs appear to be unremarkable," the M.E. was saying. "On superficial examination, I see no indication of a heart attack, which might lead to the possibility that this man suffered a stroke."

"You will need to lay bare the brain," suggested Doc Savage.

Agreeing with that determination, the Medical Examiner picked up a circular saw that was operated by electricity. With practiced skill, he commenced sawing all the way around the crown of the man's head. Bits of bone grit flew.

When this was done, the top of the skull became removable. The medico lifted this free, set down the scalp, then trained a goose-necked lamp on the exposed brain.

Doc Savage stepped closer, the golden flakes in his uncanny eyes growing animated.

The human brain is normally a grayish color, and often pink in spots. The dead man's brain was neither.

The hideously wrinkled organ looked for all the world like a large specimen of coral. It was pale white. It possessed the outward semblance of polished marble. Though it had the approximate shape of a human brain, its hue and outward appearance were not at all what the Medical Examiner was accustomed to encountering when he opened up a dead man's skull.

The medico gasped. "What on earth?"

Doc Savage's indescribable trilling filled the room. It seemed to wander about in such a fashion that it was impossible to tell whence it emanated.

So stunned was the Medical Examiner by what he had uncovered that he completely failed to take notice of the unnatural sound.

Doc Savage seldom realized that he was making the trillation, for it was entirely unconscious. But he noticed now. Sealing his lips, he stifled the vocal emanation, which had come unbidden.

"With your permission," he said. Taking up a scalpel, Doc Savage applied the sharp point to the ridges of the exposed brain.

The scalpel tip made the identical scraping sound that the bronze man had produced when he had inserted his own scalpel into the nasal passage of the deceased Ned Gamble.

"That sounds like stone!" blurted out the Medical Examiner.

"Certainly the consistency of stone," agreed the bronze man. "What it is in actuality remains to be determined. I would like to take a sample of this man's brain."

"It is highly irregular," said the Medical Examiner slowly. He appeared to be dazed. He was not a young man. There were suggestions of gray at his temples. It might be assumed he had been at his job for a number of years. But the discovery that a dead man's brain had been somehow petrified seemed to have swamped his wits.

Doc Savage said, "I will take responsibility for any repercussions."

"The big guy has my vote, too," added Hardboiled Humbolt.

Shrugging rather helplessly, the M.E. said, "Proceed."

Doc Savage used a small hammer and the kind of chisel that is often used when working with bone, and chipped off a segment of the brain about the size of a tiny cowrie seashell. He wrapped this up in a handkerchief and pocketed it.

Monk, who had been fascinated throughout, ambled up and ran his fingers along the exposed portion and grunted, "Kinda reminds me of calcium carbonate more than stone."

Doc nodded. "It may be that the brain calcified, rather than petrified. Only chemical analysis will determine that."

The Medical Examiner spoke up, "I fail to see how the human brain could do either."

"Yet you see the evidence before your own eyes," reminded Doc.

The M.E. scratched his chin, began ruminating, "Anything that could petrify the soft tissue of a brain should have petrified the eyes as well."

Taking a thumb, he lifted both eyelids, and saw that they were sunken in the man's bony sockets. Sunken unnaturally. For under the overhead lights, it seemed simply that the man's face had sunken in death. This was commonly true of decaying corpses, but the Medical Examiner realized the man had not been dead very long. The natural processes that would have rendered the facial features hauntingly ghoul-like should not have been very far along.

"This is peculiar," mused the M.E.

Doc explained, "It is possible that the brain matter has shrunk due to its chemical transformation. You know the human eyeball is directly connected to the brain, so if the brain mass did shrink, it would have tugged on the muscles controlling the eyes, causing them to retreat within their bony sockets."

The Medical Examiner nodded vigorously. "Yes, yes, that makes perfect sense."

"It is the only thing that does," complained Ham, who was hanging back in a far corner. The dapper attorney was not normally squeamish, but there was something about this procedure that bothered him greatly. Perhaps it was because it defied easy explanation.

The autopsy having produced all that it might, Doc Savage left the matter in the Medical Examiner's capable hands, saying, "You can expect another body like this before long."

The M.E.'s graying eyebrow shot up.

Doc explained, "A visitor to my office succumbed unexpectedly, and my initial examination indicated that his brain had turned into a solid mass of matter. His name was Ned Gamble. I know little else about him, except that he came from Chicago seeking my help."

"So there were *two* such victims?" the medico said incredulously.

"It may be," stated Doc Savage, "there will prove to be three, if not more. It is the more that concerns me. We must be going now."

OUT on the street, Doc conferred briefly with Inspector Hardboiled Humbolt.

"What do you make of it, Savage?" the official grunted.

"It is," admitted the bronze man, "too early to tell very much."

"Well, you got free rein on this case, since it broke on your doorstep."

"Thank you," said Doc.

Lowering his voice, the inspector whispered, "Those hardboiled yeggs I sent your way last week. How are they doing?"

"Coming along," replied Doc.

Hardboiled chuckled. "They must be pretty soft by now."

"They will be out of circulation for a long time," said the bronze man without outward humor.

"Good. That's how I like crooks—out of sight and mind. I might have a few more for you before long."

"Your confidence is appreciated," Doc told the inspector.

"See you around then," said Hardboiled, turning to go.

As they climbed back into the roadster, Ham Brooks remarked, "I take it you think that the man who died in Chicago is also a victim of this Medusa malady."

Throwing the car in gear, Doc Savage imparted, "We will look into the Chicago angle next."

Ham advised Monk, "Long Tom is already there."

"Fast work," snorted Monk.

"Nothing of the sort," Ham said dismissively. "Long Tom was already in Chicago for a scientific conference."

"Nice coincidence then," muttered Monk.

"If it *is* a coincidence," said Ham suspiciously.

"What do you know that I don't?" asked Monk.

"Nothing," snapped Ham. "I take that back. I know everything you don't. And more besides. In this instance, I am disinclined to credit coincidence."

Behind the wheel, Doc Savage said nothing. The gold flakes of his eyes were whirling briskly. Events were moving fast, but they had yet to make much headway in the mystery that had arrived, unbidden, on their doorstep.

"Mebbe we should stop by my place and pick up Habeas," suggested Monk suddenly.

"Why do such a foolish thing?" sniffed Ham.

"I got a funny feeling we're all goin' off to Chicago, and I don't want to leave him behind. Habeas gets powerful lonesome."

In the front seat, Ham looked to Doc Savage expectantly.

"I would not bring Habeas were I you, Monk. But if you insist upon it, take as much protective gear as you have designed to fit the porker."

"That don't sound good," murmured Monk.

"We are facing an unknown force that possesses the power to turn a man's brain into a substance resembling coral at a speed that defies explanation. We would not want Habeas Corpus to succumb to such a danger."

Monk's tiny eyes narrowed. He began calculating in his brain.

At last, he allowed, "When we get to headquarters, I'll call my secretary and have her take charge of Habeas. This is one trip he's just gonna have to miss."

Ham Brooks suppressed a grin of relief, knowing that if the apish chemist saw it, he would immediately reverse his decision.

Chapter VI

THE MONSTER MEDUSA

THE LIFE WORK of Doc Savage was a simple one, in theory. That was to go from one end of the globe to the other, helping those in distress, solving problems outside the domain of ordinary law enforcement. People who were in need of rescue went to Doc's headquarters to lay their troubles at his feet. Often, the Man of Bronze would help them. Few were turned away. To others, he extended assistance where their difficulties were not great and easily solvable.

Doc Savage offered charity. Not that he gave handouts. In these difficult economic times, he employed many thousands of persons.

It was a simple credo: to assist the unfortunate in any way possible.

In practicality, it was anything but simple. Many thousands beseeched the bronze man of mystery for succor, whether deserving or not. Doc turned many of these away, those who were able-bodied and capable of fending for themselves.

But the availability of Doc Savage created complications. People were continually trying to meet with him who had no business doing so. In his way, the bronze man was a celebrity. He did not like that. But he understood that to help the distressed, people around the world had to know where he was headquartered.

Because his work created enemies, Doc Savage was forced to take certain precautions. The bulletproof shield at his office was one. There were others. Many times these precautions had saved his life.

As far as it was possible to do so, the sub-basement garage Doc maintained beneath his skyscraper headquarters was a secret. But it was a discoverable secret.

His comings and goings were disguised in part by his fleet of vehicles, none of which were flashy. But in order to operate freely in congested Manhattan, many of these machines sported special number plates, such as the vehicle he now drove whose tag read: DOC-1.

To those in the know, these designations marked the automobiles as belonging to a person of distinction. Nor was it possible to completely conceal the garage since the bronze man was forced to drive up the ramp through special doors, over the sidewalk and onto the street.

The entrance door to the skyscraper basement was unmarked, and resembled the type of loading dock many larger skyscrapers boast, through which supplies are delivered. The main loading dock, in fact, stood around the corner.

The fact that the garage door was not well known did not make it a complete secret, however.

As Monk wheeled the roadster around the corner preparatory to climbing onto the sidewalk, Doc Savage's alert eyes scanned the surroundings.

It was now late afternoon, and throngs had begun to empty out of the buildings, making their way to the subways, trolleys and busses to wend their way homeward for the evening.

As Monk twisted the wheel and prepared to mount the sidewalk, Doc rapped out, "Monk, stop."

There was no great volume in the bronze man's voice, but it possessed an imperative quality that caused the homely chemist's broad foot to tramp down on the floor brake.

"What is it?" demanded Monk.

Doc Savage did not reply. He stepped out onto the running board, scrutinizing the entrance door. From their seats, Monk and Ham did the same.

On the sidewalk near the door stood an ash can, a thing of galvanized sheet steel of the type used to haul cold ashes from coal furnaces.

Normally such a container would not be found on the sidewalk at this spot. For the towering skyscraper was heated by steam piped in by the city through great system mains. No furnaces supplied it.

Doc studied the container briefly, and suddenly swung back, throwing himself behind the wheel with such violent force that Monk Mayfair's powerful bulk was slammed into the passenger seat. He grunted explosively.

The windows were open, and Doc's finger snapped out to tap a dash button. Miraculously, all open windows rolled shut. They were electrically operated.

Monk and Ham came to the same conclusion. "Bomb?" they chorused.

If Doc Savage meant to reply, it never came.

For the windshield of the roadster erupted in a flash of livid green. Of the three passengers, only Doc Savage reacted in time to preserve his eyesight.

Closing his eyelids, he threw up a great cabled arm before his face, and so the stabbing brilliance did not impact his optic nerves.

Not as quick, Monk and Ham got the worst of it. Their fingers flew to their faces, and they began exclaiming.

"I can't see a dang thing!" howled Monk.

"I cannot see at all," groaned Ham.

Nor could Doc Savage immediately. For once the green glare had ceased to paint his face, and he felt it safe to open his eyes, the bronze giant beheld only roiling smoke.

This smoke looked like something coming out of the bowels of Hades. It was black, gray, brown in turns, as if some enemy had thrown every combustible substance known to man into one hot furnace.

The roadster had been built in a factory, then rebuilt under the bronze man's direction. It was bulletproof, gas tight, capable of withstanding the detonation of hand grenades and even larger explosives.

A tank shell could certainly have done it damage, but under ordinary circumstances, the armored automobile would have turned most violent assaults.

Doc Savage sat calmly behind the wheel, waiting for the smoke to dissipate, his flake-gold eyes peering about with a trace of concern in their whirling depths.

There had been persons passing by just moments before. Even through the bulletproof glass, the bronze man could hear curses and cries of complaint.

Eventually, the smoke cleared and Doc popped open the door, stepping out.

Despite all the smoke, the explosion had not been as violent as it first seemed. The bronze giant accosted several passersby, determined that they had not been injured, merely shaken up, and waited to see if they developed any symptoms in the aftermath.

Meanwhile, having regained their sight, Monk and Ham emerged from the vehicle. Out of padded armpit holsters, the pair yanked compact machine pistols, which they waved about as if eager to unleash hot lead on the perpetrator.

But there was no perpetrator in sight. Merely thinning gray smoke, and a bitter charcoal odor. Doc Savage was quietly questioning the people who had been caught up in it.

Ten minutes passed before the bronze man felt confident enough to permit them to move on.

That was when they noticed the gruesome greenish-yellow splotch on the garage door. It was gigantic, fearsome, terrifying. Fully twelve feet tall, it loomed over them, its great snaky skull seeming alive with viper-headed tentacles.

"Jove!" exploded Ham.

Monk stared, slack-jawed, grunting, "I half expect them heads to hiss at me."

Going to the barrel, Monk discovered it was open at the top, the insides scorched black from fire and smoke.

Monk bent down as if to take a deep whiff of residue, but Doc stayed him with a quiet admonition.

"Too dangerous. I will open the garage door. Give the barrel a kick to roll it inside."

Monk pulled back with alacrity, saying, "Gotcha."

Ham went to the sedan dashboard, pressed a button. A radio signal caused the great door to roll ponderously upward.

Thereupon, Monk gave the barrel a lusty boot, and it went crashing down the ramp, finally rolling to a dead stop against a support pillar.

When Doc drove past, Monk hopped onto the running board and rode along with them to a parking area jammed with other vehicles.

Exiting the sedan, Doc Savage said, "We will examine the barrel later. Right now I wish to pursue our investigation as rapidly as possible."

As they rode the super-speed elevator up to the eighty-sixth floor, Ham gripped his sword cane until his knuckles grew white while Monk made fierce faces.

"We are bein' followed around town, ain't we?" Monk said to no one in particular.

"We are," confirmed Doc.

"And that drum down there was meant to scare us off, right?"

"Obviously," inserted Ham tightly.

Stepping off into the corridor, Monk took in the bile-colored blotch on the corridor wall and growled, "I'm gonna study this real close."

"First, let us put the residue from the hotel under the spectrometer."

"Good idea," said Monk. "That hag shadow ain't goin' anywhere."

They repaired to the great laboratory while Ham Brooks remained in the reception room, making rapid telephone calls, endeavoring to look into other angles of the growing mystery.

Doc and Monk set up the spectrometer, which burned unidentified matter, releasing their constitute spectra. This was a fancy way of saying that the colors produced by this process revealed the chemical composition of any substance being tested.

Doc and Monk took some of the residue from the hotel-room hatch and subjected it to the process.

They did not have to wait long, but when they beheld the spectrum results, Monk's eyes went wide and he gave out an inarticulate grunt.

Doc's unique trilling drifted out briefly; it had a wondering quality.

"This is new in my experience," he admitted.

"Whatever this junk is," Monk muttered, "I don't recognize it, either."

Not satisfied, Doc took another sample, and repeated the process. The results were the same. The color line produced did not match anything he knew.

To an ordinary scientist, this would not have been very significant. The world is full of unusual substances, and not all of them had been tested by man. The big bronze giant was a master of chemistry, as he was of electricity, aeronautics, medicine and virtually every other field of endeavor.

If Doc Savage did not recognize something, it was a fair bet that no other scientist on the planet would have.

As Monk absorbed this, his tiny eyes grew narrow and his mouth came back under his control.

"Blazes!" he squeaked unexpectedly. "You don't suppose that this stuff is not of this earth?"

"While we can suppose nothing of the kind," replied Doc evenly, "neither should we rule out the possibility. This matter, whatever it is, does not belong to the existing fund of modern scientific knowledge."

That last comment almost took Monk Mayfair's breath away; he did not know what to say for the longest time. Finally, he managed, "Maybe I had better take a look at the residue in that barrel downstairs."

"Be very careful," cautioned the bronze man. "We are a long way from knowing what we are dealing with."

"I'll tell a man!" Monk said fervently.

As the homely chemist sought the elevator, Doc Savage joined Ham Brooks in the reception room and asked, "Have you discovered anything of interest?"

Ham nodded. "The police have managed to trace the telephone call that Ned Gamble made from the Hotel Paramount upon his arrival. He called a Chicago number, and spoke with a woman named Janet Falcon."

Interest flickered in the bronze man's golden eyes.

"Did you get the telephone number?"

Ham tore a slip of paper off a notepad and proffered it to Doc Savage.

The bronze man took the sheet, glanced at it briefly and the number was instantly committed to his indelible memory.

Picking up a telephone, Doc Savage connected with the building switchboard operator and recited the phone number from memory.

After five rings, a nervous but professional sounding female voice asked, "Hello?"

"This is Doc Savage in New York. Am I speaking to Janet Falcon?"

"Yes, yes, you are," the woman said eagerly. "Have you met with my fiancé?"

"What is his name?" countered Doc.

"Why, Ned Gamble. He was going to visit you."

Doc Savage did not hesitate. "Your fiancé did arrive at my headquarters for the appointment, but we never had an opportunity to speak."

Puzzlement flavored the woman's crisp voice. "Why—why not?"

"It distresses me to be the one to convey this news to you, Miss Falcon, but he collapsed on my doorstep. We were unable to revive him."

Janet Falcon's voice became shrill. "What do you mean by that? Answer me!"

"We regret to inform you that Ned Gamble perished a few hours ago. The cause of his death has yet to be determined."

"Oh! Oh!" The woman sobbed. Her breathing over the telephone became rushed and ragged.

Doc Savage gave the stricken woman a few moments to compose herself, then stated, "We have some questions for you."

"Questions! At a time like this? How dare you?"

With that, the distraught woman hung up the phone with stunning finality.

QUIETLY, Doc Savage replaced the telephone receiver on its cradle, and informed Ham Brooks of what had just transpired over the wire.

"Perhaps Miss Falcon will be in a better frame of mind to talk once the news sinks in," remarked Ham.

"She appeared to be frightened," returned Doc. "She knew that Ned Gamble was coming to see me, so whatever his business was, we can extract that from her later."

"If I know women," mused Ham, "even when she settles down, we are going to have a job on our hands talking to her."

"It is conceivable that Gamble came to me at Janet Falcon's behest. No doubt she will blame herself, and possibly me, for his unfortunate passing."

Ham looked puzzled. "What makes you think that?"

"Something in her tone of voice suggested that Gamble was acting as her emissary."

"You suspect that Janet Falcon was too afraid to come by herself?"

"That is about the size of it," related the bronze man.

Just then, Monk Mayfair came up, carrying a rag which he had used to scour the barrel that had disgorged so much unpleasant smoke. It was a tattered smudge of charcoal black.

"We should see what this stuff is in a jiffy," he related.

Doc and Ham followed the hairy chemist into the great laboratory, where the spectrometer was once again engaged.

The results were disappointing, as they discovered just a few minutes later. The residue was not anything more interesting than black gunpowder and some other chemicals.

"This don't match the other stuff," Monk mumbled in disappointment.

"What was the other stuff composed of?" Ham wanted to know.

"We have no clue, Doc and me," admitted the homely chemist.

Ham Brooks seemed momentarily taken aback. He looked to Doc Savage for confirmation.

Doc told Ham, "The substance found in the hotel is unknown to us."

"What about the greenish shadow on our hallway wall?" prompted Ham.

"We will turn our attention on that next."

The three men returned to the reception room and filed out into the corridor, and were soon huddled around the yellow-green shadow.

It still discolored the marble wall unpleasantly, its aspect hideous. The wall consisted of greenish-black marble below its waist, while the facing above that was sandy in hue. The discoloration stood out starkly against both types of marble.

Monk took a chance, applied his wide nostrils to the unlovely splotch, and began sniffing.

"I don't smell nothin'," he admitted, mild voice puzzled.

Doc Savage had brought with him several vials of chemicals. Carefully, he began applying different substances at random points on the yellow-green shadow with a swab, changing swabs with every application.

They waited for the chemical reaction to take hold.

Surprisingly, nothing of the sort transpired.

Monk grunted, "Ain't painted on. So what is it, then?"

No one knew what or how to answer, least of all Doc Savage.

"This deserves further study," he said as they retreated to the reception room. "Which we will undertake with appropriate equipment, inasmuch as it is not practical to remove that section of the marble."

No sooner had Doc closed the door behind them than the telephone commenced jangling.

Leaping, Ham scooped up the receiver. He listened for a few moments and said to the others, "It's Long Tom."

Doc accepted the telephone transmitter and said, "Go ahead, Long Tom."

"I looked into this Ned Gamble fellow," Long Tom reported. "He's a mineralogist, of all things. Strictly small-time. Teaches at a local college. Doesn't have a bad reputation, doesn't have much of a reputation at all. He's on the young side. Maybe he hasn't had time to accomplish much of anything."

"Please get to the heart of the matter," requested the bronze man.

"O.K.," said Long Tom. "He's known to people at this conference. In fact, he had been planning to attend. Obviously, that won't happen now. Asking around the exposition, I found out that this Gamble is engaged to a woman named Janet Falcon. Miss Falcon is the secretary to Myer Sim. So they all tie in together."

Doc's trilling piped up briefly, then he asked, "Janet Falcon appears to be the one who sent Gamble to New York. But she refused to divulge the reason why over the telephone. Look her up, Long Tom. Talk to her. She is rather shaken up right now, but we must get to the bottom of this. So far three persons have died."

"I'll get right on it, Doc," said Long Tom, hanging up abruptly.

The bronze man turned to the others and said, "While Long Tom is pursuing the Chicago angle, we will endeavor to discover who laid the trap outside our garage door."

Monk scratched his bullet head, which was furred by rusty red bristles.

"How are we gonna do that?" he asked.

Instead of replying, the bronze man turned into the library, and passed on through its spacious expanse into the great laboratory.

Monk and Ham hastened to follow.

When they caught up with the bronze giant, Doc was standing before a large cathode-ray tube that dominated a corner of the room. This was a television device that he himself had perfected; it was far more advanced than the old mechanical scanning television devices of only a few years ago.

"As you know," he began to say, "of late we have installed television cameras at different points around the building, the better to monitor prowlers and other undesirables. These cameras are connected by special cables to this screen, and a timer causes the different cameras to cut into the screen in rotation, displaying moving images."

Ham fingered his well-shaven chin and said, "But what good will that do us without a means to record these images?"

Doc moved to another device, saying, "Of course it would be virtually impossible to film these images continuously for later viewing—not without several persons taking turns changing the film reels. That is impractical. So I have contrived the next best solution to the problem."

The bronze man broke open the back of a bulky contrivance that they realized was a large still camera pointed directly at the televisor screen. From this, he extracted a black container, which he carried over to an enclosed nook that was set aside as a photographic darkroom.

Monk snapped his fingers. "I get it! You rigged that big camera with a timing mechanism to take pictures of the screen every few minutes."

"Exactly," replied the bronze man. "Once these negatives are developed, we may be fortunate enough to capture what happened outside the garage door in our absence."

Disappearing into the darkroom, Doc toiled several minutes, patiently developing the photographic strip.

When he emerged, the bronze man held the positives in one hand. He laid these upon a work table so the others could examine them.

The angle of one television camera looked down from above the garage door, and it caught a man in the act of dropping a barrel off the back of an open truck.

The truck was in the shadow of the great skyscraper, and so the man and his features were not distinct enough to make out and were further obscured by a battered Trilby hat. But the license tag on the truck was.

Sharp-eyed Ham noticed it first. "Fortunate break! That truck can be traced."

"Without a doubt," agreed Doc. "That will be our first order of business, to locate the truck and its driver."

Monk grinned his widest. "Boy, oh boy, when I get my mitts on that bozo, I'm going to shake loose his teeth, loosen his eyeballs and anything else he's got rattlin' around in his skull."

Going to a telephone, Doc put in a call to no less than the Commissioner of Police for New York, and made his request.

The commissioner was only too happy to oblige the bronze man. Often in the past, they had worked closely together.

"I'll do everything in my power to get you this information," promised the official, hanging up.

They were not long in waiting. When the commissioner called back, he related that the tag had been traced to a truck rental agency. "Here is the name of the concern."

Doc took the information without writing it down, thanked the official, and hung up.

"We will pay a visit to the Ajax Rental Company now," he said.

As they exited the reception room, they walked past the hideous yellow-green shadow sprawled on the corridor wall.

Ham remarked, "We still have not figured out how the man who struck down Ned Gamble at our very doorstep managed to get to this floor without detection."

"If it was a man," suggested Doc.

Ham's eyes grew cunning. "You think it might have been a woman?"

"Medusa was a woman," reminded the bronze man.

Chapter VII

THE MISTRUSTFUL WOMAN

LONG TOM ROBERTS had once been a soldier. He did not look it. He was undersized, appeared to be poorly nourished, and had a complexion that suggested future business for the mortician's industry. His skin was pale as a fish belly, his hair was the color of straw that had lain too long in the sun, and his eyes were a blue so pale that sometimes sunlight made them seem colorless. Additionally, one front tooth had been knocked out in the past. The replacement was solid gold.

During the past war, Long Tom had been a major in the United States Army, and once saved the day by stuffing an assortment of knives, broken crockery, nails and other unpleasant projectiles into an old cannon of the "Long Tom" type. He had sufficient gunpowder for the operation, but lacked a proper fuse and matches. So he rigged up a small electrical detonator of the kind used to set off dynamite, hunkered down behind the safety of a fieldstone wall, and drove the plunger down.

The result was a calamity for the enemy—and a memorable victory for the young officer, who was forever after known to friends and associates as "Long Tom" Roberts.

Long Tom did not look like much when he left the great auditorium where the scientific exposition was being held in the heart of Chicago. He was bundled up in an overcoat; under one arm he toted a bulky box.

Weather had been Fall-like in New York City. Here in the Windy City, Old Man Winter had taken a firm grip. Long

Tom kicked drifts of snow out of his way as he sloped toward an idling taxicab.

Getting in, he told the driver. "Take me to the Lincoln Apartments."

"Sure, buddy." The cab, an ancient thing with an overpowered motor, made a deep grinding noise as it slipped away from the curb.

As old as the cab seemed, it had good tires. The creaky hulk held the road well as it pushed its way through slow-moving Chicago traffic.

Twenty minutes later, the hack deposited Long Tom at his destination, an apartment building of yellowish Chicago brick. He paid the fare, but offered no tip. Long Tom was stingy with his money—residue of an impoverished childhood.

Still clutching his bulky box, the puny electrical wizard entered the vestibule of the Lincoln Apartments building, ran a cold-stiffened finger down the list of occupants, found the number corresponding to *J. Falcon*, and pressed the bell.

At length, a woman's hoarse voice asked, "Yes, who is it?"

Remembering Doc Savage's admonition that the woman might not be agreeable to talk in her grief, Long Tom told a bald lie.

"Got a package for you."

"I am not expecting a package."

"Well, I have to deliver it. It has your name on it. Janet Falcon."

The woman seemed hesitant. "Does the package indicate who sent it?"

Long Tom thought quickly. "I can't read it all, but the first name is Ned."

"Ned!" gasped the woman. "Wait one moment. I will be right down."

"O.K.," said Long Tom.

He did not have to wait long. Shortly, a woman appeared and opened the inner door.

She was a cool-looking woman dressed in a tasteful business frock. Her face was marked by a thin, but not unattractive, nose. Chestnut hair was arranged in a long fall that was held together by a silver clasp. Her eyes were the clear green that sometimes suggests grass, and other times remindful of the hardness of polished jade. Right now, they had a stony quality. Her orbs were rimmed in red. Obviously, she had been crying.

Long Tom had succeeded in luring the woman into the vestibule, but he had not figured out how to open up the wormy can of lies he had served and confess the truth.

So he decided to come right out with it. Long Tom was a lifelong bachelor and he did not know women very well. Thus, he might be excused for his mistake.

The woman said, "Show me the package. I want to see it before I accept it."

That helped Long Tom get to the point. "Actually, this package isn't from Ned. Doc Savage sent me here. I'm Long Tom Roberts, the electrical engineer. Probably you've heard of me."

Long Tom's professional reputation was such that practically the whole world knew him. Declaration of this made no great impression upon Janet Falcon, however.

She attempted to slam the door in his sour face. Long Tom saw that coming, and inserted his shoe between door and jamb.

As a consequence, he let out a yelp of pain when the panel collided with his shoe. The woman was stronger than she looked. Or anger lent her greater strength than normal.

Long Tom dropped his box, which spilled its contents.

This was unfortunate, for the box proved to contain an unusual pistol, looking nothing like anything that had ever come out of a gun manufacturer's factory. The mechanism was neither that of a revolver nor an automatic. Its elongated barrel was distorted in a peculiar way. A ram's horn ammunition clip jutted out from the walnut grip.

While Long Tom was hopping on one foot, holding the other in both hands, the woman lunged down, took hold of the queer pistol, and lifted it. The weird barrel pointed unerringly. It could be seen that the hole from which bullets might be expected to emerge was unusually thin. Thin as a needle, in fact.

"This gun," she bit out, "tells me that you are lying. You mean to kill me."

Now, the normal response to having a weapon pointed at one is to raise both hands to show that you intend no attack. But the pain in Long Tom's throbbing right foot made that reflexive gesture inconvenient.

"Whatever you do," Long Tom said, holding onto his throbbing foot, "don't pull the trigger. That is no ordinary pistol."

The woman did not take him at his word. She directed the weapon at the glass on either side of the vestibule door and constricted her trigger finger.

The gun made no sound, nor did it jerk about like an automatic and spit out spent cartridges. There was no kickback, no stream of gunsmoke, no outward indication of an operating mechanism.

Instead, the door glass shivered into fragments, producing a cacophony of breaking glass.

Long Tom made his move then, grasping fingers lunging for the weapon.

Alas, he missed. The woman directed the strangely distorted barrel in his direction and suddenly Long Tom's hands were in the air and he was trying not to keel over.

"Upstairs!" she commanded. "March!"

Having no choice in the matter, Long Tom obliged. His pallid face was beet red.

Still keeping his open hands in sight, the slender electrical expert started up the stairs. The woman was canny. She stepped aside to let him pass, then dug the clumsy barrel into the small of his back, prodding him upward.

"You're making a mistake," Long Tom warned.

"I will add this error to the growing collection," the woman snapped.

When they reached the third floor, Janet Falcon directed her chagrined prisoner down a short hallway and pushed him into an apartment that was unlocked.

Locking the door behind her, she said, "Sit down, please."

There was an overstuffed sofa upholstered in faded yellow damask. Long Tom sat. He did not look happy.

The woman asked what was, under the circumstances, a peculiar question. "What kind of gun is this?"

"It's new," supplied Long Tom.

"I can see that!" the woman snapped. "That doesn't answer my question."

"What I mean is, it's a new invention. I devised it."

"This barrel of a thing—is that a silencer?"

"No. But it's complicated. It would take an hour to explain it."

Experimentally, Janet Falcon showed that she possessed a cool nerve. She directed the barrel at a horsehair easy chair that had seen better days, depressed the trigger.

The weird weapon spit out bullets without any sound, gunpowder, or recoil.

A flurry of slim holes peppered the chair, which showed no other reaction to being shot up. Neither did it shake or quiver. Perforations were too numerous to count.

"This is like no gun on earth," she marveled.

Long Tom grunted, "You have that right. I planned to show it off at the science exposition. That's why I'm lugging it around. All the rest of it was a lie. Except the part about me being a Doc Savage associate."

Janet Falcon studied the unhealthy-looking electrical wizard with earnest green eyes. "I spoke with Doc Savage not an hour ago. How is it that you come to be in Chicago so rapidly?"

Long Tom said patiently, "I just explained that. I'm in town for the big scientific conference. Doc called me. Told me to look you up. We need to get to the bottom of what happened to Ned Gamble."

At the sound of her late fiancé's name, Janet Falcon began to tear up. She fumbled into a pocket of her frock, pulled out a handkerchief that was noticeably wet, and started dabbing at her red-rimmed eyes.

"They killed him," she murmured jerkily.

"Who are they?"

Coming out of her crying jag, the woman suddenly snapped, "It is just an expression! Forget I said that."

"Doc Savage seems to think you sent Gamble to New York."

Janet Falcon made no reply, but pain brought a wince to her attractive features. For despite the pale strain on her features, she was an attractive woman—beautiful the way a marble bust can be beautiful: Cold and austere.

Long Tom decided to twist the knife. "Sent him to his death."

Janet Falcon's face fell apart at that point. "Oh, poor Ned! I should never have told you what I did."

The peculiar weapon in her hand wavered. Knowing the unpredictability of women, especially those under emotional distress, Long Tom attempted a thing he normally would not have tried.

Reaching into his coat, he found the grip of a second weapon nestled in his underarm holster, brought it out and fired two rapid shots in succession.

The machine pistol in his hand barked, and two rounds struck Janet Falcon on one bare arm. Almost immediately a combination of shock and surprise overtook her disintegrating features.

For a terrible instant, it looked as if she was going to return fire, but the weapon fell from her fingers, and she collapsed on top of it.

"Just my luck to encounter a difficult female," muttered Long Tom as he holstered the weapon, then rushed to reclaim the unusual pistol, which had tumbled to the floor.

ONCE he set this odd pistol aside, Long Tom gathered up the woman in his arms and placed her on the sofa, knowing that it would be at least an hour before she awoke again. For he had struck her with two "mercy" bullets—hollow shells that were filled with a chemical preparation invented by Doc Savage, and which were designed to disable a foe without permanently injuring them. Once the slugs struck flesh, they ruptured, introducing the anesthetic potion into the bloodstream. The speed with which unconsciousness took hold was sometimes difficult to believe. But the bronze man had formulated the stuff so that it could be used in situations exactly like this one. Janet Falcon had succumbed before she could pull the trigger on the electrical expert.

Looking at his rather large wristwatch, Long Tom noted the time and sat down on the perforated horsehair chair to await the woman's return to consciousness. At that time, he would have the upper hand and was determined to extract from her the truth, if for no other reason than to make all the trouble he had just endured worthwhile.

Unfortunately for the pale electrical wizard, he did not have an hour to wait.

A dozen minutes along, the doorbell buzzed insistently. At first, Long Tom ignored it, but when the buzzer refused to cease its annoying repetition, he went over to the electrical panel, pressed a push-button and called into the speaker grille, "Who is it?"

"This is Malcolm McLean," a thin voice returned. "I just heard about poor Ned. I've come to pay my respects and offer my condolences."

"She is indisposed," returned Long Tom impatiently.

That should have done the trick, but it did not. The thin voice became suspicious and demanded, "Who is this? What are you doing in Janet's apartment, if she is indisposed as you say?"

Long Tom had no good answer for that. So he snapped, "It's none of your business. Call another time."

"I'll call the Chicago police," snapped the voice over the calling system.

Long Tom realized this would not do. He would have to deal with the caller.

"If you insist. I'll buzz you up."

"I thank you," said the man waiting below as Long Tom pressed the push-button that electrically disengaged the vestibule door lock.

By the time a rattling knock came at the apartment door, Long Tom had inserted his unusual pistol under the horsehair chair seat cushion where the incriminating weapon would be out of sight, and went to the door.

Throwing open the panel, he was met by a remarkable sight.

The noteworthy thing about Long Tom Roberts was the fact that he looked as if death were following in his footsteps. The man who had presented himself at the door appeared as if he had been overtaken by the Grim Reaper long ago.

He was thin to painful proportions. Taller than Long Tom, he looked nevertheless far more unhealthy, to an almost unbelievable degree.

For the skin of this man was as gray as that of a corpse that had been lying in its coffin for weeks. His hair had a dry quality that made it seem lifeless. His eyes were a lighter gray than his skin, but the combination was vaguely repellent.

The corpse-faced caller took one look at the pale electrical wizard, and started. "Why, you're Long Tom Roberts, aren't you?"

"What's it to you?" returned Long Tom belligerently.

A curious light came into the other's eyes. "I've been an admirer of your work, particularly in the field of television."

Taken aback, Long Tom demanded, "Who are you?"

"Malcolm McLean. I am a chemist of some note. Perhaps you have heard of me."

Long Tom shook his head vigorously. "Chemistry is not my line."

Peering over Long Tom's shoulder, McLean asked, "May I enter?"

Reluctantly, Long Tom let the man in. As soon as he entered the apartment, his strange gray eyes fell upon Janet Falcon lying on the divan.

"What—what happened to her?"

"She fainted, I guess," Long Tom said vaguely. "So I laid her out on the sofa. She ought to wake up before too long."

Malcolm McLean looked back at the pallid electrical wizard and said thinly, "So you were not lying, after all. But what is your business with Janet?"

"My business is my business," snapped Long Tom. "Or maybe I should say Doc Savage's business, get me?"

"There is no need to be rude about it," said Malcolm McLean dolefully. "I merely stopped by to pay my respects, and to ask if there was anything I could do to help Janet in her bereavement."

"News travels fast," clucked Long Tom.

"We live in an age of scientific marvels," retorted McLean.

The two men studied one another like a pair of alley cats waiting for the other to make a wrong move. But neither man did.

When nothing untoward transpired, Malcolm McLean turned his attention back to Janet Falcon, and observed that she appeared to be sleeping peacefully.

Then he spied the two spots of moist crimson on the young woman's forearm. His gray eyes narrowed, gristle-like lips writhing with some unexpressed emotion.

"Janet appears to have injured herself," he commented finally.

"She fell when she fainted," returned Long Tom. "I was about to tend to the wounds when you showed up."

"I know where she keeps her first-aid kit," McLean offered. "Let me get it."

"Help yourself," said Long Tom casually, not taking his pale eyes off the man.

The corpse-gray man disappeared into the bathroom, rummaged around for a time. When he returned, he was carrying a small white metal box with a red cross stamped on it.

"Would you hold this while I perform the appropriate ministrations?" he requested.

Long Tom saw no reason why not, so he held out his hands and took hold of the metal box.

While Long Tom was getting a good grip, Malcolm McLean wheeled suddenly, snatched up a brass lamp on the nightstand and raised it, quickly braining the unprepared electrical wizard, who fell immediately to the floor, completely insensate.

"That will teach you!" McLean snarled vehemently. "You puny brute!"

Chapter VIII

CIGARETTE CLUE

THE AJAX TRUCK RENTAL COMPANY was nothing special.

Situated in the borough of Brooklyn, it was not much more than a dingy garage equipped with a modest fleet of trucks which were available for hire at reasonable prices.

There was a small office in one corner. Doc Savage, followed by Monk and Ham, entered to the astonishment of the proprietor.

The man's eyes popped. "Aren't you—?"

Doc looked vaguely uncomfortable. The fact of his celebrity was not something to which he had ever grown accustomed.

The bronze giant placed the photograph on the man's desk and asked, "According to the license plate, this is one of your rental vehicles."

The flustered man looked down, saw that this was true, and said, "Is this trouble?"

"Probably not for you," admitted the bronze man. "We are seeking the individual who rented the truck."

Monk inserted, "That bird, he's in a pile of trouble. And we intend to pile on him once we get hold of him."

The proprietor looked suitably impressed and said, "Just a minute."

Riffling through papers on his desk, he found a pink sheet and handed it over to Doc Savage. "This is the guy."

Doc picked up the sheet, and absorbed the name and address inscribed on the carbon paper.

"John Stone," he said. "But this address is a false one."

The proprietor blinked, stammered out, "How can you be so sure?"

Doc Savage did not reply to that. Modestly, he declined to admit that he had memorized virtually every street and thoroughfare in the greater New York area. Beyond that, the big bronze fellow was familiar with streets all over the nation, and in many foreign capitals. He had only to study a printed map for a few minutes to commit the essentials to mind. Once a detail was absorbed, it was never forgotten by his amazingly agile brain.

"Please describe the man," requested Doc.

The proprietor was not a bad painter of word pictures. He launched into his description, beginning with, "He was better than average height, I would say that he stood five foot eight high. His hair was very black. His eyes had a greenish-gray tint. Maybe you would call them hazel. He dressed like a guy who drove trucks for a living. Brown leather jacket and denim pants. Olive green hat. Paid in cash. Had the truck only two or three hours."

"Let me examine the vehicle in question," requested Doc.

"Sure. Glad to oblige."

The proprietor led them out of the crowded office and into the garage proper, where they stepped around shivering dark pools where oil had dripped out of crankcases.

The truck was several years old and the license plate numbers matched the digits in the photograph.

Climbing into the cab, Doc rooted around, but found very little. The driver had left a pack of cigarettes on top of the dashboard, and Doc took this, taking care to pick it up with a clean handkerchief in order to preserve any fingerprint impressions that might be found on the package.

Stepping out, Doc examined the tires for any telltale residue, but found nothing notworthy.

"We have what we need," he told the proprietor.

The owner blurted out, "You do? You were in there for hardly a minute."

"Sometimes a minute," advised the bronze man, "is sufficient."

With that, they left the puzzled proprietor rubbing his jaw.

Once they were ensconced in the sedan and back in traffic, Ham asked Doc Savage, "What did you discover?"

"Package of cigarettes."

Monk inserted, "Bet you five dollars the bird left his fingerprints on the package."

Doc Savage said, "The package may be more significant than any fingerprints. This is the same brand of cigarettes discovered on the person of Ned Gamble."

Ham asked, "So? Is it a common brand?"

"It is common to Chicago. It cannot be purchased here in New York."

Ham said thoughtfully, "That means the assailant hails from Chicago."

"It may mean a lot more," commented Doc. "For there is only one cigarette missing from the package."

Monk murmured, "Funny a guy would bring a package of his favorite smokes all the way from Chicago and leave it behind, after havin' only one cigarette."

"If that is in fact what happened," said Doc. Then the bronze man lapsed into silence.

THE GROUP returned to their headquarters in short order and were soon situated back on the eighty-sixth floor.

Retreating to the great laboratory, Doc Savage gave the cellophane package a thorough dusting with fingerprint powder, then used adhesive tape to lift off the print impressions. These he studied under a compound microscope.

In the normal course of criminal investigations, fingerprint patterns are analyzed mechanically and produce amazing results. Doc did none of this.

Instead, he absorbed the whorls and ridges of the lifted fingerprints, and then went to a chest of drawers similar to the card catalog in a large library.

The bronze giant seemed to know what he was looking for. Opening one drawer, which was labeled "*G*," he fingered through the closely-packed cards, then lifted out one in particular.

It showed a miniature mug shot of a man, and next to it examples of his fingerprints.

Doc compared the prints to the ones he had just harvested from the cigarette package.

"A match. The man who rented the truck is known as Duke Grogan."

Ham said slowly, "Duke Grogan. I've heard that name somewhere."

"Duke Grogan is a rising power in the Chicago underworld," advised Doc.

"The underworld!" squeaked Monk. "That don't exactly fit what's been happenin' around here. Since when does the mob go around puttin' whammies on people like they hung on Ned Gamble?"

"As much as I hate to agree with this evolutionary mishap, here," inserted Ham, "it is not like the Chicago underworld to send a hired torpedo in our direction. The consequences of failure undoubtedly would ignite the ire of Doc Savage. Chicago has been quiet since the Savoli outfit was run out of town. Why stir up the kind of trouble we could bring on their heads?"

Doc stated, "We will let the police commissioner know that Duke Grogan is in town. Perhaps they can pick him up before he leaves."

"What makes you think he's leavin' town?" wondered Monk.

"The booby trap left outside the garage door was not designed to kill us, but to deliver a warning. The warning was to stay out of Chicago. Having delivered that message, Duke Grogan is certain to be on his way home before very long."

Monk scratched his nubbin skull, muttering, "Sounds screwy to me. We never did anything to Duke or his boys."

Ham said, "Perhaps Grogan figures it is just a matter of time before Doc got around to him."

"I don't buy it," snorted Monk.

Doc Savage went over to the corner of the great laboratory where the body of Ned Gamble lay. On an adjacent table reposed the late Gamble's personal effects. Among them was the package of cigarettes found in his pocket.

Doc took this up and shook out the cigarettes, and then did an unusual thing. He began crumpling them up, producing a pile of thin white paper and coarse tobacco. Metallic fingers sifted through the pile, but he seemed to discover nothing of significance.

Then Doc did the same with the package taken from the truck cab. This pile appeared to offer no clues, either.

Lastly, Doc picked up what remained of the cigarette Ned Gamble had been smoking when he succumbed to the strange brain-petrifying influence.

Monk watched this with popping eyes. He was getting an idea of what Doc was seeking.

The bronze man took the half-smoked cigarette, and tore it open, laying the fragments on a clean sheet of paper.

"You're thinkin' that cigarette he was smokin' was doped in some way?" suggested Monk.

Doc nodded. "But it does not appear to be so. All that is discernible is tobacco. Ordinary tobacco."

Ham's eyes lit up. "You suspect that Duke Grogan somehow planted a doctored cigarette into Ned Gamble's package? Is that right?"

Instead of answering directly, Doc Savage said, "Ned Gamble knew he was being followed. Since both men hailed from Chicago, there is some question whether Gamble would recognize Duke Grogan. But it seems likely Grogan contrived to insert a poisoned cigarette into Gamble's package."

"Wild, but not impossible," theorized Ham.

"No, not impossible," admitted the bronze man in a tone that was faintly puzzled. He was studying the tobacco residue; his eyes shifted over to the other piles.

Unexpectedly, Doc produced two glass slides, and inserted samples of tobacco from the partially burned cigarette and from the package carried by the unfortunate Gamble. They were placed on separate slides.

These he conveyed over to a compound microscope, and inserted one slide after the other, studying both intently.

His trilling filtered out, low and eerie, trailing off slowly, like musical air escaping from an organ pipe.

"What is it, Doc?" pressed Ham.

"The tobacco in the partially smoked cigarette is of a different brand than the two packages from Chicago. Even the grade of paper is dissimilar."

"What does that mean?" blurted out Monk.

"It means," said Doc, "that while we were otherwise occupied, an unknown person switched cigarettes. This could not possibly have been the cigarette Ned Gamble was smoking when he was slain."

"Blazes!" exploded Monk. "Maybe that original cigarette was doped, after all."

"That remains to be determined," said Doc. "Before we solve that mystery, we must determine how that unknown individual managed to get to this floor and out again without being detected."

Doc Savage went to a cabinet and removed from it an atomizer containing a yellowish fluid, along with a lantern notable for its very dark lens. He took these items out through the big rooms and into the corridor.

Walking up and down the hallway, the bronze man began spraying this liberally about the marble floor, which was highly polished, for it was waxed weekly.

The atomizer emitted a fluid which, when applied, reacted to the scuffed patches in the wax coating left by the tread of leather soles, producing a trail of imprints. These became vaguely visible when Doc tripped a switch on the side of the lantern. No light was produced. Not light visible to the naked eye, that is.

But the scuff marks began to glow luminously—an eerie electric blue. Doc went to a wall switch and doused the hallway lights, enabling him to study the glowing prints in greater detail.

Virtually every set of footprints came from the bank of elevators, then paraded to Doc Savage's plain office door.

One, however, did not. These tracks led to a fire door, leading to a flight of stairs going downward through the building. This door was alarmed. But when Doc pushed it inward, the alarm did not go off.

Examining the door frame, the bronze man discovered the wires to the alarm bell had been severed, leaving frayed copper ends dangling.

The stairway was unwaxed concrete, and so the footprints did not proceed downward. But there was no question that the person who had reached the eighty-sixth floor had managed to find his way to the fire stairs, and disable the alarm on the fire door.

Switching off the ultra-violet lantern, Doc told Monk, "Bring fingerprint powder and tape."

The hairy chemist made haste, his bandy legs carrying him back in jig time.

Doc Savage brushed the black powder liberally on doorknobs and handrails, and picked up the residue with the sticky tape. Holding the strips up to the light, he studied the fingerprints thus collected.

"Duke Grogan has been here," he said firmly.

"Peculiar," commented Ham. "A thug like Grogan would normally send hirelings to do his dirty work. Why would Duke take the risk himself?"

"When we catch up to him," Doc said firmly, "we will ask Grogan."

The bronze man's grim tone left no doubt in the minds of his two aides that that hour was shortly at hand.

Chapter IX

THE PHONIES

LONG TOM ROBERTS returned to conscious awakening with difficulty.

His first reaction was to let out a moan of pain. His skull throbbed. It felt as if every blood vessel winding through his brain was on fire.

Long Tom had walked the trails of danger for a long time. He knew how incapacitating a skull concussion could be, so he took pains not to move until he could ascertain how seriously he was injured.

His low moaning caused a woman's voice to say thinly, "He's coming to."

"That ruffian!" complained a thin, male voice. "What is to be done with him?"

"I have no wish to speak with Doc Savage, or anyone associated with him, until I know more of what happened to poor Ned," replied the woman.

Long Tom recognized the female voice. It was Janet Falcon speaking. The man's voice he could not immediately place. The blow on the head had left him groggy.

"Perhaps it would be best if you went into hiding," suggested the man.

Long Tom's memory was slowly returning. The image of a face like a gray corpse came back to him. Malcolm McLean.

Janet Falcon was saying, "I think you are right, Mr. McLean. I do not wish to involve the police. Not until I think things through."

"I know a place where you will not be found," said McLean. "Get your things, and come with me. You will be perfectly safe. Doc Savage and his associates will not bother you until you're ready to speak of this tragedy."

There followed a bustle of activity. Long Tom took stock of his surroundings. He did not open his eyes. But he could tell from the rough textures pressing on his face and hands that he was lying on the carpet.

When he opened one pale eye a crack, the light was almost blinding. He sealed it.

Deep within him, the electrical genius felt a strong urge to jump to his feet and take control of the situation. But every limb felt hollow, like empty milk bottles. His wiry strength was absent. That told Long Tom that if he sprang into action, he would be swiftly overcome. It was aggravating. He wanted to use his fists on someone.

He remembered that corpse-faced Malcolm McLean had brained him with the brass lamp. Long Tom was inclined to return the favor.

As the prone electrical wizard tested his fingers to see if they would respond to his aching brain, Malcolm McLean and Janet Falcon stepped briskly around him and exited the apartment, drawing the door shut with a click.

After that, there was an interval of silence in which Long Tom endeavored to pull himself together.

It was a slow and painful process, but before long his arms and legs were obeying his mental commands. First, the fragile-appearing electrical wizard sat up on the rug. Then he crawled over to the overstuffed horsehair chair and, with agony warping his pallid features, pulled himself up into a seated position.

The perforated cushion was anything but comfortable. That was when Long Tom remembered the peculiar gun he had stashed there. He did not feel up to excavating it now. He merely settled into the cushion, and tested his eyes against the lights.

When at last he opened them, the electrical expert saw only blackness. For a terrible moment, he thought he had lost his eyesight. Concussions can do strange things to a man.

"This is bad," he muttered to himself. With relief, it dawned on him that the duo had switched off the lights when they left the apartment. That was all.

Long Tom felt around his person, and discovered his compact superfiring machine pistol still snug in its underarm holster.

"Be thankful for small favors," he told himself forlornly.

Long Tom judged that more than an hour had passed, inasmuch as Janet Falcon had shrugged off the anesthetic effects of the mercy bullets, and was back on her feet. But that was all he understood. Why the woman had been so recalcitrant and why she didn't wish to speak to him remained a baffling mystery. Her fiancé had been murdered visiting Doc Savage. It stood to reason she would want to know the whys and wherefores.

Instead, she had disappeared into the night, to hide out like a common criminal.

It took another twenty or so minutes for Long Tom to feel up to standing, and when he did, he weaved a little. Experimentally, he attempted to walk to the wash room, barking one bony shin against an end table, but managed to stumble to the sink, where he drew running water. This he splashed on his face, which helped somewhat.

Long Tom had flipped on the lights upon entering. This enabled him to make his way back to the rather dilapidated horsehair chair and dig out the strange gun which he had brought with him.

The pistol was apparently in good working order. It could be seen that the curled ram's horn magazine still jutted from the grip. A numerical indicator told that the weapon held a significant quantity of ammunition.

Ordinarily, Long Tom would have made a thorough search of the woman's apartment, looking for clues. But he did not feel that he possessed the mental presence to do so.

Instead, he decided to take his leave, return to his hotel and get word to Doc Savage. Doc would know what to do next.

But Long Tom Roberts was destined not to return to his hotel that evening. Just as he was making his way to the door, the vestibule buzzer sounded again.

At first, the sound hardly penetrated his headache. He had a faint ringing in his ears, which did not help, either.

Finally, the noise got through and Long Tom diverted to the wall panel housing the inter-communicator.

"Who is it?" he asked foolishly. Realizing that it was probably not the wisest thing to answer someone else's door, he made a sour face.

A gruff voice barked, "Police. Let us up. It's about Ned Gamble."

Long Tom could hardly decline to admit a Chicago police officer. So he pressed the electric door-release button, and went to the apartment door. This he threw open.

Clinging to the door frame, the pale electrical engineer awaited the arrival of the police.

The two men who stepped off the elevator wore plainclothes and the stolid expressions habitual with city detectives. One sported the heavy beard growth of a man sorely in need of a shave.

"Are you the cops?" Long Tom asked.

The blue-jawed arrival nodded curtly and demanded, "Who the hell are you?"

"Thomas J. Roberts, one of Doc Savage's men."

Hearing that declaration, the two men acquired startled expressions. No doubt they had heard of Doc Savage. Few in the civilized world had not.

Instead of greeting Long Tom as a respected associate of the Man of Bronze, the two stolid-looking men drove their hands into their overcoats and drew out stubby revolvers.

"In that case," one snarled, "you're coming with us."

"Am I under arrest?" stammered out Long Tom, taken by surprise.

"You're going to wish you were," said the other. "We ain't cops, wise guy."

Now Long Tom was really flummoxed. "Who are you birds?"

"I'm called Blackie, and this here's Blue. We are a team—kind of like a vaudeville act." He wiggled his revolver barrel, whose barrel had been bulldogged until it protruded barely an inch in front of the fat cylinder. "There are six lead honeys in there, brother!" he confided laconically. "Every one has been scratched on the nose and rubbed in garlic."

Long Tom gulped, found his voice.

"What does that mean?" he demanded.

"Makes blood poisoning," Blackie elaborated genially. "Gangrene. You get slugged with one of these and you're same as in the dead box."

"What's the idea?" Long Tom asked indignantly.

"No idea at all," rasped Blackie, moving closer. "Now come with us."

"Where?"

"Nowhere," chuckled the other, then both he and Blackie laughed loudly.

"In that case," returned Long Tom, "count me out."

The men stepped up and took positions on either side of Long Tom, their stubby .38s digging into his scrawny ribs.

Blue taunted, "We're kind of a couple of tough eggs. Are you a tough egg, too?"

"Yeah," said Long Tom, making hard fists. "I'm plenty tough."

"Is that right? Then show us how tough you are, tough guy."

Long Tom did not need a further invitation. He took a seemingly wild swing. It was a bolo punch—combining a hook and an uppercut. It connected with the nearest man's jaw, rocking it backward.

Evidently, the man on the receiving end of the powerful punch had sized up Long Tom as a lightweight. Long Tom's hard knuckles striking home disabused him of that notion.

As he stumbled backward, Blue said to the other, "Slug him!"

Blackie's bulldogged revolver lifted, chopped downward—and Long Tom was promptly brained for a second time. He went down like a sack of potatoes falling off a farmer's truck. He did not get up again.

Methodically, the two tough men pocketed their revolvers. One grabbed hold of Long Tom's ankles, while the other took him by the shoulders.

Hauling the insensate electrical genius over to the automatic elevator, Blue elbowed the call button, and when the door slid open, they threw Long Tom in as if he was no more than a sack of household refuse.

Fortunately for Long Tom, he did not land on his head.

The two tough men stepped aboard, closed the door and sent the cage sinking toward the foyer.

Since it was now the dark of night, they had no difficulty lugging the limp electrical expert out through the vestibule and into a flashy roadster parked at the curb. Long Tom did not receive the dignity of the back seat. Instead, they threw him into the rumble seat, slamming down the lid.

Taking seats in the front of the machine, one said to the other, "This is a hell of a note, Blue."

"It is, at that," replied the blue-jowled one. "But maybe it will work out all right in the end."

"Where Doc Savage is concerned," observed Blackie, "I'm not sure anything works out all right in the end, or otherwise."

"What do you mean?"

"I had a pal down in Cincinnati what got grabbed by Doc Savage. He disappeared for about a year. I ran into him one day. My pal, who I knew since I was a kid, didn't recognize me at all. I called him by his right name, and he insisted that wasn't his name. But I knew the guy. It was him. Only it wasn't him anymore. Get me?"

"No, I don't," said Blue, rubbing his unshaven jaw.

"Doc Savage done something to him. Something horrible. Not only did he call himself by a strange name, but the guy had gone straight. Straight as an arrow. I couldn't talk him into any crooked stuff. He gave me the air. And me, his pal since we were both squirts in short pants."

Blackie got the engine going. It made a contented sound, indicating quality of manufacture.

As the flashy machine muttered into traffic, Blue groused, "That Doc Savage is a devil."

"You got that right," grunted Blackie. Then they fell into an interval of comfortable silence as they moved through city traffic.

Chapter X

"WATCH FOR DUKE"

DOC SAVAGE'S FATHER, a great humanitarian in his day, had laid out the course of his only son's life when the latter was still in swaddling clothes. The aim was to fit the youngster for his life's work. It commenced when Clark Savage, Sr., voluntarily placed the child in the hands of a seemingly endless parade of scientists and other knowledgeable men. Thus, while other children played with toys, young Clark had begun as intensive an education as any mortal had ever experienced. The lad was trained in many scientific disciplines. There existed no field of study the bronze man had not touched, and many he ultimately mastered.

Among them was criminology in all of its manifestations. As a scientist, he was an acknowledged wizard, a modern Mercury with a dash of Merlin. As a follower of clues and deductions, he passed for a latter-day Sherlock Holmes.

By modern means, Doc had determined that Duke Grogan was in Manhattan. But the trail had gone cold. There seemed no way to get on it again.

Thus it was to the mutual astonishment of Monk and Ham that their bronze chief suddenly announced, "If we act fast, we may prevent Duke Grogan from boarding the Twentieth Century Limited back to Chicago."

Monk and Ham swapped befuddled glances.

Ham began to object. "But how do you know he plans to train back to Chicago?"

Instead of responding, Doc Savage said, "We have no time to waste."

Monk beamed. "This might be a good time to bring along the special ammo I've been workin' on."

Ham asked waspishly, "What ammunition is that? I have heard nothing of this."

Instead of replying, the homely chemist waddled into the laboratory and came back, lugging two metal cases. One was his portable chemical laboratory. The other was a bulky ammunition locker which the hairy Monk toted with simian ease.

Soon, they were dropping to the sub-basement garage and climbing aboard a subdued gray sedan.

The auto roared up the concrete ramp and jounced over the sidewalk and onto the avenue.

Monk looked back at the garage door as it was closing.

"Heck! That green shadow is gone."

Doc Savage's active eyes flicked to the rear-vision mirror and noted that this was so.

"What happened to it?" blurted Ham.

"Action of direct sunlight may have obliterated it," suggested Doc.

It was a short distance to Grand Central Terminal. During the drive, Monk asked Doc Savage, "What makes you think Grogan is lammin'?"

"In Ned Gamble's billfold was a return ticket to Chicago. We can surmise that he was followed from Chicago. It stands to reason that the person doing the following occupied the same train or, at least, one not many hours behind it."

"Makes perfect sense," offered Ham.

"Having slain Gamble and warned us off, Grogan has no reason to remain in town. It follows that he would depart as quickly as possible. The next train to Chicago leaves in fifteen minutes."

Monk eyed his wristwatch.

"Better step on it, then. It's gonna be tough to run down one guy in all the hubbub at Grand Central."

Doc Savage touched a lever and a concealed siren sprang into full voice, clearing the traffic as efficiently as any police prowl car.

Doc Savage had amassed a considerable fortune in recent years. Its source was a mystery to the general public. With the business depression, the bronze man had ploughed some of his funds into various businesses, helping them back on their financial feet. Among these enterprises were various railroad companies.

As it happened, Doc owned a large stake in the branch of the railroad that maintained the New York to Chicago run.

Parking in a spot reserved for bigwigs, Doc alighted, then entered the station. Monk and Ham followed close on his heels.

Doc Savage went directly to an office, and conferred with the station master in charge of Grand Central Terminal.

"There is reason to believe a known criminal is planning to depart on the Twentieth Century Limited," Doc told him.

The station master looked aghast.

"I understand that you have the authority, but I am reluctant to have the train held up," the official gulped.

"There is no need." Doc produced a photo of Duke Grogan and added, "Have every red cap and conductor look for this man."

"That will take several minutes," the man pleaded. "And the train is due to depart momentarily."

"There is no need to hold up the train. If Grogan can be taken off, the train may depart without him."

Relief washed over the station master's pale visage.

"At once, Mr. Savage," he clipped.

"Discretion is of paramount importance," cautioned Doc. "My men and I are too conspicuous to infiltrate the throng without being identified by Grogan."

The station master rushed out to show the photo to his employees.

"This will be a lead-pipe cinch," Monk chortled.

Ham frowned. "I don't know. Duke has a reputation of being a wily customer."

"Well, we're more wily," retorted Monk confidently. "We'll get him."

IT WAS not fear of Doc Savage, nor any inkling that the mighty bronze nemesis was on his trail, that compelled Duke Grogan to take certain steps once he had boarded the Twentieth Century Limited train.

Duke had secured a Pullman compartment, which was the epitome of luxury, for the simple reason that he liked to travel in style, and his nefarious activities had caused his picture to appear in a great many news sheets. That much of this exposure was limited to Chicago was not significant to Duke. He was in the habit of taking precautions wherever he traveled.

Grogan was walking down the aisle of the train, seeking his private compartment when Dame Fortune tapped him on the shoulder.

Coming from the other direction was a pinched face he knew well.

"Well, well," Duke growled in a friendly manner. "If it ain't my old pal, Ed Waco."

The man thus addressed stopped in his tracks, and his crafty eyes lit with a challenging light.

"Duke! As I live and breathe. What are you doin' in this burg?"

Grogan chuckled. "I'm on my way back home. Got a private compartment with all the trimmings."

Ed chuckled back. "You don't say! Same here. You sure come up in the world since you were an alky cooker."

"Those were the days, eh?" Duke lowered his voice and said, "Do a pal a favor?"

Ed Waco looked crafty. "What's the favor?" he asked suspiciously.

"I'm leaving town after finishing a big job. I don't think the bulls are on my trail, but you never know. You said you got a private compartment and so do I. What say we swap?"

"Swap?"

"That's right. In case any bull pats you on the shoulder, thinking you're me, you could set them straight pretty quick. Cover for me. Get it?"

Waco rubbed his jaw dubiously. "I could get into trouble. What's in it for me?"

Duke looked injured. "For doing what? Sitting in another guy's Pullman compartment? You can just say you got confused."

"What's in it for me?" repeated Waco.

Duke growled unhappily. "If you're going to be that way, two hundred smackers."

Waco returned a wise grin. "Three hundred, to make it worth my trouble."

Duke Grogan didn't hesitate. Removing a gold money clip from a pocket, he extracted three crisp new one hundred dollar bills and handed them over. The two men swapped tickets in silence.

As he passed Duke Grogan, Ed Waco gave the brim of his dark hat a tug in salute and said, "Nice runnin' into you, Duke."

"Same here, brother," returned Grogan.

The two men moved on to their respective private compartments, took their seats, closed their doors, and awaited the departure hour, which was imminent.

Not long after that, there was a commotion.

A conductor came barreling down the aisle, looking for a specific compartment. One that was reserved in the name of Duquesne Grogan, which was Duke's legal name.

This conductor had been shown the picture of Duke Grogan, as had other train employees, but since there was only one picture, it could not be carried around by all the searchers. So they were forced to rely on their memories.

When he arrived at the private department, the conductor didn't bother to knock first. Instead, he threw the sliding door open, and barged in.

"You Mr. Grogan?" he barked.

"Not me. My name's Ed Waco."

"Then what are you doing in this private compartment reserved for Mr. Grogan?"

"Am I in the wrong spot?" asked Ed Waco, reaching over to his overcoat draped over the seat next to him.

"Don't give me that malarkey," snapped the ticket taker. "I seen your picture, and you are the spitting image of Grogan. No more backtalk. You come with me."

"Hold the phone, you railroad bull. I got identification in my wallet that says I'm Ed Waco. Not any Duke Grogan."

That last remark was a mistake. The conductor grinned and said, "Never said your first name, Duke."

Ed Waco knew he was sunk then. But he had another ace up his sleeve. "My driver's license will prove that I'm Ed Waco."

"That may be so," grunted the conductor. "But you'll be doing your proving in the police room at the station. You're getting off this train."

Ed Waco did not like the sound of that. He decided to bolt.

Unfortunately for him, the only way out of the cramped compartment was through the one door. And the conductor had grown up in a tough section of Brooklyn.

ED WACO attempted to shove his way out, but the conductor uncorked a meaty fist that connected hard, then drove him backward. The crook's backbone collided with the compartment table, over which he sprawled.

The conductor leaped in, took Waco by the coat lapels, jerking him to his feet.

A brief tussle ensued. Ed Waco was not any sort of lamb. He had fists and knew how to use them. Alas for Ed Waco's immediate future, his first swing was wild and the conductor's horny-knuckled response was decisive.

Waco went flying backward again, this time striking the back of his head against the table's edge. That did for Ed Waco. He was out like a light. Pleased with this outcome, the conductor once again reached down. This time he threw Waco over his shoulder the way a fireman carries a helpless victim out of a burning building.

The railroad man made quite a spectacle as he carried Ed Waco off the train and down to the platform.

Duke Grogan, safely ensconced in Ed Waco's private compartment, heard some of this altercation. Easing his sliding door open a trifle, he pasted one wary eyeball to the opening slit and peered out.

When he saw the unconscious Waco being borne off the train, he grimaced and said, "Looks like I made a smooth move. Too bad about Ed. But he wasn't the brightest boy ever hatched."

With that, Duke Grogan ran the sliding door shut, and settled back to await the rattling commotion that would signify the Twentieth Century Limited was leaving the station.

Word reached Doc Savage of the capture in the police room of Grand Central Station. The spot was where New York's finest would bring various pickpockets and other malefactors, whom they collected in the course of policing the busy railroad depot, for questioning.

The burly conductor came in with an air of triumph and a great big grin rounding off his square features.

"Found him right away," he announced to all. "He didn't come that easy, but I persuaded him. Where do you want him?"

Doc Savage said, "The table will do."

There was a long table that was used for interrogations, and the big conductor clucked, "With pleasure."

Dropping Waco on the table, he all but slammed the body on its back.

Doc Savage, Monk Mayfair and Ham Brooks gathered around the exposed face.

Doc took one look and pronounced, "This is not Duke Grogan."

"Well, he was squatting in Grogan's private compartment. Who else would he be if he's not Duke?"

Doc studied the face briefly and said, "This is Ed Waco, a notorious police character."

The conductor scratched his head and muttered, "He was the only mug in the Pullman."

Doc Savage said, "There are only two possibilities here. Grogan convinced Ed Waco to take the train to Chicago to throw us off the scent. Or the two exchanged compartments."

The Grand Central Terminal station master held a list of the passengers who had booked tickets and private compartments. He went down the list. "There is a Mr. Edward Waco on this list."

"In that case," Doc said quickly, "Duke Grogan may yet be on the train."

The station master eyed the clock on the wall, which was approaching the top of the hour. With a distinct click, the minute hand touched the numeral 12.

"If that's so, he's pulling out of the station now," he moaned.

The station master looked aghast. One could tell from his slack expression that he would rather lose a pint of blood than to have to stop the train, whose reputation for punctuality was unrivaled.

Doc Savage looked thoughtful for a minute.

"Duke Grogan's clever substitution may indicate that he knows we are on his trail, but it hardly seems likely. Perhaps it would be the wisest course of action to let him take the train all the way to Chicago."

The station master looked relieved, but he was responsible enough to ask, "How is that wiser than stopping the train?"

"If the train is halted, Duke may do something rash. And a gun fray on a crowded passenger train is not a pleasant prospect."

"You can say that again!" snapped the station master.

Doc continued, "If the train is allowed to proceed all the way to its destination, Grogan will be convinced that he is in the clear. He will not expect us to be waiting for him when the train pulls into LaSalle Street Station."

"How are you going to beat the train? It's one of the fastest in the nation."

"By private aircraft," stated the bronze man.

Ham Brooks asked, "Do we have time to question this man when he wakes up?"

Doc shook his head, saying, "Not if we merely wait."

He removed from a pocket a flat case which contained a hypodermic needle and a small vial. He selected the syringe, charged it from the vial.

Rolling up one of Waco's sleeves, Doc Savage introduced the contents of the syringe, saying, "This stimulant should bring him around quickly."

It did. Waco was soon snapping his eyes, flapping his hands. Abruptly, he pushed himself up into a seated position.

The first person Ed Waco laid eyes upon was the unfamiliar station master. The face meant nothing to him. Then he saw Ham Brooks and Monk Mayfair, and a vague light of recognition leapt into his uneasy orbs.

Doc Savage spoke up, asking, "We are interested in knowing what you were doing in Duke Grogan's private compartment?"

Ed Waco's eyes veered to the speaker, and drank in the imposing form of Doc Savage. He recognized the big bronze man. Every crook knew him. And feared him, if they were smart.

"I ain't done nothin'!" he bleated.

"We did not say that you did," replied Doc calmly, his flake-gold eyes steady, like the penetrating orbs of a bird of prey.

There was something about the fixed expression of the bronze man, combined with his impassive voice, which unnerved the small-time crook. Waco had heard stories of companions in perfidy who had run afoul of Doc Savage, and had never been seen again. All the underworld heard such stories. No one could explain them.

For a second time, Ed Waco decided to bolt.

Sizing up the men surrounding him, he took sartorially foppish Ham Brooks to be the easiest to bowl over. He was correct in that assumption.

Ed Waco shot off the table top and drove one shoulder into Ham Brooks' immaculate chest.

The dapper attorney went sprawling, and Waco dashed past him.

Growling, Monk Mayfair unlimbered his supermachine pistol from his underarm holster.

Ed Waco lunged for the door, seized the knob, and wrenched at it. That was as far as he got.

Squeezing one eye shut, Monk lined up the lean snout, and fired two shots.

The slugs struck Ed Waco in one calf.

Normally, the effect of being felled by a supermachine pistol was to bring about instant unconsciousness.

Squirming about on the floor, Ham Brooks caught a glimpse of the man's retreating feet, and expected him to go down. The fleeing crook did not. Waco kept going, possibly stimulated by fear of the bronze man of mystery.

He got out of the room, and flung himself into the crowd outside.

Ed Waco immediately began hopping on one foot. The hopping did not take him very far. He soon stumbled, falling to the ground, and grasped the calf that had been shot as if it were on fire.

"What the hell!" he cried. "What's got into my leg?"

Monk grinned broadly. "It worked!"

Scrambling to his feet, Ham Brooks asked, "What do you mean? It clearly did *not* work. The mercy bullet should have knocked him out by now."

"Oh, I didn't hit 'im with a mercy slug," returned Monk airily. "But with a new bullet of my own invention."

Monk and Ham quickly surrounded Ed Waco, who was struggling to keep his left leg still. The limb seemed to be in intolerable agony.

"What was in that bullet?" demanded Ham. "Rattlesnake venom?"

"Naw," beamed Monk. "It was a hollow shell with the chemical preparation that once it gets into a man's muscles does a job on them. I call it my Charlie horse bullet."

On the ground, Ed Waco squirmed and moaned. "That's what I got! A Charlie horse! A damn Charlie horse. Make it go away."

Monk told him, "It'll go away on its own. You just gotta wait it out."

Doc Savage gathered up Ed Waco and brought him back into the interrogation room, this time planting him in a wooden chair. The bronze giant held him down with both hands pressing on the miserable crook's shoulders.

"The story of you and Duke Grogan on the train, please," requested Doc.

Between grimaces, Ed Waco, in the parlance of the underworld, spilled his guts.

"I happened to bump into Duke. He made me a deal. Swap rooms and I got three hundred simoleons in the bargain. That's all. I hadn't seen him in a couple years before I ran into him. I swear."

The station master said, "We have nothing to hold him on, if that's the truth."

"Nonetheless," advised Doc Savage. "I will take custody of this man."

"Fine by me. I know you have the rank of inspector with the police."

Ed Waco heard these words, and sheer terror gripped him. He began to tremble all over, not just in his afflicted leg.

"Look at that guy!" chortled the station master. "You just mention you're taking him into custody, and he's falling apart like he's being sent to the electric chair."

"This man has many crimes to his name," said Ham Brooks. "Doc will make sure that he pays for them."

Hearing that, Ed Waco simply fainted.

The train conductor looked thunderstruck. "Imagine that! A hard-boiled egg like him, fainting at the sound of justice."

The man's amazement could be understood and forgiven. He had no inkling that Doc Savage was not about to turn Ed Waco over to the police for commonplace justice. Doc Savage had other plans for Ed Waco.

For the bronze man maintained a secret institution hidden in upstate New York. To his private sanitorium, Doc consigned criminals who fell into his hands, and whom he did not wish to turn over to the police.

There, a trained staff subjected the captured crooks to the strangest rehabilitation regimen ever imagined. First, their memories were removed through delicate brain surgery. Then they were taught a useful trade and to hate crime in all forms.

Once this stringent moral and spiritual renovation was completed, the former felons matriculated into the normal world. As a graduation gift, they were provided new identities—hence they were termed "graduates" of Doc's "crime college."

Only Doc, his men and the staff—and Inspector Hardboiled Humbolt of the New York City Police—knew of the existence of the facility. It was too radical a solution to the problem of the career criminal to make public.

Within the hour, a private ambulance would convey Ed Waco to this facility.

Doc Savage and his men would not accompany the nervous crook; they had a different destination in mind.

Chapter XI

CHICAGO BOUND

MONK AND HAM were having an argument. As usual. "A Charlie horse bullet!" sneered Ham. "Only a brainless anthropoid such as yourself could come up with such a harebrained idea."

"There's nothing harebrained about it," growled Monk. "When a guy's muscles get overtired, certain lactic acids build up, creatin' that Charlie horse crampin' that you sometimes get. I just whipped up a batch of sodium lactate, and poured some into our mercy-bullet capsules. It sure done the trick."

"Nonsense!" jeered Ham. "It's ridiculous. You'll make a laughingstock of us yet."

"And that's only one of my new bullets," said Monk proudly. Tapping an ammunition case, he added, "I got me a pile of nifty ones. You watch."

Ham frowned, but interest came into his dark eyes. "What kind of bullets?" he demanded.

"You'll see, shyster. Stick around. The best is yet to come."

With that, Monk subsided, confident that he had the dapper lawyer's interest.

They were winging their way over upstate New York, having taken off from Doc Savage's private warehouse-hangar on the Hudson River. In this somewhat ramshackle edifice, the bronze man housed his fleet of boats, aircraft and other aerial conveyances.

Doc had selected his tri-motored speed plane for the hop to Chicago, the so-called Windy City. The aeronautical marvel was driving for the Great Lakes at a speed which topped two hundred and fifty miles an hour. It was streamlined to a degree that few other planes had yet achieved. The cabin was electrically heated and soundproofed to an amazing degree.

Thus, Monk and Ham were seated in comfort behind the cockpit. Doc flew the craft.

As the argument abated, Ham Brooks asked Doc Savage, "Duke Grogan is going to be beside himself when he steps off the train and discovers us waiting for him."

"We will arrive in Chicago half a day ahead of the Twentieth Century Limited," stated Doc Savage. "That will give us time to hunt up Long Tom, and see how his investigation is going first."

"This is sure spooky business," muttered Monk. "People's brains turnin' to stone for no reason. And grisly green shadows found on the walls afterward."

Ham Brooks was a learned man and his reading had not been limited to law books. He had perused the classics, and knew Greek and Roman literature, as well as mythology.

"It is not reasonable to think that Medusa is walking around in modern times," he declared.

Monk snorted, "And it sure ain't reasonable for a bird's brains to turn to stone. But some did. Make something of that."

Ham could not. He fell back on a recitation of what he could recall of the mythological Medusa.

"Medusa was a horrid creature in the shape of a woman, but with a head full of twining serpents instead of hair. Her awful stare was anciently said to turn any mortal to stone in an instant."

Monk made thoughtful faces. "Well," he said, "this modern edition doesn't have the act down completely. Nobody's turnin' to stone. Just their brains."

"I fail to see how," commented Ham.

Monk Mayfair's chemical mind began to work. "The brain is made of a substance kinda like bean curd. It's soft. Nothin' to it that could harden into stone—not by any chemical action."

Always poised for an argument, Ham retorted, "Don't living things petrify into fossils that were once soft in nature?"

Homely Monk was not stumped by that. "The human brain can only live as long as the skull holdin' it. Once a person is dead, the brain will liquefy pretty dang quick."

"Ned Gamble did not die in an ordinary manner," reminded Ham. "It appears that his brain suddenly fossilizing is what struck him down."

"When archeologists dig up fossils, they never find the brain," scoffed Monk. "It just won't fossilize. Besides, the process of fossilization can take millions of years."

"Then explain the sorry state of Ned Gamble's brain," retorted Ham.

Monk entertained some mental counter arguments, but decided there was no point to playing devil's advocate. The dapper lawyer was correct. The unfortunate Gamble appeared to have died because his brain had turned to a stony substance, and not the other way around.

Calling ahead to Doc Savage at the controls, Monk asked, "Doc, do you reckon what happened to Ned Gamble's brain is what croaked him?"

"Undoubtedly," returned the bronze man.

"Any notion what might've done it?"

Doc did not reply. He was not being rude. It was one of his few quirks that when he heard a question he preferred not to answer, he fell into a somber silence, pretending he had not heard the inquiry.

Often, this meant that Doc was still formulating theories, other times it indicated he had arrived at a definite conclusion, but was unwilling to share it pending actual proof.

It was impossible to tell from the bronze giant's silence into which of the two categories his lack of comment belonged.

The subject apparently exhausted for the moment, the cabin fell silent, as Doc Savage sent it hurtling through the night. It was a long way to Chicago but the bronze wings of the big plane devoured them with the speed that would have impressed another mythological figure, the wing-footed Mercury.

AT THE exact time Doc Savage was flying to Chicago, Long Tom Roberts was experiencing difficulties.

The undersized electrical genius was being drowned.

The persons doing the drowning were the two thugs who had abducted him from Janet Falcon's apartment. They were taking turns.

One, whose unshaven jaw had a bluish tint, was saying, "What's it going to take to get this mug to wake up?"

"We conked him pretty good, Blue," grated Blackie.

"Yeah, maybe *too* good. He ain't coming around."

"Dunk his head again. Even a guy who's out like a light needs to breathe."

The one addressed as Blue seized Long Tom's neck, and shoved his face underwater. The water in question was an overflowing bathtub that had once been used to make bootleg gin. Long Tom became immersed; immediately bubbles of air began popping on the surface of the water.

Blue held the electrical wizard down, waiting for a reaction.

The reaction was not coming. The two men watched with cold-eyed interest, as Long Tom continued to drown, completely unresponsive to their hearty calls to wake up.

Blue looked up at his confederate and said, "We got to find out what Doc Savage knows, Blackie."

"Don't I know it?" grunted Blackie, throwing a well-smoked cigarette into the water. The burning butt made a hiss, but that was all; it soon sank.

The paucity of air bubbles breaking the surface became alarming.

Blackie's nerve broke. "I can't go through with it. It just ain't fair, guy."

"O.K., O.K., lift him up."

Blackie hauled Long Tom's head out of the water, and laid him flat on the bathroom floor. The puny electrical wizard just lay there, seeming beyond all appeal.

The two blows to his head had done a job. Long Tom would not wake up until nature permitted this.

Blackie and Blue looked at one another in exasperation. Blackie said, "Duke will want to know everything this guy does."

"Well, Duke ain't here. We gotta think for ourselves."

The two men lit cigarettes and threw themselves into comfortable chairs while they gave the matter thought.

The pair were hardened killers, products of the Chicago underworld. Killing a man was not something that bothered them particularly. Bumping off one of Doc Savage's men was another matter entirely. They were afraid to do that until they had wrung from their captive everything he knew of Doc Savage's interest in Janet Falcon.

"What if the punk don't ever come around?" Blue asked Blackie. "Some birds don't."

"Well, we got to wait until he does. Can't chill him until we get the word from Duke."

Blue looked at his wristwatch and said, "Duke won't be in until tomorrow. That's a long time from now. I don't feel like babysitting this runt. I got a hot babe itching to go out on the town."

Blackie gave the matter thought as he puffed slowly, threw his head back, and blew smoke rings expertly. Silently, he watched the vaporous circles strike the ceiling and dissipate like expiring ghosts.

"I got an idea."

Blue regarded his partner expectantly.

"This idea is a peach. It may cause Doc Savage to think twice about sticking his nose into our business."

Interest grew on Blue's unshaven features.

"I'm going to send the bronze guy a telegram. We'll make up a story, put them on a wild goose chase. Plus, we need to buy us some extra insurance."

Blinking, Blue rubbed his purplish jowls. "Insurance? I don't get you. Insurance from what?"

"Not life insurance. But *death* insurance. Insurance that we don't disappear like my pal who disappeared."

Now Blue's interest was acute. But Blackie did not enlighten him. Instead, he grunted, "Help me drag this punk into the cellar."

Shrugging, Blue stood up, and the two men took hold of Long Tom Roberts, and proceeded to convey him to the basement.

SOME hours later, Long Tom began to emerge from his prolonged period of unconsciousness. He opened his eyes painfully, but saw nothing. Only darkness.

Smells that came to his dilating nostrils suggested mustiness, stored coal, and other indefinable odors that are found in cellars and basements everywhere.

Long Tom tried to move, but found he could not. His right arm appeared to be fixed. When he gave it a tug, he discovered that the limb felt as heavy as concrete. He could not move so much as his fingers. They would not even wriggle.

"Blast it! What have I gotten myself into now?"

Long Tom attempted to lift his right hand, but it seemed to weigh a ton. In fact, the member felt as if it was composed of rock-hard cement.

The exertion was too much for the feeble electrical wizard. Once again, he lapsed into unconsciousness.

His last wild thought before oblivion overtook his brain was that his entire arm was turning to concrete....

Chapter XII

THE TELEGRAM MYSTERY

OWING TO PERSISTENT headwinds, Doc Savage arrived in Chicago at the crack of dawn.

Although his plane was an amphibian, and capable of landing on water, the bronze man chose to set down at the Chicago Municipal Airport.

Thanks to the rising sun, the bronze paint of his speed plane was evident to anyone loitering at the busy airport when the amazingly streamlined ship came in for a landing.

One happened to be a Chicago newspaper reporter. When he saw the metallic hue of the plane taxiing discreetly into a hangar, he rushed to a pay telephone, his hungry-looking face excited.

Shoving his lanky frame into the wooden call box, the reporter demanded that the operator connect him with his city editor.

"Sam! It's Jack. Guess who I just eyeballed down at the airport. No less than Doc Savage himself. No, I didn't see him exactly. But his bronze plane is scooting into a hangar right now. Sure, I'll try to snag a story. You know me. If I can't get one, I'll make one up!"

Hanging up, the reporter snapped the door open, and hotfooted it toward the hangar in question. He made excellent time, managing to reach the structure just as Doc Savage, trailed by Monk Mayfair and Ham Brooks, exited the building.

Excitedly, the legman raised one arm, calling out, "Hey! Doc Savage! Is that you?"

Behind the bronze man, Monk Mayfair growled, "Dang! Looks like a local newshawk."

Ham frowned. "No avoiding him."

Doc Savage commented, "I had hoped to avoid such a situation by landing in the dark, but headwinds were against us."

The scribe jogged up and came to a halt, a yellow pencil poised over his dingy notepad.

"What brings you to the Windy City, Doc?"

Monk got in front of the bronze man and waved his massive paws about, saying, "Scram, you! Don't you know Doc never gives interviews?"

The scribe grinned crookedly, "Sure. But rules are made to be broken. What say you? What's doing in Chicago that interests the Man of Bronze?"

Doc Savage imparted, "We prefer to offer no comment at this time."

The reporter had a hunch, or perhaps he took a wild stab. "Is it anything to do with the mysterious death of Myer Sim?"

Ham Brooks interjected, "My good man, Doc Savage does not wish to speak on the record."

The newspaper legman was persistent. He followed them to the operations building, pestering them with questions but getting no response.

Doc Savage resembled a statue of bronze, except that he moved with a fluidity that belied his metallic solidity. He was such an impressive sight in motion that the reporter began wishing he had a photographer along. Candid pictures of the bronze man of mystery were rare.

Entering the building, Monk made a point of going in last and slamming the door behind him, holding the knob firmly in both hands, preventing the lanky reporter from so much as turning the knob.

Seeing the way of it, he ran back to the public telephone, and began filing his story.

"Sam! It's hot! Doc Savage blew in to town to look into the Myer Sim mystery. I got the whole scoop! Put a rewrite man on the wire."

For the journalist in question was one of the members of his fraternity who rarely wrote his own stories. Instead, he phoned them in to someone who took down the facts verbatim, typing them into publishable form.

ONCE he had made arrangements for securing his aircraft, Doc Savage rented a dark sedan, and he, Monk and Ham piled in and began the push into early morning traffic.

"Where to for us, Doc?" asked Monk.

"We will check in at Long Tom's hotel, and find out what progress he has made. By now, he should have spoken with Janet Falcon."

The Hotel Chicago was one of the best the city had to offer. But this early in the morning, it was quiet.

Doc Savage entered the lobby, Monk and Ham following him. He went to the front desk clerk, swiftly cut through the man's flustered excitement.

"We wish to secure a suite of rooms," said Doc, "but first ring the room occupied by Major Thomas J. Roberts."

"Wait one moment." The clerk looked up the room number and rang. A few minutes later, he hung up, reporting, "Mr. Roberts does not answer, sir. But there is a telegram for you."

No expression registered on the bronze giant's metallic features, but Monk and Ham looked vaguely baffled.

"No one knew we'd be coming here," declared Ham.

"Long Tom might reasonably suspect that we would show up," stated Doc, taking the telegram and tearing it open.

Once Doc read the message, he passed it around, first to Monk. Ham crowded in.

The two aides read it together. The text ran:

JANET FALCON LIT OUT OF TOWN. GOT A LINE
ON HER. TAKING MIDNIGHT TRAIN TO KANSAS
CITY.

It was signed, "THOMAS."

"Long Tom didn't write this!" exploded Monk. "It's more
than ten words. That runt is too cheap to pay the extra word
charges."

"Although I detest crediting this brainless baboon," chimed
in Ham, "he is correct. Also, Long Tom would never sign a
telegram with his formal name."

Doc nodded. "Nor are any of our usual code words employed
to verify that this message is genuine. Someone has waylaid
Long Tom, not suspecting that such a ruse would never get by."

Monk asked, "So what do we do? We ain't gotta clue where
that runt went off to."

Doc said, "Long Tom was to visit Janet Falcon. We will start
there."

After securing lodgings, Doc and his aides returned to their
rental sedan, and drove through early morning traffic to the
apartment of Janet Falcon.

They made good time, inasmuch as it was too early for most
commuters to be on the road. South of the Loop, rising out of
Lake Michigan, reared a fantastic sight—a cluster of futuristic
buildings, most of them windowless.

This was the waterfront site of Chicago's late world's fair,
the Century of Progress. It had recently closed. Now its impressive layout, built around a pair of artificial lagoons, awaited
demolition.

Ham remarked, "I wonder if cities will really look like that
in coming years?"

Monk grunted, "Don't act so impressed. Those overgrown
shacks are built out of plywood and gypsum. They're mainly
for show."

Ham added, "I read that the fair's success led to the establishment of the scientific exposition Long Tom is attending. It is intended to be an annual affair."

"It is a direct continuation of the fair's Hall of Science exhibit," inserted Doc. "By all reports, it is off to a promising start."

Pulling up before the modest yellow brick structure, they alighted. Doc Savage strode into the vestibule, and depressed the push-button next to the name of *J. Falcon*. He did this several times.

"Kinda funny not to be up and about," muttered Monk suspiciously.

Doc reminded, "Remember that her employer is now deceased. She is likely out of work."

Doc Savage wore a bulletproof vest of many pockets. From an inner pocket of his carry-all garment, the bronze man produced an unusual key of his own devising. He carried several of these. The exact properties were not known to his aides, but the ingenious mechanical gadget possessed the ability to adapt itself to certain kinds of locks.

Doc inserted the device, manipulated it in a way that neither Monk nor Ham could clearly discern, and the door immediately fell open.

They mounted the stairs, found Janet Falcon's door, and noticed that the hallway carpet runner was somewhat askew.

Drops of blood had spattered here and there.

Doc Savage looked at those drops, and to Monk and Ham's profound astonishment, announced, "That is Long Tom's blood."

"Jove!" exploded Ham.

Monk's jaw sagged alarmingly. "Blazes! How can you tell, Doc?"

It was such an uncanny deduction that Monk and Ham were momentarily flummoxed.

"If you were to kneel down," informed Doc, "you would see blond hairs mixed in with the fluid. They are the exact color of

Long Tom's hair. This leads to the inescapable conclusion that Long Tom was struck upon the head on this very spot."

Monk and Ham looked a little sick.

They considered how to enter the apartment after first knocking and receiving no response.

Doc began to go through his miracle keys, but Monk proved to be impatient.

Stepping back, the gorilla-like chemist threw his burly form against the door. The panel was solid. But its hinges were not. The door went flying inward, its lock smashed out of the jamb.

Monk puffed out his barrel chest, boasting, "Renny could hardly have done as nifty a job of door wreckin'."

Renny was Colonel John Renwick, esteemed civil engineer and one of the absent members of Doc Savage's band of trouble-busters. Renny was possessed of a pair of horny-knuckled hands the size of the wooden mallets employed by circus roustabouts for the purpose of driving the pegs with which to stake down bigtop tents. When balled into fists, they became intimidating monsters. For some reason known only to the big engineer, Renny liked to haul off and smash down inoffensive doors with one devastating punch.

They entered the room, snapped on the light.

The living room disclosed at first appeared ordinary, its furnishings categorizable as shabby-genteel. Dominant was a horsehair armchair covered in faded yellow damask. The high back and seat cushion were freckled with tiny, uniform holes, no bigger than the lead shaft of a mechanical pencil.

Doc Savage's keen gaze absorbed these details, then came to rest on something even more unusual.

On the floor of the parlor lay a pile of what appeared to be construction debris. This consisted of chunks of irregularly-shaped stone or concrete. Much of it had been thoroughly pulverized, as if persons unknown had taken sledgehammers to the pile of rock.

In fact, impressions found on the rug were greatly suggestive that exactly this had happened.

"Whoever took hammers to this rock pile, wanted to make sure it was unrecognizable," Monk decided.

Flake-gold eyes active, Doc Savage moved around the rock pile, staring at it intently.

That was when he noticed spots of crimson on the divan. They were still somewhat moist, and sticky. A bronze finger touched one spot, lifted it to his sensitive nostrils.

The bronze man sniffed the sticky stuff carefully. Then he said something that stunned his aides.

"Someone in this room had been shot with a mercy bullet."

Ham stared. "How the deuce can you tell?"

"Mixed in with the vital fluid are faint traces of the chemical contained in our mercy bullets."

The fact that Doc's olfactory senses could detect the potion was not as remarkable as it might seem. As a part of a routine of daily exercises followed since childhood, he subjected his five senses to a regimen of tests. These included smelling the contents of an ever-changing variety of vials while blindfolded, and correctly identifying the odors bottled therein.

Other apparatus tested the upper limits of the bronze man's vision, hearing, touch—even his taste buds were challenged, for sometimes it was necessary to identify substances by application of his sensitive tongue when no other means was available.

"Any idea whose blood it is?" asked Ham, half hopeful of a positive reply.

"None," said Doc, his active eyes going to the pile of grit spread over the carpet.

It had been virtually demolished, but something stuck out of the gritty pile.

Employing the toe of one shoe, Doc nudged it, bringing a pale object to light.

The others gathered around.

Kneeling, Doc Savage reached in and extracted the thing.

It proved to be a human hand, but apparently composed of stone. Despite possessing a somewhat swollen thumb, the hand looked vaguely familiar to them.

Ham blanched. He struggled to form words, but his tongue failed him.

So Monk did it for him. "That kinda looks like Long Tom's hand. I recognize a scar on the back."

Doc Savage said nothing, but from a pocket he withdrew a small magnifying glass. The bronze man began studying the tips of the stone hand's digits, and now he put them under the glass one by one.

As he examined each pad, his trilling seeped out, eerie and ethereal.

"What is it, Doc?" bleated Ham.

"This stone hand exhibits seemingly lifelike fingerprints. The thumbprint is the only one that is clear, but unquestionably it matches Long Tom's print."

Monk and Ham took turns going pale. The hairy chemist pointed at the debris pile, and his eyes were sick.

"Is that—" Monk said thickly.

Doc Savage stood up, holding the hand. His next words made them all feel ill at ease.

"If this hand in fact belongs to Long Tom Roberts, it follows that this pile of pulverized rock comprises his mortal remains."

No one spoke after that. The ticking of a wall clock was the only sound heard.

Then Ham noticed something odd. It was an unusual gun, being larger than a common pistol and possessing a long, distorted barrel and no sign of its operating mechanism. He picked it up.

"What is this?"

Doc Savage took it, and said, "This is a new gun Long Tom has been working on. He was planning to display it at the scientific exposition. He would never have left it behind."

Ham groaned. "That's further proof that Long Tom is no longer with us."

Doc Savage said nothing. The monotonous ticking of the wall clock was the only noise audible in the apartment.

The place was as quiet in a macabre way as a funeral parlor.

Chapter XIII

THE GRAY GHOUL

DURING THE DRIVE back to the hotel, the mood was pensive.

Doc Savage drove. Monk Mayfair sat in the passenger seat beside him. In the rear, Ham Brooks was examining the strange pistol found at Janet Falcon's apartment.

"This looks bally familiar," he said somberly.

"It's a magnetic gun," offered Monk. "You remember that time we tangled with that Arab, Mohallet. He had a bigger version of that contraption. It fired bullets that were so quiet, you could hardly hear them whistle past your ears."*

A light of understanding flared up in the dapper lawyer's intelligent eyes.

"I remember now! We almost fell into a trap in which one of these infernal devices figured."

"Yeah," said Monk. "After we captured it, Long Tom put it in that private museum of his. He got to tinkerin' with it, and started believin' that he could miniaturize it. Mebbe make one small enough it could be toted around in a holster."

"So this is what he produced," marveled Ham.

Doc Savage inserted, "It was Long Tom's belief that magnetic guns such as those could be developed to a degree of proficiency that they might one day replace our superfirers."

---

* *The Phantom City*

122

Monk snorted derisively. "I got wind of that. It gave me a better idea. Not a new gun. Different bullets for our regular supermachine pistols."

Ham had been examining the magnetic pistol and saw that the barrel consisted of a shielded coil, and reasoned that sending power into the coil was the means by which bullets could be emitted at high speed in utter silence, the gun mechanism having no moving parts beyond its trigger and ammunition feed.

The dapper lawyer looked up and remarked, "So that is why you developed that Charlie horse bullet."

"And others besides," said Monk proudly. "Long Tom and I were kinda havin' a contest to see who could do a better job of improvin' the weapons we chose."

"And now Long Tom is no longer with us," said Ham sadly. His eyes went to the woman's hatbox on the seat beside him. Doc had appropriated this from Janet Falcon's apartment, and into this receptacle he had poured several handfuls of the powdery rock, as well as the petrified hand which bore the electrical wizard's unique thumbprint.

"Could that really be Long Tom's remains?"

Doc Savage said, "Whatever turned the brain of Ned Gamble to stone—or a substance the consistency of stone—could conceivably do the same to human flesh and blood and bone."

Neither Monk nor Ham responded to this assertion. They lapsed into an uncomfortable silence.

Doc Savage added, "Only a rigorous scientific analysis of the material will tell us for certain."

They said no more about it after that.

The morning was getting along, and the rental machine was wending its way toward the famed Loop in the heart of downtown Chicago. A cold wind blew off Lake Michigan, biting in the extreme, and the skies looked vaguely threatening.

Snow on the ground was several days old and, while a good deal of it had been plowed and picked up, much of the soiled stuff remained.

Doc Savage drove expertly, managing to avoid the worst streets as if he could see around corners. It was nothing of the sort, of course. Doc knew Chicago well. He had visited the Windy City many times, in different seasons, and had retained virtually all memory of his previous experiences.

The bronze man recalled from past experience which streets were favored during inclement weather and which thoroughfares the city was less diligent about plowing. He merely followed his mental map as he drove along.

Abruptly, he pulled over into a side street in the Jeweler's Row District.

Braking, Doc lifted his golden eyes to the rear-vision mirror and waited.

Monk and Ham looked about them, faces baffled, thinking they had arrived at some undisclosed destination.

But Doc Savage made no immediate move to quit the vehicle.

They saw that the bronze man was studying the view out the back window through the rear-vision mirror. They swiveled their heads about to look.

Traffic swept by, moving at an energetic pace.

Then one machine—a purple convertible phaeton—slithered forward, slowed, seemed about to take the turn, then hesitated.

Doc Savage got out, went to the trunk and opened it. He began removing chains from the trunk, as well as a jack and tire iron.

Monk clambered out, and watched with a curious light in his gristle-pit eyes.

"Are we plannin' to drive out into the country? We don't need chains for the streets. They're pretty well plowed."

In Mayan, a tongue understood by few outside of a tiny enclave in Central America, Doc said, "Observe the phaeton behind me."

Monk was canny about it. He did not react suddenly. Standing close to Doc, he squinted one eye, and seemed to be observing the bronze man, but in actuality was sizing up the phaeton.

"Blazes!" he breathed. "Glim that driver."

By that time, Ham Brooks had joined them. He had caught the exchange, understood it perfectly. All three men spoke the ancient Mayan language as a result of experiences encountered during their first great adventure together.*

Ham caught a glimpse of the driver through the windscreen, as he dawdled at the corner.

"Has that fellow been following us?"

Doc nodded almost imperceptibly.

Ham decided to take bold action. Stepping away, he began walking toward the slushy corner.

Drawing near, the dapper lawyer observed the driver's face more clearly. He all but paled.

For the face of the driver looked like nothing natural. It was an unlovely gray, exactly the color of a corpse that had lain in his coffin for some weeks.

The prospect of the man's unpleasant cast of countenance caused Ham to hesitate. Some sights are unnerving, and this was especially so. The face appeared to be dead and gray, yet the eyes were very much alive and active. They locked upon Ham Brooks.

Baring very white teeth—so white that the contrast around the surrounding gray lips was uncanny—the driver abruptly backed up, evidently intent upon fleeing with alacrity.

"He's tryin' to get away," Monk growled in Mayan.

Doc Savage dropped a tire chain in the snow, and left off all pretense of putting it on the rental machine's tire. Wheeling, he dashed down the street, just as the purple phaeton was straightening itself out.

---

* *The Man of Bronze*

With a frantic shifting of gears, the corpse-face driver threw the car forward. Malodorous exhaust jetted from the tailpipe. With a grinding noise, the phaeton shot ahead.

It was well underway when Doc Savage broke into a sprint, and raced behind the vehicle. Traffic inhibited the phaeton, of course, so it could not accelerate to its upmost speed. Still, it was making a good clip. The machine apparently possessed a very fine motor.

Doc Savage raced up behind the fleeing vehicle, overhauled it, then did something that was seldom seen outside of Hollywood extravaganzas.

Pacing the phaeton, he grabbed hold of one window post, and leaped to mount the running board.

The corpse-faced driver at first did not realize that he had picked up an unwanted passenger. His almost too-alive eyes were bugging out of his head as they stared at the traffic before him, seeking an opening in which to insert his fleeing machine.

Only when bronze knuckles began rapping on the driver-side window did his head jerk around and his eyelids fly wide.

The effect was very weird. The whites of his eyes, combined with the ivory of his bared teeth, looked rather like a skull that still possessed some of its living parts.

The man emitted an inarticulate cry. He began wrenching the wheel from side to side, as if to violently throw off his unwanted passenger.

Calmly, Doc Savage reached down with one free hand and attempted to pry open the car door.

Seeing this, the driver panicked. He attempted to get at the push-button lock of the door. For the bronze man had seen that it was not pushed down.

They engaged in a tug-of-war, a test of strength between the man frantically pushing down on the door button while Doc Savage actually forced the door handle up.

The bronze giant's tremendous strength quickly won out.

Opening the door was not easily accomplished since the bronze man's own body was blocking it. But he managed to crack it enough to let in cold air, as well as his ringing voice.

"Pull over," ordered Doc. He was polite about it, but something in the metallic ring of his voice also carried a compelling vibration of command.

The corpse man would have none of it. He took one hand off the push-button, grabbed the wheel with both sets of gray fingers, and began rocking it back and forth.

"That will do you no good," cautioned Doc.

Nor did it. The driver began to clash nearby fenders; it seemed as if an accident was imminent.

That was when Doc Savage stepped back along the running board, found the handle to the back door, and let himself in.

The bronze giant landed on the rear seat cushions with such force that the suspension springs groaned and the car body jounced alarmingly.

Reaching forward, Doc Savage seized the man by his thin neck, and began applying pressure to certain spinal nerve centers there, so as to effect a sense of creeping paralysis in his extremities.

Feeling the strength go out of his fingers, the driver's evident panic redoubled. He understood he was about to lose control of his machine. So he did all that he could.

Throwing the steering wheel hard to the left, he flung the auto up onto the curb, simultaneously stomping on the brake pedal.

The phaeton slammed to a sloppy halt. One headlight cracked.

Doc left the vehicle, threw open the driver's door and hauled the gray man out bodily.

He attempted to place the man on his feet, but the fellow's knees had gone rubbery and Doc's spinal kneading had pretty much turned his nerve strings into limp spaghetti. Doc had to catch him before he fell to the sidewalk slush.

There being no appropriate place to set him down, Doc lay the unusual fellow on the hood of his own vehicle, holding him in place with nothing more than the strength of one corded hand. The grisly-looking man struggled in vain.

Reaching into his pockets, Doc found the man's billfold, opened it up and began examining what he found within.

"This identification says that you are Malcolm McLean," the bronze man said. "Is this true?"

The man found his voice. Through chattering teeth, he admitted, "I am Malcolm McLean."

"Why are you following me?"

"Because you are Doc Savage. The morning newspaper said that you had come to town to look into the Myer Sim matter."

"What business is that of yours?"

"Myer Sim was a colleague, and a friend. I am interested in knowing what happened to him, as well."

"What is your business, McLean?" pressed Doc.

"I am a chemist of some note. Myer was an inventor, as you may know," the man chattered. "We sometimes worked on projects together."

"That does not completely explain your behavior."

"If I may," said McLean, pushing himself off the hood and finding his feet.

Standing up, the man tried to compose himself. Either nervousness or the cold or a combination caused his teeth to chatter uncontrollably. It was an unnerving sound, given his corpselike countenance. Even his hair had a kind of dead look to it.

Doc asked, "Were you born with this condition?"

McLean shook his head vigorously. "When I was born, I did not possess this gruesome pallor. No, my unfortunate affliction is the direct result of experimenting with colloidal silver, which as you certainly should know as a medical man, results in the condition called argyria."

Doc nodded. His flake-gold eyes continued to scrutinize the unfortunate individual. In his general contours, Malcolm McLean appeared to be an ordinary man, but in his skin tones he was anything but. A Hollywood movie director could have cast him in a horror picture, and raked in considerable box office. That was how unpleasant Malcolm McLean looked.

By this time, Monk and Ham had caught up with Doc Savage.

The homely chemist eyeballed the human corpse and remarked unkindly, "Who dug you up?"

The gray face swiveled, took in Monk's gorilla physique and his eyes became bright with recognition.

"I recognize you, sir," said Malcolm McLean. "You are Andrew Blodgett Mayfair, the renowned industrial chemist. I am pleased to make your acquaintance. We are in the same line. For I, too, am a chemist by trade. Malcolm McLean is my name."

"Never heard of you," grunted Monk. "What's the idea of followin' us?"

The man's face fell momentarily, as if he were expecting recognition from a presumed colleague.

Malcolm McLean was momentarily tongue-tied. His teeth chattering resumed. A pink tongue came out and licked grayish lips like old gristle. The combination of colors was vaguely nauseating in a human face.

Ham Brooks interjected, "Speak up then. We are not to be trifled with."

Some inner dignity asserted itself, and Malcolm McLean took firm hold of his chattering jaw. When he resumed speaking, his voice was deeper and more resolute.

"You gentlemen may wish to explain why one of your associates—I am referring to the celebrated electrical expert, Mr. Long Tom Roberts—injured an acquaintance of mine last night."

Suspicion made Ham's eyes darken. "Make yourself plain, my good man."

"I am referring to Miss Janet Falcon, the personal secretary of Myer Sim. Last evening, your man Roberts paid Miss Falcon a visit and an altercation ensued in which Mr. Roberts assaulted Miss Falcon most cruelly. I happened to be paying a call upon her, and discovered this. Seeing the way of it, I rendered Roberts unconscious, and escorted Miss Falcon to a safe refuge until the matter could be straightened out. It does appear that her life is in danger."

Doc Savage had been listening patiently. Now he put in a question. "Where is Miss Falcon presently?"

"Where no one is likely to find her. Living under an alias."

Monk bared teeth that looked big enough to double as the tops of picket fences. This made his entire simian face ferocious in the extreme.

Balling two fists, he lifted one in warning. "We got ways of makin' guys like you talk."

"I am innocent of any wrongdoing," protested McLean. "You cannot apply such brutish pressure upon an upstanding citizen such as myself. Also, Doc Savage has an impeccable reputation. I doubt very much that he would countenance a bruiser such as yourself giving me a physical workover."

"Don't think we don't take care of guys who hurt our friends," growled Monk.

Malcolm McLean was about to utter something cutting when Doc Savage broke in to ask, "Where did you last see Long Tom Roberts?"

"I left him unconscious in Miss Falcon's apartment. No doubt he has returned to wakefulness by now."

"We did not discover Long Tom in Miss Falcon's place," said Doc, not going into any further details.

This did not sway Malcolm McLean. "No doubt he let himself out. If you wish to locate him, I would advise you to go to the hotel where the scientific exposition is being held. I myself am planning to attend later today. For I have something to exhibit there."

Doc Savage studied the man, and was thoughtful in a stoic, composed way.

"We were on our way to look into the Myer Sim matter," he stated. "Perhaps you would like to serve as our introduction to his survivors."

Malcolm McLean appeared momentarily taken aback. He seemed at a loss for a proper response. His eyes narrowed and his teeth commenced chattering anew. They sounded like castanets.

The unpleasantness of the man's demeanor was almost shocking. His eyes jerked about in his head and his teeth continually clashed. McLean might have been a puppet whose maker had not yet finished painting normal human hues on his wooden features.

Finally, he announced, "Since you are investigating the death of my good friend, I will acquiesce on his behalf. But for no other reason. For the behavior of your man Roberts last night was reprehensible—inexcusable in the extreme."

Doc Savage said nothing about that.

Instead, he offered, "We will bring our vehicle around, and you may lead us to Myer Sim's residence."

A strange relief washed over Malcolm McLean's leaden countenance and he said, "The home is in the suburb of Lincolnwood, not ten miles away. Kindly follow me."

Chapter XIV

THE GHASTLY STAIN

THE DRIVE TO Lincolnwood was not very long, but at one point Doc Savage pulled over to install the snow chains on his tires in order to navigate certain thoroughfares.

During the stop, which occupied a short interval, Malcolm McLean stepped out of his purple phaeton to watch the bronze giant jack up the sedan's tires in order to set the linkages in place. Somewhat bored, his gaze wandered, and so noticed a hatbox resting on the back seat cushions.

"That is Miss Falcon's hatbox!" cried the gray-visaged chemist.

Monk Mayfair growled, "What's it to you, you walkin' zombie?"

An indignant expression, so comical it almost caused Ham Brooks to burst into laughter, took over Malcolm McLean's unlovely features.

"Why, this is theft of personal property! I've always understood you fellows were men of sterling character. First, Long Tom Roberts shoots a defenseless woman in cold blood, and now one of you has made off with her hat."

Impulsively yanking open the door, McLean grabbed the hatbox and lifted it. The stupefied look on his face when he almost dropped it was something to see.

"Why, this is quite heavy," he said wonderingly.

Surrounding the hatbox with one arm, McLean lifted the lid and exposed the powdery grit contained within. Atop it was the stone hand whose freakishly fat thumb bore the print pattern of Long Tom Roberts.

McLean lifted this up, studied it and asked, "What the devil is this?"

Monk Mayfair, always happy to shock someone, said matter-of-factly, "We think it's Long Tom's remains. We found it on Miss Falcon's rug."

"Nonsense! This appears to be mere crushed rock."

"That is correct," interjected Ham. "We suspect Long Tom was reduced to stone."

The incredulous look that overtook Malcolm McLean's gray features was bestowed upon Doc Savage, Monk and Ham in equal shares.

"Speaking as a chemist, I doubt this is conceivable—except perhaps as a result of the action of millions of years. In which case, it might be possible for a man to become fossilized. But this does not resemble a fossil to me."

McLean studied the hand, noticed the whorls of the thumb-print, the lifelike wrinkles at the knuckles and joints, and his changing expression suggested that he was doubting his own professional opinion.

His too-white eyes skated over to Doc Savage as if to ask the bronze man his opinion.

Doc had finished attaching the last jangling web of linked chain and straightened up simultaneously, dropping the front of the vehicle with a quick twist of the jack.

"The truth remains to be seen," he stated noncommittally.

Gingerly, McLean placed the lifelike hand back in the box, closed the lid and restored it to the back seat of the sedan. He appeared to want nothing more to do with the hatbox.

After Doc stowed away his tools, the two-vehicle procession continued on.

Some twenty minutes later, they were pulling into the circular drive of the rather fashionable brick Victorian home in the suburb of Lincolnwood.

As they exited the vehicle, Doc asked Malcolm McLean, "Does Myer Sim have any family?"

McLean shook his gray head, and said, "He lived alone, although there were servants. The maid should still be in residence. I understand she is quite shaken up."

McLean led them to the front door, lifted the brass door knocker and rapped on it several times insistently.

The maid soon answered, and she seemed not particularly alarmed by the sight of a human corpse at her door. She was a Negro girl, young and rather pretty. She wore the neat black-and-white uniform of a housemaid.

"Why, Mr. McLean!" she said politely. "What can I do for you?"

McLean said, "With me are the famous Doc Savage and his associates. They are interested in what happened to your late employer. May we come in?"

The maid looked uncertain. Then Doc Savage stepped up and showed his New York police credentials, and it seemed to do the trick.

"Do come in," invited the maid, stepping aside.

They were quickly led to a paneled study that was partly a library and personal business office. It had the look of a room that had been maintained over several generations, with only small personal details changing with each occupant.

Doc Savage went to the desk, and examined the items upon it. For the most part, they were unremarkable.

Malcolm McLean addressed the maid, saying, "You were the only one in residence when Mr. Sim was stricken. Why don't you tell us what happened?"

"But I don't know what happened!" she said sincerely. "I was moving about the house, doing my bounden duty, and I thought I heard Mr. Sim arguing with someone in this very study."

Doc Savage asked, "What was the nature of the argument?"

"I was too far away to tell, but it was mighty peculiar. I hadn't let anybody in. Yet I heard two voices. Mr. Sim was getting rather hot in his arguing, for his voice was raised several times. It was not like him to raise his voice; he was not that sort of man."

"Did you make out any of it?" asked Doc.

"It sounded like he was saying. 'I refuse! I refuse!' There was a long silence, and I thought I heard him speaking to the telephone operator. Then he called out, saying, 'What is this ringing I hear?' Lastly, there come a noise like something had fallen. It was quiet for a while after that. Then it seemed to me to be *too* quiet, if you know what I mean. So I knocked on the door. Mr. Sim did not answer. So I opened the door."

The maid, whose name was Polly, became shaky in her composure.

"I found Mr. Sim on the floor, the telephone in one hand, the telephone stand knocked over. He wasn't moving none. He wasn't moving at all."

"Go on," invited Doc.

The maid closed her eyes and took in a slow sip of air. When she resumed, she was more in control of herself.

"I knelt down, and I could hear the telephone operator calling out, but I was afraid to take the receiver out of Mr. Sim's cold hand. I knew he was dead. I could tell. A body knows."

Doc Savage had been hovering around the desk, his eyes very active, and unbeknownst to the others, his keen sense of smell was also at work.

Ham questioned, "You said you heard two voices. Were there any signs of a second party in the room?"

The maid shook her head vigorously. "None. I couldn't touch the telephone, so I went to a neighbor woman and she called the police. The police done came and took poor Mr. Sim away. He was definitely dead. Not that I needed anybody to tell me. I know a body when I see one."

The servant closed her eyes again. It was a painful memory they were stirring.

Doc Savage asked a question which, in the moment, seemed peculiar.

"What time of day did this happen?"

"It was afternoon. The day before yesterday, as a matter of fact."

Doc drifted over to one window. All blinds except for this one were pulled down for privacy. These were fabric window shades. The center one was rolled up quite high, and a decent dose of sunlight was coming through to help illuminate the study.

"Was it sunny when you entered this room?" prompted Doc.

"Yes, sir. It was a very sunny day."

"What were the positions of these shades?" Doc queried.

The maid looked momentarily puzzled, and thought hard.

"Mr. Sim likes the shades set halfway down so the sun doesn't get into his eyes when he is sitting at his writing desk. Except the center one, he likes it down pretty low most days."

"Why is it up now?" asked Doc.

The maid looked a trifle embarrassed. "On account of the stain. I pulled it up all the way before the police arrived because I didn't want it to reflect poorly on Mr. Sim, or on my house-keeping."

Reaching up, Doc found the woven ring and hauled down the shade.

Monk and Ham were startled by what they beheld on the shade, although on reflection perhaps they should not have been.

IMPRINTED on the pale surface was a bilious greenish-yellow splotch. It had a shapeless quality, but the head portion was unmistakable. It resembled a nest of snakes, their wedge-shaped heads twisted all about, bristling with fangs and forked tongues.

Malcolm McLean strode up to the window shade, and examined the gargoyle-shaped outline with professional interest.

"I do not recognize what type of stain this could be," he said slowly.

Monk grunted, "Join the parade."

McLean continued to study the outline, and seemed not to recognize what it signified.

"Rather large for a stain," he pronounced.

"It may not be a stain precisely," commented Doc. "But the outline is very suggestive."

"Of what?" McLean wondered.

"Step back a few paces," suggested Doc.

McLean did so, and seemed to struggle with his eyes. Finally, Ham Brooks lent a hand.

"The top portion suggests a being with a head full of darting serpents, while the rest of the form might be a garment of ancient cut."

McLean frowned, and the deep corrugations of his unlovely forehead did not look natural.

Monk completed the thought for him, asking, "Don't you recognize Medusa when you see her?"

McLean got it then. But he continued to look baffled.

"Why would anyone paint that hideous outline on a common window shade?"

"It may not have been painted," said Doc. "Monk, take it down, please."

While the homely chemist climbed onto a chair to retrieve the widow treatment, the bronze man drifted over to the wastebasket and was rummaging through the detritus found within.

"There are burnt granules on the desktop," he stated. "What was Mr. Sim in the habit of burning?"

The maid replied, "Mr. Sim suffered from asthma. When he was having an attack, he would burn some of his asthma powder on the desk and inhale it."

Doc found the residue of burnt powder at the bottom of the wastebasket and poured this onto a blank sheet of paper he took from the desktop. It smelled faintly of peppermint oil, which was a common ingredient in many of the commercial powders that aided suffering asthmatics.

"Was this powder on his desk after the body was discovered?"

"Yes, sir," said the maid. "I cleaned it up only this morning."

Doc Savage took the sheet of paper and folded it in a shape that was similar to the paper sailor hats young boys create. He inserted this into an inner pocket. But he said nothing more about it.

"Did you look at your employer's face when you found him?"

"I did."

"And what did you perceive?"

"Poor Mr. Sim's eyes were sunken and hollow, like someone dead for a few days. But that plain couldn't be so. He was alive and talking only moments before."

"Thank you," said Doc, who then turned to the others and announced, "We are finished here. Our next course of action is to locate Janet Falcon."

All eyes turned to Malcolm McLean. A stubborn look came over his dull face. He folded his arms defiantly and said, "I refuse to divulge Miss Falcon's present whereabouts until we get to the bottom of her mistreatment."

Monk and Ham looked to Doc Savage, who went to the telephone and picked it up.

"Operator, get me the Superintendent of Police of Chicago. This is Doc Savage speaking."

In short order, the bronze man was in low conversation with the party who came on the line. He turned his back to further conceal the exchange. And when he was done, he turned and announced, "By the time we get back to the city, we should have a line on Miss Falcon's present whereabouts."

This comment immediately struck Malcolm McLean as humorous. He began cackling in a macabre way that was forced and unpleasant.

"Oh, I will believe *that* when I see it!" he tittered.

Monk Mayfair eyed him and said, "Brother, be prepared to believe. When Doc Savage says something, it comes plated in gold."

Malcolm McLean's tittering came apart, and his eyes got a little worried. He essayed another attempt at laughing, but it failed miserably.

Doc told him, "Nevertheless, you are welcome to accompany us to our destination."

The moribund-looking chemist did not hesitate. "I have heard astonishing things about you, Mr. Savage. I'm intrigued to see if your reputation is as stellar as the newspapers would have it. Also, in the unlikely event you do manage to unearth Miss Falcon, I wish to be present to guarantee her safety."

Now it was Monk Mayfair's turn to laugh.

"Follow us, ghastly," he said roughly. "It might be educational at that."

Chapter XV

UNPLEASANT INTERVIEW

DOC SAVAGE DROVE rapidly into downtown Chicago, and pulled up before the central police station on Michigan Avenue. McLean's garish purple phaeton coupe pulled in behind, brakes jerking, tires cutting into the curbstone.

"Wait here," Doc informed the others. "Watch McLean. Do not let him out of your sight."

Ham asked, "You do not trust him?"

"We do not wish McLean to call Janet Falcon and warn her that we are on her trail."

The bronze giant went inside.

Minutes later, Doc returned and said to Monk and Ham, "I have a line on Janet Falcon. But first we will go to Long Tom's hotel and look into the situation there."

When this was conveyed to Malcolm McLean, assorted expressions paraded across his deathly-gray features.

"As I told you before, I planned to attend the exposition today. I will be happy to detour to that particular hotel on our way to wherever you imagine Miss Falcon to be."

"Thank you," said Doc politely. He reclaimed the wheel of the rented sedan, and the two vehicles moved into traffic.

The hotel was equipped with a rather sizable underground garage. Since Doc had previously registered, they were able to park the sedan there. As a member of the scientific exposition being held within its halls, Malcolm McLean was extended a similar courtesy.

140

They rode a rather narrow service elevator up to the lobby, and Doc Savage strode up to the front desk, and what he said caused Malcolm McLean to practically jump out of his rather tight shoes.

"In which room is Miss York staying?" he asked.

Had a man of less sterling reputation asked such a question, he might have been politely rebuffed. But this was Doc Savage, a world-renowned figure.

The desk clerk had no hesitation in responding, "Miss York has taken Room 612."

"Thank you," said Doc.

Turning, his flake-gold eyes rested upon Malcolm McLean, who was trying to gather his wits, and not doing a very good job of it.

"You—you tricked me!" he burst out.

"How so?" asked Doc calmly.

"You informed me that we were coming to this hotel before going to meet Miss York—I mean Miss Falcon," he sputtered out.

"No," corrected Doc. "You were told that we would visit this establishment on our way to visit Miss Falcon. You assumed that we were bound for two separate destinations."

Now McLean sealed his lips so tightly they disappeared. His eyes narrowed. It seemed as if his normal reserve was becoming undone. Dark gleams came into his bone-gray eyeballs that were not pleasant to see.

"You may accompany us," invited Doc unemotionally.

They took the elevator to the sixth floor. As the lift toiled upward, Doc Savage, for reasons that were not clear to Monk and Ham, launched into a brief explanation of his amazing deduction.

"Two clues were provided by your statement, McLean," he said. "One that Janet Falcon was safely hidden away, and the other that she was using an alias or assumed name."

McLean said tightly, "It is not possible to deduce anything useful from those minuscule facts."

"I did deduce from your apparent professional connection with Miss Falcon that you did not hide her in your own personal residence. That suggested a hotel. Under the circumstances, a respectable hotel. That narrowed the possibilities down considerably."

McLean sniffed, "But there are dozens of good hotels in the Chicago area. Many more immediately outside of it."

Doc nodded somberly. "Which prompted our visit to police headquarters where I requested that they assemble a list of female residents who had checked into local hotels in the last twenty-four hours. Women do not frequently travel alone, so the list was rather scanty. When the police superintendent showed me the list, I concluded it could only be a woman named Jane York who had lately registered at this hotel."

"That is quite a leap in assumptions," sneered McLean.

"Not if one understands human psychology," supplied Doc as the lift came to a halt, and the door rolled open.

They stepped out, turned left, and walked along the carpeted hall runner.

"Assuming that the woman chose her own alias," continued Doc, "and knowing that normally persons are uncomfortable with assumed names, it was a safe bet that Janet Falcon would have chosen a first name close to her own. Before seeing the list, I planned to look for women whose first initials began with the letter J. Evidently, due to the speed at which she was forced to go into hiding, Janet Falcon chose a first name that was only one letter short her own name."

Monk snapped his thick fingers. "I get it! Janet became Jane."

"That was so simple even *you* could follow it," sniffed Ham.

They came to the correct room, and Doc Savage said, "It was too close to be coincidental."

Malcolm McLean said in a low, disgruntled voice. "You make it sound elementary."

Ham interjected, "Perhaps because it *was* elementary."

In response to Doc's knocking, a female voice asked cautiously, "Who is it?"

To Malcolm McLean's complete dumfoundment, he heard a voice very much like his own emerge from Doc Savage's metallic lips. The tone that was identical to his own said, "Malcolm McLean calling."

McLean's jaw sagged downward, and he looked about to shout a warning. Monk Mayfair swept in, and clapped a hairy hand over the man's open mouth.

McLean struggled strenuously, but was unable to speak or wrest free.

Sound of footsteps approaching the other side of the panel came. Monk abruptly removed his paw and thrust Malcolm McLean's dazed features in front of the door panel, where there was a tiny peephole.

McLean realized too late that he was being used to allay Janet Falcon's concerns.

The door came open, and Monk pulled McLean away. Doc Savage stepped into view, a tower of bronze.

The woman responded as one might expect a woman would. The back of her hand flew up to her open mouth, and she seemed torn between letting out a shriek of surprise and stifling it.

Doc said directly, "Apologies for the subterfuge. But we must speak to you about the whereabouts of Long Tom Roberts."

"You are Doc Savage!" Janet Falcon gasped.

"We would prefer to come inside," said Doc. "In order to converse in private."

Janet Falcon's fear-widened eyes went from the bronze man to Monk, Ham and finally Malcolm McLean, who was grabbing his tie and attempting to straighten it out. At the same time, his features resembled dirty gray water that had become disturbed.

"Mr. McLean! What is the meaning of this?"

"I was tricked by these men," he burst out. "I did not mean to bring them to you. Please forgive me."

This proclamation alarmed Janet Falcon, who suddenly stepped back, and attempted to slam the door shut.

Monk Mayfair inserted a huge foot, effectively blocking the panel from closing.

Doc stepped in, easing the door open with gentle but irresistible strength.

"We mean you no harm, Miss Falcon. We are merely making an investigation."

"I do not wish to speak with you," she said flatly.

While Ham was closing the door behind them, Doc Savage scrutinized Janet Falcon.

"Your employer was found dead under mysterious circumstances," he related. "And now your fiancé has also met his end. One would think you would wish to cooperate."

"She does not have to, you—you wooden Indian!" Malcolm McLean inserted.

Monk ambled up to the deathly-gray individual and growled, "Pipe down, you! Or I'll fetch you a fresh coffin to go with your graveyard looks!"

The corpse-faced chemist gasped, then subsided.

Doc Savage continued, "What about it, Miss Falcon? Why did you send Ned Gamble to New York?"

"I decline to answer. Please go away. You have no standing in Chicago."

From an inner pocket, the big bronze man produced an envelope. It was unsealed. Opening it, he unfolded a sheet of paper, and handed it over.

Janet Falcon accepted this and read it in silence. The letterhead belonged to the Superintendent of the Chicago Police Department.

"This says that you have been authorized to conduct an official investigation into the death of Myer Sim," she breathed.

"And, per my New York credentials, that of Ned Gamble," added Doc.

"I see," said Janet Falcon vaguely. Her eyes darted about the hotel room. She twisted her pale fingers together, made a bony knot, nervously undid them.

"I—I have nothing to offer you," she said miserably.

Doc Savage produced another sheet of paper. Handing this to her, he said, "Here is a list of recent visitors to Myer Sim's residence. Chicago police detectives compiled it, sharing it with me. Do you recognize any of those names?"

The distraught woman looked over the list. It was short. Only a handful of names.

"I know all of them," she admitted. "These are men of high position in the scientific community. Surely you recognize them as well. Are you not yourself a scientist?"

Recovering the list, Doc Savage stated, "All are familiar to me. I merely wished to know if they were frequent visitors to Myer Sim's residence."

"In recent weeks, yes. Some of them came often. But that means nothing. All of these men are present at the exposition being held at this very hotel." Her tone becoming brittle, she added, "Why don't you simply go to the exposition hall and inquire of them? I wish to be left alone."

Doc looked to Monk Mayfair. "Hand me that, please."

The homely chemist had been studying the trim lines of Janet Falcon's frock. He lifted the rolled-up window shade taken from the Sim residence den.

"Here you go, Doc."

Accepting the tube, the bronze man unrolled it with a sudden snap of his metallic hand.

The laminate sheet dropped open, displaying the yellow-green imprint that was so hideous.

Janet Falcon's emerald eyes went to the image. She immediately paled. Her eyes rolled up and her knees suddenly buckled.

Monk moved then. He leaped in and caught the woman's suddenly limp form, depositing it on the couch.

"Fainted!" said Ham. "The image meant something to her."

"What do you know about that?" muttered Monk. "What do you say, Doc?"

The bronze man furled the shade and commented, "You overlooked something."

A puzzled expression roosted on Monk's wide features that bordered on the comical.

Doc Savage helped him out by asking, "Where is McLean?"

Monk and Ham looked around wildly.

"He must have ducked out!" Ham exclaimed.

Monk snarled, "I thought you were watchin' him!"

Ham waved his slim stick in frustration. "I assumed that you were. But of course you had your eyes on the girl. Or should I say—on her legs?"

Doc Savage said, "We will get no more out of Miss Falcon at present. McLean doubtless retreated to the exposition hall. We will follow him and begin interviewing the participants."

"Sounds kinda dull," muttered Monk.

But it proved to be anything but.

Chapter XVI

GATHERING SCIENTIFIC

THE SIGN OVER the great exhibition hall attached to the Hotel Chicago read:

CHICAGO EXPOSITION OF SCIENCE

Doc Savage, accompanied by Monk Mayfair and Ham Brooks, arrived at the entrance after a brief stop at their hotel room to leave the unusual window shade collected from the home of Myer Sim. Doc secreted it, along with Long Tom's strange magnetic gun, in a large upholstered chair.

During that stop, he had also left the hatbox containing the grit believed to be the late Long Tom Roberts' mortal remains behind, but asked Ham to pocket the intact stone hand without further explanation.

There were ticket takers stationed at the front of the building, and they were so awestruck by the giant bronze man they neglected to ask if he held a ticket. All recognized him.

When Doc entered the exhibition hall itself, heads began turning.

Almost immediately, one individual approached. He wore an extremely serious countenance whose cragginess bespoke of middle age, and resembled an investment banker down to his conservative haircut and wire-rimmed eyeglasses framing frank gray eyes.

"Dr. Savage," he greeted. "I recall we met a few years ago at a conference in Washington. Warner Rockwell is my name."

Doc Savage took the offered hand, and shook it firmly, saying, "I remember you, Dr. Rockwell. At that time, you were working along certain lines in brain surgery."

A tremor touched Dr. Rockwell's craggily handsome features.

"Lines upon which you improved. For before I could conclude my research, you announced a superior version of my procedure."

Doc nodded. "An unfortunate circumstance. But I had been pursuing similar clinical studies prior to our meeting."

"Well, that's all in the past," said Rockwell. "I read in the papers that you're in town to investigate the strange death of Myer Sim."

As he spoke, Dr. Rockwell's penetrating gray eyes never left the bronze man's face. He had a rather peculiar gaze. He did not seem to blink. He just stared.

Doc admitted, "The newspapers have jumped to a conclusion. In this case, it was the correct one. It is my understanding that you were often a visitor to his home."

"I was. Nothing unusual about that. A great many of us were excited about this exposition."

"Did Sim have any known enemies?" pressed Doc.

"I doubt it. But you might want to talk to Marvin Lucian Linden about that. He knew Sim better than I. Come, let me introduce you to him."

Walking with a purposeful stride, Dr. Rockwell led the bronze man through the maze of exhibitions that was the exposition.

The assembly was, in fact, composed of multiple exhibitions. There were booths in which well-known commercial companies were represented. Individual inventors also showed their prized developments.

The latest industrial projects, modern conveniences destined for homes across America, were on display.

As they passed by, Monk looked some of these over with great interest. He had a keen eye for the latest developments in his field, and others. The work which Doc Savage and his men did required that they be at least one jump ahead of their enemies. Most of their tools were scientific.

They came to a booth which stood empty. There was a banner over it, proclaiming that here was the exhibit belonging to Thomas J. Roberts, the noted electrical engineer.

The sight of the vacant booth brought a pained expression to Monk Mayfair's incredibly homely features.

Ham Brooks likewise looked faint. Firming up his lips, he said nothing. The thoughts of both men were easily read on their faces. They were thinking of a hatbox containing a gritty powder which might be the mortal remains of their comrade in arms.

No doubt Doc Savage noticed the empty booth as well, but the bronze man showed no outward sign that he did. From childhood, he had been schooled to control his emotions. His face might have been a metal mask.

They came at last to a booth not far from where Long Tom had planned to hold forth. This was in the section of the exhibition hall segregated for advancements in the field of electrical engineering.

The person manning the booth was small and spry, and rather on the excitable side. His hair stuck out in a frizzled halo, as if he had accidentally electrocuted himself and the individual strands of hair had fried to the proverbial crisp. In spite of the fellow's comparative youth, their color was a rather neutral gray.

When he saw Doc Savage approaching, the crispy-haired individual leaped from his chair, and proclaimed, "Do I spy the Man of Bronze himself? Doc Savage in the flesh! Although flesh might not be the best description to use for, if you were not moving, I might have mistaken you for the legendary warder of ancient Crete, Talos. He, too, was a man of bronze."

The effusive one grinned with what appeared to be genuine pleasure.

Dr. Rockwell made introductions. "Doc Savage, please meet Marvin Lucian Linden, a close friend of the late Myer Sim."

Doc and the excitable electrical inventor shook hands, Linden rather too vigorously. Doc managed to detach himself, however.

"I have been keeping my eyes peeled for your comrade, Long Tom Roberts, all morning," said Linden. "But I have yet to spy him."

"Long Tom is indisposed," replied Doc Savage matter-of-factly.

This brought startled looks into both Monk and Ham's eyes, but they said nothing. Doc Savage was doubtless concealing the truth for reasons of his own.

Marvin Lucian Linden went on breathlessly. "I had hoped to discuss with Roberts his latest theories on television. I believe that television will become an important medium in the future. Of course, your theories would interest me, as well. A few years ago, I had begun work on a new-type scanner to replace the old mechanical ones then in development. Imagine my displeasure when I read in a scientific journal that you had already achieved a breakthrough in that area."

Doc Savage said, "Television has a long way to go before it has been fully explored in all of its potential. A great deal of work remains."

Marvin Lucian Linden grinned rather lopsidedly. "That is a rather gracious way to put it. But no hard feelings. Although I was beaten to the punch, it was fair and square, and I have not yet been knocked to the canvas."

Doc Savage changed the subject without skipping a beat. "I am interested in the activities of Myer Sim in the days leading up to his untimely passing."

The lopsided grin collapsed, and Marvin Lucian Linden became grim of feature.

"I am keen to read the autopsy results," said Linden. "For I cannot imagine what struck down poor Myer. The man was in his prime."

"What did you two discuss when last you spoke?" pressed Doc.

"Why, the coming exhibition, of course. Sim was most eager to appear. He had invented something rather novel, but refused to divulge the details. There was nothing personal in that, of course. Secrecy is important to an inventor working alone. His booth in the northwest corner is rather large, so I imagine that what he planned to display was not a small discovery."

"What was Sim's particular field of endeavor?" asked Doc.

"He did not have one. Sim was rather a scientific gadfly. He had invented many things on a small scale. But now he had moved up in the world to something he thought was momentous. What it was, I have no idea. Nor did I need to know in advance. I fully expected to view it here today." Linden shook his head morosely. "Alas, it was not to be."

Doc Savage then asked, "Do you know Malcolm McLean well?" This question was not directed to Marvin Lucian Linden alone, but to Dr. Warner Rockwell as well.

Both men exchanged quick glances, as if to see who wished to reply first.

Dr. Rockwell did. "Malcolm McLean," he began, "is from a good family here in Chicago. His background is impeccable and his work, while not well known, is showing great promise."

"Along what lines is McLean working?" queried the bronze man.

Marvin Lucian Linden answered that one. "McLean was interested in rare minerals and elements, their properties and applications. His father owned several coal mines south of here. Consequently, he has always been keen to explore what minerals have been dug out—outside of common coal, naturally."

Steady-eyed Warner Rockwell laughed explosively. "If I did not know McLean suffered from chemical poisoning, I would suspect his gray complexion was the result of spending too much time in the family mines."

Doc Savage absorbed this information without a flicker disturbing the continuous whirling of the golden flakes in his eyes.

"We were speaking with McLean earlier," he advised, "and he is believed to have come here. Have either of you seen him recently?"

Both men shook their heads firmly.

"I have not," snapped Linden.

"Nor have I," echoed Dr. Rockwell.

"What is your interest in McLean, if I may inquire?" wondered Marvin Lucian Linden.

"We are interested in anyone who might know anything about Myer Sim's last hours," replied Doc.

"I imagine the police are already investigating this," said Dr. Rockwell.

"Our investigation is running parallel with theirs," stated Doc. "Are either of you acquainted with Myer Sim's personal secretary, Janet Falcon?"

The two men attempted to reply at once, and their words blurred together.

Marvin Lucian Linden nodded in Dr. Rockwell's direction deferentially.

The medical man allowed, "Only in passing."

"The same is true with me," said Linden. "I have encountered Miss Falcon without forming any close association."

The line of questioning did not seem to be getting anywhere. Monk and Ham became fidgety, having nothing to contribute.

Noticing this, Doc directed, "Endeavor to locate McLean. No doubt he is among the crowd."

"Righto, Doc," said Ham, snapping up his sword cane.

Monk added, "I'll look for him in the chemistry section; he's probably there."

The two aides departed, going their separate ways.

Doc Savage resumed his interrogation. "The persons in charge of this exposition may have something important to reveal," he stated.

Dr. Rockwell and Marvin Lucian Linden looked momentarily blank.

Doc explained, "In order to arrange for his new invention to be displayed, prior accommodations must have been made. The persons in charge of the exposition may know some of the details."

Dr. Rockwell said, "That is sound thinking, Savage." His steady regard never left Doc Savage's face.

"In that case," Linden offered, "you will want to speak with Mr. Lubeck. He is the exhibition organizer."

"Thank you," said Doc. "I may have more questions for you later."

With that, the bronze man took an abrupt departure.

Melting into the push of people like a hot knife through butter, Doc Savage shouldered his way through the crowded hall, his great presence causing people to step aside as he approached, while simultaneously arresting their attention. It was an uncanny sight. Normally, celebrity-seekers are drawn toward the object of their interest. Crowds typically gather, inhibiting progress.

The human Hercules in bronze captured the attention of all who beheld him. There was something awe-inspiring about his gigantic presence which caused people to press closer, yet also maintain a respectful distance.

Thus, no one asked for Doc's autograph as he moved purposefully through the busy assemblage.

Doc Savage made quiet inquiries and was directed to a small office where Mr. Lubeck held forth. He was a roly-poly fellow with damp blond hair.

Lubeck was only too eager to accommodate the bronze man.

"Yes, yes, of course," he said. "Poor Myer Sim's invention was trucked here two days ago, in anticipation of being put on display. Of course, we could not undertake that, since the man has passed on. Especially now, having no instructions to the contrary."

"Where is this invention?" asked Doc.

"It was taken off the truck and stored in the garage. I can show it to you."

"Please do so," invited Doc.

The two men took a handy elevator to the basement garage, and walked through the ranks of parked machines. The bronze man noticed that most of the empty parking spaces were now occupied. Visitors were continually arriving for the scientific exposition.

One section of the garage was reserved for hotel employees and managers. Thus it was safe from prying eyes. Lubeck was waddling toward that quadrant.

Lubeck was saying, "We concealed it from view with a tarpaulin, so that it appeared to be simply another motor vehicle parked in an out-of-the-way spot."

"Myer Sim's invention was an automobile?" asked Doc.

"Not exactly. But you will soon see for yourself."

That statement was, on the face of it, an honest one. But very swiftly it proved to be overly optimistic.

The garage lights were arrayed in banks nestled among the concrete ceiling joists. As the two men walked toward the far reaches of the garage, these lamps went out.

This did not bring utter darkness. But it did create a moment in which all was rather dim. The garage lacked windows, but there were far doors that were open and some light bled downward.

Somewhere in the near distance, a powerful engine roared into life.

Then something shiny as aluminum came hurtling through the twilight dimness in their direction.

The thing showed no headlights, but suddenly a single ray of light snapped into life.

Lubeck was immediately blinded by the blazing illumination. Doc Savage, throwing one hand before his face, managed to fend the worst of it.

Whatever the thing was, it came hurtling in their direction, like a low-slung cyclops running on all fours.

There was no question that the juggernaut was bearing down upon them.

Lubeck stood, momentarily paralyzed, directly in its path.

Doc Savage moved like a bronze flash, seizing the plump man and carrying him out of harm's way.

The metal monster screeched around the corner, and went leaping for the ramp that led up to the street.

Doc sat Lubeck down on the hood of a nearby auto and demanded, "Was that Sim's invention?"

Lubeck had a handkerchief out and was mopping his suddenly moist features, "Yes, yes, it was. Someone appears to have stolen it! This is terrible."

"Alert the police. I will attempt pursuit."

Without another word, the bronze giant flashed for his rented sedan.

Getting behind the wheel, he urged the motor into life.

Immediately, Doc Savage was charging up the ramp, his metallic features determined.

Chapter XVII

ANOTHER STONE BRAIN

DOC SAVAGE HAD selected his rental sedan for its efficiency of engine, as well as its inconspicuousness. It was not by any means the equal of his personal autos with their supercharged motors, but it was a sound stock car, one of the best on the market.

Easing up onto the ramp, the bronze giant twisted the steering wheel and spun into traffic. His foot depressed the gas-feed. The car shot ahead, lunging. The motor gave forth roaring horsepower.

Through a typical Chicago congestion of automobile traffic and winding streetcars, Doc could see the fleeing vehicle darting into scrambling motor traffic.

The automobile—or whatever it was—was remarkably narrow, and wove in between dodging autos. Drivers, startled by the strange thing slipping and sliding between them, careened in the slushy sleet.

One machine went up on a curb and knocked over a mailbox. Another lunged into a cigar stand with predictable results.

Doc leaned on his horn in an effort to part traffic before him. In that, he was only partially successful.

The vehicle was the burnished silver of a duralumin aircraft. It had some of the qualities of a Bluebird racer in that it was low-slung and not very wide. Vanes resembling stubby wings were visible on either side of the careening bullet of a car. They seemed to run the length of the streamlined vehicle.

Seen from behind, there seemed room for no more than a single driver in the careening car.

Jockeying through traffic expertly, Doc Savage began to overhaul the lean machine.

A taxicab, coming up a side street, cut in front of him, forcing the bronze man to brake and slew his machine.

This cost him some time.

Working around the scattered taxi, Doc got his sedan straightened out, and picked up speed again.

At that point, the chase was truly on. The strange vehicle had the advantage of being narrow and nimble, being not much wider than a motorcycle sidecar.

For his part, Doc Savage was handicapped by his snow chains. While they improved the traction of his tires, they hardly aided in the sedan's performance as the speedometer crept higher and higher.

Still, by dint of blasting his car horn, and expert manipulation of the heavy machine, the bronze man once again began to overhaul the strange bullet car.

The driver did not appear to have a rear-vision mirror of any sort. In fact, the back window was circular, rather resembling a porthole.

More than once, the driver turned his head to look out that circular pane, and no doubt became aware of the pursuing sedan.

As seen through the safety glass, the features of the driver were indistinct, but they confirmed what Doc Savage had already suspected. The weird motorcar carried a solitary passenger in a single seat. Otherwise, the driver's face would not be centered in the round rear window.

Doc Savage managed to keep the odd automobile in sight, but soon discovered that the drag of his clanking tire chains were not going to permit him to overhaul his quarry.

The fleeing driver did not seem to appreciate that fact. For, abruptly, perhaps thinking he was not going to escape, he wrenched his steering mechanism hard to the left, and suddenly flung himself into opposing traffic, cutting in front of a clanging streetcar.

As the queer automobile veered away, Doc Savage got a better glimpse of the driver.

It was corpse-faced Malcolm McLean!

Doc Savage was forced to continue along until he encountered a cut-through. Then, as luck would have it, a motorcycle policeman came popping into view.

Abruptly, Doc reversed course, and cut the officer off.

The bluecoat dismounted his steel steed with his face turning crimson and his teeth baring in something that was definitely not a smile.

"What's the idea!" he roared.

Doc Savage stepped out, and immediately the full extent of his height as well as the metallic bronze of his features became apparent.

The cop was saying, "I'm gonna run you in for that," when he suddenly swallowed his words. One leather-gloved hand popped a quick salute.

"If you aren't Doc Savage, I'm the Queen of Spain."

Doc strode over and said, "Pursuing a suspicious person. I will need to borrow your motorcycle. You may take my rental sedan."

Even in Chicago, it was a highly irregular request, but the motorcycle officer took only a moment to absorb it. He politely waved Doc onto the motorcycle's worn leather seat, offering his goggles.

"Please take the sedan to the Hotel Chicago," requested the bronze man.

The kick-starter banged into life, and Doc went charging off.

There were two reasons for this switch. He did not wish to drive a full-sized automobile against traffic, which would tempt catastrophe. Free of his snow chains, the bronze giant could now make better time.

Two, the nimbleness of the motorcycle was certain to match, if not outperform, that of the peculiar bullet machine.

Doc went chasing after the thing, veering and sliding around oncoming traffic. To a great degree, the queer machine cleared the way for him. All Doc had to do was shoot between separating cars, some of which were sliding out of control as they frantically dodged the hurtling aluminum juggernaut.

Weaving in and out again, the silver car took dangerous risks, and once swapped ends, but managed to get itself oriented again and resumed its mad, reckless path.

The chase soon approached the waterfront, and the cold-looking waters of Lake Michigan.

Doc Savage's flake-gold eyes, protected by the officer's borrowed goggles continued to scan the way ahead as if to somehow divine the destination of the careening torpedo of a thing.

Passing before an imposing lakefront hostelry named the Drake, the machine continued along. Without warning, the driver wrenched the wheel hard, and was suddenly crashing across oncoming traffic, heading for a sandy beach. There was a sidewalk fronting the beach, and the weird wheeled contraption vaulted this to plop onto the sand. Narrow tires dug in, gaining traction. The thing lurched forward, toward the lapping lake waters.

It seemed as if the beach sand would inevitably drag the driver's progress to a halt.

Instead, the laboring vehicle moaned along the beach, charging for open water. As Doc Savage watched, a peculiar extension began to rise from the narrow roof. This proved to be a pipe. The tube was bent at the top, the bend angling forward.

The contrivance looked for all the world like a periscope.

So it was that Doc Savage was not greatly surprised when the narrow silver vehicle plunged into the frigid water and kept going.

The bronze man followed, wrestling the motorcycle in its wake, but was forced to brake to a halt when he hit beach sand.

Dismounting, Doc plunged after the thing, which, seen from the rear, possessed some of the qualities of a silver fish.

Miraculously, the car kept going; water closed over the aluminum hull and diving vanes, and the periscope pipe continued to lift upward, as if being cranked higher the deeper the vehicle proceeded.

A wave created by the fleeing machine spread out as the body of the car began to submerge. A disturbance churned the water at the thing's stern, and it shot ahead. Quickly, the roofline was awash. It vanished and the periscope-like pipe was all that was visible.

Doc Savage immediately began kicking off his shoes and removing his coat, shirt, tie and outer garments. He stood in black silk underwear, which doubled as swimming trunks. Without regard for the bitter coldness, the bronze man plunged into the water.

It was icily frigid. The cold was so great that it felt as if a vise had clamped over his magnificent bronze chest. Doc commenced swimming in an overhand matter, making remarkable time, but if he expected the automobile engine to flood and cease functioning, Doc Savage was greatly disappointed.

The combination periscope and snorkel—for that was what Doc deduced it must be—continued onward as the incredible machine raced along the lake bed. It was not making outstanding time, owing to the irregularities of the muddy lake bottom, but it was still moving faster than Doc Savage could swim.

Reluctantly, the bronze man broke off pursuit. He treaded water for a time, eerie golden eyes tracking the snorkel through which the driver was apparently able to breathe.

Doc had noted that the remarkable machine produced no exhaust, proof that the engine was not of the internal combustion type. Probably, it was electric in nature and ran off batteries. A screw-type propeller had been briefly visible at the stern;

this was the source of the violent churning. The device had not been visible before the machine reached water. Apparently, it was retractable.

When it was no longer prudent to remain still in the water, Doc reversed course and started swimming back to shore.

Back on the beach, a crowd had gathered, and Doc Savage soon found himself surrounded.

"What *was* that chariot?" someone wanted to know.

Doc Savage did not reply. He strolled stolidly toward the pile of clothes he left behind and began dressing—rather self-consciously since a number of the growing crowd were women eyeing his magnificent physique with admiration.

His bronze hair and skin dried rapidly, a peculiar property they possessed.

Once he finally had his tie in place, Doc went to claim the motorcycle.

A police radio car pulled up and Doc changed course to confer with the arriving officer briefly. The bronze man explained what had happened.

"Have a police launch undertake a search for the silver submersible," directed Doc.

"It's a big lake," the bluecoat reminded.

"The snorkel's length will limit its operations to a mile or less off shore," Doc pointed out. "Confine the search accordingly, for it will have to beach somewhere. I would like to swap this motorcycle for your machine," he added, producing the letter from Chicago's Superintendent of Police.

The officer did not exactly salute. In fact, he looked a little put out. But the exchange was made without complaint, and the bronze man was soon driving back toward the Hotel Chicago.

WHEN he pulled up in front, Doc Savage received a surprise.

There were several police machines and an ambulance arriving.

Joining the procession, Doc pulled into the garage with the group, whose sirens were caterwauling.

Parking, Doc Savage stepped out and began asking questions.

A bluecoat told him, "We got an urgent call that one of the bigwigs attending this thing has keeled over dead."

"What name?"

"The bird's name is McLean."

Doc Savage's trilling leaped into life. He throttled it before it careened out of control.

"I will join you," the bronze man rapped.

Together, they took the elevator up to the exhibition hall.

It was not difficult to locate the stricken man, not even in the great exhibition hall with its swarms of people. A circle had formed around the scene. Rubberneckers were elbowing one another aside, others vying to peer over the shoulders of persons shorter than they, all in a futile effort to get a clear look at what was transpiring.

Knowing that tapping such persons on the shoulder and requesting that they step aside would be futile, the police began blowing their traffic whistles, shouting at the top of their lungs.

"Make way! Make way! Ambulance attendants coming through. Make way!"

With reluctance, the push parted, forming a lane through which the ambulance men and their police escorts shouldered strenuously through.

The stricken individual had been laid on the empty booth that bore Long Tom Roberts' banner. It was obviously the only raised space available, and there was no other significance to it.

Dr. Warner Rockwell and Marvin Lucian Linden were in attendance. Their faces wore worry like masks of grief.

Monk and Ham, seeing the approach of Doc Savage, rushed up to greet the bronze giant.

"There was a green flash of light," began Ham.

"Let me tell it!" Monk interrupted. "I saw it better than you."

"Go ahead," invited Doc.

"Like the shyster said," Monk said excitedly, "it was a flash of green light. I was lookin' in the general direction. And that's what I saw. Knowin' what it might mean, I rushed over fast as I could run. That Malcolm McLean was already on the floor. When I got down beside him, he wasn't movin'. He was like a stick of wood."

Ham sniffed, "You made so many cracks about him looking like a dead man, now you have your wish."

Doc Savage said, "Had you seen McLean before the flash of green light?"

Both Monk and Ham shook their heads in the negative. Ham offered, "We were looking for him, but there was no sign in this deuced crowd."

Swiftly, Doc Savage filled his associates in on the bizarre theft of the submersible automobile, for that was what it obviously was, and the fact that the driver appeared—at least from a distance—to be the same Malcolm McLean.

Monk squawled, "Blazes! How the heck could that be?"

Doc Savage imparted, "It would not have been possible for the driver of that submersible machine to have doubled back in such a short period of time. Therefore, one of the gray-featured men is not who he seems."

Ham frowned thoughtfully. "A dead-looking face like that of McLean's would lend itself to an artificial mask—should someone go to the trouble to make one up."

"That is one possibility," said Doc Savage. "Let us see to the condition of the Malcolm McLean who was stricken."

"Don't we kinda know that already?" husked Monk. "On account of the green flash, I mean."

"Say nothing of that," cautioned Doc.

Turning, the three men drew near the table where the gray corpse lay, its closed eyes strangely sunken.

Dr. Rockwell was folding up a doctor's stethoscope as he told the ambulance attendants, "I am sorry, gentlemen. You are too late. This man has expired. You may take my word for it, for I am a physician. Dr. Warner Rockwell is my name."

The two orderlies evinced no skepticism on that score, for the ashen coloration of the corpse told a clear story.

One asked, "Was it a heart attack?"

Rockwell shook his head somberly. "I doubt it. McLean was altogether too young to suffer from such a sad fate."

The other interne wanted to know, "Then why does he look so dead?"

"The unfortunate fellow acquired that skin condition as a result of careless chemical experiments with silver. It is a rare, but not unknown, thing."

The ambulance attendants looked vaguely skeptical. They had encountered many dead bodies before this, and this was a new one on them.

"Whatever happened to McLean, it seems to have affected his brain," pronounced Rockwell grimly.

Doc Savage interjected, "What leads you to that conclusion, Dr. Rockwell?"

"Step closer, Savage. I will show you." Bending over the inanimate form, the medical man lifted one eyelid, exposing an orb that rather resembled an old oyster shell. "Observe McLean's eyes. They appear to have become crusted over with some stony substance I do not recognize."

Doc Savage lifted the other eyelid, and exposed a matching ball of stone. There was the faintest suggestion of iris and pupil, but it was so indistinct only the bronze man's impressive visual acuity perceived it.

Rockwell explained, "This was like nothing I ever before encountered, so I examined McLean's mouth and ears, but found nothing. When I shone my pen light into his nostrils, however, I encountered an obstruction in both. Inserting a scalpel probe into one nostril, I encountered a hard substance that I imagine resembles the matter that now comprises his eyeballs."

"What is your conclusion then?" asked Doc.

"By some means beyond my comprehension," said Rockwell suddenly, "I am forced to conclude that poor Malcolm McLean's brain has turned to stone, and whatever effected the transformation, it was sufficiently potent to petrify his eyeballs, as you can plainly see."

"That was very astute of you, Dr. Rockwell," complimented Doc. "Most medical men would not think to make an examination of the nasal cavity."

Dr. Rockwell nodded his head slightly in recognition of the professional compliment.

Doc placed a hand over McLean's chest, detected no heartbeat, and transferred his attention to both wrists. Finding no pulse, he placed the lifeless hands atop the dead man's chest.

"There is no question that this individual is now deceased," he pronounced.

Warner Rockwell shook his head slowly, saying, "None at all."

"He is wearing a suit and tie identical to those Malcolm McLean wore earlier in the day," added Doc.

Dr. Rockwell looked slightly confused. "There is no doubt but that here lies poor McLean," he said gravely.

Doc met the craggy-faced physician's frank gaze with his own unnerving regard. "Yet a man strongly resembling McLean made off with the invention of the late Myer Sim and drove it into Lake Michigan, evading all pursuit."

Marvin Lucian Linden had been hovering nearby. Interest flared in his eyes. "What invention was that, Mr. Savage?"

"It appeared to be some form of snorkel car."

Linden looked blank.

"An automobile designed along the lines of a one-man submarine capable of moving on roads and sea beds," explained Doc. "The snorkel doubles as a periscope, providing both breathable air and navigational assistance."

"To function properly," Linden mused, "a periscope would have to be sealed."

Doc offered, "No doubt the tube was double-barreled."

Linden's eyes lit up. "Ingenious!"

Dr. Rockwell asked, "You say the driver resembled McLean?"

Doc nodded firmly. "At several points, he turned around to track my pursuit. His features were gray and, although I could not see them clearly, I naturally assumed they belonged to McLean. Men with his condition are rather rare, as you well know."

Dr. Rockwell's unblinking eyes went from the bronze man to the body of Malcolm McLean and back again. He shrugged elaborately.

"Of course, I must take you at your word. But the proof of McLean's innocence lies on the table before you."

"A submersible automobile," breathed Marvin Lucian Linden, half under his breath. "What a remarkable achievement, provided the thief who stole the machine has not drowned in Lake Michigan."

The ambulance internes fell to gathering up the body, and Dr. Rockwell put in a request.

"I would like to accompany the body to the hospital."

"You mean the morgue," returned one orderly.

Rockwell shook his heavy features resolutely. "No, I would like the body to be conveyed to Mercy General Hospital, where I do much of my work. This is an unusual case, and it interests me as a medical man. I would like to study the circumstances before this body is consigned to the city morgue for autopsy."

The two medical men conferred with one another briefly.

One spoke for both when he said, "Well, I guess there's no reason not to. We'll do just that."

Dr. Rockwell turned to Doc Savage and his aides, saying, "If you will excuse me, gentlemen, I must be going."

After the body was hoisted onto a wheeled gurney, Warner Rockwell followed it out through the milling crowds, and to the ambulance waiting in the garage.

Doc Savage's gaze was thoughtful as they departed, his golden eyes shifted about the room, looking here and there, as if seeking something specific.

Ham noticed this and asked, "What is wrong?"

"I fail to see the green shadow that accompanied all previous incidents where men were struck down, their brains petrifying in some mysterious fashion."

Monk burst out, "That's right! Maybe we should start nosin' around."

THEY did not need to nose around very much, for Doc Savage discovered something intriguing on the floor not far away.

"Was this the spot where McLean was struck down?" Doc asked Monk.

"That's right. After the flash went out of my eyes, the first thing I saw was the poor stiff lyin' right here, lookin' even worse than usual."

"Observe the floor," requested Doc.

Ham and Monk did. There was no doubt but that both men expected to see another hideous snake-headed outline, but that was what not what their uneasy eyes fell upon.

Instead, there were ragged letters—black letters as if they had been burnt there—inscribed on the floor. The words spelled out:

Gorgones Vincit Omnia

Ham knew Latin, and translated it immediately.

" 'Gorgons Conquer All,'" he intoned. "This is new."

Kneeling, Doc Savage touched the letter G, brought up a blackish residue and examined it carefully with aureate eyes.

"These scorched letters suggest a substance which was ignited, possibly producing the green glare," he ventured. "Since Long

Tom's booth was empty, there were no other persons close enough to be stricken by the phenomenon."

"Could this be the same burnt matter found on Myer Sim's desk?" asked Ham.

"Unquestionably," replied Doc, scraping up scorched residue into a plain white envelope he produced from a pocket.

Doc stood up, features grim in their metallic way.

"What are we gonna do now?" asked Monk.

Doc Savage suggested, "Perhaps news of Malcolm McLean's apparent demise will change the mind of Miss Falcon, insofar as her willingness to talk."

Chapter XVIII

VIOLENT ABDUCTION

TOGETHER, DOC, MONK and Ham made for the corridor. Monk hammered a tattoo on the elevator call button with his thumb. It seemed as if the cage would never arrive, but at last there came a *whirr* and a *click* and the door slid back.

The trio stepped aboard and waited in silence while the lift climbed.

Monk and Ham were uncharacteristically silent. The presence of the elevator operator might have had something to do with that.

Just as the cage toiled to the level of the sixth floor, up the elevator shaft rattled a racket that seemed out of place in the genteel hostelry.

Monk made a face. "Sounds like—!"

"Gunfire!" rapped out Doc Savage.

Just then the cage came to a halt, and the elevator boy threw it open.

Doc Savage stepped off, turned, and instructed his aides, "Go directly to the lobby and investigate this. I will check on Miss Falcon."

The white-faced elevator operator grabbed the control and sent the cage whining downward.

Doc Savage moved to the left, glided up the hallway, seeking Janet Falcon's room. It was not fear for his own safety that caused him to send his men down into the fray below. Rather, it was the concern that the gunfire had something to do with the woman. Better to check on her while he was on the same floor, than to have to turn back if gunmen were now rushing up the stairs.

Doc did not expect to be long. He went directly to the door, and applied his knuckles to the panel.

The hotel room door proved to be unlocked; it jarred open. This was immediately suspicious.

Cautiously, Doc Savage retreated and stepped off to one side.

From an inner pocket of his vest, he took a small folding grappling hook which he habitually carried. This was attached to a coil of silken line. At the bottom portion, the thin line had been tied into an open loop. The bronze man widened the loop somewhat, drew back further, and made an expert toss.

The miniature lasso caught the doorknob, and Doc gave the line a hard tug. This brought the door slamming shut again. It elicited another reaction, too.

Suddenly, splinters started flying from the door as large caliber bullets punched jagged holes in the thick wood.

Back of the door came a staccato rattle, one instantly recognizable to anyone who had dwelled in Chicago over the last decade or so. It was a Tommy gun in violent operation.

The sound it made resembled that of a riveting gun, and the so-called Chicago typewriter continued spewing lead until the entire door was perforated with splinter-edged holes.

It was not possible to count the number of shots being fired, but Doc Savage was familiar with the Thompson submachine gun. The sub-gun emptied its hundred-round drum in approximately ten seconds.

Doc counted the seconds. He did not bother with his watch. His sense of time was superb.

When the Thompson fell silent, the bronze man hit the door. There was not much left of the panel. His shoulder, striking in the center, caused the wood to come apart like a giant jigsaw puzzle. Biting gunsmoke wafted out.

The gunman attempting to remove the ammunition drum from his Thompson submachine gun looked up, and took in the awesome sight of the metallic human juggernaut charging at him. That was all he registered. His jaw fell open, the cigarette dangling from his lower lip hung precariously for a moment, then fell to the carpet.

A bronze fist struck him square in the center of the forehead. The knuckles actually left four deep indentations that were still present an hour later when the underworld torpedo was carried out on a stretcher.

Doc Savage had no time for the man, knowing he would be out for a considerable period of time. Instead, he flung from room to room, looking for any signs of Janet Falcon. He found none.

There was a sprinkling of blood drops here and there, suggesting recent violence. But they led in no particular direction.

Plunging back into the hallway, the bronze man sped for the elevator bank, saw by the indicator dials that they were all on different floors, and ran for the fire stairs.

Possibly no other man living could flash down the winding staircase faster than an elevator could climb its shaft and collect him. But that is what Doc Savage did.

When he reached the lobby, it was a mess.

Flowerpots had been shot to pieces, and the front desk man was cowering behind the desk, clutching his lapel gardenia as if it were a protective talisman.

"What year is this?" he moaned, an apparent reference to the era not long in the past when wild bullets flew in Chicago on a daily basis.

There was a man lying sprawled in an overstuffed chair where he had been reading the morning newspaper.

Perforations showed in the newspaper. Equivalent holes stood behind them in the man's vest. These latter holes were leaking crimson. A cigar had fallen out of the unfortunate's mouth, and was smoldering in his lap. The man did not seem to mind. The glassy stare in his open eyes indicated that he was beyond all earthly concerns.

Doc saw from a badge visible on his vest that this was the hotel detective. Whatever had happened, the unfortunate man had been caught unawares.

Doc flashed outside—just in time to see figures piling into a pair of matching touring cars. These machines were curtained.

Into the lead car being bundled by force was Janet Falcon. Someone had her by a knot of long hair and was trying to force the woman into the back seat. Seeing Doc Savage, her mouth flew open.

"Mr. Savage! This is about—"

A hand leapt up, seized her mouth and wrung it closed. But the green-eyed brunette was having none of that. She bit the kidnapper's thumb.

The hand withdrew, and she tried again.

"Gorgoni—" she shrilled.

The stubby barrel of a .38 revolver struck her a glancing blow on the head, and she collapsed into the back of the car.

Doc Savage had cleared half the distance between the lobby entrance and the first touring car when one of the kidnappers pulled a dark object out of his trim overcoat, then bit off a steel ring before tossing it in Doc Savage's direction.

The bronze man did not need acute vision to know what that was. Doc had had hand grenades tossed at him more than once in the past.

Although he wore a bulletproof undergarment, it was not proof against grenade shrapnel, he knew.

Veering to the right, the bronze giant flung himself onto the hood of a waiting taxicab and continued on, to land hard on the other side, where he crouched behind a fendered front wheel.

The grenade let go with a bang and a flash—and the immediate vicinity was suddenly filled with flying objects battering themselves into whatever stood in their way. Glass broke, the side of the hotel was altered in many respects, but no one was injured.

Both touring cars charged off as Doc Savage leaped to his feet, flinging himself behind the wheel of the taxicab.

The driver was not present. The key was in the ignition. Doc gave it a twist. He got the motor going, endeavored to wrench the wheel around.

Turning mushily, the machine moaned away from the curb and refused to pick up much speed.

Doc Savage did not need to exit the vehicle and look to confirm that more than one tire had been punctured by shrapnel. But when he did step out, a quick examination told him that all four tires were beyond repair.

Doc looked around; there was not another vehicle at hand. So he began running.

He was soon following behind the second touring car. Through the rear window glass, he could see Monk and Ham's faces turning toward him.

Monk tried to mouth something. It was so big that Doc Savage could easily lip-read his outcry.

"Call us dunces!" Monk was saying. "We walked right into it."

Doc continued running, and was actually doing fairly well, given that the slushy streets inhibited the touring cars from making the best headway.

Then one of the car doors flung open and a man in a dark overcoat and olive green Trilby hat stepped out onto the running board, cradling a Thompson submachine gun.

The Tommy gunner was either very brave or very foolhardy. For he used both hands to manage the weapon, leaving no way to hold onto the careening vehicle. Perhaps he saw the same reckless stunt done in a gangster movie and thought he could do as well.

Grimacing, he squeezed down on the firing lever and the mechanism began chattering.

Once again, Doc Savage was forced to leap for cover. He barely made it. If he had worn a hat, it would certainly have been knocked off his head. As it was, the whistle and snap of bullets around his ears came uncomfortably close.

In mid-leap, Doc was suddenly sent into a somersault not of his making. Knocked off course, he fell against a fire plug, and lay there a moment, stunned.

The bronze man had not struck his head. But at least one slug had caught him in the back. The chain-mail undergarment he habitually wore had prevented the lead from biting into his flesh, but offered no protection against the stunning force of impact.

Doc lay on the slushy sidewalk, trying to get his breath organized.

TEARING up the street and turning the corner, the reckless Tommy-gun jockey got the last laugh, and swung back into the tonneau of the touring car.

His face was beaming under the downturned brim of his rather rakish Trilby hat.

As he sank into the cushions, he chortled, "I smoked him good, Patches."

"That you did, Duke," snickered the driver. "Doc Savage is bound for the morgue."

In back, Monk and Ham gave out two very different groans.

Composing himself, Ham Brooks warned, "You will not be the first gangster to think he got the better of Doc Savage, only to learn differently."

Duke Grogan began disassembling the smoking Tommy gun, placing the large sections into an open bass violin case at his feet. "Maybe," he murmured. "Maybe not. But I don't see him following me anymore. Put that in your pipe and smoke it."

Ham subsided. Then he asked, "The police were alerted by Doc Savage to meet your train and take you into custody. How did you elude them?"

"My boys telegraphed me that Doc Savage had blown into town. I put two and two together. So I got off in Albany, and chartered a plane. I figured that the harness bulls might try to nab me at the railroad station, anyway."

Monk Mayfair growled, "Pretty slick, Duke."

"Thanks, you dish-faced ape," drawled Duke.

"Where are you takin' us?"

Duke Grogan grinned cruelly. "Nowhere. Nowhere at all. Just going for a little ride, all of us. Get me?"

Ham Brooks said, "I thought the underworld custom of 'the ride' was a thing of the past."

Grogan laughed nastily. "You're thinking it went out of style, along with the speakeasy. But I'm a traditional sort of fella. I'm thinking we'll keep it, strictly for old time's sake. Now settle down. We got a ways to go before we get to nowhere."

The gangster's chuckle was maliciously cruel.

Chapter XIX

DEAD ENDS

A POLICEMAN, STANDING in the street near the Hotel Chicago, a bewildered expression on his red face, gave Doc Savage the bad news.

"I called the snatch into the station house, Mr. Savage. We got cars in hot pursuit, but no luck so far."

Doc nodded. "Did you witness any of it?"

"Just two guys fleeing the scene," said the cop. "They dived into a car and drove off."

"Describe them."

"One was some kind of a mug with a heavy growth of beard. Didn't see the other bird's face. He was average size. Both wore the kind of flashy duds you associate with gangsters."

The officer did not know it, but he was describing Blackie and Blue, the abductors of Long Tom Roberts.

The patrolman looked at Doc and shifted uncomfortably. He had recognized the bronze man. Not only did he know Doc's reputation, but he was also aware of an order posted in the precinct station, signed by the police superintendent himself, which directed that Doc Savage was to receive every cooperation, and no questions asked.

"Sure sorry I didn't get a good look at him, Mr. Savage," mumbled the cop. "They were gone before I could do a thing. You see, I heard some shots, and was coming down the street to investigate."

Doc Savage glanced up the street, saying nothing.

The cop began again, "I'm sure sorry—"

"Phone your precinct station," Doc directed. "Have a general pick-up order issued for a gangster named Duke Grogan."

Doc gave a rapid, accurate description of Grogan—a word picture that would have astounded Grogan, who thought Doc had not so much as seen his features.

"Also have a general search started for my associates, Monk Mayfair, Ham Brooks and Long Tom Roberts," Doc instructed.

"What do they look like?"

"Your superior officer will have their descriptions on file."

Doc slipped into the hotel building. The policeman departed for a run to the nearest departmental telephone. He would have preferred to remain, having heard much of the remarkable detective ability attributed to this bronze man.

Had the cop looked on, he would not have been disappointed.

Doc Savage crossed the hotel lobby, which was swarming with police officers lately arrived.

The unconscious body of the machine gunner the bronze giant had kayoed up in Janet Falcon's room was being conveyed out of the establishment on a stretcher, the livid knuckle marks of Doc's metallic fist plainly etched on his noticeably bruised forehead.

The desk clerk was giving a full account of the events that had all but wrecked his sumptuous lobby.

"These men stepped off the elevator, and they were hustling a green-eyed woman through the lobby," the jittery clerk was saying. "Anyone looking at her face could tell that she was being abducted. The hotel detective was sitting in that chair over there, reading a newspaper, and I signaled to him. The gunmen must have seen me give the high sign. Because before the hotel dick could finish rising from his chair, they shot him in cold blood."

The poor detective in question was still sprawled on the easy chair, staring vaguely into space. Someone had thrown water in his lap to put out the smoldering cigar.

The clerk continued, "The next thing I knew, they were trying to bundle the woman into a touring car. That's when the two men came bounding out of the elevator, waving strange-looking pistols. They gave chase."

"Then what happened?" Doc asked him.

"There was a lot of shooting, and I ducked," admitted the clerk.

"In other words, you didn't see anything further?"

"No, but I heard plenty. Bullets zinged everywhere. Sounded like a hand grenade went off, too. It reminded me of the bad old days just a few years ago. I thought those times were done with."

One cop rocked back on his heels and remarked, "So did we, brother, so did we."

Doc Savage made his presence known. "The two men were my assistants, Monk Mayfair and Ham Brooks. Somehow they have been abducted, along with a woman whose name is Janet Falcon. She is a private secretary of the late Myer Sim."

"What is this all about, Mr. Savage?" asked one officer.

"That is entirely unclear. But it all seems to have started with Sim's death."

The police officers look nonplussed. Here was the famous Doc Savage, renowned as a scientist, medical genius, and investigator of unparalleled skill, confessing that he had not a clue.

"Well," concluded one cop, "I guess we'll have to get the stiff to the morgue, and try to sort things out."

They got to work on that. At one point, an officer suddenly thought of a question. He turned to voice it, blinked at the spot where Doc Savage had been standing a moment before. The space was now empty.

"Well, where did he go?"

There was a general search for Doc Savage, beginning with the bank of elevators. None of the operators had taken the bronze man upstairs, so it was clear that he had quitted the hotel. To where, was a complete mystery.

Doc Savage went out, and began to study the slushy sleet, which was firm enough to hold the imprints of the tire tracks of the two touring cars. The bronze man committed these to memory. Then he reclaimed the rental sedan he had been previously using, and sent it out into the street. The police officer whose motorcycle he had commandeered had seen to it that the machine was returned to the hotel.

Doc was able to follow the tire tracks of the two touring cars for quite a distance—almost three quarters of a mile—when the last traces of the machines became lost in the general confusion of crosstown traffic.

Changing course, Doc Savage next drove out to the municipal airport, parked the sedan, and entered the operations building, where he requested permission to take off without delay. This was summarily granted.

That matter settled, Doc went to the aircraft hangar where the great bronze speed plane stood waiting, its three propellers gleaming.

Climbing aboard, Doc saw that it had been refueled as instructed, and gunned the engines.

The hangar door was already up, so Doc ran his speed plane out onto the tarmac, warmed up the engines, then released the brake.

The bronze ship scooted down the runway, vaulted into the air, and began climbing for altitude. Presently, Doc leveled off at only five hundred feet. Then the bronze man sent the speed plane out over Lake Michigan's watery expanse.

From the air, he spotted the beach in front of the Drake Hotel where the weird submersible automobile had plunged into the water.

It stood to reason that a rubber-tired vehicle rolling along the lake bed would stir up mud. It had. A spreading trail of discoloration led deep into Lake Michigan. Doc followed it from the air for approximately three quarters of a mile.

The muddy tail seemed to cease, ending in a diffused patch of brownish water.

Abruptly, the bronze man dropped the plane, and began skimming the wavelets that wrinkled the lake surface. The afternoon sun was high in the air, and the lake sparkled with myriad solar jewels.

Again and again, Doc hiked the speed plane about, peering down as if to penetrate to the lake bottom. But the lake was not clear enough to permit such viewing.

Finally, Doc turned the plane toward the spot where the spreading fan of mud petered out. Aiming for that point, he brought the amphibian plane down, dropping onto its pontoons. He chopped power. The whirling props went still, freezing in place.

Doc was an expert pilot and what he next accomplished showed that clearly. The aircraft struck the water, bumped along, then wallowed. Doc steered the pontoon's water rudders and jockeyed the plane toward the spot he desired to reach.

The speed plane coasted to a stop at almost that precise point.

Stripping to his black silk undershorts, the bronze man donned a diving lung of his own invention, which consisted of a canister which strapped to his chest, and an air hose leading to a rubber contrivance that covered his mouth and nose. Opening the hatch, he dropped down.

The lake water was just as frigid as he recalled; fortunately it was not freezing.

Doc commenced swimming downward, using kicking motions of his feet and great sweeping motions of his mighty bronze arms.

In a surprisingly short time, he discovered the aluminum automobile resting on the lake floor.

Sweeping in, Doc saw that the retractable snorkel was entirely submerged. He went for the angle near the top, took hold of it, and began examining the contrivance.

The projection was as he judged it earlier. A combination periscope and snorkel. Two channels were built into the steel pipe, one for air, the other for viewing. Under pressure of pursuit, the driver had misjudged the depth of the lake, and apparently driven it beyond the point at which the retractable snorkel could be extended.

Using his hands, Doc worked down the snorkel barrel until he was kneeling on the roof. Ducking his head, he peered through the windshield.

There was a single seat, a steering wheel, various levers not found on an ordinary automobile. But no sign of the operator.

The interior, however, was filled with muddy water which was slowly settling.

Stepping off the roof, the bronze man alighted on his feet and discovered that the driver-side door was not latched. The gray-faced man who had driven the submersible car out into the lake had clearly quitted his outlandish vehicle when the driver's compartment began to flood.

He must have possessed a ration of nerve, for he had retained the presence of mind to close the door after him, even if he did not finish sealing it.

No trace of disappointment showed in Doc Savage's flake-gold eyes as he left the strange machine empty-handed. It would not be possible to take fingerprints off the vehicle, since it was completely immersed.

Pushing upward, Doc swam back to his waiting plane, climbed aboard one pontoon, got inside, and toweled himself off. His hair had dried by itself, a peculiar property it possessed.

The cabin was electrically warmed, so Doc did not bother dressing again as he ran the aircraft along the tops of the choppy waves. Soon the tri-motor was back in the air and Doc pointed the howling snout upward, seeking altitude.

Again, he leveled off at about one thousand feet. Flying past the municipal airport, Doc aimed for the city. The purpose in this endeavor was difficult to discern. The big bronze man began flying meticulous circles, no doubt seeking the whereabouts of his missing men, Monk Mayfair and Ham Brooks—not to mention the abducted woman, Janet Falcon.

Chapter XX

JOE SHINE

HAD HE BEEN born in Naples, Italy, Giuseppe Athalentia Shinola would probably not have made much of a mark on the world. But his Neapolitan parents had immigrated to America before he was born. When he came squawling into the world, Giuseppe Athalentia Shinola had done so in the city of Chicago. That, conceivably, had made all the difference.

His childhood was not remarkable. He had got into no more trouble than any other shaver his age. Growing up near the stockyards, young Giuseppe had naturally been drawn to the sprawling slaughterhouses when it came time to make his first living.

A beef killer is a man with a peculiar occupation. The beef killer stands at a chute in the stockyards and sticks a thing like an icepick into the base of the beef's brain. Most beef killers use a hammer, though.

Giuseppe Athalentia Shinola—he was going by the name of "Joe" by that time—became a beef killer. He had a knack for it. He hadn't minded all the blood. In truth, he rather enjoyed it. He customarily wore a heavy smock and wading boots to protect his street clothes and shoes from the constant splashing of bovine blood.

For how long Joe Shinola would have stood the strenuous work of being a lowly beef killer is difficult to guess. Not long, certainly. For in those days Chicago was changing. Prohibition became the law, and where there is law, there inevitably follows lawlessness.

By the time Joe Shinola had grown weary of the stockyards, he was mentally prepared to participate in the brawling boom town that the Windy City was fast becoming. He was physically prepared as well. The stockyards had seen to that, too.

When young Joe Shinola, dressed in his best Sunday suit of clothes and highly polished shoes, had presented himself to Angelo Moroni, who in that day had controlled the South Side of Chicago and all its rackets, he wasn't laughed at, exactly.

"What do you got to offer me, kid?" Moroni had demanded.

Joe Shinola had had trouble being heard over the raucous noise of the speakeasy that day a decade ago.

"I know how to kill," he insisted.

"Is that right? How many men have you killed, punk?"

"None so far. But I've slaughtered hundreds of heifers."

Angelo Moroni did not laugh. But he did smile. Craftily.

"Killing a man is not like killing an animal. Come back when you've got some real blood on your shoes. Now beat it."

Joe Shinola beat it. He did not go far. He ran over to the North Side and found Red Gains. Red Gains was having his hair cut in a barber shop.

The bootlegger listened to Joe Shinola patiently. At the end of the spiel, he did not look up from the newspaper he was reading. Nor did he address the eager young man with the shiny black shoes directly.

Instead, he remarked casually, "That Angelo Moroni is gettin' too big for his britches. Somebody oughta run that grifter out of town. I'd do it myself, but the coppers might take offense."

An avid light came into Joe Shinola's shoe-button eyes.

"Well," mused Red as he turned to the sports page, "maybe some day I'll get around to that chiseler."

When the silent barber expertly whipped the sheet off Red Gains' lank form, the young beef killer was no longer standing there.

They found Angelo Moroni sitting in the Gem Theater the next day. The Gem Theater had been showing another cowboy picture. "Wyoming Guns," the picture was called.

A sail needle had been used on the victim. It would be some time before they found the needle there.

The police had been rightfully baffled. The press had had the proverbial field day. Accusatory fingers were pointed all over the Chicago underworld. But the murder was never solved, nor was the slayer ever named.

Only two individuals suspected the truth. One was Red Gains and the other the ill-fortuned barber who had been privy to the first meeting of the crime boss and his new assassin.

Later, the barber was found in his barber chair, sitting glassy-eyed in death. The only reason the medical examiner discovered the sail needle buried at the base of the man's brain was that recent experience had told him where to look. For there had been no blood in evidence.

That killing was never solved, either.

The years had passed by swiftly. During that interval, Joe Shine—as he now styled himself—rose to prominence in the Red Gains outfit, becoming a lieutenant in the North Side branch of the Chicago underworld, which by then had grown fat from the profits made from distilling illicit liquor.

Came Repeal, and all that changed. The brutal gang wars had weeded out the weak. Angelo Moroni was long gone. The Savoli mob were likewise no more.

Red Gains was a philosophical gangster. He looked at the sorry state of affairs and called a meeting of his lieutenants, among them Joe Shine.

"Boys, this racket is cooked," he announced through heavy cigar smoke. "We've skimmed the cream. I got mine. I'm cashin' out. My advice is that you all do the same. Find yourselves respectable wives, and start families. It's all over. This Prohibition cow has been milked dry."

There was the expected grumbling, but it was soon drowned by newly-legal whiskey. The party lasted long into the night, breaking up before dawn.

None of the participants remembered much the next day when the maid found Red Gains lying asprawl his magnificent bed, dead to the world.

It was two days before the police were called. The M.E. by this time was a new man. He had not been around during the bad old days of the gang wars.

Consequently, he never found the sail needle that had been driven by a small hammer into the base of Red Gains' skull.

No one questioned Joe Shine when he announced to a convocation of the North Siders that he was the new head of the rackets. Without a shot being fired, the former Giuseppe Athalentia Shinola became the latest crime czar of Chicago.

That was not very long ago.

JOE SHINE was having his shoes buffed when his afternoon was interrupted. Most men have their shoes shined once a week, if that. But Joe Shine was different. He had his own personal bootblack.

The rackets king of the North Side was seated at his private table at the Neapolitan Restaurant, which he owned. It was his headquarters, as well as a front for his illegal activities.

The bootblack was liberally applying shoe polish to Joe Shine's expensive brogans. This was the third time today that the shoe-shine boy was performing this task. If needed, he shined these same shoes four or five times a day. It was a ritual with them. Nothing quite explained this ritual, but a psychologist might have harkened back to Joe's days in the Chicago stockyards, when his work boots were literally splashed with bovine fluids on a daily basis.

It was as if Joe's shoes could never be polished enough for him.

Into the restaurant came charging one of Joe Shine's lieutenants.

"Joe! You gotta hear this!"

"What is it?"

"Duke Grogan. He's back in town, and he pulled a funny move."

Joe Shine all but jumped out of his seat, and demanded, "Is he trying to muscle in on the North Side again?"

"No, it's not that. He and his boys just snatched two of Doc Savage's men."

"Doc Savage! I heard he was in town. Looking into some killings. But that doesn't have anything to do with us."

"Maybe it don't," said the other. "But all hell is going to rain down on this town after what Duke pulled. Doc Savage is poison to crooks like us. Everybody knows that."

Joe Shine's shoe-button eyes narrowed in thought. "What's Duke mixed up in that he pulls a stunt like that?"

"I don't know," the lieutenant returned. "But Duke don't mix into any business that he can't chisel a few dollars out of it."

Joe Shine scowled. "You don't chisel Doc Savage. Can't be done. I know that much."

"I'll say! I had a pal that went up against the bronze guy a few years back. He up and disappeared." The man snapped his fingers adding, "Just like that. Like he popped out of existence. I've searched from Walla Walla to Sing Sing, and never found my pal what got nabbed by Doc Savage."

"You say that it was Doc Savage's men who got snatched, but not the bronze guy himself?"

"That's right. And you know what *that* means."

"Yeah," grinned Shine. "Doc Savage is gonna go to town on Duke Grogan and his boys. He'll be lucky to see the sunrise."

Joe Shine was standing up now and inserting his arms into his velvet-collared overcoat.

"Let's look into this. Maybe there's something in it for us."

The lieutenant looked blank of face and more than a little queasy about his immediate future. "Like what?"

"If I know Duke Grogan," said Joe Shine, hard-heeling out of the restaurant, "he's taken those two mugs for a ride. And I know where he likes to bump people off. Let's see if we can head him off."

Now the lieutenant looked truly uneasy.

"What are you thinking of doing?" he asked, following closely.

Settling a black Homburg atop his slicked-down hair, Shine growled. "I haven't figured out that angle yet, but it'll come to me. All I know is this: if Duke Grogan is muscling in on Doc Savage, I wanna know why, and I want my piece of the action."

"I don't know, Joe," the other said vaguely, "any piece of the action involving Doc Savage is liable to get us a one-way ticket to nowhere, just like my pal."

"Doc Savage," bit out Joe Shine, "ain't the king of the North Side of Chicago. Now get a move on. We got places to go and things to do."

Chapter XXI

GANGNAPPED

TWO TOURING CARS rocked as they tore through the city streets.

In the back seat of the lead automobile, Monk, Ham and Janet Falcon shifted with each lurch of the swerving machine. Curtains were pulled so that they were not visible through the side windows.

That was not the only precaution taken. The abductors had driven to a dingy garage outside the city limits, where they ditched the kidnap cars, changing to fresh machines in order to foil police pursuit.

During the exchange, Duke Grogan had ordered the three prisoners into the back of one automobile, whose curtains were tightly drawn.

Two of the thugs doing the shoving were Blackie and Blue, but inasmuch as neither Monk nor Ham had previously laid eyes on the hard-faced duo, they failed to realize they were in the presence of the crooks responsible for Long Tom Roberts' disappearance.

Swiftly, the autos melted into traffic, unsuspected.

Duke Grogan sat in front. He had collected Monk and Ham's compact supermachine pistols during the initial abduction. The pair had blundered into the muzzle of a Tommy gun, and so had not gotten off a single shot, despite having their weapons out and ready for action.

Grogan was fiddling with one of the ingenious guns, saying, "Not bad, not bad at all. I could use a brace of these. How do you unlock the mechanism?"

Ham Brooks answered that. "Very carefully. For if you work the safety catches in the wrong order, a vial of acid breaks open and the weapon will sear the flesh off your finger bones."

That casual warning sounded so intimidating that the gangster leader shoved both weapons into the glove box, saying, "You can show me later."

A thudding rain had commenced. It produced a dismal tattoo on the canvas tonneau roof, and rapidly turned the slushy avenues into rivers.

Behind the wheel, the driver growled, "I wish this foul weather would make up its mind."

Beside him, Duke turned in his seat and said, "We don't have far to go now."

"Is that so?" muttered Monk. "Where exactly are we headed?"

"Nowhere," chuckled Duke. "Just plain nowhere. You fellows should have stayed back in New York, just like Ned Gamble should have never left this burg. Too late for him, and now it's too late for you."

"Is that a confession of murder?" chided Ham.

Beside the dapper lawyer, Janet Falcon was chewing at her ragged lower lip, and fighting back hot tears. But she said nothing.

Ham demanded, "Doc Savage knows you're involved in this affair, Duke. Do you have any idea what he will do once he catches up to you and your gang?"

Duke Grogan let out a rough guffaw. "Doc Savage is yesterday's news. This time he's up against something that can't be beat."

"Are you referring to yourself?" Ham asked suspiciously.

The gang leader looked as if he was about to make a biting retort, but thought better of it. He licked his lips with a trace of nervousness.

"There is somebody bigger than Doc Savage now," he boasted. "Put that in your pipe and smoke it."

The dapper lawyer ground out, "There is no one bigger than Doc Savage. Get that through your head."

Grogan said nothing. The expression on his half-turned profile told that he was eager to boast, but thought better of it.

To the girl, Ham Brooks said, "It appears as if we are about to be put on the spot. Have you anything you'd like to tell us before that happens?"

Monk grunted, "Just like a lawyer to go cross-examining someone before they get killed."

"Shut up!" Ham insisted. To Janet Falcon, he prodded, "Well?"

Janet Falcon chewed her lips in extreme distress. She was succeeding in holding back tears, but all her efforts seemed to go in that direction. Shaking her head, she refused to speak.

The touring car, followed by another, wended its way out of the city and began following a shore road that skirted Lake Michigan.

By this time, dusk had given way to darkness.

Seeing city lights reflected in the vast lake's expanse, Monk muttered, "Somehow, I get the sinkin' feeling we're all goin' for a swim."

"Not all of us," said Duke thinly. "The dame stays above water. For now."

The driver laughed cruelly, inserting, "You can't exactly swim when you're wearing concrete overshoes."

"We don't have time for that, Patches," snapped Duke.

"Well, there's two of them. How the heck are we gonna weigh them down?"

"Snow chains, that's how."

"Well, that might work, at that," Patches allowed.

Monk and Ham exchanged looks. Although no word passed between them, they seemed to arrive at a mutual understanding without need for conversation.

Their hands were tied behind them, but that did not inhibit their next move.

Leaning back into the seat cushions, they brought up their feet, set the soles of their feet against the backs of the front seats.

Exerting pressure in unison, they tested the seat backs.

Duke noticed this pressure, turned, and started to say, "What the—?"

Simultaneously, Monk and Ham reared back, then slammed their feet forward.

The maneuver sent Duke Grogan and his driver slamming forward violently.

The driver crashed into the steering column, breaking it. For his part, Duke's skull bounced off the windscreen on his side of the automobile, knocking off his olive green hat.

Losing control, Patches began swerving madly, using the broken spokes of the wheel to steer.

The touring car swapped ends, slid around, and threw up great sheets of rain water mixed with slush on all sides.

It was still spinning when Monk Mayfair turned in his seat, and kicked the passenger door open on his side. It was not the most foresighted maneuver.

Centrifugal force sent him flying out of the careening car.

Ham bleated, "Monk!"

As Ham watched in horror, the hairy chemist went tumbling onto the shoulder of the road. Fortunately for Monk, it was a wet mass of soil and slush.

When the homely chemist ceased rolling, he sat up, and did something that most men could not imagine doing.

Monk's gorilla-like arms were incredibly long, and by dint of strenuous effort, he was able to work his tied-together wrists down and around his folded legs, which were rather short in comparison, and bring his fists before him.

The ropes used to tie the wrists were not stout, but they were tightly woven.

The apish chemist brought his teeth to bear, and began chewing ferociously. Fibrous strands parted, popped. It was all Monk needed.

His neckless head hunkered down between his sloping shoulders, Monk Mayfair grated his teeth with the exertion, and snapped the rest of his bonds by main strength alone.

It was an impressive feat of muscular might, but there were no witnesses.

The touring car continued sliding and sloughing around, until the radiator collided with a tree. That brought the machine to a rather forceful dead halt.

The touring which was following careened up, braked hard, and men piled out of the jouncing automobile.

"Duke! Duke! Are you all right?"

Duke Grogan was dazed by the crack on his head. He did not respond.

The gunman called Patches was untangling himself from the broken pieces of the steering wheel. He had a bruise on his chest from the impact of his breastbone against the steering column that would not go away for weeks. He was also out of breath.

Climbing out of the machine, he said breathlessly, "We got to get Duke out of here. We don't want the cops happenin' along. This is a snatch, remember?"

"Sure, sure." Gunmen began helping to assist Duke Grogan to exit the wrecked machine, half dragging him over to the other one.

"What about the ones in the back?"

"Grab the girl. Shoot the other one."

"Happy to," said one minion, bringing out a .38 caliber revolver, and striding over to the upright machine.

Pulling open the door, he reached in and hauled out the unresisting Janet Falcon.

When he had her entirely out of the machine, the gunman pointed his revolver in, and fired three times. Yellowish flashes illuminated the back of the machine, but that was all that was visible to witnesses.

Janet Falcon turned her head away, and fought back moaning words.

She was unceremoniously shoved into the back of the second touring car. Doors clapped shut and the machine took off, gathering speed in the growing darkness.

By the time it had departed, Monk Mayfair was on his bandy legs and charging toward the ruined touring car. He had not heard the verbal exchange that had taken place, but the sound of gunshots had given him renewed vigor.

Growling, the simian chemist sprang up on the running board, looked in, and saw Ham Brooks sprawled in the back, his eyes wide open and a thread of blood crawling down out of one corner of his mouth.

"Ham! What'd they do to you?"

The dapper lawyer did not reply. He did not move. He did not do anything. It was not even certain that he was still breathing.

Monk's tiny eyes veered up to the road ahead. Through the pounding rain, he saw the departing tail-light of the touring car and knew he could never catch up to it.

Falling upon the machine in which Ham lay, Monk began disassembling it by brute strength. First, he pulled off the door. It had already been damaged. He flung this away. The hairy chemist seemed intent on tearing the car to pieces as a way of venting his rage and frustration.

He was well along when a blue limousine flashed by, slowed to a halt, and then began backing up with a grinding noise.

Coming to a halt, the driver of the limousine rolled down his window and asked, "What's the problem, buddy?"

Monk was too busy taking out his frustrations on the wrecked touring car to reply.

Two doors popped open; the driver and his passenger stepped out.

The passenger wore a black pinstripe suit, a matching Homburg, and his shoes were incredibly shiny.

"If I believed in luck," remarked Joe Shine, "I would say that Lady Luck has caught up with one of us."

At those words, Monk Mayfair seemed to snap out of his spell of rage.

Turning, he calmly said, "Need to borrow your car. My friend's been shot up. We gotta get him to a hospital."

Joe Shine put a hand into his overcoat pocket, and taking it out, showed Monk Mayfair the destructive end of the heavy automatic pistol.

"We'll give you a ride, all right. We're going to give you the ride of your life."

Monk's sunken eyes narrowed, and his knees bent as if he were about to spring on the gunman.

Joe Shine took this all in, and decided in an instant what he must do.

Without a change of expression, he placed three shots in the center of Monk Mayfair's barrel chest, striking the area over his beating heart.

The gorilla-like chemist actually turned a complete somersault from the impact of the slugs. Hammering lead drove him into the back seat of the wrecked touring car.

The driver was so taken aback, he said nothing for a full minute. When he got control of his tongue, he cried out, "Boss! We gotta lam outta here!"

"We will. But we're takin' them along."

"But they're dead."

"Dead or alive," said Joe Shine carefully, "they got to be worth something to Doc Savage."

Chapter XXII

FURTIVE MOVEMENTS

THE EVENING WAS well along, and the hour one where honest folks were fast asleep in their beds. The thudding rain which had marked the transition from daylight to night had abated to a pattering that freckled the puddles that had collected in the gutters.

In the suburb of Cicero, only streetlamps glowed. The occasional nighthawk taxi splashed light about as it prowled the rain-washed thoroughfares.

In one modest house, however, lights still showed. These lights were in the basement. And from time to time, shadowy forms moved, interrupting the light as seen through the narrow casement windows in the granite foundation.

Two o'clock had come and gone when finally these lights were doused. After a short interval, one of the casement windows cracked open. It was of the type that lifted upward, and out of this narrow aperture crawled what appeared to be a man.

The man was black from head to toe. Every inch of him. All that could be discerned of this darksome figure was that he was slender enough to squeeze out of the open casement window—a feat that would have defied a man of average height and build.

By wiggling his narrow-hipped body, the fellow managed to pull his legs free, and finally stand erect.

The nearest streetlight was not close, and its light showed rather feebly.

The figure who stood up in the cloud-smeared night was not black in the manner of a gentleman of color. His blackness was flat and powdery, as if he had spent the night sleeping in a coal bin, and accumulated a residue of anthracite.

Conceivably, that is exactly what must have taken place. For the narrow window was situated next to the household coal-delivery chute. Then the man looked at his sooty hands, and instead of holding them up to the drizzle, he smeared his face and hair liberally, further darkening them.

A furtive shadow, he wandered the streets until he came to a public telephone. Entering the booth, he dropped a nickel in the slot, and asked the operator for a local taxicab concern.

When his party came on the line, he began speaking in a peevish tone, saying, "I'm stranded in Cicero. I need a ride. Tell the driver to look for me on the corner of Atlas and Canberra. And tell him to hurry it up. It's pouring out here."

A few minutes later, a taxicab came scooting along, its tires throwing up sheets of spray whenever it rolled over chug holes filled with dancing rain water.

The driver watched the way ahead intently. The dispatcher had told him to pick up a passenger who would be waiting on the corner directly ahead. If the passenger was not there, the dispatcher had directed the taxi driver to go on about his usual business. Late-night passengers were often impatient. Rather than wait in the rain for the summoned cab, they were as apt to hail any passing hack, leaving the original driver to wander the streets in vain for his vanished fare.

The taxi neared the corner where the fare was to be waiting. The driver slowed a bit, although he could see no one. His perspective passenger was not in sight.

Grumbling, he decided to circle the block. This produced no tangible results, so the increasingly irate cabbie returned to the designated corner and parked.

He craned his head all around, but saw no one. A leafless tree planted on the sidewalk creaked and groaned unpleasantly in the wind-whipped rain, but no one appeared to be standing beneath it. The bare branches offered little shelter from the midnight tempest, anyway.

Finding a call box, the hack driver called his dispatcher and reported, "Looks like a bum fare. Got anything else for me?"

"Not a thing," he was told through a line crackling with static created by rain falling on old telephone wires. "Slow night."

Muttering choice words, the driver hung up and returned to his machine. Crowding behind the wheel, he engaged his motor. It was noisy. Carbon knock was distinctly detectable. This covered the slight noises made by the furtive ebon figure who detached himself from the groaning tree and, crouching so as not to be seen, settled onto the broad running board.

The individual was such a bantam that the cab did not rock from his added weight. Nor was he visible as he cracked the door open, for he was as black as a living lump of coal.

Slipping in, the stealthy one laid down on the cushions, the better to remain invisible.

As he left the curbing, the driver did not notice that he had acquired a passenger. The incessant drumming of rain on his roof saw to that.

The cabbie rolled around, hunting fares. But it was hopeless. Sensible citizens were in their beds. Few automobiles were seen on the streets.

"Maybe I'll call it a night," he grumbled to himself as he halted at a stop light.

A moment later, the sound of a powerful motor muttered up, causing his head to turn.

For beside him had appeared a long touring car, its curtains open.

It was an expensive machine.

The dash light showed one man seated in the driver's compartment. The man behind the wheel was not visible. But a passenger in the rear was.

The passenger was hunkered down in his seat, applying a handkerchief to his battered features. They were impossible not to recognize.

"Duke Grogan!" gasped the cabbie. "And he looks like he just went fifteen rounds with Max Baer!"

Beside the gangster, only half visible in the shadows, sat a long-haired woman. She looked over toward the idling taxi, and her pale face was painted by a streetlamp's muted glow, causing the emerald glint of her eyes to shine eerily. Her expression was strained, expressing a pleading fear.

"Wonder who the dame is?" muttered the cabbie.

In the rear seat behind him, a low voice husked out two words: "Janet Falcon!"

Duke Grogan could not have heard those whispered words any more than the cab driver did, but his eyes snapped around, alighted on the shocked cabbie, and went brittle as quartz.

The notorious gangster drew a forefinger sharply across his own throat in warning. The meaning was clear. The hack driver contemplated it as the light changed and the touring car powered off.

"When the Duke is out so late, it can't be good news for someone," he breathed.

Regaining his composure, the cabbie watched the dwindling tail-light fade off into the dismal curtain of rain, then abruptly wheeled his machine into a side street, not wanting to encounter the sinister touring again.

Slowing to negotiate a turn, the man started violently. "What the heck!"

A rear door of his car had apparently slammed shut!

He twisted in his seat. It sounded like somebody had left his machine, although the driver had thought he was carrying no one.

The rear seat was empty. It was smeared with coal dust, but from the vantage point of the front seat, that was not apparent. The cabbie peered around the street, seeing nothing but the shadows of the night. They were dark shadows. Some of them seemed to sway and change in shape.

"Now that was queer!" The driver scratched his head in a puzzled manner. Then he grinned, convinced he was imagining things. The sound must have been a rock the wheels had thrown against the under part of the car, instead of the door closing.

But the driver was not entirely convinced. His encounter with the Duke Grogan machine had spooked his nerves, as had the fruitless run out to this deserted side of town.

At the corner, the hackie turned his machine in the street and ran back. In passing the spot where he thought the door had slammed, he stared intently at the shadows he had noted before.

He saw nothing particularly strange about them.

"Sure, it was my imagination!" he declared.

The taxi was hardly out of sight, however, when one of the strange shadows moved.

It was the sooty-looking individual. The dreary drizzle had not cleansed him appreciably. Where he stood, black water was pooling.

In furtive silence, the ambulatory shadow left the vicinity, making grayish-black tracks. After he had walked some distance, a cruising cab drew near. Hailing it, he got in. He gave an address of a residential home in the neighborhood. Huddling in a corner of the vehicle, the damp passenger did not make a perceptible movement en route.

The driver was a curious sort. He called back, "What happened to you?"

"Mind your damn business!" gritted the passenger.

"Happy to. Only you look like you went tumbling into a coal scuttle."

"I don't want to talk about it," snapped the darksome fare.

Shrugging, the hack conveyed his passenger to an address on Atlas Street. The house was dark.

Half a block up the street, lights were coming on in another residence. This was the home from which the dusky passenger had recently crawled. But the cabbie could not know this. A garage door was being closed on a recently arrived touring car. It was the machine that had carried Duke Grogan through the night.

The driver could not know that, either. He waited patiently as his fare paid him carefully out of a coin purse, adding nothing to the amount registered on the taxi meter.

Shutting the coin purse, the darkly damp passenger dismissed the cab.

"Cheapskate!" hissed the cab driver after him.

Working his way through monotonously falling rain, the inky one made his way back to the still-open basement window, loitering there as if considering wriggling through the narrow slit once more.

Examining his streaked and smeared appendages, he evidently decided against this course of action. Heaving a resigned sigh, the dark one commenced creeping around to the front of the dwelling, from which low voices were emanating.

During this prowl, a wan shine emanating from a streetlight fell upon the stealthy creeper, bringing his narrow features to light, and disclosing eyes so pale they were almost colorless. A golden glint showed between thin lips, indicating that the mouth concealed a gold tooth.

Despite his inky aspect, the face of the man could be recognized. It was one that would be familiar to many who followed the amazing career of Doc Savage. Indeed, the fellow was famous in his own right.

For the sooty individual was none other than the renowned wizard of the juice, Long Tom Roberts!

Presumed dead, the puny electrician had escaped captivity only to reverse course once he discovered that the gangster behind his misfortunes, Duke Grogan, was returning to his Cicero hideout with the missing Janet Falcon.

The hardness of Long Tom's fists predicted a determined effort to settle the score in that regard.

Chapter XXIII

DUKE BOWS OUT

LONG TOM ROBERTS took shelter in some ornamental bushes.

Nothing happened for perhaps ten minutes. During that interval, he crept closer to the house into which the touring car had gone. Lights appeared behind a bank of windows. Once he saw the slender form of a long-haired young woman silhouetted in shadow. Janet Falcon, no doubt.

"Never mind crying, sister!" a voice growled loudly.

"I don't like your manners," the woman snapped.

"You're going to find a lot of things you don't like besides manners if you get funny with me," the tough one promised in a most ominous tone.

The woman's sobbing could be heard, choking and anxious.

Another tough voice asked. "Want me to hold her down, Boss?"

"No, I want no witnesses. Take the car, Patches. Go get yourself some smokes. Come back in an hour. Get me?"

"I got you, Duke. Catch you around, girlie."

All but invisible in the streaky shadow of a tall privet hedge, the prowling electrical engineer considered this development. It did not bode well for Janet Falcon.

A minute later, the touring car left the garage, disappearing into the damp night.

Long Tom wriggled closer to the entrance and investigated. The front door had not closed forcibly enough to actuate the spring lock. It stood slightly ajar. He crawled onto the stone-paved stoop and strained his ears.

The voices Long Tom heard were faint, evidently coming from an inner room. An inch at a time, he shoved back the front door, then got to his feet and stepped inside. The entrance hall was deserted, and the voices grew louder.

Stealthily, the slender electrical wizard stepped across thick rugs into another room, which was unlighted. Then he whirled, scuttling wildly into the shelter of a ponderous, tapestry-upholstered divan, and listened. Long Tom was blessed with big ears. They caught everything.

Lights sprang out in the room. The tough-talking voice and the girl had entered.

"So you won't spill, sister?" the male voice demanded harshly.

"I told you I have no idea what you're talking about!" the woman retorted. Her voice was frightened, laden with wracking sobs.

"You're a liar! Maybe this will change your mind! What happened to your boyfriend could easily happen to you. Don't think it can't."

"Oh! So it was you who murdered Ned!"

"I ain't owning up to nothing," the tough talker chuckled harshly. "Especially not a murder rap."

"I don't understand what you are driving at!" the woman wailed.

"You want my proposition?"

"I don't care to have anything to do with you, Mr. Grogan. Please let me go!"

Duke Grogan laughed unpleasantly. Unseen, the smoky eavesdropper heard scratching sounds as if the gangster thumbed his cigarette lighter.

"Get me straight, sister," he barked. "I've been chasing you all around town. But you kept getting away. Until now."

"Doc Savage stopped you, didn't he?"

"That high and mighty meddler!" he snarled. "By now he's cooling his heels on a slab in the morgue, so I guess we're even."

The woman gasped. "He—he is dead then?"

"Doc Savage," rasped the other, "is as defunct as Old Man Prohibition."

"Will you let me go, please! I don't care to listen to you."

"I don't please, lady. Paste that in your bonnet! I want to know all you know about what Myer Sim spilled to you. And you're going to tell me."

The girl remained silent.

"Aw, don't be a dumb dame, honey," Grogan suddenly continued in a wheedling, suggestive tone. "I could hit it off with a classy dame like you. Me and you can go ahead with this thing together."

"What do you mean?"

"Just this: I got the word not to rough you up too much. Get me? The big brain back of this don't want you hurt. To me, that means you're up to your neck in it. Maybe more...."

"Just what sort of theories have you?" the woman asked with chilly curiosity.

"It ain't theory. It's fact. Myer Sim and this Gamble bird were all set to blow the whistle on something big. Gamble went to see Doc Savage, to put him in the know. But somebody got wise and sent a certain someone to bump Myer Sim. That certain someone got your fiancé, too, but you outsmarted him. That leaves you without a partner. I'm thinking of taking the job."

"You're insane!" snapped the girl.

Long Tom heard the woman move swiftly across the floor. The telephone receiver rattled.

"You don't call anyone, I said!" Grogan snarled.

A feminine scream was choked off in its inception. A chair upset.

Peering furtively from behind the big divan, Long Tom saw Duke Grogan jerk the young woman away from the telephone.

One hand enveloping her mouth, he replaced the receiver, then flung her into a chair and pounced.

"Working on a cute trick like you is going to be a pleasure!" he rumbled. "You and me have got all night to get acquainted, baby!"

He seized one of the girl's wrists and twisted her arm cruelly at her back.

"Talk, you miserable wren!" he snarled.

Janet Falcon squirmed and tried to kick him. Her efforts were futile against the gangster's bulk.

Long Tom had heard all he expected to. He gathered his feet beneath him and leaped from the concealment of the divan. His hands closed over the first weapon handy—a heavy floor lamp. He swung it over his head as he sprang forward.

He wasted no words, knowing that Duke Grogan would probably shoot him on sight.

The cord attached to the floor lamp spoiled the effectiveness of his swing. Although the cord broke, the weighty lamp thumped off Duke Grogan's skull with no more force than if it had fallen a few inches.

The gangster staggered back, pawing for the long-barreled revolver holstered in his armpit.

"You punk!" sneered Duke. "I'll fix you!"

There was no time for another blow. Long Tom pitched himself upon the gangster, pinioning the fellow's arms. They thumped to the thick carpet.

DUKE GROGAN saw his unexpected nemesis looming. His strength was impotent against the wiry muscles of his undersized opponent. But Duke already had a hand on his gun.

Janet Falcon sprang out of the chair. Her hands clasped at her open mouth. She did not scream. Nor did she help Long Tom. Instead, she whirled and fled through the door.

Duke Grogan wrenched his pistol free.

"You lousy crumb!" he barked. "I'll croak you good."

He swung the barrel of his weapon against the side of the puny prowler's skull. His head swimming in a Milky Way of colored sparks, Long Tom Roberts felt his muscles grow watery and useless. He toppled off the gangster. He was not completely unconscious, only stunned.

The finishing shot he expected did not come. Duke Grogan leaped to his feet and plunged into the open doorway through which the girl had vanished.

Long Tom heard the girl scream once, piercingly.

Four shots blasted out so swiftly that they were a roll of deafening sound.

Duke Grogan backed into the room. He was doubled over, both arms clamped across his stomach. The long-barreled revolver dropped from his limp fingers. Another shot roared.

That slug struck Duke Grogan between the eyes. He folded to the floor.

Long Tom floundered groggily to his hands and knees. The shatter of breaking glass penetrated the ringing in his ears.

Crawling on all fours, the slim electrical wizard got the gangster's pistol. Cautiously, he crept into the room from which the shots had come. It was empty. The glass was smashed from a window in the front door. It had been slammed shut.

Long Tom clutched a chair and hoisted himself erect. He peered about. Duke Grogan was dead.

Janet Falcon's purse lay on the table. Long Tom scooped up the handbag. Then he dashed out of the house.

There was no sign of the woman. The undersized electrical genius searched the ground for female footprints, but saw nothing that told him in which direction the woman had fled.

Five smoking cartridges lay in the slush. Evidently, this was the spot from which the fatal shots were fired. The ground was a tangle of slushy indentations which led nowhere.

Stooping, Long Tom snatched up the spent shells.

"Whoo!" he exclaimed, for they were yet hot to the touch. Bouncing them in one palm, he saw that they were .22 caliber rounds, from a small gun such as a woman might employ.

Standing up, he again peered about. No sign of Janet Falcon.

Had Long Tom possessed sufficient presence of mind to go to the open cellar window from which he had earlier escaped, he might have detected signs that a slim form had slipped silently into the dim coal bin. Emerald green eyes hung back in the inky dark, regarding him like a silent cat.

As it happened, a taxicab was passing by. It was the nighthawk machine Long Tom had earlier commandeered.

Turning a corner, it was rapidly gathering speed, the driver hunched fearfully over the wheel. Long Tom sprinted madly into the street and flung himself upon the running board.

Reaching out through the open window, the driver tried to knock him off. Long Tom flourished Duke Grogan's smoking revolver.

"Stop!" he shouted.

The driver snarled an oath and subsided. Opening the rear door, Long Tom scrambled into the back cushions.

"Get away from here as quick as you can!" he ordered.

"I ain't getting mixed up in a croaking party," growled the driver. "How many did you bump? I heard four shots."

"Don't talk! Drive! We've got to clear out of here."

"You can bet I'll clear out!" grumbled the other. "I've got three convictions on my record. One more and I'll get the book. Why didn't you—"

"Shut up!"

The driver shut up. Long Tom's voice sounded desperate enough to convince the man he was hauling sudden death.

"Where do you want to go?"

"Back to the city," Long Tom told him.

"You got it."

As the taxicab rolled along, Long Tom went through the girl's handbag. He found lipstick, a powder compact, a handkerchief and a tiny platinum wristwatch set with diamonds. He vented a grunt of surprise when he discovered a key stamped with the name of the Hotel Chicago. It was the same hotel where he was staying.

Using a compact mirror, Long Tom discovered a trickle of blood had run from the spot on his scalp where Duke Grogan's revolver barrel had struck and dried on the side of his face. He moistened a frilly handkerchief and erased the gore.

Eventually, the taxi rolled into the city. Long Tom halted the machine and gave the driver a ten dollar bill from the purse.

"You better forget this," he warned.

"You said it!" the man snarled. "And I hope I never see you again."

As he watched the machine roll out of sight, Long Tom waved vehemently at another cab.

The driver almost failed to spot him, a slender shadow in the darkness of night. Then his brakes squealed to a stop.

"Take me to the Hotel Chicago," he told the pilot of that conveyance.

"Good luck walkin' into the lobby in the middle of the night, lookin' the way you do," the hackman commented.

"Who asked your opinion?"

"I know the doorman. He's tough as they come. He'll kick you around like an empty tin can."

"Well, I'm tougher," snarled Long Tom.

"Think I'll stick around after we get there," remarked the driver. "I'm figurin' I might see a free show."

"You might, at that. But I'll write the ending."

Chapter XXIV

SNATCH

AFTER A DRIVE of nearly an hour along the shore of Lake Michigan, the swanky blue limousine carrying Joe Shine and the unconscious Monk Mayfair and Ham Brooks approached a dockage.

Here was tied up a solitary lake freighter. The laker was distinguished by having a forecastle rammed up at the bow and a bulky doghouse at the stern containing extra cabins. The center of the ship was flat. Only open decking and closed hatches showed there.

Except for periods when the Great Lakes were frozen over in the winter months, these freighters carried ore and other commercial cargo from mines and ports all over the region.

This particular laker was tied up and, from the way her rusty hull listed in the water, it was evident that she was barely seaworthy.

"Pull in here," directed Joe Shine to his driver, a man named Rollo Wheels. That was not his real name, any more than Joe Shine's was authentic, but it suited Chicago.

Two automobiles sat in darkness in the lee of the long laker and, as the approaching sedan headlights washed their rounded shapes, doors opened and hard-faced men emerged, their blocky jaws unshaven.

These were some of Joe Shine's men, who had been summoned to the spot. Rollo the driver had pulled over en route, and made a telephone call from an all-night drugstore, summoning them.

"What's up, Boss?" asked one from the side of his mouth.

"That crazy Duke Grogan put the snatch on Doc Savage's men." Joe Shine cocked a thumb over his shoulder. "That's them in back there."

The assembled gunmen looked properly impressed.

One asked, "If Duke grabbed them off, how did you end up with 'em?"

Joe Shine beamed, showing ivory teeth whitened by moonlight.

"Why, I snatched 'em away from Duke."

Frowning eyebrows shot up. Men took drags on glowing cigarettes.

"Duke dead?" one grunted.

"I didn't stick around long enough to find out," said Joe Shine casually.

Another gunman evinced a cruel smile. "There'll be a hot time in the old town tonight if Grogan's in a pine box."

"We'll worry about that in the morning," snapped Shine. "Right now, we're holding these Doc Savage henchmen until we figure out what Duke wanted with them."

One man paled in the moonlight. "You ain't thinkin' of askin' Doc Savage for ransom?"

Joe Shine looked down and admired the way his polished shoes reflected moonlight. He teetered back on his heels. "I haven't thought that far ahead yet. Let's get them aboard the scow and work them over until they open up. Once I know the score, we can plan our day."

These hired men went to the back of the blue limousine, yanked open one door, and pulled Ham Brooks out first.

The well-dressed attorney looked less than elegant. It would have distressed him to see how disheveled his appearance had become. But Ham was entirely dead to the world. Two men took hold of his shoulders and hauled him out while a third grabbed up his limp legs.

While they were carrying Ham up the rickety gangplank, another group attempted to do the same with Monk Mayfair.

This proved to be more than they could easily handle. The gorilla-like chemist weighed no less than two hundred and sixty pounds. Most of that was tough muscle and gristle coated in rusty hair.

They attempted to pull out Monk by his feet; it took two men each grabbing one bowed leg to get the homely chemist off the cushions and onto the ground.

Monk landed heavily on the seat of his pants, and then seemed to do something unexpected.

One of Monk's eyeballs opened a sliver. Unnoticed, the piglike orb shifted back and forth, taking in his surroundings. He did not otherwise move, or betray the fact that he had returned to consciousness.

Monk threw a swift glance at each of his captors. Both had their eyes on his stubby legs. One was smoking a fat cigar.

Monk slapped a hairy hand against the lighted cigar in the fellow's mouth. Heedless of the blistering of his palm, he knocked the glowing end up and rubbed the fiery particles into the gunman's eyes. With the other hand, he shoved a fist into the unprepared man's midriff.

The rodman howled, pawing at his eyes with both hands, completely forgetting his burden.

Meanwhile, the other one drove a hand into his overcoat and brought forth a dull blue automatic. It was equipped with a tubular extension—obviously a silencer.

Monk lunged and clamped both hands upon the man's gun wrist. He gave a frenzied shove and turned the muzzle aside a fraction of a second before it exploded. The silencer was not in place properly, and the apish chemist had further jarred it out of plumb, with the immediate result that instead of silencing the report, it completely blocked the passage of the escaping bullet. The back-pressure blew the breach mechanism of the gun to bits.

Monk scrambled to his feet and flung himself clear of the vehicle. He rolled like a football. This enabled him to escape the descending gun barrel wielded by the third gunman. Monk was fortunate enough to throw an elbow in front of his face as he rolled, saving his homely features from being battered.

The simian chemist came to a halt on all fours, dizzy and bruised. He bared his teeth and growled with a primitive feroc- ity. Standing erect, Monk resembled a slovenly dressed ape. Crouching on all floors, he was a sight to behold.

The man with the intact revolver hesitated, the hackles on the back of his neck rising in fear.

Monk saw his chance. Scrambling to his feet, he sprinted for a shack. It was perhaps ten yards away. He leapt and sprang high, throwing himself over the structure. A gun barked at his back and the bullet made a loud hiss passing perilously close to one deformed ear.

This brought him to the wharf. More bullets whined, split- ting the night. Legs churning, Monk raced along the ram- shackle dock. One foot stubbed a loose board, and he went down, momentum causing him to tumble head over heels, yelling, "Daggone it!"

Lead gouged the weathered wood all about him. One bullet mashed itself into a shiny lump close to one hirsute hand.

"Ye-e-o-o-w!" squawled Monk, scrambling to his feet. The apish chemist made a flying jump and went over the dock. There was no splash. Instead, the nimble Monk had managed to catch the rungs of the rickety ladder dropping into the water. There he clung, his bandy legs poised to propel him away if slugs started nipping at him.

Joe Shine had been an angry witness to all this.

"Don't let him get away!" he yelled out. "We need them both."

"Alive or dead?" a rodman demanded loudly.

Joe Shine had to think about that a moment. "Alive! But dead if you have to."

Monk heard every word, and considered dropping into the water. It was not deep, and powder-driven pistol lead, entering dense lake water, had a tendency to lose momentum and corkscrew about. His chances for living might be improved by immersion.

The apish chemist was on the verge of doing exactly that when another gunman cried out, "I got me a bright idea."

"Cough it out," demanded Joe Shine.

"These two are Monk and Ham. They're supposed to be thick as thieves. If that ape don't climb out of the water peaceably, we shoot the lawyer."

The idea seemed to appeal to Joe Shine, except that he said, "No more shooting. We had enough of that." From a pocket, he produced a small tack hammer and a long sail needle. Marching up to sprawled Ham Brooks, he kicked the dapper lawyer onto his stomach, knelt down at the top of his spine, and touched the needle's vicious point to the base of Ham's skull.

"You listen, you there under the dock," he yelled out. "I used to kill beeves in the stockyards. I gotta sharp pick stuck in the back of your friend's skull. If I bring this hammer down, he's dead in an instant. The pick will part his spinal cord like old twine."

Monk heard that and did not hesitate. "Suppose I climb out and you just shoot me anyway?"

"Well, what if you climb out and I don't?"

"That don't sound very reassuring," Monk grumbled loudly.

"Well, it's the deal I'm offering. Take it or leave it. But say goodbye to your friend if you welch."

Monk accepted the offer. He clambered up the ladder and onto the dock, lifting his hairy hands to show that they were empty.

The simian chemist was miserable, but he said nothing. Finally, his eyes could see the sail needle gleaming in the moonlight. In the upraised arm was the small tacking hammer, ready to drive it home.

"Go get him," barked Joe Shine.

Monk did not resist. Not even after the gangster stood up, pocketing his grisly tools of death.

"Hustle them aboard," said the gang leader with satisfaction.

Ham had to be carried by two men, but Monk went under his own power. Guns were trained on him. Blunt steel muzzles ground into his burly back and ribs.

Monk bestowed upon Joe Shine a surly look, and growled, "Where do you figure into this?"

"Funny," returned Shine. "That was going to be our first question to *you*."

"We're two of Doc Savage's men."

"That's what makes you valuable to me. Name's Joe Shine. Ever hear of me?"

Monk thought that over, as if tasting the name. "Can't say that I have."

"I'm the next king of the Chicago underworld."

"I thought Duke Grogan was shootin' for that throne," muttered Monk.

"Duke is out of the running as long as Joe Shine has anything to say about it. He don't matter. Now Duke went to a lot of trouble to snatch you two, and I want to hear all the details."

Monk's tiny forehead wrinkled as he realized he had scant details to offer. But he said nothing.

Soon, they stood on the laker's broad deck where Joe Shine told his men, "Let's take them back to the doghouse. It will be quieter there, in case we have to get rough."

Shine's dark eyes went to Monk Mayfair. "In this situation, I'm thinking we're going to have to. Am I right, mug?"

Monk shrugged negligently. "To tell the truth, I don't know much about it. Ham is the one who knows everything Doc knows."

"I don't believe you," snapped Shine.

"If you know anything about Doc Savage's organization," said Monk casually, "you know that Ham is the lawyer of our group. Naturally, he knows a lot of confidential dope the rest of us don't."

It was a shameless lie, but it possessed plausibility. Monk was quite the prevaricator, when he put his mind to it. Eyeing Monk Mayfair, Joe Shine sized him up as dwelling on the stupid side. Many enemies of Doc Savage had made that identical mistake.

"If you're lying, it's going to go hard on both of you," warned Shine.

"Do I look like I would lie in front of all these crook guns?"

Shine considered. "You look dumb, but not that dumb. All right, I'm going to throw you in a cabin until the mouthpiece wakes up. Then it's going to be all business. Get me?"

"I get you."

Monk was marched to a cabin. Ham was carried in his wake.

The dapper lawyer was flung in unceremoniously, but they made Monk stand outside the cabin while they removed various articles of clothing, including his armpit holster, which was empty. Monk had lost his supermachine pistol during his abduction by the Grogan gang.

While Monk was shucking off his battered coat, one hirsute paw plunged into a pocket and captured something. Surreptitiously, he transferred this object to his wide mouth. Then he sealed his lips.

Monk's shoes, socks and most of his outer clothing were deposited on the deck. Stripped to his shorts, he more than ever resembled a squat bull gorilla. Sans attire, Monk was as fuzzy as a baboon, his knotty muscles resembling those of a football halfback.

The assembled gunmen looked him over carefully.

"He's clean!" one pronounced.

Joe Shine nodded, growling, "March in there! And get that lawyer ready to talk his head off when he wakes up."

Monk ambled in without any backtalk. His trousers and belt followed him in. The door was dogged shut behind him.

Drawing on his pants, Monk surveyed the space in which he was confined. There was not much to it but steel walls and a bare floor. Illumination was entirely natural. The two portholes were too small to permit egress by a man's body. Monk and Ham would be secure herein, until released.

"If you know what's healthy, you'll keep quiet in there," Joe Shine called through the shut steel door.

Monk said nothing. Kneeling down, he examined Ham Brooks, saw that a fleck of blood and foam had crusted on the corner of his wide, mobile mouth. Unbuttoning the starched shirt, the apish chemist saw the bulletproof vest which had taken the impact of the bullets driven into Ham Brooks. They had, no doubt, left punishing bruises, but Ham was otherwise uninjured.

Standing up, Monk went to the two portholes. They were filthy with grime. Swiping them clean with his broad palm, he stared out over the water and then extracted from his mouth a small object.

This resembled an ordinary stick of chalk. Taking it in both hands, Monk exerted considerable pressure, reducing the chalk to a powder. Soon, his palms were coated with the stuff.

The hairy chemist wiped them off on the porthole glass, doing so carefully, smearing every inch of glass, then repeating the process on one other porthole.

That accomplished, Monk sat down on the floor to await developments. Despite the direness of his predicament, he did not look in the least bit worried.

Chapter XXV

DOOM DECKS

THE MIDNIGHT HOURS passed slowly, and still Ham Brooks did not emerge from his coma.

The first flickers of concern twitched at Monk's homely features. From time to time, he checked on the recumbent attorney, who lay supine on the scuffed steel floor.

His breathing appeared normal, yet Ham did not come to when Monk snapped impatient fingers on either side of his head.

"Come on, you fashion plate. Snap out of it. We got things to do."

Ham Brooks slumbered on.

When he was not tending to the stricken barrister, the homely chemist pressed his nose against the twin portholes. When he wasn't watching the wavering lights on the dark waters of Lake Michigan, his tiny eyes continually scanned the night skies. Autumn clouds raced along, but that was all.

Eventually, the door rattled, and Monk sprang to his feet, ready for anything.

In stepped a thug he recognized. It was the one whose automatic had exploded because of the improperly fitted silencer. His gun hand was bandaged in white. The bandage was soaked in scarlet now.

A nickel-plated .45 caliber revolver showed in his good hand. It shook a little. Monk was a primitive sight stripped to his trousers.

The thug wiggled the heavy gun barrel, saying, "March!"

"Ham ain't woke up yet," protested Monk.

"Well, ain't that too bad?" sneered the thug. "Get out of there!"

The gunman stepped aside and Monk lumbered out, long arms dangling.

The gun muzzle pointed forward, and Monk obligingly padded along on his bare feet. They made mushy noises along the moist deck. For the moment, the rain had stopped.

Small eyes shifting left and right, Monk walked slowly and carefully, pausing once.

The hard probing gun muzzle ground into one spot on his backbone. That told Monk that his captor walked only a pace or two behind.

"Keep movin'," the gunman urged. "If I have to blow your spine in two, don't think I won't."

Monk continued ambling along, looking about, but showing signs that he was not watching where he was going. He made his way forward several paces, then managed to hook his toes into a coil of Manila rope lying on the deck.

Giving out a yowling yell, the hairy chemist threw up his great arms, and pretended to trip. Down he went, in a pile of rusty red fur.

Caught flat-footed, the startled gunman held his fire.

Monk muttered, "Well, dang me for a lowdown dog. I didn't see that coil of line."

"Get up!"

Monk gathered his hirsute limbs together, and pretended to look dazed.

The gangster stepped closer, features darkening with fury. "Damn you, quit stallin'!"

Monk shook his head as if to clear cranial cobwebs. Abruptly, he sprang to his feet and snatched the automatic from the gunman's good hand, at the same time smearing a furry paw over the fellow's mouth before he could scream.

The gunman quivered, kept his feet. Monk hit him with the barrel of the revolver, then caught him as he sagged, easing the body gently to the deck.

Monk stripped the belt around the hapless one and employed it to bind the fellow's hands, then used his own belt on the gunman's ankles. The gunman had two handkerchiefs and a plug of chewing tobacco in his pocket. Monk wrapped the tobacco in cloth squares and jammed the resulting wad in the man's mouth, tying it there with one of the straps which formed the shoulder harness that supported the holsters of two big automatics. Extra clips of ammunition reposed in the man's coat pocket. The apish chemist carried these in his left hand and thrust both guns under a makeshift belt he tied around his waist, using the thug's gaudy necktie for that purpose.

Murmur of voices came from a spot toward the bow. Apparently, the short fray had attracted no attention. Monk made for the sounds.

They were coming from the forecastle.

A gunman was saying, "I'd like to blow a hole in him for rubbing that cigar in my eyes! I can't see out of my left eye yet."

"Will you put a tackle on that jaw, you mug?" Joe Shine ordered.

Monk gripped his captured automatic tightly. His piggish eyes narrowed. Now was the time to act, while all of the gang were confined in one spot. Otherwise, his handiwork on the unconscious guard would be discovered soon.

Monk pitched through the door.

"Stick them up!" he rasped savagely.

Joe Shine gulped, pouring part of a glass of whiskey down his shirt front. Another was massaging an inflamed eye. He squinted foolishly, his hands remaining over the orb. The third gunman was tipped back in a chair, hands clasped behind his head. A fourth just stared, a burning cigarette balanced on his slack lower lip.

The group became perfectly motionless. Then their hands crept above the ears.

"Line up along the wall!" snarled Monk.

The quartet hesitated.

"Do what he says!" ordered Joe Shine. "He looks like he's willin' to fling lead."

"You got that right," growled Monk.

As one, the cowed gunmen turned meekly and put their noses against a rusty bulkhead. Monk relieved them of their guns and piled the weapons on the table. One rodman snarled an oath when Monk's fingers felt over his person. He half turned.

"Do you want your bile splashed all over the wall?" Joe Shine hissed out of the side of his mouth. "Let him have his fun."

"Shut up, you!" Monk gritted.

The simian chemist stuck his fingers through the trigger guards of the automatics he had collected. They made a big fistful.

A glance had shown him that the stateroom door was fitted with a substantial lock. The gunmen would be secure there, as long as they did not smash down the door.

Monk seized a flashlight off the table.

"Make yourselves comfortable," he barked.

The four leaning against the wall made no answer. Relieved at the ease with which the capture had been executed, Monk backed toward the door. "Now to collect Ham," he muttered.

He fumbled at his back to transfer the key from the inside of the door to the outside.

Vesuvius, the whole galaxy of planets and a half dozen anvil choruses seemed to land on the back of his head.

Joe Shine roared, slapped both hands against his thighs and doubled over with a burst of ribald laughter. Monk heard his bellowing mirth fade away in the hellish echo as he folded down on the floor.

THE LAUGHTER ceased for a time, then sounded again. It became louder—a fiendish cackle. Monk decided he was having a nightmare, hearing things in the delirium of unconsciousness. There was an agonizing impact against his nose and mouth. Scarlet curtains, like glowing streams of gleaming blood, rose and shattered in front of his eyes.

"He likes it, Rollo!" Joe Shine chuckled. "He's wakin' up so he can enjoy it better!"

Monk struggled and reached his feet. He opened his eyes just in time to have the chair Rollo wielded close them again. The blow knocked the stunned chemist across the table. He lay there with only his toes touching the floor.

Joe Shine dashed whiskey into the homely face. The alcohol smarted Monk's split nose and lips. Monk kept his eyes shut, feeling that if he moved, he would be hit again.

"Use your fist, Rollo," growled Joe Shine. "You'll croak him with that shillelagh."

"And skin my knuckles on him? Not much I don't. Anybody got a pair of brass knucks?"

"Lay off!" Joe Shine snarled. "You'll have him so he can't talk."

"Can't talk, eh? I'll make him cackle like a rooster."

Rollo slapped the side of Monk's face with his open palm. The force of the slap rolled the gorilla-like chemist off the table. He fell onto the floor.

Rollo stepped back and kicked at the face and the most tender portions of Monk's stomach. Monk moaned and tried to crawl under the table. Someone seized his leg and pulled. Monk tried to hang onto a leg of the table. Rollo drove a toe against his spine and Monk's grip went numb. Clawing feebly, he was dragged into the middle of the floor.

"Give me that bottle!" a voice ordered. "I'm gonna to cut his ears off!"

Monk suddenly recognized that voice. It was the thug with the injured hand, the one he had brought low. Evidently, he had recovered his smashed senses and sneaked up on the hairy chemist unawares. How he had gotten loose from the thorough job of trussing Monk had performed was a question.

There was a bang as the gunman brought the bottle down on the table, accompanied by the shiver of breaking glass.

Monk opened pain-curtained eyes, then squirmed feebly toward the door. He was jerked up and slammed into a chair. Three gunmen accomplished that feat of strength. The tough ran the jagged funnel of the bottleneck in front of Monk's flat nose, then deliberately opened an ugly gash in the side of his face.

"Your ears come next!" the fellow promised gleefully.

Joe Shine stepped in then. Shoving the hoodlum back, he snapped, "Hold up, Alonzo."

He thrust his head down and blew foul breath into Monk's face.

"Cough up, you gorilla!" he snarled. "What's Duke Grogan's interest in you? How does Doc Savage tie into this?"

Monk rolled his head and ran his gaze about the cabin. One gunman was conspicuously absent, but the other sprawled in another chair, grinning malevolently.

Two newcomers were present. One was gnarled and bullet-headed, with a balloon of a chest and bowed legs. His head and hands were pale, as if they had been made out of ivory that had become dirty. He had a shock of red hair which was as stiff as piano wire and he wore a dark, pinstripe suit. One eye appeared larger than the other.

The other man was a shriveled wart of a fellow with a rat's narrow face.

Joe Shine slapped Monk himself, and the impact of his palm splattered blood on Monk's rust-furred chest.

"Loosen up!" he barked. "Get your chin going!"

"What—what happened?" mumbled Monk, fishing for time.

"Big Eye and Percy, here, were keeping watch at the stern," Joe Shine chuckled. "They found Alonzo trussed up on deck, then came below and kissed you on the noggin with a blackjack."

"Ooo!" Monk moaned. "My achin' head!"

"Now let's get down to brass tacks. Fill our ears."

Monk had been considering possible answers to that query from the moment he had regained consciousness. He could tell them the truth, or he could bluff. In either case, the outcome was pretty certain to be disastrous for himself. He didn't know enough to be worth much. And he knew that Joe Shine would not accept his story.

"What I told you before," said Monk. "Ham knows the deal. I'm just Doc Savage's hired muscle."

Joe Shine frowned. "I heard you were a famous chemist."

"That's what I do for side money. But working for Doc, I'm mostly his muscle man."

Which was far from the truth, but the simian chemist was speaking a language Joe Shine and his gang knew well. Many of the rodmen in the room doubled as muscle men, judging from their physical appearances.

Joe Shine rocked back on his heels, considering.

Looking over his men, he directed, "Big Eye, you go back to the doghouse and haul that mouthpiece forward. I don't care if he's awake or not. Get it done."

Big Eye departed without a word.

A FEW minutes later, Big Eye stumbled back into the cabin, blinking in the glare of the light, his brick-red face registering puzzled curiosity.

"What's eatin' you—?" demanded Joe Shine.

"He's gone!" Big Eye blurted.

"Gone!" Shine exploded. "Did you chill that lawyer?"

"No, of course not. But he ain't there anymore."

Joe Shine turned to Alonzo and demanded, "Didn't you lock that door when you collected this stupid-looking ape?"

"Sure. I thought I did."

"Thought! Saint Peter on the footstool! I told you to lock the door behind you. Did you?"

Alonzo the guard looked uncomfortable.

"Did you?" Joe Shine howled.

"Aw, he was out cold. He wasn't going anywheres."

"I'll kill you!" Shine informed Alonzo with a calm anger that was horrible. "Only it wouldn't do any good. You already fixed things, you iron head. Sit down there and listen to what this ape has to say."

Joe Shine spun on Monk. The mobster's eyes were hard and his voice had a buzzsaw quality.

"Why is Doc Savage in Chicago?"

"Doc is givin' a big speech at the scientific exposition," Monk bluffed boldly. "We just blew into town and queer stuff started to happen."

"What kind of stuff?" Shine demanded.

"It started with Duke Grogan. He barged in and began throwin' lead," recited Monk. "I don't know for sure, but I think Doc comin' to town made Duke nervous. It got into the papers. Maybe Duke thought Doc was after him." Monk shrugged elaborately. "That's how I figured it anyway."

Joe Shine and his hoodlums swapped dark looks.

"In that case…" murmured Big Eye, rubbing his hands together expectantly.

"Yeah," said Joe Shine gruffly. "We got to have a croaking bee, then lam. Take him down in the hold where nobody will hear him squawk."

Joe Shine tangled the fingers of one hand in the guard's hair and propelled him bodily in the direction of the cabin door.

"Since you gummed up the works, it'll be your job. Don't get a lot of blood smeared around in the hold, either. Our fingerprints are all over this tub."

"Don't worry, boss," Alonzo promised cheerfully. "I'll take care of that."

"Stick the corpse in a sack with a piece of chain and dump it overboard. Somebody go with him. Make sure the deed gets done right."

"Sure, boss," said Alonzo. "Come on, Big Eye. I'm gonna show you what happens to guys who smear fire in my eyes."

And to the prod of gangland guns, Monk Mayfair was marched out onto the deck, and then into a companionway leading below decks.

The simian chemist feigned an even greater exhaustion than he felt and forced Alonzo and Big Eye to have to drag him through a tangle of corroded and rust-eaten metalwork.

"Geez! You're a picture," Alonzo chuckled. "Get some life into you so I'll have something to kill."

"Maybe we oughta skin him alive first," Big Eye suggested fiercely. "I could use an ape skin rug." The hoodlum laughed maliciously.

Too busy enjoying his ghoulish jest, Alonzo failed to look where he was going and tripped over a rusty can that stood against a bulkhead. With a startled squawk, he went down—his jaw encountering Monk's fast-rising fist.

Alonzo literally lifted off his feet. Coming back down, he folded messily, like a boneless bag of clothing. His jaw slammed the floor, and his face went slack.

Cursing, Big Eye slammed Monk to one side, and threw his shoulder against a steel panel. It gave inward with the complaining screech from the hinges.

"The execution chamber," laughed Big Eye. "Something like the old dukes used to have. Get in!"

Monk slid down the bulkhead and lay on the floor. He did not move. Big Eye kicked him in the stomach.

"Get in there," he snarled. "Or I'll kill you out here."

On all fours, Monk crawled over the raised threshold. Big Eye threw the flashlight beam about. A swift glance about the hold compartment showed a wooden crate with an empty bottle balanced atop it. A pallet that had been laid on the floor, and covered in what looked like horse blankets.

Monk squinted at the pallet, wondering why anyone should wish to sleep in the odorous hold of the ship. The stink of foul bilge water was a stuffy clog in his wide nostrils.

"You'd better say your 'now I lay me down to sleep' if you got any!" Big Eye suggested callously, locking the door behind him.

"Wait a minute," Monk groaned. "Do you want to make some money?"

"No," snapped Big Eye. "I don't."

"Five thousand smackers."

Big Eye squirted his light into Monk's eyes.

"Do you have the roll on you?" he asked with healthy interest.

"No, but I can get it in the morning."

Big Eye chuckled. "No. Can't be did. Joe Shine is in a stew now because that lawyer pal of yours up and vanished. He'd croak me."

"You're a sucker to pass up five thousand smackers," Monk told him.

"Listen, guy!" grated Big Eye. "Five grand doesn't mean a thing to me, see! It ain't even chicken feed. We're playing for millions—control of all of Chicago. You oughta know that."

Monk blinked. Stalling for time, he demanded, "Huh—what do you mean?"

Big Eye came closer and bored the glare from the lens of his flashlight into the homely chemist's broad face. He swore under his breath, a puzzled oath.

"You must be a dumb cluck," he decided.

"How come?"

"I don't think you even got an idea what this is all about."

"You got that right," Monk lied. "Listen, I can tip you off to where the five grand is. You can get it easy."

"A bird in the hand is worth a flock in the bush," sneered Big Eye. "I know." Thoughts of the five thousand had made Big Eye garrulous, if it had done nothing else. Nevertheless, Monk had about given up hope of bribing the fellow.

"Ha, Ha! You're great on expressions. You ought to have seen your own puss when that blackjack kissed you."

Unexpectedly, he kicked Monk in the stomach again. The hairy chemist fell on his back and writhed in agony that was not entirely pretended.

Big Eye rocked back the hammer of his revolver.

Monk twisted to his feet.

"At least, let me take it standing up, pal," he groaned.

Big Eye skinned his lips off his teeth in a cruel, knowing smile. "Sure, sure I appreciate a guy with guts. Get to your feet; make it snappy."

Monk clutched with the fingers of his right hand at the improvised table crate. He wrapped hirsute fingers around the neck of the bottle which stood there before Big Eye sensed trouble and spun.

The apish chemist hurled the bottle. It exploded to bits on Big Eyes' temple. The fellow staggered. His gun gushed flame at the floor plates. The flashlight dropped and the lens broke, but the bulb continued to glow.

Monk leapt and kicked Big Eye's feet from under him. As the man fell, Monk leapt into the air and came down stiffly on the back of his head. Something snapped audibly under his bare feet—the man's neck.

Springing for the low bulkhead, Monk felt along it until he found the door by which Big Eye had intended to depart after the dirty deed was done. It was secured with a rust-eaten lever arrangement which had originally been intended to draw it sufficiently tight against a rubber batten to make it waterproof. He wrenched the steel panel open and plunged through.

A light was dancing back out in the corridor and feet were crunching debris.

Someone was approaching, perhaps drawn by the commotion.

"Need any help, Big Eye?" The query belonged to the rat-faced Percy, who had followed, perhaps out of curiosity.

Monk scooped up the revolver Big Eye had carried, then doused the wan gleam of the flashlight.

Percy appeared in the aperture of the rear bulkhead. Unable to see the sights of the automatic, Monk leveled it by guess and stroked the trigger. The flame from the muzzle seemed to leap completely across the compartment.

Percy screeched, grabbed his shoulder and staggered back the way he had come.

An instant of fumbling disclosed that the panel could be secured from either side. Monk threw the levers. He looked about, scratched his bristly head and asked himself, "What the heck do I do now?"

An answer of sorts soon came. It sounded above his head. Short, at first, and muffled. But to the apish chemist, the commotion was unmistakable.

A series of ferocious bullfiddle blasts erupted. These were the sounds of Doc Savage's supermachine pistols in violent operation!

"I knew Doc wasn't dead!" Monk cried exultantly.

Chapter XXVI

PISTOL PARTY

THE BULLFIDDLE ROAR was not a familiar sound as it smote the ears of Joe Shine, the gangster leader of the North Side of Chicago.

He had been leading a search of the lake freighter, seeking the missing Ham Brooks, when his senses were assaulted by the distressing racket.

Shine and one of his cohorts were poking about the cargo hold amidships. The latter was his burly driver, Rollo Wheels.

The sound came from above. It came again. In three long and short bursts.

Pounding of feet running pell-mell on deck soon followed. Cries, curses and the occasional ungodly screech punctuated the cacophony.

Joe Shine blurted out, "What's all that racket?"

Rollo mumbled, "I don't know. It sure don't sound like a Tommy gun."

Nor did it. The familiar *rat-tat-tat* stutter of a submachine gun was of a different quality. This sound was a blur of percussive reports in which it was impossible to distinguish among the individual shots.

"They say Doc Savage's men tote guns that sound like that," Joe Shine undertoned.

For the first time, the mob boss looked nervous. He mopped sweat off his brow.

"But they didn't have their gats on them!" Rollo yelled. "Duke Grogan musta grabbed them."

Joe Shine scowled blackly. "Well, somebody got hold of one of them. It sounds like a regular war up there."

The shooting continued, and there was briefly the sound of a Tommy gun in operation. It ran out a stuttering bray of a sound. Then came a bullfiddle roar that drowned it out, after which the sub-gun went silent.

In the quiet interval that followed, nothing seemed to move.

"Do you suppose that rusty ape got loose?" Rollo mumbled.

The gangster leader did not reply. He was listening hard. His hands, fumbling in his coat pocket, produced his sail needle and tacking hammer. This was obviously a nervous impulse, since these tools of sudden death would hardly avail him in a gunfight.

Came a few brief stuttering reports, then silence again.

"What do we do, Boss?" Rollo hissed nervously.

"We lay low," returned Shine slowly. "At least, until we get the lay of the land," he added, lest his underling think he had turned yellow.

In the gloom of the hold, they stood motionless, ears straining for every sound. But all they captured was silence. It was a very disquieting silence.

"If Doc Savage or one of his men tangled with our boys, somebody must've just come out on top," muttered Shine.

Rollo nodded. "Yeah. But who's top dog?"

Further listening did not lead to any concrete determination. Joe Shine continued waiting, his implements of murder squeezed tight in his well-manicured fists.

Above, there came the rattle of one of the cargo hatches.

Shine and his confederate retreated into a corner, and pressed their backs to a bulkhead, pulling the brims of their hats low to conceal the pale patches that constituted their faces. They were expert in this latter operation, having had to conceal their features from photographers' flashbulbs during their rise to prominence in the Chicago underworld.

The hatch creaked open, and spectral moonlight flooded the spacious hold.

A cultured voice called down, "If anyone is down there, step out into the light."

Rollo Wheels hissed to his boss, "Who is he kidding?"

"Ix-nay!"

The hood subsided.

An extremely white pencil line of light shot downward, and quested about the hold, disclosing piles of iron pellets.

"There does not seem to be anyone down here," the cultured voice reported.

A metallic response came, "Close the hatch, Ham."

The hatch came down with a great rattling clang, restoring darkness to the hold.

Joe Shine and his nervous driver looked up, saw that the hatch was sealed. They quietly congratulated themselves in the dark.

"We got away with it!" enthused Rollo.

Shine nodded. "Looks like we did. And that sounded like Doc Savage himself. Guess that means my mob is down to you and me for now."

"If we get off this boat alive," muttered the other.

"Don't worry, we will. They'll search everyplace else, and then give up on us. Just have to wait them out."

"But how did Doc Savage get on board?"

"Never mind that. We got a lot of waiting ahead of us, and I got a lot of thinking to do."

Silence filled the hold. The regular ticking of Joe Shine's expensive wristwatch, along with the somewhat nasal noises made by their nervous breathing, were the only sounds.

The unrelieved darkness surrounding the hiding crooks began to prey upon their minds.

At length, Joe Shine muttered, "I'm gonna light a match."

"Is that smart?" asked Rollo nervously.

"If anyone's creeping up on us, I want to see for myself."

Shine took a wooden match from a coat pocket—he carried them because he liked to smoke cigars and paper matches would not do—and, lifting one foot, rasped the sulfur head against the sole of that shoe.

The flaring light made them blink rapidly.

When his eyes became accustomed to the fitful illumination, Joe Shine looked about. He saw nothing but shifting shadows. In his visual inspection, the crime czar noticed that the polish on one shoe had become dull from tripping about the old ship. The other gleamed nicely.

Flicking a handkerchief from a breast pocket of his coat, he sat down and began to buff the tops of both shoes in turn. Under the circumstances, it seemed like a foolish thing to do, but Joe Shine took great pride in his appearance in general, and in his footgear in particular.

When he had buffed the leather uppers to a high gloss, the gang lord stood up and tossed his soiled silken handkerchief aside.

Turning to where he last had left his associate, Joe Shine requested, "Hand me that flashlight."

But the gloomy dark gave back only silence.

"Did you hear me? I said, 'Hand over the flashlight.'"

But no flashlight was offered.

The silence was suddenly unnerving. Joe Shine had pocketed his deadly sail needle and hammer, but now his fingers slipped to his pockets, ready to remove the slender weapon at a moment's notice.

"Rollo?"

Silence. Not even the sound of breathing.

"Rollo, talk to me," Shine whispered.

There was a single companionway leading down into the hold. Joe Shine's dark eyes careened toward that dark void.

There was nothing to be seen, so deep was the murk.

Still, it was the only way in and out. Carefully, the gangster began creeping toward the companionway stairs that led up to the deck.

He stepped carefully, mindful of the litter of iron pellets, and using one hand to feel along a bulkhead wall to guide him.

Shine had a pretty good idea of where he was going, so when he encountered an obstacle, it caused him to freeze in his tracks.

The obstacle felt like a bulkhead, so hard was it.

Reaching up, Joe Shine encountered, not hard steel, but what felt like cloth.

"Rollo?"

But instead of the voice of his associate, a metallic voice intoned, "The shine of your shoes gave you away."

Joe Shine jumped back like an alley cat that had encountered a rattlesnake. The sail needle leapt into his hand, and he plunged forward, driving it toward the source of the voice.

The needle was not designed for stabbing purposes, yet in a pinch it could do the job. In times past, it had.

In the dark, Joe Shine could only make a wild stab at the human obstacle before him.

The needle point struck something, but scraped along before it slid off into space.

The strange voice said, "Chain-mail vest. It will turn bullets and blades alike."

Warm metallic fingers took hold of Joe Shine by the throat, and began squeezing. Suddenly, he was flailing helplessly, and the suffocating darkness of the hold became deeper and blacker than any darkness he had ever known.

A brilliant ray of light split the dark, illuminating the giant figure of Doc Savage standing over the conquered Joe Shine.

The ray was emanating from the free hand of lawyer Ham Brooks, who was clutching his unsheathed sword cane in the other. There was a tiny bit of crimson on the tip of the blade, where the point had broken the skin of Rollo Wheels, who lay on the floor nearby.

The blade's narrow tip was coated in a brownish substance that was a powerful narcotic. Once it broke skin, a victim lost consciousness almost immediately.

This was what had transpired in the darkness. Ham Brooks had slipped down the companionway and found Rollo, rendering him *hors de combat.*

This had prompted Joe Shine to seek escape, which brought him into the terrible hands of the Man of Bronze, who could render any foe helpless by applying his trained fingers to special nerve centers on the man's neck.

Now Doc Savage picked up the gangster leader under one mighty arm, walked casually over to Rollo Wheels and threw him up and across the opposite shoulder. The metallic giant seemed not to exert himself, despite carrying a combined three hundred and thirty pounds.

Ham Brooks leading the way, they ascended the companionway.

"Now to find Monk," remarked the dapper attorney.

"Monk will be upset that he missed all the fun," commented Doc.

"If I know that ape," rejoined Ham, "he will have had more than his share before you arrived to rescue me."

MONK had indeed had his share of entertainment before Doc and Ham showed up to release him from his ignominious imprisonment. It showed on his homely face in the form of numerous cuts, abrasions and a shiner that was a beauty.

These souvenirs did not mollify the hairy chemist, who took one look at his elegant sparring partner and snarled, "Don't tell me the scrappin' is all done and over with."

"Very well," returned Ham. "I will not. But it is."

Bare-chested, Monk was a sight. From the waist up, he resembled an enormous steel-wool pad that had gone to rust. His knuckles were skinned, his wide face was bruised and it looked as if one gristled ear had become a blood blister.

Doc Savage simply said, "That was good work smearing the portholes with our special luminous chalk."

Monk grinned. "It was the best thing I could think to do."

Doc nodded. "I was able to see the portholes while flying around the city. Thanks to the ultra-violet projectors built into the craft, coupled with the mechanical goggles we employ to pick up the invisible rays. From the air, the ship appeared to possess two goblin eyes glowing blue."

Monk's grin grew broader. "I take it you released Ham, and then the two of you went to town."

Doc nodded. "First, we slipped around the ship, taking out what guards we happened upon. Then when the mêlée became too thick for stealth, Ham was forced to use his mercy pistol, which I had brought with me, along with a spare sword cane."

The dapper lawyer holstered his supermachine pistol, and was restoring his narrow blade into the dark tube of the barrel.

"Your assistance was not necessary," Ham remarked waspishly.

Monk made formidable fists that caused blood to seep from skinned knuckles, and began growling words that could not be understood, assuming that these utterances were in fact words. Despite his college education, the hairy chemist sometimes acted the part of a primitive caveman.

"Well," Monk said at last, "I got in some good licks before you showed up."

Ham sniffed, "It looks rather like you got licked yourself."

Monk squinted one blackened eye almost shut, and the other one glared bloody murder at Ham.

"I have half a mind to lock you in this icebox and see how you like it!" he snarled.

"Half a mind," returned Ham acidly, "is twice the number of brain cells I credit you with."

Monk snapped back, "At least I got to work out. You look like you didn't even muss your hair."

Ham made a distasteful face. "I did more than my part. Which is more than I could say for you, you hapless hillock of hair."

Doc Savage interjected, "We might want to see what Joe Shine has to say for himself."

Monk and Ham abruptly called off their glaring and face making. They were very interested in what the crime boss had to divulge.

"You got nothing on me!" snarled Shine, after Doc Savage had brought him back to consciousness by kneading at the same nerve centers that had rendered him insensate. "I want to talk to my lawyer."

Ham said crisply, "I will serve as your lawyer."

"Not you! I got a mouthpiece. I pay him plenty. Fetch him."

"I am the only lawyer you're likely to see for some time," remarked Ham coolly.

"I don't like the sound of that!" snapped Shine. "Now get me my attorney."

When no one moved, Joe Shine realized that he was in a different situation than if he had fallen into the hands of the Chicago police.

Doc Savage said, "Tell us how you came to enter this affair?"

"I don't know what you're talking about."

"You kidnapped two of my men."

"No, I rescued them from that no-good grifter, Duke Grogan. He kidnapped them. I got them loose. The least you could do is thank me."

"Don't hand us that!" Monk exploded. "You grabbed us, dragged us to this tub. You got something up your sleeve. Shake it out. We want to see it."

Defiantly, Joe Shine shucked off his coat and rolled up both shirt sleeves, one at a time, displaying bare forearms.

"See? Nothing up my sleeves. Now cut me loose. You ain't cops. You can't pinch me."

Doc produced a letter from Chicago's Superintendent of Police and held it before Joe Shine's shifty eyes. The gangster scanned the lines quickly, and that seemed to take a great deal of the starch out of his demeanor.

"O.K., O.K. You got some pull, after all. So what's next?"

Doc Savage did not reply. Instead, he produced a hypodermic and a vial of some liquid.

Joe Shine was not dumb. He eyed the bronze colossus as Doc charged the needle and said, "I get it. That stuff is truth serum. You're going to drag the truth out of me."

"One way or another," said Doc Savage calmly.

"Well, I'm no rat. I'm not squealing on anyone. Not even myself. Do your worst."

Monk and Ham moved in as one, took hold of the man's arms, and the hairy chemist wrestled Joe Shine's forearm until he was holding it straight out.

Doc Savage applied the needle and plunged the truth serum into a pulsing vein.

Shine did not have much resistance. He literally sat down where he was standing, and his face became slack and his mouth loose and rubbery.

"This stuff is hittin' him awful fast," clucked Monk.

In no time at all, Joe Shine was mumbling semi-coherently as if in a drunken stupor. This behavior told Doc Savage the potent chemical had gone to work and the tough-talking gangster was ready for questions.

"How did you come to capture my men?"

In the slurred voice, Joe Shine said, "Heard you blew into town. Figured something was up. So I muscled my way into the deal."

"For what purpose?"

"For the purpose of knocking Duke Grogan out of the picture and grabbing off a piece of his action."

"What do you know about the death of Myer Sim?"

"Nothing."

"What about a man named Ned Gamble?"

"Never heard of him."

Doc asked a few more questions. Ham Brooks threw in some of his own, but the result was a great quantity of nothing. Mob leader Joe Shine seemed not to have any direct knowledge of the events in New York, never mind the confounding mystery that had brought the bronze man and his aides to Chicago.

"Dead end," muttered Monk. "Too bad."

Ham Brooks spoke up, "I imagine you will wish to make arrangements to ship Joe Shine and his mob off to our college."

Doc nodded. "They are of no further use to us."

The "college" to which the elegant barrister referred was Doc Savage's secret institution hidden in upstate New York, the one to which the unlucky Ed Waco had been spirited away.

The disposition of the Joe Shine mob was only a little complicated.

Doc Savage had arrived in his speed plane, which breasted down onto Lake Michigan a fair distance away, alighting on silenced engines. The silencers had been of the bronze man's own invention. They were remarkably efficient, producing only a steady hissing that might have been the wind whipping across the lake.

Doc had launched a collapsible dory, and brought it into the stern of the lake freighter.

Climbing the anchor chain was a job for a circus acrobat, but Doc Savage had surmounted the obstacle with speed and silence, easily locating the glowing portholes, then freeing Ham Brooks without being detected.

Getting the Joe Shine group back to the speed plane for conveying to the airport was a cumbersome operation, requiring that they be ferried over to the aircraft two at a time. Not possessing the impressive muscular strength of his comrades, Ham Brooks stood guard over those who remained on deck.

They made quite a collection, but soon the mob was lying in a disorderly pile in the rear of the plane.

Had these activities transpired in New York City, it would have been necessary only for Doc to summon a private ambulance to whisk the captured ones upstate, as they had with the ill-fortuned Ed Waco at Grand Central Station. Here in Chicago they had no such resources.

Looking over the unconscious group, Monk muttered, "What are we gonna do with these clowns?"

"Dose them with anesthetic and leave them in the plane hangar until they can be collected," replied the bronze man.

"Think they'll keep?"

"For their own sakes, they had better," said Doc ominously.

Chapter XXVII

RUN AROUND

THE DOORMAN STATIONED before the Hotel Chicago thought he was tough.

When he spotted a soot-black figure step from a taxicab and attempt to gain entrance to the hotel lobby, the uniformed fellow blocked his way.

"Where do you think you're going, shorty?" he challenged.

"To my room," said Long Tom peevishly. "Now step aside before I knock you flat on your can."

The puny electrical wizard was in no mood for ceremonies or civilities. He wanted to take a hot bath.

The doorman took Long Tom not as a guest in good standing, but as a gentleman of color who had wandered over from Bronzeville. Long Tom was coated in soot, and although the rain had caused the stuff to run, he was still dark of hue. Furthermore, although the electric lights outside the hotel showed good illumination, it was still drizzling, inhibiting vision. Hence, the doorman's blunder.

"My name is Long Tom Roberts and I'm registered at this hotel."

"If that's so, you'll have a key. Show it."

Long Tom turned his pants pockets inside out and complained, "Some lug lifted my wallet, not to mention my key."

"In that case," returned the doorman distastefully. "Kindly beat it."

From the time that he had been waylaid at Janet Falcon's apartment, and held captive at Duke Grogan's Cicero hideout, Long Tom Roberts had had a tough time of it. He had grown sullen and ill-tempered, and dangerously in need of a bath. Moreover, he had had enough of the doorman's guff.

"Watch me beat *you!*" Long Tom barked.

The doorman had his beefy fists set on his uniformed hips, and stood before the revolving door like a brick wall. He did not think much of the little man confronting him with ill-disguised hostility.

So the functionary was not prepared when Long Tom hauled off, and connected with his compact but powerful fist.

The doorman landed on the seat of his pants and Long Tom Roberts walked across the brass buttons of the flunky's resplendent coat, scuffing the braid of his uniform as if the man were a ceremonial red carpet. His uniform happened to be crimson.

Barging into the lobby, Long Tom stormed up to the front desk. The clerk almost jumped out of his skin, thinking that the intruder was someone who had been caught up in a particularly smoky fire.

The clerk did his best to smile and inquired, "How may I help you, sir?"

"Thomas J. Roberts. Lost my key. Need the spare."

The desk clerk squinted as he peered at the sooty features and said, "I will need to see some identification."

"Don't make me bust you in the snoot, too," warned Long Tom. "Just hand over that room key."

There was a hotel detective seated nearby, a new one. He could be forgiven for not having recognized Long Tom, either.

Putting down a magazine, he sprang from a lobby chair, and made his way over, his truculent features reddening.

"Haven't we had enough trouble in this establishment?" he challenged.

Long Tom turned, said, "What do you mean?"

"Don't you read the papers? There was a big shootout right here in this lobby a few hours back. A woman was kidnapped and Doc Savage got on her trail."

"I'm one of Doc Savage's assistants," Long Tom returned. "Has Doc come back yet?"

"Nobody's seen hide nor hair of the big bronze fellow. The police are keeping a lookout for him, though."

"What about my pals, Monk and Ham?"

"There is talk that Duke Grogan kidnapped them. Cops are looking for them, too. Now are you going to scram, or am I going to have to get muscular?"

"Duke Grogan could never grab off Monk and Ham."

"And why not?"

"Because Duke put the snatch on me, but I got away."

The hotel detective cracked a derisive grin, and his belly shook with barely-repressed laughter.

"A little runt like you? That'll be the day!"

At that point, the doorman shook his head violently and clambered to his feet, pushing angrily into the lobby.

"Let me at that little squirt! I'll give him a paste in the snoot."

Waving a hand magnanimously, the hotel detective stepped aside and invited, "Be my guest."

At which, Long Tom hauled off again and repeated the operation that slammed the doorman flat on his back. The hotel dick flopped down and neglected to rise.

Witnessing this, the doorman decided he was urgently needed out on the sidewalk.

Turning back to the desk clerk, Long Tom drawled, "When he stops hearing little birdies, tell him he owes me an apology for trying to keep me out of my own lodgings. Now hunt up that key."

The desk clerk had been grinning up to that point, but now he had discovered a newfound respect for the sooty claimant. A worried eye shot to the hotel dick, who had been favorably impressed by Long Tom's lightning right hook, inasmuch as he seemed in no hurry to stand again on his feet.

"What did you say your room number was?"

"I didn't, but it was 308."

The hotel detective looked to the desk clerk and gave him the high sign. The clerk consulted the register and reported, "It says here that Thomas J. Roberts has 308."

"That you?" asked the detective, groping the carpet in search of his hat.

"None other," returned Long Tom. "Now do I get my key?"

They seemed to be at an impasse when Doc Savage, followed by Monk and Ham, entered the lobby from the street.

Monk and Ham did not immediately recognize the slender electrical wizard, but Doc Savage did.

"Long Tom," he said. The bronze man did not sound surprised.

Monk and Ham's eyes grew wide. They charged up, and got on either side of Long Tom. They looked as though they wanted to hug him, but his sooty appearance gave them pause.

"What have you been rolling in?" exploded Monk. "Mud?"

"I got tossed into a cellar coal bin by Duke Grogan and his boys. Managed to escape through a basement window. I would have been here hours ago, except Grogan rolled up with Janet Falcon. So I doubled back to rescue her."

"Where is she?" asked Doc Savage.

"She got away from us both—after shooting Grogan down."

Doc Savage's trilling piped up, low and wondering, and then shaded into an alarmed note.

"Did you witness this with your own eyes?" asked the bronze man.

"I saw Janet Falcon flee the hideout house, Grogan pounding hard after her. Five bullets cut him down, four to the stomach and one square between the eyes. He's dead as a doornail."

Ham Brooks interjected, "We went to Janet Falcon's apartment looking for her and you. We found a pile of grit and in it was a petrified hand. The thumb bore your fingerprint."

Long Tom looked as if he did not know what to say to that.

Monk inserted, "We kinda thought you'd been turned to stone and then pulverized by hammers."

Long Tom eyed the hairy chemist skeptically. "Why would you think a fool thing like that?"

"Because people all over town have had their brains turned to stone and we thought maybe your whole body got the same treatment."

A memory seemed to creep into the electrical expert's mind. "When I was trapped in the dark, I remember my right hand felt heavy, like it was turning to stone. I could hardly lift it. In the dark, I couldn't see what was going on, and I lost consciousness after that."

Long Tom lifted the specified hand and flexed his fingers. "Seems all right now," he muttered.

Ham Books had been listening intently, his lawyerly mind sifting through facts.

"It is obvious what transpired," he declared.

"Not to me," grunted Monk.

Pointing at the dark right hand of Long Tom, Ham said, "Duke Grogan's boys simply inserted Long Tom's hand into a tub of wet concrete and made a cast of it, later creating a lifelike copy, which they planted to make us believe that you were no more."

"Makes sense," admitted Monk. "Grogan would have the ingredients for concrete on hand, since guys like him like to stick guys' feet into tubs of dryin' cement and drop them in the lake."

Doc Savage interjected, "Have you any idea where Janet Falcon went?"

Long Tom shook his head violently. "By the time I found a taxi, there was no sign of her."

Ham went over to the desk clerk, asked, "Has Jane York been seen? Her room number is 612."

"Not that I am aware. But I can have the bell captain check her room."

"That will not be necessary. We will do that."

Doc led the way to the bank of elevators, and the starter waved them aboard the next available cage.

AS THEY rode the lift upward, Long Tom commented sourly to Monk and Ham, "You two don't look so happy to see me, considering you thought I was defunct."

Monk grinned. "We're still not sure it's you. You look like something the cat drug through a charcoal pit and then set on fire."

The puny electrical wizard eyed Monk's shiner, and assorted cuts, abrasions and bruises. He shot back, "You don't look so hot yourself!"

Monk's grin got a little lopsided. "We had a run-in with Duke Grogan and then another fracas with Joe Shine."

Long Tom commented, "Isn't he another gangster?"

Monk waited until the elevator let them off on the sixth floor and had closed behind them before saying, "*Was* a gangster. We mopped up on his entire mob. They're all at the airport, sleepin' off a dose of mercy-bullet dope. We gotta figure a way to get them to the college before they wake up."

Long Tom offered what conceivably might have been an understatement when he remarked, "It sounds like we've all had a busy night."

By this time, they had rolled up to Janet Falcon's hotel room. The bullet-shattered panel had been replaced. Doc Savage did the knocking. There was no answer.

Going to a house phone, the bronze man requested the front desk ring the room. This was done. They could hear the ringing, muffled by the door, going on and on.

"No one could sleep through that," remarked Ham impatiently.

Doc told the desk man, "Never mind. It appears that Miss York is not in her room."

Going to their own suite of rooms, Doc Savage consulted a telephone book and found Janet Falcon's apartment number. He put in a call.

The telephone was picked up on the second ring and a voice that did not sound so much sleepy as it did nervous asked, "Yes? Who is it?"

Strangely, Doc Savage did not reply. He merely tapped the switch hook several times, breaking the connection. Dropping the receiver onto its cradle, he picked it up again, this time requesting the police.

"This is Doc Savage. Please send a squad car to the following address and pick up a woman named Janet Falcon. Do not take her to the local police station. Instead, bring her to the Hotel Chicago. I wish to question her myself."

"At once, Mr. Savage," said the crisp voice at the other end of the line.

Terminating the conversation, Doc Savage said, "Janet Falcon will be delivered here shortly. In the meantime, we need to make ourselves presentable." The bronze man's golden eyes went to Monk and Long Tom, in particular—although Ham Brooks looked as if he could have stood a change into fresh clothes as well.

While his men were climbing out of their rags and into proper attire, Doc Savage said, "This affair has taken a turn that was not expected."

"What do you mean?" asked Ham from another room in the suite.

"Our arrival in Chicago appears to have aroused half of the underworld. Yet Joe Shine insisted that he knew little about the happenings in New York, or their continuation here."

The sound of running water indicated that Long Tom Roberts was drawing a bath. Soon, he was splashing away.

Through the closed wash room door, he called out, "For some reason, Duke Grogan's men are interested in Janet Falcon. But I couldn't make out why. In fact, I couldn't make heads or tails of anything. Where does Joe Shine fit into this?"

Ham answered that. "Shine is a rival of Grogan's. It appears that the events of the last twenty-four hours stirred up that rivalry. Shine thought he could muscle in on whatever Grogan's racket was."

"Well, what *was* it?"

"We do not know," advised Doc.

"There's another skunk in the woodpile," said Long Tom, stepping out of the bathroom, looking human once more. His pale hair was still streaked with gray grime, and a bath towel was tied around his waist to ensure modesty.

Doc Savage eyed him. "Yes?" he prompted.

Long Tom then launched into a succinct recitation of his first encounter with Janet Falcon, which involved her attempting to shoot him with his magnetic gun, and Long Tom having to fire back in self-defense.

Eyes going wide, Monk blurted, "You shot a woman down?"

"It was either her or me," Long Tom retorted. "Now listen, while I was trying to figure things out, this creepy gink calling himself Malcolm McLean showed up. Said he was a chemist. I had to let him in because he was going to call the cops on me. And after I did, he brained me with a lamp."

Doc Savage imparted, "We encountered McLean later. He appears to have stolen Myer Sim's secret invention that was set to be unveiled at the scientific exposition."

Long Tom looked interested. "What was it?"

Doc elaborated, "A submersible automobile that the thief drove into Lake Michigan, and later abandoned. It was equipped with a retractable snorkel, permitting it to navigate in shallow water. Evidently, the tires were not equal to the muddy lake bottom and the machine became stuck. The driver escaped, abandoning the vehicle."

Ham asked, "Do you suppose Myer Sim was killed over that machine?"

"Very little is clear at this juncture," admitted Doc. "But we have our work cut out for us. For another individual fell victim to the strange petrifying power at the scientific exposition. It was Malcolm McLean."

Long Tom whistled. "So whatever it was striking men down is traveling around."

"Exactly," said Doc. "And it remains up to us to discover the motives behind this unusual phenomenon."

Long Tom ducked into the bedroom and began to search for fresh clothes, emerging moments later with nothing but a sheepish expression.

"I just realized this isn't my hotel room. My duds are downstairs. Who wants to be a pal and go fetch me a fresh suit of clothes?"

Neither Monk nor Ham looked eager to come to the electrical expert's rescue, so Doc Savage suggested, "Why don't you both go?"

Before either man could exit the hotel room, the telephone commenced jangling and Doc swept up the receiver.

He was not on the line for very long, listening more than speaking. But his questions were distinct.

"When did this happen? Did anyone see the kidnap car?"

After he was done, Doc Savage hung up. Everyone looked at him expectantly. The big bronze man did not disappoint.

"Janet Falcon has been kidnapped from her apartment," he related.

"Again!" exploded Long Tom.

"That woman is the most kidnapped frail in all of Chicago." muttered Monk.

"We had best get going," said Doc urgently.

All four men left immediately, stopping only on a lower floor so that Long Tom Roberts could collect fresh clothes.

"I guess we ain't gonna get any shuteye tonight," said Monk, who did not appear displeased at the prospect. The simian chemist would rather fight than sleep most any day.

Chapter XXVIII

VANISHED VICTIM

ON THE RIDE over to Janet Falcon's apartment in the suburbs, Doc Savage and his men fell to checking their weapons. These were spare supermachine pistols stored in their hotel suite.

Long Tom had brought along the strange magnetic gun which Doc Savage had collected on his first visit to the Janet Falcon apartment.

"This might come in handy," he was saying. "It's completely silent in operation, and fires hollow slugs tipped with hypodermic needles. They work faster than our mercy slugs, even though they carry the same anesthetic inside."

"Rather like the hypodermic thimbles Doc sometimes wears on his fingertips to catch foes by surprise," mused Ham.

Long Tom nodded eagerly. "That's what gave me the idea when I started tinkering with one of those captured magnetic guns."

Beside him, Monk Mayfair was swapping out drums on his superfirer. "I brought along a bunch of the new bullets I've been fiddlin' with. I already got some good use out of the Charlie horse bullets. Now I'm itchin' to try some of the others."

Ham Brooks patted the padded underarm holster beneath his elegant frock coat, remarking, "I will stick with mercy bullets, if you don't mind. They have never failed us."

"We gotta keep up with the times," grunted Monk.

"Exactly," agreed Long Tom. "And the magnetic gun will soon supplant the ordinary firearm. That is my prediction."

As he returned his strange weapon to his lap—it was a trifle too large for a common holster—the pallid electrical wizard showed an oversized watch on one skinny wrist.

"My word!" remarked Ham. "That is the largest wristwatch I have ever seen a man wear."

Long Tom yanked back his sleeve to further display the timepiece. It was a monster.

"This is what I call my shock watch," he said. "I was wearing it when Duke Grogan's boys grabbed me. They worked me over good, but I wouldn't say a thing. So they tossed me into the coal bin while they figured out what to do."

"How did you get loose?" Doc asked.

Long Tom said, "With this. Grogan and his boys took off somewhere, leaving one guard behind. I convinced the bird that the watch was worth a pile of dough and if he let me go, he could keep it. He fell for the ruse, right enough."

Long Tom cracked a thin grin. "What he didn't know was that the watch was hooked up to a dry cell battery in my pocket, and all I had to do was set it a certain way and it gave off an electric shock. When the guard reached his hand out for it, I tossed it. The dope received a jolt about equal to grabbing hold of an electric eel. That knocked him out long enough for me to crawl out of the basement window."

"Clever," said Ham. "Why didn't they find the battery when they searched you?"

"They did, but they didn't think anything of it. It was hooked up with an insulated wire as thin as a hair that ran down my shirt sleeve. They weren't the brightest bunch of crooks I ever ran up against."

Soon, Doc Savage piloted the rental sedan into the correct neighborhood, and after they turned the final corner, they were surprised to see an official police limousine among the radio cars.

The Superintendent of Police of Chicago was among those gathered. That indicated something serious had happened.

Exiting their machine, they drew close, and discovered sprawled on the sidewalk a police officer in blue, his brass buttons shining, the rest of him in a sickening pool of blood.

Seeing Doc Savage, the Superintendent turned and said, "It was the Grogan gang. This officer told us that much before life fled his body."

The police official was holding his hat in his hands, as did the other officers, who stood bare-headed and downcast. It was clear they were awaiting a hearse, not an ambulance.

"Were any of the abductors recognized?" asked Doc.

"One bad apple. Patches Cordovan was fingered by my officer. He's Grogan's right arm."

"What else did this man tell?" pressed Doc.

"Only that there were three of them, and they dragged the poor woman into a touring car and took off like the very devil was snapping at their heels. I have the entire city looking for that machine," the Superintendent added. "What can you add to our knowledge of the situation?"

Doc told him, "Miss Falcon and my associate, Long Tom Roberts, were lately prisoners of Duke Grogan and his men. Long Tom got away from their hideout in Cicero, but had to go back when he realized Miss Falcon had been abducted. There ensued a fight, during which Janet Falcon just managed to escape. Evidently, she returned to her apartment, thinking it was safe to do so."

"Where is this hideout?"

Long Tom provided the address, adding, "When you bust in, you may find Duke Grogan. He'll be plenty dead. I think that Falcon dame shot him. I didn't see who fired the gun, only where the bullets landed. They landed pretty hard on Grogan."

The Superintendent of Chicago Police whistled low and slow. His eyes gleamed. "So Duke Grogan got himself croaked!"

Doc said, "It may be that Grogan's gang is seeking revenge on Miss Falcon. Her life is in immediate danger."

"If I know Grogan's lads, by now they're doing their dirty work. But I'll send a car over to that address just the same. In fact, I'll send a squad of men."

"It is unlikely that the Grogan gang returned to that house," advised Doc. "But no possibility should be overlooked."

The Superintendent went to his limousine, and the driver handed out a radio microphone. The police official spoke forcefully, words coming out of his mouth like bullets.

"I want that house turned upside down! Send the riot squad. And put out a dragnet for anyone known to associate with Duke Grogan."

Returning the microphone, the Superintendent rejoined Doc Savage saying, "That means the way is clear for Joe Shine and his mob. No doubt they'll be looking to take over Grogan's old territory."

Doc Savage said nothing. It was not his way to turn over criminals to local authorities. The bronze man did not believe in prisons, incarceration, and especially capital punishment. Disposal of Joe Shine and his men would forever remain a secret, so long as Doc Savage had any say in it. The bronze man was devoted to rehabilitation, not punishment.

A hearse pulled up, and the unpleasant task of loading the draped corpse in blue onto a stretcher and bundling him in the back was conducted in respectful silence.

Every officer held his uniform cap before his heart and bowed his head as this solemn duty was concluded.

After the somber hearse pulled away, the Superintendent instructed the remaining men to fan out and comb the city for the fleeing touring car.

Doc Savage was looking down at the rain-washed street, studying the impressions made by the kidnap car. No one seemed to notice this.

"Good luck with your hunt," advised Doc. "We will be in touch as developments call for it, Superintendent."

"Thank you," shot back the official as the bronze man took his departure.

ONCE they were safely ensconced in their rental sedan, Ham wondered aloud, "Chicago is a large metropolis. Where do we start?"

"We will begin by following the tire tracks of the touring car whose tread I recognized."

The trail twisted along several streets, seeming to go nowhere in particular. Eventually, it turned up Wabash Avenue, a street which would normally be clogged with streetcars, but the trail soon petered out as a result of the incessant drizzle and the fact that other night-traveling automobiles criss-crossing the dry portions under the Elevated train trestle had erased all sign.

After less than a mile, Doc Savage was forced to admit that the promising trail had been lost.

"This is a fine turn of events," murmured Ham.

"Yeah, they're probably dumpin' Janet Falcon's body into the Chicago River even as we speak," said Monk glumly.

"I don't know," mused Long Tom slowly. "From what I saw, Janet Falcon can kind of handle herself."

Ham arched a skeptical eyebrow. "Up against the Grogan gang?"

"She shot Duke in the belly and finished him off with a slug between the eyes. That's pretty fair shooting. Not to mention cool nerve."

Silence fell over the rolling sedan after that observation.

Presently, Ham Brooks asked, "I'm still in the dark. Have we made any progress in this investigation so far?"

"None whatsoever," admitted Doc Savage, with a trace of self-reproach in his tone. His flake-gold orbs held a bleak light. This once, the bronze man felt helpless in the face of the rushing events of the night.

Doc Savage filled Long Tom in, describing the events precipitated by Ned Gamble's arrival at Doc Savage headquarters, his subsequent demise, and the grisly discovery that his brain had been petrified in some fashion.

"You left out the weird silhouette of Medusa found at several murder scenes," Ham interjected.

"Medusa!" Long Tom exploded. "You mean the old crone with the head full of snakes?"

"The same dame," admitted Monk. "It was like she left her awful shadow behind after doin' her evil deed."

Long Tom seemed to repress a shudder that was probably not caused by the dampness of the night.

"Medusa," he murmured reflectively. "She was one of the Gorgons, wasn't she?"

Ham nodded resolutely. "Yes, there were three Gorgon sisters in the olden days. Medusa is the most famous." Suddenly, the dapper barrister snapped his fingers and burst out, "Gorgon! That's terribly close to Grogan, isn't it?"

That thought sunk in, and everyone in the rolling machine grew momentarily reflective.

"What could that possibly mean?" wondered Ham.

"It is clear," stated Doc, "that Duke Grogan is connected to the petrified-brain murders—for murders they obviously must be. As for the similarity in names, Gorgon means 'terrible' in the Greek language, while Grogan is an Irish name translating to 'fierce.'"

"Kinda close for coincidence," muttered Monk. "But I still don't get it. Is Duke Grogan our phantom Medusa?"

"Well, if he is," suggested Ham, "he has been put out of the petrifying business. And by a woman whose fiancé he murdered. That seems rather fitting to me."

For once, Monk agreed with the dapper lawyer. "Justice, I call it. Plain and simple justice."

"If Grogan is truly the Gorgon," offered Ham, "that means the reign of terror by petrification is drawing to a close."

"Yeah? And with us havin' done hardly anything about it!" complained Monk.

"What do you mean, nothing?" said Ham caustically. "We've had the daylights scared out of us, and we've practically shattered the Chicago underworld. I call that a good night's work!"

"The night is not yet over," reminded Doc Savage.

Chapter XXIX

VERMILION TRAIL

RACING AROUND THE streets of Chicago in the pre-dawn hours produced exactly no results whatsoever.

Traffic was sparse, although a few horse-drawn milk wagons were already trudging from door to door. By far, the greatest amount of traffic consisted of the prowling black-and-green Chicago radio cars, which were also intent upon locating the missing Janet Falcon.

Seated beside Doc Savage in the front seat, Monk Mayfair complained, "We're gettin' no place fast!"

To which Long Tom added, "It's like looking for a needle in a haystack in a fog."

Perhaps it was the mention of the needle that prompted Doc Savage to abruptly pull hard on the steering wheel and reverse course, causing the rubber of his automobile tires to smoke and burn.

"Where are we going?" wondered Ham.

"Airport," said Doc. "We are unlikely to make any progress here that the Chicago police cannot achieve on their own."

It did not seem to be much in the way of a direct answer, so Ham followed up with the question. "Do you intend to conduct a search by air?"

Doc shook his head slowly. "It may be that Joe Shine possesses information as to where Grogan's gang take bodies to be disposed of. Rival criminals often know such things, inasmuch as they prey on one another as much as they do the general public."

Doc Savage's mention of bodies made them all fret that Janet Falcon was by now deceased. It was a reasonable assumption, for it appeared by all evidence that the distraught woman had slain the gangster leader, and now his surviving hoods were taking her on a one-way ride to oblivion.

Monk grunted explosively, "Dang! It's not a bad idea, at that. I'll be happy to wring that hood's neck until he coughs up whatever he's got."

Doc said nothing. But the bleakness in the bronze man's eyes told that he did not hold out much hope for the missing woman.

Arriving at the private hangar where Doc Savage's speed plane was temporarily housed, Doc and his men jumped out of their machine, and entered the corrugated steel barn.

Unlocking the hatch to the airplane, they found Joe Shine and his men sleeping off the anesthetic doses they had been given. There was a fair amount of twitching and snoring going on, but otherwise the Joe Shine mob was oblivious to their surroundings.

Doc Savage fell upon the crime lord, lifted him up as if he were but a child, and placed Shine in one of the plane seats.

From his gadget vest, the bronze man extracted a flat black case which contained a syringe and small vial of restorative solution. Doc's men recognized the stuff. It was a concoction designed to bring a person out of the anesthetic rapidly without harming him.

Rolling up one of Joe Shine's sleeves, Doc administered the stuff, and stepped back, pocketing the case and its contents.

Shine's shoe-button eyes snapped and fluttered, and suddenly he jerked erect.

Looking about wildly, he demanded, "Where am I?"

"In trouble," advised Ham. The dapper lawyer had exposed the blade of his sword cane, and the tip was now hovering beneath Joe Shine's slack jaw.

The elegant attorney transferred the point from Shine's Adam's apple to the tip of his nose. This did not do the awakening mobster's state of mind any benefit.

Joe Shine got right to the point. "What's goin' on?"

Doc Savage told him, "A woman has been kidnapped by Duke Grogan's gang. The city police are searching for her, as are we."

Shine blinked. "What's that got to do with me, if anything?"

"No doubt some of Duke Grogan's rivals have been disposed of secretly. Where would Grogan's men take someone they intended to kill?"

As the question sank in, Joe Shine's black eyes glittered with an avid light. He took his time answering, letting his brain clear. It cleared rapidly.

"What's in it for me if I tell you?"

At that point, Monk Mayfair stepped in. His hairy paws seized the racket chief. One hand went around Shine's throat, while the other clamped down on the top of his head. In prehistoric times no doubt cavemen possessed hands such as this, heavy and hirsute as a gorilla's.

Shine struggled, but all that happened was that Monk pointed the criminal's face upward so that the simian chemist's fierce visage loomed over him.

Now Shine found himself caught between Ham's wicked-looking blade and Monk's muscular manhandling.

Monk growled, "If I start twistin', I'll bet I can unscrew your head like the cork on a wine bottle."

Joe Shine's head was suddenly jerked to the left, and hot lights danced in his eyeballs.

"There is a place!" he screeched. "It's where Grogan dumps the stiffs he bumps off. It's a mine south of here. A coal mine."

"What is the name of this coal mine?" asked Doc Savage.

"I don't know the name! It was closed down years ago, after a big gas explosion. I just know where it is."

"Where?"

"Near a town called Ryerson. Due south. Down in Vermilion County."

The mob leader was so frightened that every word rang true.

"Monk," said Doc. The bronze man did not need to elaborate, for Monk took his hands away and warned, "You better be tellin' the truth, guy."

"Cross my heart and hope to die in bed," vowed Joe Shine sincerely.

Doc Savage said, "Ryerson is too far to drive. We will have to fly there."

Waving his blade, Ham asked, "What about these scoundrels? We can't leave them behind. If they are found in the hangar, difficult questions will be asked."

Doc Savage seemed to have already given the matter sufficient thought, for he replied, "We will have to haul them with us."

Joe Shine heard this and said, "I ain't much for flying. I get air sick, as a matter of fact."

To which Long Tom commented, "Who said you're going all the way?"

"Yes," seconded Ham. "We might just drop you and your boys in a nice lake we happen to pass over."

"There ain't any lakes between here and Ryerson," Shine pointed out.

"It don't matter," shrugged Monk casually. "From that height, hittin' a wet lake and hard ground amounts to the same thing. Splat!"

Everyone began claiming their seats and preparing to take off. Doc Savage started the three big radial engines.

"Bet you never thought you'd be taken for a ride in an airplane," added Monk with bloodthirsty relish.

Joe's Shine's dark orbs widened in horror. "You wouldn't kill me!" the mobster gulped.

"No, we wouldn't," assured Ham Brooks smoothly. "In actual fact, hard ground will cause your demise."

Joe Shine's eyes narrowed. "That's a technicality."

Ham said carelessly, "I happen to be an attorney. I trade in technicalities."

"You sound like my mouthpiece," Shine said bitterly.

"I am not your lawyer," returned Ham stiffly, inserting the tip of his blade into Joe Shine's right cheek. The point went in and out so quickly that at first the nervous gangster did not realize he had been stung.

By the time awareness of the puncture dawned on the criminal, his eyes rolled up into his head, and he slumped into a seat, once more stupified.

Restoring the blade to the barrel of the cane, Ham Brooks took a seat as the big aircraft started rolling forward.

Long Tom got out and opened the great hangar doors, then hopped back aboard while Doc Savage ran the tri-motored aircraft out onto the tarmac.

THEY were soon in the air, and Doc pointed the moaning nose due south.

The flight was brief, for Doc opened up all three engines, inducing the greatest speed possible.

Finding the town of Ryerson at night would have been a challenge for a seasoned airline pilot. Doc Savage was no ordinary aviator. He knew all the tricks.

First, he found a set of railroad tracks that led in the general direction of Vermilion County, and followed those as far as he needed, then changed course, going southeast, until he announced, "We are approaching Ryerson."

Monk Mayfair, sprawled in the co-pilot's bucket, was duly impressed. The urgency of the situation was still grave.

Doc flew low and cut the floodlamps that he was using to illuminate the ground, not wishing to alarm his quarry—if in fact Joe Shine's information proved reliable. There was no doubting the gang chief's sincerity, but neither was there certainty that his information fit the present situation.

Every reason existed to believe that Janet Falcon had been marked for death, but no assurance that she had not been already murdered, and her body dumped into Lake Michigan.

This weighed on all of their minds. They barely knew the woman, who had not been cooperative. Indeed, her behavior had been inexplicable, given the fate of her fiancé, Ned Gamble.

But she was a woman, and Doc Savage and his men were determined to rescue her—if this were possible at this belated hour.

In the cockpit, Doc Savage donned infra-red goggles, and Monk did the same. The bronze man now illuminated infra-ray lamps set in the nose of the aircraft. These lights could not be seen from the ground, but anyone wearing the goggles could perceive what went on below—although everything would be akin to watching a grainy black-and-white film.

Monk said suddenly, "I spy the mine! The big coal-washin' house is up ahead."

Doc Savage nodded silently. He had spotted the bulky structure first; his ever-active eyes were taking in all the details.

The coal mine appeared to have been abandoned sometime back, no doubt for good. The operational structures had been allowed to go to seed, much the way barns in the Middle West are sometimes permitted to sag and fall into ruin by the relentless action of wind and the elements, rather than the owners spending the funds to raze them.

Doc flew on, passing over the coal bed, and his remarkable memory told him that there was no landing field within reasonable driving distance.

"Monk, take the controls," directed Doc. "I will have to parachute down in the darkness."

"I'll go with you."

Doc shook his head firmly. "No. If there is any chance of surprising the gang, utmost stealth will be necessary. I will go alone."

That settled the argument. "Want me to land this bus on the highway nearby?" asked Monk.

"Do so unobtrusively," Doc told him. "Park the plane out of sight." Then he vaulted out of his seat.

At the rear of the plane, Doc removed his coat and shoes.

Almost from the beginning of his remarkable career, the bronze man had taken the sensible precaution of going about wearing a bulletproof vest of chain mail. Over time, he had found it necessary to expand this protective garment so that it covered his arms and legs under his shirt. Gunmen often aimed for the chest or arms, rarely for the head, and less often for the legs.

However, Doc Savage had been struck or nicked by a fair amount of slugs in recent months. So by this time, he had taken to wearing what amounted to a union suit of chain mail under his street clothes. Wading into a nest of hardened gunmen such as the Grogan gang, this would not be sufficient.

For this reason, the bronze giant took the precaution of donning a remarkable suit of jointed stainless steel armor, which he extracted from a numbered case in the cargo area at the tail of the night-winging plane.

This consisted of a flexible helmet of chain mail, which draped over his head and permitted vision through a pair of eyeholes which he then covered over with a pair of goggles designed to work with an infra-red headlamp mounted over the lenses.

Gloves and boots of flexible steel were added to this ensemble.

When the bronze giant had finished, he looked like an ultra-modern knight in armor. He carried no weapons, other than his many-pocketed vest, which was stuffed with handy gadgets of all varieties.

Lastly, Doc Savage shouldered into a canvas parachute pack.

"Let me know when we are near the coal mine," he called forward to Monk.

"Want me to drop you smack in the middle?"

"No," returned Doc. "Put me on the lee side of the big coal-washing plant. I wish to approach from the southwest."

"Gotcha!" enthused Monk. "Comin' right up."

The simian chemist banked the big plane and banked it again, bringing it around. The hissing of its silenced motors could not be heard in the soundproofed cabin. Nor was it likely to be detected from the ground.

Doc Savage went to the hatch, and flung it open. Cold slipstream ripped into the interior of the plane, causing the hats and neckties of the unconscious Joe Shine mob to fly about wildly.

One hat flew out the open door. Doc attempted to intercept it, but he was encumbered by the cumbersome armor, and the hat went flying outward.

"Get ready," warned Monk.

Doc stepped to the edge of the open hatch, and held himself in place with his metallic fingers.

"Go ahead and jump!" yelled Monk.

The bronze man disappeared from view, and Ham Brooks scrambled to pull the door shut by using the gold knob of his cane to hook the door latch. He almost fell out attempting this, but managed to get the door closed with a little help from Monk, who, without warning, stood the plane on its right wing, causing the door to clap shut, and the flailing attorney to slam across the cabin and into the opposite bulkhead.

When Monk righted the plane, Ham jumped to his feet and squawked, "Remind me to brain you when you are not flying this plane!"

Monk yelled back in an injured tone, "You would've fallen out if I hadn't pulled that stunt."

"I almost had a heart attack!"

"Next time, try to succeed," snorted Monk, slanting the plane in the direction of the nearest country road.

They did not attempt to follow Doc Savage's progress to the ground, for the bronze man had donned a parachute that was as black as octopus ink, which could not be seen from the ground or from the air.

Clouds had obscured a fingernail moon, which would minimize the chances of the chain-mail armor being picked out by moonlight. There was no guarantee that Doc Savage might not be spotted as he neared the ground, assuming that guards were picketed below on watch.

The unpleasant thought was on all of their minds and caused Long Tom to snap, "Plant this crate on the ground, fast. If Doc needs help, we've got to be Johnny on the spot."

"Hold your horses," retorted Monk. "I gotta find a stretch of road that's sheltered so the landin' lights don't show."

"Just get this thing on the ground," groused Long Tom. "I'm looking forward to trying my magnetic gun on these mobsters."

"Wait'll you see the new bullets I'm packin', Long Tom," Monk chortled. "Some of them are doozies."

"Doozies is right," sniffed Ham. "I hope you can live down those Charlie horse misfires before this night is over."

"Look out I don't nick you by accident," warned Monk. "When I get to fightin', I don't have time to look where I aim."

"You wouldn't dare!"

"Just watch yourself, that's all I'm sayin'."

Chapter XXX

THE COLLIERY

DESPITE THE SEASON, there was no prevailing wind. The air was still, although chilly in the extreme.

That might explain why no guards were posted outside the colliery. No doubt they preferred the comparative shelter of the big coal-washing plant, which bulked fantastically in the night, looking like a barn that had been constructed to house gigantic, otherworldly beasts. For the coal preparation structure stood many stories tall, but not in all of its angular portions.

The faint moonlight etched out a shiny area which Doc knew must be a slurry impoundment, where the sludgy byproduct of coal separation called blackwater was collected.

The bronze man had more than a passing familiarity with coal mining operations, as he did with almost every field of endeavor, human or industrial.

In the not long-ago days when the plant was active, bituminous coal was brought up on conveyor belts and put through the processing plant where it was washed, crushed, separated and loaded into railroad hopper cars for transport to market.

As he fell in silence, suspended from the great black silken parachute bell, the mighty Man of Bronze directed the dark lens of his infra-red headlamp on the ground below, searching for any signs of movement. He saw none.

The gangster hat that had tumbled out of the aircraft had managed to land on the roof of the plant. It was an incongruous touch, but it was not likely to be spotted from the ground.

There were a few windows in the washer structure, but very few. He could not assume that someone might not be picketed behind the broken glass of one of those opaque panes of glass.

Such a guard would as likely as not tote a high-powered rifle. Depending on the rifle and the caliber of bullet, Doc Savage might withstand any sniper's handiwork. Too, his steel armor was blued like a knife blade, so that it tended to absorb stray moonbeams, rather than reflecting them. But this precaution was not perfect.

The bronze giant's chief concern was a rifleman puncturing the canopy of his parachute. His chain mail armor would not protect him from a sudden fall, of course.

So Doc played the invisible rays of his infra-red lantern toward every shadow and crevice of the ground, seeking signs of lurking gunmen.

Not even the pooled shadows moved, however.

Pulling on his shroud lines, the bronze man attempted to steer the billowing black bell close to the big separation plant, figuring that he stood a better chance of gaining entry to the structure if he had less distance to traverse. Landing on the outskirts of the coal pit might be safer in the short run, but more risky if he had to cross open ground.

Briefly, Doc had considered attempting a landing on the roof of the plant, but the structure looked too flimsy to risk it. The roof was a tarpaper patchwork, and there were visible holes attesting to its state of disrepair.

Doc endeavored to land as close to the looming building with its weather-beaten sides of unimproved lumber as practical.

His metal boots touched the ground, slamming firmly. Doc's knees bent only slightly, as his tremendous leg muscles cushioned the impact, such as it was.

Absence of wind caused the silken shroud to collapse over him, and Doc knelt in place, rigid as a statue, permitting this to happen.

When the thing finally finished collapsing, Doc drew a knife from the scabbard, pierced it with a blade as blued as his chain-mail armor. Working swiftly, he sliced out a square of silk, cut a roughly circular hole in its center.

He drew this over his head like a wide, billowy poncho.

When he was done, Doc Savage was all but invisible, the makeshift black silk garment covered all but his helmeted head.

Moving with uncanny soundlessness, the bronze giant advanced on the washery building. It cast a gray shadow as large as the giants of Greek mythology known as Cyclopes. A randomly-placed window at the top floor suggested a vacant orb, completing the illusion.

Moving past the touring cars parked near the main door, Doc Savage paused long enough to study the license plates, and to feel of their long hoods.

Both engines were still warm, indicating that they had lately arrived. Since he had not previously spied them from the air, this could only mean that the drivers had pulled in while Doc's plane had been circling in advance of his preparing to jump.

Neither machine was locked, so the bronze giant slipped inside and worked swiftly and silently with a set of miniature tools. When he emerged, the ignition coils of both cars reposed in one pocket.

Moving on, he drifted up to the door, a fragment of darkness taken on life.

Pausing there, Doc listened, but no sounds reached his ears, which were only a little handicapped by the fact that a metallic helmet covered them.

The door stood slightly ajar, and Doc maneuvered his head so that he could point the infra-red helmet headlamp inside. This revealed no lurking forms.

Carefully easing the weather-beaten panel in an inch at a time to prevent rusty hinges from creaking, the bronze man slipped in as elusive as a drifting shadow. Once inside, he was able to move about freely past abandoned cyclone separators and other bulky equipment used to wash, separate, and crush raw bituminous coal for transport by rail. These had all gone to rust.

The odor of cigarette smoke drifted to his sensitive nostrils. Doc Savage changed direction, moving toward that telltale smell.

He began hearing voices—those of men in low conversation.

"But we can't wait around all night," one was saying.

"Can it, Blue. We're parked here as long as we need to. With Duke out of the picture, I am in charge of this outfit."

"Sez you."

"That's right. Sez me. If you want to put it to a vote, you better use bullets, on account of we're fresh out of ballots."

"I ain't going against you, Blackie. But Patches Cordovan might have something to say about that. He was Duke's number two. Five slugs promoted him to number one."

"We'll see about that."

"Go ahead and arm wrestle Patches for the privilege," Blue said truculently. "That ain't my big worry right now. Without Duke bossing us, I don't think we know what we're doing anymore."

"That moll won't talk. And we need her to talk."

"Why don't we just bump her off and dump her down a shaft? No one will ever find her there. They never found the others, did they?"

"Not until we get the word. Only Duke had the ear of the head snake. And we don't even know who that is. We just know what number to call."

"Well, why don't you call the number then?"

"Do you see a telephone around here?" snarled the other. "Besides, I don't want to call with the bad news that Duke is gone unless I have some good news to add to the pot."

"Aw, you're just trying to curry favor with the king snake."

"What if I am? Without this new deal, we're gonna need a fresh racket. Repeal put the kibosh on the old racket. That's why we hooked up with this Medusa dame."

"Well, Patches is gonna be back shortly," muttered Blue. "He'll give the word."

"I wonder why he took some of the boys into the mine like he did," mumbled Blackie.

"That part of it we were never made wise," said Blue. "Duke figured it wasn't our business. Patches probably figures the same thing."

The other was silent for a time. Finally, Blue broke the silence, saying, "Another twenty minutes in that holding pen oughta crack that twist's nerve."

"I'm not so sure," considered the ambitious thug called Blackie. "I'm almost one hundred percent certain she burned down Duke. A woman who can kill a man in cold blood doesn't crack easily."

"Duke greased her fiancé," commented Blue. "I'm not sure how cold her blood is about that. If you take my meaning?"

In the darkness, cigarettes glowed like tiny coals, and suddenly one described a downward arc and exploded in a brief uprush of sparks.

"O.K., then. Let's go back there and work her over. I'm getting tired of this dismal joint."

Blue took a long draw of a cigarette and the tip glowed more brightly, showing his face in satanic profile.

He made as if to dispose of the cigarette when there was a faint tinkle followed by another, and without warning, both men keeled over on their faces, and began breathing heavily in the darkness.

DOC SAVAGE entered the chamber, stepped over the unconscious bodies, and moved deeper into the great shadow-clotted structure, finding his way with the infra-red lamp whose rays could not be seen by the unaided eye.

There was a guard posted before a rough door and this individual also smoked a cigarette, whose fiery glow etched out the barrel of the Thompson submachine gun cradled under one arm, tracing long red gleams.

Doc Savage eyed the sub-gun warily. Its punishing power was something he did not wish to confront, even enveloped in chain mail as he was.

From a pocket of his leather vest worn over the chain mail, the bronze man removed another sphere of glass, and tossed it at the feet of the Tommy gun wielder.

Then he faded back.

The tinkle was the sound of a thin-walled globule of glass breaking. The grenade released a potent chemical brew which volatilized immediately, producing a colorless and odorless gas that soon found the nostrils of the guard.

The man was looking down at the glass shards at his feet, blinking in the bad light, when he unwittingly inhaled the potent anesthetic.

He collapsed where he stood, tangled up with his Tommy gun. Gliding up, Doc Savage reached down, lifted the weapon and quietly and efficiently began dismantling it, starting with the heavy drum which rattled with its load of .45 caliber bullets.

Doc took his time removing every single bullet casing, throwing the slugs in all directions so the weapon could not be easily reloaded.

Not satisfied with that, the bronze man took the deadly thing in one hand and while he held the weapon down with one knee, exerted a steady pressure while the barrel groaned slowly until it was bent out of plumb.

When that was done, Doc stood up, and tried the door.

It gave easily, the hinges squealing. Deep inside, a woman gasped.

"Don't you dare come in here!" the woman yelled fiercely. Her voice was defiant, and if there was any fear in it, the bronze man did not detect it in her cultured timbre.

Doc switched off the infra-red helmet lamp, and now he pulled one of the handy spring-generator flashlights from his vest. This he had wound before leaving the plane, so he thumbed it on, simultaneously throwing back the helmet and goggles which concealed his features.

When the bronze man stepped in, he was instantly recognizable, at least from the neck up.

The woman had a stone in one hand; her arm was already cocked to throw.

Before she could recognize Doc Savage, she pitched the dornick.

Doc Savage faded to one side and the missile struck a supporting timber and rebounded away.

"That is not much of a welcome for someone who is coming to rescue you," he said firmly.

The woman's voice lost its defiance. "Oh! I recognize you now. Doc Savage."

Chapter XXXI

THE HIDEOSITY

"**WHEN I LAST** saw you," murmured Janet Falcon breathlessly, "I never dreamed I'd be as glad to see you again as I am now."

Doc Savage entered the room.

The young woman was alone. She still wore her business frock. She had ripped off several inches at the bottom in order that she might move about more easily. Her green eyes were sharp and unafraid.

The ravishing smile she gave Doc was as calm as if it had been delivered in a New York Library reading room.

"I rather hoped someone would rescue me before those men could decide what to do," she said. "But I dared not dream it would be you, for I was told that you had been killed. You see, I was terribly afraid that I was to be left here to die."

"After chasing your captors half the night, it is quite a relief to find you," Doc said politely. He guided her toward the exit. "We had better clear out of here."

Janet Falcon held back. Her features were anxious in the glow of the flashlight, which Doc was now using to examine the chamber interior.

The woman grasped the bronze giant's arm, seemed astonished by the hardness of the armor he wore. "Malcolm McLean is being held in this awful place," she said with low urgency. "Aren't we going to rescue him?"

For four or five seconds following that announcement, Doc's weird trilling sound came into being and penetrated to the far corners of the room. Having no tune, yet melodious, inspiring without being awesome, the fantastic note seemed to come from everywhere.

Janet Falcon evidently did not realize from where it emanated. She looked around in perplexity. She remained wide-eyed with wonderment even after the sound died.

"McLean?" Doc queried softly.

"Yes. Duke Grogan's gang seized him in Chicago."

"Where is he?" Doc questioned sharply.

"In a room in the opposite wing of this building," supplied Janet Falcon.

"You are sure he is there?"

"Mr. McLean was placed there when we first arrived," declared the young woman. "I was in the adjoining room for a few hours. But they moved me."

"Malcolm McLean was brought all the way from Chicago—as a prisoner?" Doc asked sharply.

"Yes." Janet Falcon wrinkled her attractive brow.

"Did you know that he was supposed to have been murdered yesterday?"

Janet made a round mouth of surprise. "I did not hear that!"

"Did you overhear them say why they were holding any other prisoners?" Doc inquired.

"No!" The young woman made a bewildered gesture. "Are there two Malcolm McLeans?"

"There's only one real Malcolm McLean," Doc assured her. "However, two men are going about passing as the gentleman. One of them is a fake."

"I'll show you where Mr. McLean is being held," Janet Falcon advised.

Doc nodded and grasped her arm lightly.

They hurried through the cobwebbed gloom of the washing house. When they crossed the cavernous room where lay the motionless figures of the men who had been overcome by Doc's gas, the girl stared wonderingly. Evidently, she had reason to know just how tough these fellows were. Great admiration was in the gaze which she turned upon Doc.

"Did they ever say why they were holding you prisoner?" Doc asked.

"No. But I surmised that they intended to use my safety as a club to keep you in line," Janet Falcon replied.

"In line?" Doc asked swiftly.

"I am not with them," the girl snapped defensively. "What I meant was that they intended to use my safety to keep you from molesting them."

Doc said nothing. They plunged down a long corridor. The walls were stout, made of rough planks resembling barnboard. Doors were massive, and as crude as those on a barn.

"Here it is," breathed Janet Falcon.

Doc loosened the locking bar and heaved the door open. Blackness packed the room beyond. He spiked his flashlight beam inside.

"Malcolm McLean is not there!" Janet Falcon cried.

Doc Savage seemed to be giving all of his scrutiny to inspecting the empty cell. Actually, he gave close attention to the tone of the girl's voice. He was trying to tell whether she was genuinely surprised or acting.

She sounded genuine.

"I don't understand this," she said wonderingly. "I thought he was here."

"What made you think that?"

"The talk of the guards, which I overheard."

"What was that talk?"

"They were merely grumbling about having to watch prisoners in widely separated parts of the building."

Then Doc Savage had a realization that made him feel faintly foolish.

"How many captors in all?"

"Seven."

"I encountered only three," imparted the bronze man. A faint suggestion of disgust tinged his vibrant tones.

Janet Falcon hissed, "The others went somewhere in a group. I suspect to that horrid mine. More than once, they threatened to cast me down a shaft and leave me there."

"It is remarkable that they did not do so, for they believe that you gunned down their leader, Duke Grogan."

Doc Savage studied the woman in the flashlight glow. She turned her face away, and her green eyes grew brittle as glass.

"Did you?" pressed Doc.

"I—I would rather not say."

Flake-gold eyes studied Janet Falcon intently. "That does not sound like a denial."

"Nor is it an admission of guilt," she returned firmly.

Doc Savage said nothing more. Although the bronze man was schooled in many disciplines, one subject had always baffled him. And that was women. The female mind and its inner workings Doc had never been able to fathom. Janet Falcon was no different. Doc could not tell whether she was lying, or simply being contrary.

"Come on," he urged. "My men should be arriving any minute."

DOC SAVAGE plunged out of the washing plant, Janet Falcon in tow.

The bronze giant moved in the direction of the slurry impoundment. Doc Savage had given the still pond careful scrutiny as he descended from the sky, and noticed something that had caught his attention.

Seen from the ground, the impoundment displayed a scummy surface that was unbroken except for a hole at the edge of one limb. Doc Savage stopped at this spot, and switched on his helmet headlamp, simultaneously clamping the special goggles used in conjunction with the infra-red lantern. Directing the unseen beam downward, he stared into the inky waters a long time without speaking.

"What are you looking at?" Janet Falcon wondered uneasily.

Before the bronze man could respond, there came a noisy commotion from the general direction of the road leading to the mine. A flurry of movement was visible beyond the impoundment.

Pounding into view came Monk Mayfair, Ham Brooks and Long Tom Roberts. They appeared to be loaded for bear. Monk and Ham waved supermachine pistols, while Long Tom, the electrical wizard, clutched the peculiar-looking magnetic gun that he had invented.

The two groups came together, and the eyes of Doc Savage's men went wide at sight of Janet Falcon, only dimly visible in the thin moonlight.

Long Tom was no appreciator of the feminine sex. He took one look at Janet Falcon and said, "We figured you for dead."

The woman flushed. Her green eyes bathed the slender electrical genius with a frigid stare. "I am pleased to make your acquaintance once again," she returned frostily.

Ham Brooks put in gallantly, "What Long Tom means is that we had all but assumed that by now Duke Grogan's killers would have done away with you out of revenge."

"Anyone could see that they have not," Janet Falcon returned thinly.

Doc Savage interjected, "Three of Grogan's gang have been rendered insensate. They lie back in the coal-washing plant. But there are at least four others in the mine."

Monk said eagerly, "Let's charge down there and clean 'em out!"

"Not so fast," cautioned Doc Savage. "Abandoned mines are extremely dangerous. We cannot just blunder in without risking a cave-in, or worse."

Long Tom suggested, "Why don't we just wait for them at the mine entrance, and pick them off when they emerge?"

Doc told him, "There is another complication."

"What's that?"

"Janet Falcon insisted that Malcolm McLean was a prisoner of the Grogan gang. He was not in the separate cell in which he is supposed to have been confined."

Monk howled, "That walkin' cadaver! Ain't he dead?"

"We all saw his body after he was struck down at the scientific exposition," agreed Doc. "Yet I followed a man who bore a strong resemblance to McLean as he absconded with the late Myer Sim's submersible automobile only a few minutes before."

Ham frowned. "Could McLean be twins?"

All eyes went to Janet Falcon questioningly. It was a moment before she realized that she was expected to respond.

"I do not know Mr. McLean very well. He never spoke of a brother, much less a twin brother. Given his unusual medical condition, it is difficult to conceive of two of him."

Doc stated, "His condition is not so unusual that others who follow chemistry as a career might also conceivably suffer from the affliction."

No one knew what to say to that. For now, they had more pressing matters at hand.

Doc addressed Ham Brooks, saying, "You remain here with Miss Falcon. The rest of us will investigate the mine."

The dapper lawyer looked momentarily taken aback. He did not wish to be left out of any action, yet Janet Falcon was a ravishing beauty, and had already caught his eye.

"I will be more than happy to make certain that Miss Falcon is safe," he said graciously.

Monk Mayfair took the elegant attorney aside, growling low, "Normally, I would match you for it. But I'm hot to test out my new bullets on the Grogan gang."

"So am I!" said Long Tom eagerly. The sour-faced electrical expert was not normally of gleeful disposition, but the prospect of inflicting punishment with his magnetic gun seemed to have turned him into a walking spark plug.

Led by Doc Savage, who had restored his metal helmet and was blending into passing shadows like an ebony ghost, they made their way up the rocky soil of the coal mine, a low hillock rising from the earth.

The mine entrance was a horizontal gash of a thing called an adit. The stony portal seemed clogged with inky shadows. A fading wooden sign read:

DANGER! UNSAFE MINE! DO NOT ENTER!
Per Order Ryerson Coal Corp.

Climbing carefully, dislodging rocky scree with every step, they reached the portal, and began listening.

No voices were heard, but there came the distant sound of scraping and digging.

Monk muttered, "Are they diggin' for coal?"

Doc said, "Someone is digging for something. It is very peculiar."

Long Tom offered, "Maybe they've got a small stove back at the washing plant, and they need to keep warm. This place could be some kind of temporary headquarters for the gang."

Doc said nothing. Instead, he directed, "Wait here. All of you. I will reconnoiter."

Not waiting for any objection, the bronze man melted into the shadowy maw of the portal, and vanished utterly into the drift.

Doc Savage switched on his infra-red helmet lantern. The dark-lensed goggles were drawn over his eyes. The invisible rays permitted him to walk carefully into the mine along a winding tunnel, following an old coal seam. From time to time, he came upon a vertical shaft that he was forced to work around.

The timbers ahead shoring up the fissured ceiling were stout, but dried out with age. They did not look as if they had much strength left in them.

Intermittent sounds of digging and scraping continued, and Doc Savage moved toward them.

The difficult passage was littered with so-called "gob" piles—broken bits of coal and loose rock, and the bronze man had to employ his greatest stealth in picking his way forward. This cost him a great deal of his customary speed.

As he moved along, Doc took note of his surroundings. It became evident that the method of extracting coal had been the room-and-pillar variety. Passages were cut through the coal seam at cross angles to one another, creating standing pillars of unclaimed coal ore, which served to support the roof until the seam was exhausted and the mining operation retreated, where-upon the pillars would be taken and the roof permitted to collapse.

All indications were that the mining company never reached this latter stage. For Doc moved past dark pillars still extant after the operation had shut down.

Doc came to a widening of the drift, signifying a space carved out of the immense seam that loomed gigantic.

Sounds grew louder, and a shrill voice was speaking. Echoes reinforced the bronze man's sense of a great yawning space ahead.

"When you men are finished, you will return to guard the girl and await further instructions."

"If you say so," a man said. His voice was nervous.

The first speaker continued, but the shrill voice had a muffled quality.

"It will not be necessary to hold the girl for long—merely long enough."

"What does that mean?"

"It is not for you to know, Patches Cordovan. But now that you are the leader of the Grogan gang, you will take orders, like the late Duke."

The second speaker laughed roughly. "You mean the Cordo-van gang."

"Call it whatever you wish, but the arrangement with your outfit will continue unchanged."

"Just don't forget to hold up your end of the bargain. Starting with that backstabbing rat, Joe Shine."

"Leave Joe Shine to me. His demise has already been or-dained."

Sounds of banging, cutting and scraping continued, followed by what sounded like clinkers of coal being dropped into scuttles or pails.

Doc Savage eased closer. He had hung back in order to catch every word, but now he advanced with the eerie silence that marked his often ghostly comings and goings.

Turning the corner in the workings, Doc came to a zone where flashlights played. There, kerosene lanterns were also giving off a weak yellow glow.

Those combined lights threw towering shadows along a great ballroom of a space.

Most of the shadows were ordinary, although they loomed gigantic. One, however, was not.

The bronze man perceived the enormous shadow before he saw the being who cast it.

The silhouette was intensely black, and manlike, except for the head. The head was hideous. It was a mass of tentacles, which writhed and waved with ophidian life.

Seeing this, Doc hesitated. Although a brave man, he did not plunge blindly into the unknown. Ordinary gangsters did not frighten him. The bronze giant had disposed of many of their ilk thus far in his career.

But the gigantic shadowy head with its squirming serpents of hair was like nothing he ever before beheld.

Carefully, Doc directed the ghostly beam of his infra-red lantern toward the form that cast the unnerving shadow.

Viewed from the back, it soared seven feet in height or more, and was attired in a tattered gray garment rather like an old-fashioned nightshirt. It was impossible to tell the sex of the owner. But the head was a wonder.

Even seen from the rear, it fascinated. The knot of serpents writhed. They were predominantly green, but a few stood out scarlet. No two seemed of the same species. Some were lividly banded, a few speckled; others striped. Some fat and others lean. Pale light gleamed along the glossy skin surfaces of each individual viper.

It was impossible—an astounding sight! Doc Savage watched with flake-gold eyes flickering weirdly.

Movement of the clumped vipers was limited, for they were packed close together, but there was no mistaking the semblance of life as they writhed about the crown of the weird figure dominating the great chamber of rock.

Perhaps it was the uncanny apparition, perhaps it was simply the difficult conditions. Doc Savage was considerably hampered by his steel armor and enveloping poncho of parachute silk, a portion of which clutched in a mailed fist so he could reach his vest.

Doc Savage was attempting with his free hand to remove the flat case containing his anesthetic grenades when one metal-shod foot shifted, creating a clatter of loose stones.

This did not go unnoticed.

With a violent hissing, the snake-haired monster turned, revealing its face.

This countenance was bizarre beyond any expectation of imagination. The thick features were as white as marble, expression frozen in a fixed rage. The eyes glared horribly, for they were slit like those of a lizard and as green as the twitching serpents surrounding it.

Rubbery lips were pulled back against grotesque fangs, and a hand as yellow as snakeskin pointed an accusing finger in the bronze man's direction.

"What is that?"

The group of gangsters broke off their work, dropping their pick axes, hands flashing to armpit holsters. Guns came out.

"No!" shrieked the snake-haired one. "Do not fire."

But the command came too late. One nervous gunman, seeing only a weird helmeted head, squeezed off a shot. The passage quaked, became filled with the gory flicker of gun lightning.

Doc Savage had already faded back around the corner when the slug from a heavy caliber automatic struck a leaning timber, spraying the vicinity with splinters mixed with needles of hot lead created when lead struck a steel spike.

Results were disastrous.

The ancient, dried-out timber had several punky spots, and the bullet had gouged out one of those. Under the considerable strain of supporting the ceiling, the old wood crackled and broke.

Dust, debris, cries of horror, suddenly filled the tunnel passageway.

Doc Savage understood old mines. They were nothing to fool with, especially when they became unstable.

Having no choice in the matter, he pitched backward, using great speed, but taking every precaution as he retreated.

Behind him, there was a stampede. Yells, curses—much of it profane.

And above those complaints, the voice of the Medusa shrieked, "Keep your heads! Keep your heads!"

Then, with a resounding cracking of timbers and rock, the mine began sundering.

Doc Savage redoubled his speed. Throwing caution aside, he abandoned his infra-red helmet lantern. Behind his weirdly flashing form, a cloud of dust and grit coughed out, and began chasing him the length of the ancient tunnel.

Chapter XXXII

REVERSALS

AT THE MOUTH of the old coal mine, Monk Mayfair and Long Tom Roberts were debating the relative merits of their weapons.

Monk was saying, "I've got a drum full of slugs loaded with bee venom. Bein' hit by a mess of 'em is like bein' stung by a swarm of yellowjacket wasps. What do you say to that?"

"Sounds goofy," Long Tom retorted. "I'll take Doc's special anesthetic anytime. But my hypodermic bullets do the job much quicker than mercy slugs."

"I'll believe that when I see it with my own eyes," grunted the hairy chemist.

The argument was quite muscular, but carried on in low tones. Neither man wished to draw attention to himself.

"How do you think Doc is doin' in there?" Monk wondered aloud.

"Why ask me?" returned Long Tom peevishly. "Do I look like I'm toting a crystal ball?"

"Well, you don't have to be wrathy about it," said Monk indignantly. "I'm just makin' conversation."

"Make sense instead," snapped the slender electrical expert. "Your goofy bullets and your fool notions go together, if you ask me."

"Nobody asked you," said Monk in an injured tone. The homely chemist was normally not so thin-skinned, but he was inordinately proud of his new ammunition.

Monk and Long Tom lapsed into silence, their ears striving to capture any sounds emanating from the old mine. But nothing came.

"Spooky hole," muttered Monk.

"I don't much cotton to mines," agreed Long Tom. "They give me the heebie-jeebies."

"Someone who also gives me the creeps is that Malcolm McLean," said Monk thoughtfully. "The guy looks like someone dug him up a month after his own funeral. I wonder why the Grogan gang glommed him."

Now it was Long Tom's turn to grunt, "For a dead man, he sure gets around. First, he steals an automobile that thinks it's a submarine, then he gets killed over at the science exposition, and now he pops up in this joint."

Monk shrugged. "Maybe he's triplets."

"Bushwa," snapped Long Tom. "There could be only one such guy. So that's out."

They paused again to listen, knowing that it was all but impossible to hear Doc Savage when he was on the warpath, as he was now. Although a veritable giant, Doc Savage combined the tracking skill of a Cherokee brave with the jungle cunning of a hunting tiger.

Their first indication of trouble brewing was a deep rumble.

"I don't like the sound of that," muttered Monk.

The rumble swelled until it grew into a throaty roar like the teeth of some monster clashing together, grinding and pulverizing great boulders.

Instinctively, the hairy chemist and the pale electrical wizard faded away from the portal, knowing that something was about to erupt from the shadowy mouth.

Something did. But it was not what was expected.

Like a streak of blue-steel lightning, Doc Savage flashed into view, all but invisible, except for his metallic helmet.

Close on his heels, a terrible cloud of blackness that smelled of must and coal dust and more noxious things.

"Hold your breath!" Doc rapped out.

"What?" yelled back Monk.

"If you have gas masks, don them," urged Doc.

The crashing urgency of the bronze man's voice seized them by their throats.

Pocketing their weapons, Monk and Long Tom dug into their clothing, and extracted simple gas masks consisting of nose and mouth pieces, and an oxygen canister hanging by a flexible hose.

As they put on the contrivances, their eyes took in Doc Savage. He whipped off his flexible helmet, dug into his pocketed vest. It did not contain an elaborate gas mask, but he did produce a device that consisted of a spring clip that clamped his nostrils shut and a separate but connected chemical filter which he clapped over his mouth.

Once that was in place, the bronze giant seized Monk and Long Tom by their coats, and began sprinting, driving them ahead of him.

Long Tom wanted to know, "What's the big deal? That's only coal dust, isn't it?"

Doc Savage did not reply. Instead, he redoubled his efforts. The elemental power of the bronze colossus was never more evident. Neither Monk nor Long Tom were slouches in the running department. But their feet struggled to keep up with the urgent velocity imparted by the bronze man's shoving arms. Similar to being pushed along by a locomotive, the fear of being swallowed under the cow catcher was alarming.

Finally, Doc conveyed them to the sheltered spot where Ham Brooks had been guarding Janet Falcon. Ham had heard the commotion, and his face was stiff with white shock. For the elegant barrister had not moved, mindful of Doc Savage's instructions.

"Run, Ham!" Doc Savage called ahead. "Hold your breath. Keep running."

Ham did not have need of further explanation. Seizing Janet Falcon by one arm, he sprinted hard.

They all dashed as far from the coal works as possible.

Ham looked back once, and spied a black cloud coming out of the mine, and he thought the worst.

"Did someone touch off some old dynamite?"

"No," said Doc. "If you have a gas mask, put it on."

Ham did.

"What about me?" screeched Janet Falcon.

"We have no spares," said Doc. The bronze man eyed her steadily, awaiting her reaction.

"She can have mine," said Ham.

Janet Falcon surprised them all. She said, "No, I shan't. I—I will take my chances—whatever they are."

Removing his contrivance, Doc offered it to the woman. She pushed it away stubbornly.

There was no time to argue about it, only time to keep running. So they ran, but Janet Falcon finally accepted the protective device. Doc Savage possessed the remarkable ability to hold his breath for an astonishing period of time. Compressing his lips, he applied a spare spring clamp to his nostrils, effectively sealing them.

When, winded, they reached a point where they felt they had put sufficient distance between them and the collapsing coal mine, they stopped for breath.

As a group, they turned around and tried to make out what they could in the absence of moonlight.

The uproar had caused roosting birds to fling themselves up out of the trees, and any bushes where they might be.

Birds were circling around, fluttering and twittering. An unsettling thing began happening then.

Many of the birds started dropping from the sky. They fell in groups; others, seeing the uncanny fate that befell their fellows, took wing for distant parts.

Soon, there were no birds visible in the sky.

Monk muttered, "There musta been some poisonous stuff like chokedamp or firedamp in that old mine."

"No," said Janet Falcon slowly. "It was not poison gas. Not in the way you imagine."

They all looked at her.

Doc Savage asked quietly, "Do you know something you wish to share with us?"

Janet Falcon shook her head numbly. "No. Not at this time."

"Is it your opinion that anyone trapped in that mine could not possibly survive?"

"Yes, that is my firm opinion. There would be no survivors."

Her voice was dull, and all the light seemed to have drained out of her.

"That was the last of the Grogan gang, wasn't it?" she asked.

"All but the ones left in the coal-washing plant," said Doc. "And they were likely overcome, as well."

Janet Falcon stared out into the night, as if measuring distances.

"My guess is that the fumes would have reached the plant. If so, there could be no survivors there, either."

THEY waited an hour before Doc Savage investigated.

The gas masks of the others had already run empty of their supply of oxygen. Doc Savage's simple device worked to filter out chemical substances, for he breathed through his mouth only via the sponge filter. He had reclaimed this from Janet Falcon.

The bronze man considered whether to enter the coal-washing plant for some time before he drifted down in that direction. He had great confidence in his filter, but once again he was facing an unknown danger.

Doc reached the two men who had been put to sleep by his anesthetic gas balls, and they were not breathing.

Taking a scalpel from one pocket, he inserted the implement into one nostril and then the other of both men. This produced a gritty sound that he had come to know well.

Next, Doc went to the machine gunner who had stood guard before Janet Falcon's makeshift cell. Doc did not need to use a scalpel to ascertain the man had died as a result of his brain petrifying. The lack of respiration and strangely-sunken eyes told him all he needed to know.

Doc Savage made a thorough search of the coal plant, and found no other bodies. Only the gangster hat that landed on the roof. The outrush of violently expelled air had blown it to the ground.

Next, he moved toward the mine, and shone an ordinary flashlight into the portal. The powerful beam did not penetrate very far, but there was no sound, not of digging or cries for help or anything. All was still. Deathly still.

Doc worked his way around the face of the mine, looking for other means of egress, but the air was so cloudy with grit, his eyes struggled. The special goggles were only useful with the infra-red lantern, which was now lost. So they did not help.

Finally, Doc Savage rejoined the others, saying, "It appears that there were no survivors."

Monk offered, "So the Grogan outfit has been snuffed out."

"No great loss," commented Long Tom.

Ham's brow furrowed. "Is this then the end of the brain-petrifying menace we have been investigating?"

Once again, all gazes turned toward Janet Falcon.

"I confess that I do not know," she said wearily. "I would like to go home now."

"You will have to make a full statement about what you do know," advised Doc.

Janet Falcon nodded. "I understand that. But not here. I am very tired."

That seemed to be final, so they made their way back to the big bronze speed plane that Monk had left parked on the approach road to the mine.

As they trudged back to the waiting aircraft, they saw police lights flashing red.

Reaching the roadway, they saw that the way was blocked. A police roadblock had been established on either side of the shelter belt of trees behind which rested the big bronze-skinned bird.

"Looks like the local cops found our bus," remarked Monk.

"Let us hope they did not discover Joe Shine and his mob inside," murmured Ham.

The police had. For they had forced open the hatch door, something that took special tools and a great deal of patience, for Doc's planes were armored against bullets and burglary both.

There was a police sergeant in charge of the detail, and Doc Savage approached him. There was no issue of the bronze giant's identity, even fantastically armored as he was. His metallic features and close-fitting hair so remindful of a skullcap identified him instantly.

"Is this your plane, Mr. Savage?" the sergeant asked.

"It is," admitted the bronze man.

"We found Joe Shine and his mob sleeping inside. What can you tell me about that?"

Doc said, "I have full authority from the Superintendent of Chicago police to make arrests."

"What are the charges?"

"Attempted murder, kidnapping and several others."

That seemed to satisfy the sergeant. "Well, we'll take them off your hands now. You might explain it all to the superintendent when he wakes up in the morning."

Dawn had yet to creep as far west as Illinois, but it was not far beyond the horizon.

Doc Savage said nothing. He did not wish to turn Joe Shine and his boys over to the police, but there was no getting around it now.

Doc told the officer, "There was a cave-in at the mine yonder. Inside were some of Duke Grogan's men, but it appears that they perished in the cave-in. There is no hope for them."

The sergeant beamed. "That's a hell of a good night's work, Mr. Savage. You bagged the Joe Shine mob and put a period to the reign of Duke Grogan. The state owes you a debt of gratitude."

Doc said, "Thank you. It has been a long night. We would like to take possession of our plane and return to the city."

"Be my guest. Go catch up on your sleep. We can sort this out later today."

Joe Shine's sleeping mob were loaded into the backs of assorted squad cars. There was not enough room or sufficient seats, so the police flung some of them into the trunks of their machines, rudely slamming down the lids. They appeared to be quite pleased about the matter.

Doc Savage had neglected to mention that the woman accompanying him was the missing Janet Falcon. He did not wish her to fall into police custody just yet.

Once the plane had been emptied, the police departed in a procession, a gaudy gangster necktie flapping from the closed trunk lid of the trailing squad car.

Everyone climbed aboard and while Long Tom closed the cabin door, Doc Savage started up the engines.

No one had much to say. It had been a long night and now that it was concluding, fatigue was setting in. Even Doc Savage showed faint traces of strain on his metallic features.

Easing the throttle open, Doc urged the bronze aircraft rumbling along the macadam road, until the tail lifted and the plane climbed, striving for altitude.

Pointing the bawling engines north, Doc Savage set a course for Chicago and its municipal airport.

No coddler of criminals, Doc nonetheless regretted very much the Joe Shine outfit falling into police custody. He knew that some of those men faced long prison sentences for their past crimes—and conceivably the electric chair for a man or two.

"Too bad about the police nabbing the Shine mob," murmured Ham.

Monk said callously, "As long as they're out of circulation, that suits me."

"What were you going to do with them?" Janet Falcon wanted to know.

No one bothered to respond. Janet Falcon took the hint. She subsided in her seat. Her emerald eyes took on a faraway look, and her composed face had a drained, bloodless cast to it.

Silence dominated the flight all the way to the metropolis of Chicago.

Chapter XXXIII

TWISTS

IT WAS FULL morning by the time the taxicab had dropped Doc Savage and his party off at the Hotel Chicago in the heart of the Loop.

As they exited, Janet Falcon remained seated. Poking her disheveled head out the open window, she said plaintively, "If you do not mind, Mr. Savage, I would much prefer to travel on to my apartment."

Doc told her, "That would not be wise. Two attempts to kidnap you have already taken place. You will be safer with us."

Firmness showed in her set features. "I am afraid that I must insist."

Doc showed her the Superintendent's letter and said, "Consider yourself in my custody."

The woman's lips thinned bloodlessly. "Very well, if you insist."

Getting out, she allowed herself to be escorted into the deserted lobby and on to the elevator.

There, Janet Falcon hesitated. "I rather prefer my own hotel room—the one Mr. McLean arranged for me."

"Time enough for sleep later," advised Doc. "I would like to take your statement as soon as possible."

"I—I am not up to any such ordeal," she said evasively.

They were in the elevator now, rising to the upper floors.

Doc said firmly, "It should not take long, Miss Falcon. Afterward, you will no doubt wish to make arrangements for your late fiancé's funeral."

Janet Falcon's pale face turned starkly white.

"Ned!" she choked. "Where… is… he—his body, I mean?"

Doc Savage stated, "Arrangements were made for his remains to be returned to Chicago for burial."

Fighting back tears, the woman nodded. She seemed like a delicate handkerchief that had been wrung out of all its absorbed tears.

They entered the suite, and Janet Falcon threw herself on the divan, looking more than a little lost.

Doc Savage was moving about the hotel suite, evidently uncomfortable with the woman's display of grief. He slipped into the next chamber. He was out of sight but a minute.

Monk Mayfair froze, startled, listening to an eerie sound which had come into being. Remindful of ghostly cicadas, it swelled into a unitary chorus of disembodied musical notes before dwindling to nothingness.

The homely chemist looked at Ham, puzzled. It was Doc Savage's sound, which he only made in moments of mental stress. Moved by the same thought, Monk and Ham rushed to the connecting door which led to the other rooms of their suite. They got the door open.

"What is it, Doc?" Monk exploded.

The bronze man stood in the center of the room. He was holding in one hand the cushion of a sofa chair, the seam of which he had opened.

"The evidence we had collected," the bronze man said. "The piece of Ned Gamble's petrified brain and the asthma powder Myer Sim had inhaled which evidently caused his death."

"What about them?" queried Ham.

"Gone," Doc Savage said quietly. "They were concealed in this cushion."

"Someone's been prowling in here," Monk muttered. "Whoever it was knew what he wanted and got it."

"Something else is missing," the bronze man pointed out. "The window shade bearing the Medusa silhouette we discovered in Myer Sim's den. I secreted it under this chair, but it is no longer there, either."

Monk peered about, shook his head. "This place don't look like it's even been searched."

"It *has* been searched," Doc Savage assured him. "The person who did the job was an expert. No ordinary examination would show that anything had been disturbed. Whoever did this has done the same thing a great many times before."

"You think that is significant?" Ham asked.

"It might be."

Ham firmed his lips. "Anyway, we still have one piece of evidence left."

From his coat pocket, the dapper lawyer produced the stony hand that had been found at Janet Falcon's apartment—the artifact they had for a time believed was the petrified hand of Long Tom Roberts. It was wrapped in a silk handkerchief. Ham unwrapped the thing.

The little casting of pale stone was a marvelous bit of workmanship. In every respect but one, it was very lifelike. The thumb was large and out of proportion to the rest. It revealed the expected tracery of fingerprint markings upon examination with Doc's pocket microscope.

"What is that?" asked Long Tom.

Ham told him, "This is the broken hand we found in a pile of rubble back at Miss Falcon's apartment. We thought the pile was all that was left of you, and this hand the only intact portion."

"That's crazy!" Long Tom exploded.

"That sore-lookin' thumb has your fingerprint," Monk pointed out.

Long Tom snatched the thing from Ham and examined the thumbprint with one doubtful eye, the other squeezed tightly.

"I don't know my own fingerprints from Adam," the puny electrical wizard related. "But this thumb is too big."

Monk allowed, "We kinda thought whoever turned you to stone and smashed your corpse with a hammer hit your thumb while you were still livin', and the thing kinda swelled up."

Long Tom favored the hairy chemist with a dubious look.

"Did it ever occur to you," he retorted, "that the thumb was made big so that the fingerprints could be cut into it?"

Monk's mouth dropped open, proving that it had not.

"That is the most reasonable explanation," imparted Doc.

Tossing the grisly relic back to Ham Brooks, the undersized electrical wizard snapped, "I'm going down to the lobby and collect some newspapers. The local press should be having a field day with last night's activities."

With that, Long Tom took his departure.

Ham shook his well-tonsured head violently.

"This whole thing is getting to be an incredible puzzle!" he snapped. "Men have been found dead in two cities, hideous greenish shadows near them. I can't understand that part of it."

"That," Doc Savage told him, "is probably the least significant part."

"Eh?" Ham looked interested.

"Let us talk to the young woman," Doc suggested.

Monk and Ham, realizing they had left Janet Falcon alone, whirled and dashed wildly into the other room. Much to their relief, she was still there.

The attractive young woman seemed not at all interested in what was going on.

Doc Savage addressed Janet Falcon.

"When we last saw you, Miss Falcon, you were being kidnapped by Duke Grogan. Why?"

Janet Falcon flushed. Her head came up and she bathed the bronze man with a frigid stare. "You should ask him."

"Grogan is believed to be dead," continued Doc, unperturbed. "He was shot by an as-yet unidentified person."

The bronze giant's words seemed to sting the woman. She patted at her head. Her long fall of hair had become undone. She was absently toying with it, a faraway look in her eyes.

Doc reminded, "During the abduction, you attempted to impart something before your outcry was smothered."

"You will have to refresh my memory," Janet Falcon said thinly. "It has been a difficult night."

"I distinctly heard you say, 'Gorgoni,' which in the Italian language is the plural for Gorgon. But I do not think you know that fact. Therefore, you were trying to communicate something else entirely."

"Perhaps you misheard me. I believe I was berating Duke Grogan. The names sound similar, as I am sure you are well aware."

Lowering her head, she turned her back on the bronze man.

Doc said, "Monk, prepare a dose of truth serum."

"Gotcha." The homely chemist went in search of his portable chemical laboratory.

That seemed to shake the young woman of her resistance. "No! Please, I am prepared to divulge all that I know."

At a glance of Doc's golden eyes, Monk subsided.

Doc Savage attempted another approach. "How did this chain of grisly events get started?" he queried.

The girl showed a little spirit. "With Ned Gamble, my fiancé. As you know, he is a mineralogist—or was. He made a discovery so terrible that it got out of hand. Ned was being threatened in some way, but refused to share details. Ned did not know which way to turn, then he had lighted on a way of bringing you into the affair. He was going to get you to come to Chicago."

"For what purpose?"

"There is some kind of a horrible mystery behind this whole affair. Ned wanted to get you working on it, hoping you would clear it up without involving the authorities. But something went wrong."

"This is rather a circular explanation," Doc stated. "What went wrong?"

"The master mind, whoever is behind all this, found out that Ned was going to New York," said the girl, twisting her handkerchief miserably. "Shortly before he left, Mr. Sim was found dead. Then I received a letter. It informed me that if I did not do exactly as I was told to do, Ned would be killed next. I was scared. The writer of the letter telephoned me, speaking in a horrible, hissing voice. I pretended to agree to do what he or she wanted. My first order was to refuse to speak with you."

"During the rest of the affair, you were under threat to be quiet?" Doc Savage demanded.

"I was."

"Where is this letter?" queried Doc.

"I am afraid that I burned it. The telephone voice instructed me to do so."

"Was the letter signed?"

"It was. *M.S. Euryale.* The name meant nothing to me. It seemed unreal. And there was no such person in the Chicago telephone directory."

"Or any other," stated Doc Savage. "For the name is one plucked out of Greek mythology. Euryale is one of the three Gorgon sisters. The other two are Medusa and Stheno. By invoking all three names, this unknown person was attempting to incite terror."

Ham put in, "I still do not understand what Myer Sim has to do with this?"

"I never did learn," replied the girl. "But I do know that Ned spoke to Mr. Sim about the matter, and Mr. Sim gave a statement to the press just before his death that he had learned something of grave medical significance. It was his going public that alarmed Ned, and prompted Ned's mission to New York City. I gather that Ned confided in Mr. Sim, but I was never told what they feared—no doubt to protect me, I can now see."

"And where did Malcolm McLean come in?" Ham pressed.

"He was merely an acquaintance. I knew him through Ned. They were friends, and often spoke of working together, but as far as I know, nothing ever came of this talk. The other day, Mr. McLean happened to telephone my apartment looking for Ned, and I blurted out that Ned was packing for a trip. Mr. McLean became very solicitous."

"Who knew that Ned Gamble was coming to New York to see me?" asked Doc.

"Only Ned and myself—and Mr. McLean, in whom I confided."

Monk grunted, "Someone tipped off Duke Grogan that your boyfriend was takin' a train to see Doc Savage. If it wasn't you, it had to be McLean."

Janet Falcon looked stunned. "I—I can scarcely imagine such an act of treachery. It—it seems so out of character. While he never came out and declared such, I have always harbored the suspicion that Mr. McLean rather had a crush on me. Of course, he would keep any such feelings to himself, out of respect for poor Ned."

"A motive!" exploded Monk. "That cinches it. McLean tipped off Duke Grogan, then Grogan trailed him to New York."

The woman jumped up from her seat, paling. "Oh! That cannot be. It isn't possible."

Ham Brooks interjected coolly, "Men have been slain for much weaker motivations."

Janet Falcon was again wringing her sopping handkerchief. Her composed features were white as bone.

"And now Mr. McLean is himself dead." She shuddered uncontrollably. "If what you say is true, he has paid for his misdeeds—for no doubt he was killed during the cave-in."

Monk and Ham looked to the bronze man for confirmation of this theory, but the expression on the bronze giant's metallic features was as unreadable as that of a cigar-store Indian.

JUST then, the telephone rang. Doc Savage glided to the instrument stand and scooped up the handset.

"Doc Savage speaking."

The voice on the other end launched into what appeared to be a wordy speech. At its conclusion, the bronze man said, "Thank you."

Restoring the telephone to its cradle, he addressed the others.

"That was the Superintendent of Police with some unfortunate news. Joe Shine's attorney turned up at police headquarters with a judge's order to release the gangster on bail. Shine has been freed."

"How is that possible?" howled Monk. "We got him dead to rights on kidnappin' and attempted murder. Any judge woulda thrown the book at him!"

Ham frowned, saying, "Any honest judge, you mean. You are forgetting that this is Chicago. And a writ of habeas corpus was filed to facilitate the man's release."

Doc Savage said, "This might be for the best, after all."

"How's that?" wondered Monk.

"No doubt Shine will go directly to his home. We will go there and return the favor."

Ham blinked. "What favor?"

In recognition of the fact that Janet Falcon could hear every word spoken, the bronze man switched to speaking Mayan, the almost unknown language which they used amongst themselves when they did not wish to be understood by outsiders.

"The favor of kidnapping you and Monk," replied Doc. "We are going to kidnap him ourselves and spirit Joe Shine to our college, where we intended to consign him in the first place."

Monk grinned. "While we're at it, we should look up that crooked judge and add him to the pile."

"Time enough for that later. When Long Tom returns, we will go after Joe Shine."

But when Long Tom Roberts showed up a minute later, he was as excited as a human spark plug.

"Doc! Take a look at this headline. It's about Malcolm McLean."

"They found his body?" suggested Ham.

"Body? According to this, he's not even dead!"

Chapter XXXIV

DEAD MAN ALIVE

THE HEADLINE TOOK their breath away:

MEDICO RESTORES DEAD MAN TO LIFE!

Word of a medical miracle rocked Chicago this morning when it was announced that Malcolm McLean, a chemist who was mysteriously struck down at the scientific exposition yesterday and transported to Mercy General Hospital, has been brought back to the world of the living.

The miracle man behind this modern medical wonder is the esteemed Dr. Warner Rockwell. Dr. Rockwell was one of the first on the scene when the corpse was discovered yesterday. The quick-witted medico requested that McLean's body be taken to Mercy General rather than the morgue, as is custom when individuals are pronounced dead.

By all accounts, Malcolm McLean had lost his life. Arriving at Mercy General, the supposedly deceased man was subjected to a battery of medical tests, including a fluoroscopic examination which showed that his brain had been turned into a solid mass. It is at this writing unknown what had struck down McLean, but the agency was so malign that not only was McLean's brain petrified, but his attached eyeballs had also taken on the appearance of stone.

"During my initial examination," Rockwell told reporters this morning, "I had assumed that the patient's brain had been petrified in some strange manner. Close examination revealed that it had actually been calcified, which is an entirely different matter. By whatever means, a deposit of calcium had built up very rapidly in the man's brain and I reasoned that, if I acted swiftly, it might be possible to reverse the process. Since the patient no longer evinced a heartbeat or respiration, it seemed that there would be no compelling reason not to undertake the procedure I had in mind. The exact details I must keep to myself. Within hours, the process had begun to reverse itself. By early evening, Malcolm McLean had been restored to normalcy."

The article went on to delineate the fact that the procedure had been so effectual that McLean had been released from the hospital by early evening, to all appearances perfectly normal and healthy once more. This was against the advice of Dr. Rockwell, but McLean appeared outwardly unaffected by his ordeal, and desired nothing more than to return to his home and hearth.

Dr. Warner Rockwell was being hailed as a hero. There was no doubt but that he had pulled off a Lazarusian resurrection against all odds.

There was passing mention that the noted scientist and surgeon known publicly as Doc Savage had also been present at the discovery of the stricken man, but had not contributed to the medical resurrection.

Long Tom had brought up several different Chicago news-papers and distributed them among the others. So each of Doc's men had his own sheet to peruse.

Except for an understandable amount of sensationalism, every report agreed in the basic particulars. Malcolm McLean, who in life resembled a walking corpse, had been restored to life, still looking like a freakish animated cadaver, but no longer a victim of the uncanny power that petrified human brains.

Ham Brooks was the first to speak. "I don't believe a word of this!"

Monk Mayfair was raging, "It can't be done! You can't calcify a man's brain and then decalcify it, any more than you could leach the accumulated minerals out of a fossil and end up with a livin' organism. It just ain't possible."

Doc Savage stated, "Every newspaper seems to agree that this has been done."

Long Tom said disgustedly, "I'll believe that Malcolm McLean is alive when I punch him in the snoot—which I intend to do at my earliest opportunity. I still owe him for braining me with that lamp."

Turning to the others, Doc Savage said, "This changes our plans. Monk, you will accompany me to the hospital. Ham, you and Long Tom go to Joe Shine's residence, and seize him if you can. Bring him to the airport and lock him in our plane until we can make arrangements for his transportation."

They held their conference in a room apart from Janet Falcon, and now Doc Savage went out to her and said, "You may repair to your hotel room. But be advised that you should remain there until you receive permission to return home."

"Why am I being held prisoner like this?"

"Because your life is clearly in danger. And it is my duty to protect you."

That seemed to mollify the anxious woman. Without another word, she took her departure. The fact that she did not slam the door behind her indicated that she was in a better humor than previously.

After the door shut, Ham Brooks remarked, "Her behavior is sometimes reasonable, but more often not."

"You can't trust a dame!" observed Long Tom. This was not considered to be an objective opinion, for Long Tom Roberts was no fan of the fairer sex. "Besides, wasn't Medusa a woman?"

All eyes went to Doc Savage.

Doc said, "Miss Falcon's responses to our questions have not been satisfactory. Her story has holes. At the mine, she definitely stated that the escaping gasses were not ordinary. Nor was she forthcoming about her cryptic reference to Gorgoni."

Ham asked, "You suspect her, then?"

"When we return," stated the bronze man firmly, "we will see how her story holds up under truth serum."

For the first time, Doc revealed the vision he had encountered in the coal mine, before the tremendous cave-in.

"For the love of Mike!" yelled Monk. "A livin' Medusa in the modern age!"

Ham marveled, "That sounds positively unreal."

"By all appearances," said Doc, "it *was* unreal. Regrettably, that apparition appears to have perished in the mine collapse, along with the last of Duke Grogan's gang."

"Sounds like this Gorgon problem is about wrapped up," remarked Monk.

Doc shook his head somberly. "Hardly. For I spied something in the slurry impoundment pool that greatly resembled the body of Malcolm McLean."

Ham frowned. "If you discovered McLean's body, then that man has died a second time."

"So it appears," said Doc cryptically. "But appearances, as you know, are often deceiving."

With that, the bronze man led them out of the hotel suite and down to the street, where they claimed separate machines. Ham took the rental sedan while Doc hailed a taxicab. The vehicles promptly whirled them off in different directions.

THERE was a police cordon around Mercy General Hospital when the hack deposited Doc Savage and Monk Mayfair a block away.

"I can't let you off any closer," apologized the cabbie, "on account of the cops."

"We understand," said the bronze man, paying the driver.

Doc and Monk approached on foot, and Doc Savage, towering over the crowd, soon saw the reason for the commotion.

Fully all of Chicago's Fourth Estate were clamoring to get into the hospital lobby, and the reason was evident from their excited shouting.

"We just wanna talk to Dr. Rockwell!" one yelled.

The police sergeant retorted hotly, "He's already given the press a statement. There will be no more interviews for today. Now kindly be on your way."

The assembled Chicago reporters were having none of it. They looked as if they were prepared to lay siege to the hospital building until they got their way.

Looking around for another way in, one of their number spotted Doc Savage's metallic features looming over all.

"Hey!" he shouted. "That sure looks like Doc Savage. Maybe he'll give us a statement."

The press was soon surging in the bronze man's direction, and the police could do nothing about it, since their efforts were concentrated on keeping the reporters out of the hospital.

Growling a warning, Monk Mayfair stepped before the bronze man, looking like a football player preparing to block the opposing team by dint of might and menace.

Doc Savage stated quietly, "If we are to enter that hospital, the press cannot be avoided."

"I don't mind knocking a few blocks off," returned the apish chemist, "just so we don't get tied up all day."

Instead of replying, the bronze giant stepped around his aide, and stood for questions. They came in a wordy flurry.

"Mr. Savage, what do you think of Dr. Rockwell's miracle cure?"

"Until there is an opportunity to confer with Dr. Rockwell," stated Doc, "comment on that subject would be inadvisable."

Another demanded, "What do you think is petrifying all these people's brains?"

"That is unknown," replied Doc.

"Is that why you came to Chicago?"

"We do not speak publicly about our investigations," Doc told the man.

Reporters were swiftly scribbling in their notepads, and a few flashbulbs popped, capturing perfect likenesses of Doc Savage's impassive features.

The bronze man disliked publicity, and did not care to have his photograph taken. Under the circumstances, there was nothing he could do about it—if he intended to enter the hospital.

"What about that scrape you got into with Duke Grogan's gang yesterday," one scribe pressed. "What can you tell us about that?"

"The police will no doubt be offering an official statement later today," Doc related.

Monk Mayfair spoke up in his squeaky voice, saying, "That's enough for today. Make way, you dog-eared mutts. Doc Savage has business in that hospital."

The reporters were stubborn, and they pressed forward with more questions. One was Jack Swangle, the reporter who had broadcast Doc's arrival in Chicago, resulting in unnecessary complications.

"Looks like Dr. Rockwell stole a march on you, Savage," he suggested meaningly.

That was not a question, but it was cleverly calculated to elicit a quotable reply.

The bronze man said nothing, however. Monk began using his long arms to pry open a hole in the press of reporters through which the bronze giant could navigate.

Hats began falling off heads and smoldering cigarettes dropped out of slack mouths.

"Hey!" a scribe shouted. "Watch who you're shoving there!"

"Make a hole," Monk growled. "We're comin' through if I have to step on faces."

The burly chemist's unusually long arms began flinging reporters about, and he took care to step on such toes as strayed near him.

Between pushing, shoving and stepping on tender corns, Monk created a passage through which Doc Savage moved easily.

The police stepped in at that point and started using their nightsticks to prod close-pressing reporters into giving the bronze giant a wide berth.

In this way, Doc Savage and Monk finally reached the hospital entrance and entered the lobby, which was at the moment forbidden to all reporters, regardless of their standing.

At the nurse's station, Doc Savage asked, "Where is Dr. Rockwell at this moment?"

"In his office," the bronze man was told.

"And the patient, Malcolm McLean?"

"The patient was released last night, at his own insistence."

"That is rather unusual for a man who came close to death, is it not?" queried Doc.

"Very unusual," the nurse agreed. "But Dr. Rockwell gave him a clean bill of health, and there was no medical reason to keep him overnight."

Monk made a skeptical noise in his throat, but said nothing.

Dr. Rockwell's office was on the fourth floor, the helpful nurse imparted to Doc Savage.

"Thank you," said the bronze man, moving in the direction of the elevators.

Neither he nor Monk spoke until the elevator closed. It was a modern elevator, having its own push-button and no operator.

"A guy who had his brains turned to stone doesn't just up and walk out of the hospital after treatment," commented the apish chemist.

Doc Savage said nothing. His flake-gold eyes flickered speculatively.

The elevator soon let them off and they found their way to Dr. Rockwell's office.

"Who is it?" asked Rockwell gruffly, after Doc knocked twice.

"Doc Savage. May we enter?"

Dr. Rockwell appeared at the door, throwing it open. He regarded the bronze man and Monk with his unnerving eyes, which seemed never to blink.

Mouth warping with humor, the medico remarked dryly, "I imagine you've received word of McLean's rather miraculous revival."

"We are interested in your findings," stated Doc.

Rockwell stepped aside to allow his visitors to enter and gestured toward two empty seats arrayed before his desk.

Taking the chair behind his own desk, Rockwell steepled his fingers and said in a measured tone, "I do not know what I am prepared to share with you, Dr. Savage. The significance of what I've accomplished is only just now sinking in."

Doc said, "You yourself pronounced McLean dead less than twenty-four hours ago."

Rockwell nodded. "So he appeared. But I had a hunch. I do not have to tell you, Savage, about rare conditions such as catalepsy, or suspended animation."

Doc nodded. "In unusual cases, persons have been revived after being immersed in frozen ponds, or even have come alive on the autopsy table, after having been pronounced expired."

"Every doctor has heard of or encountered such situations. Throughout history, there have been reliable reports of people who have actually been interred, only to awaken in their own tomb, calling out for help. Medical science has yet to explain these cases, yet the facts are beyond dispute."

"Go on," prompted Doc Savage. Nothing in the bronze man's features indicated doubt.

Rockwell continued, "Knowing that McLean had died very rapidly with no external injuries, I considered the possibility that his condition might be reversible. I confess I do not yet understand the nature of what afflicted him, only that I had a hunch and I acted upon it."

"You and McLean have been friends for some time," suggested Doc.

"As a matter of fact, I am McLean's personal physician. And that gave me a certain interest in his case, as well as a professional responsibility to do all I could to assist the man."

Doc vouchsafed. "We are very interested in how you managed to reverse the calcification of Malcolm McLean's brain matter. As a physician, this is of interest to me. Additionally, my associate, Monk, is curious about the chemical processes involved."

"It don't make any sense to me!" exploded Monk. "Every school boy knows how bodies of animals are fossilized, but that takes millions of years. Turnin' it around beats me all hollow."

Dr. Rockwell smiled thinly. There was a light in his dark eyes that seemed to be a mixture of professional pride and perhaps a touch of ego.

"I never thought I would see the day that I would baffle the great Doc Savage," he murmured. "Rather an interesting turnabout, isn't it?"

Crisply, Doc cut the man off. "There are other victims of this petrifying influence. It is probably too late for them, having perished days ago, but if there is any chance of reviving any of them, you are obligated to share your discovery."

Rockwell compressed his lips. "The only other victim I am aware of is poor Myer Sim. And he has already been autopsied." He frowned distastefully. "There is no reversing that procedure, unfortunately. As for sharing my discovery, I will have to consult my attorney about that. This process may be patentable."

Monk yelled, "Patentable! People have been droppin' like flies, and you claim to be the only guy who can save them."

"Do not fear," returned Dr. Rockwell patiently. "If another victim turns up, I stand ready to move on a moment's notice and apply my process in the hope of restoring that unfortunate one to life."

"That is your final word?" said Doc Savage.

Craggy features firm, Rockwell remarked, "I am sorry to disappoint you, Dr. Savage. I hold you in very high esteem, as does every other medical man in the country, if not the world. In this case, a peculiar Fate had anointed *me* Man of the Hour, and I wish to savor it before making any decisions."

With that, Warner Rockwell stood up, signaling that the meeting was over.

Doc and Monk likewise left their seats and Rockwell offered his hand in farewell. But Doc Savage appeared to miss the gesture, and quickly departed, Monk Mayfair following behind him, his tiny eyes narrow with suspicion.

Once they were on the elevator, Monk growled, "Do you buy his story?"

"There is insufficient basis to either accept or reject Rockwell's assertions. But the fact that Malcolm McLean is alive and walking about suggests that this process of brain calcification may not be as final as previously thought."

"I don't get you."

"Up to this point, we have believed, based on our own investigations, that victim's brains had been turned entirely to calcium carbonate. It may be possible that only a shell of calcium forms around the brain matter in some cases."

"You mean that the brain just stops operatin', but is still alive under that shell?"

"It is difficult to know what to believe, since the victim's heart stopped beating and respiration also ceased. All of these biological activities, as you know, are regulated by the brain. But if there is a way to dissolve that shell, normal life processes might be persuaded to return."

"This is startin' to get my goat," complained Monk.

"And mine," stated the bronze man frankly.

The elevator reached the ground floor. As they stepped off the cage, Monk asked, "Where to next?"

"Let us pay a visit to Malcolm McLean, if we can find him," said Doc. "I wish to see with my own eyes that he is still living."

Monk grunted, "How are we gonna be able to tell? The guy makes Count Dracula look to be in the pink of condition."

Stepping out into the lobby, they ran into a fresh hubbub.

The noisy press of reporters was back to trying to force their way through the police cordon, and the bluecoats were pushing back with all their muscular might.

A lobby guard saw Doc and Monk and rushed over in a lather.

"What's going on now?" demanded Monk.

"Aw, they're all riled up over the news."

"What news?" inquired Doc Savage.

"The news that Joe Shine got out on bail, only to wind up dead."

"Dead!" roared Monk. "What got him?"

"They think his brain got turned into a rock," related the guard.

Chapter XXXV

THE BLACKEST MAGIC

OWING TO THE necessity of transporting in secret the gangster Joe Shine to Doc Savage's hangared plane, Ham Brooks had taken the bronze man's rental sedan, a public taxi hardly being appropriate for the task.

Ham piloted the nondescript machine toward Little Sicily, on the north side of Chicago. The neighborhood soon became a monotonous thing of brick row houses whose roofs were festooned with radio receiving aerials.

In the front seat beside the dapper lawyer, Long Tom Roberts was fiddling with his clumsy-looking magnetic pistol.

"Watch you don't set that thing off prematurely," Ham scolded.

"Don't worry about it," Long Tom retorted. "This beauty has a safety just like an ordinary pistol. It won't go off until I want it to."

Ham sniffed, "I fail to see why you think such a contraption is superior to one of Doc's supermachine pistols."

Long Tom took no special umbrage at that remark. "Sometimes we've got to rush into situations, and all the racket of a mercy gun gives our positions away. This nifty device is built around a magnetic coil. When I pull the trigger, instead of a firing pin dropping on a cartridge primer, the coil is charged and steel slugs race down the barrel. They hardly make any sound at all. Just kind of a whispering noise. And that's the sound of the bullet, not the noise of the gun."

Ham nodded somberly, saying, "I can see your reasoning. Speaking for myself, I think the roar of a supermachine pistol is so frightening that it often unnerves our foes. Some just throw up their hands and surrender, instead of firing back."

Long Tom made a face as he thought about that. "Good point," he allowed. "Maybe I can add a noisemaker to this thing that can be switched on when we need to make a fuss."

Ham said, "You say it fires hypodermic needles?"

"Yep. They go right in, injecting the knockout stuff. You know, mercy bullets will sometimes break against thick layers of clothing, and don't get through. These hypo needles will puncture anything. The needles operate pneumatically. Once they hit, the dope squirts out from the reservoir portion of the round."

This explanation appeared to satisfy the elegant attorney. At length, he declared, "I believe I would like to see that gun in operation one day."

Long Tom spanked the mechanism energetically. "Maybe today is that day. I don't think Joe Shine is going to go quietly. Especially when he sees our faces."

Ham frowned. "With his mob all in jail, he may not put up much resistance."

"Hoods like Joe Shine can whistle up fresh muscle any time they want. By now he may be surrounded by new bodyguards."

"We shall soon see," said Ham determinedly.

THE RESIDENCE of gangster Joe Shine was rather modest for a man of his means. This was calculated. In recent years, hoodlums of Shine's ilk had been incarcerated, not upon conviction for their crimes, but due to their failure to pay income tax. Therefore, it behooved the gang lord to give every appearance of a modest style of living.

The house stood in a nice residential neighborhood on a quiet street. The home was two stories tall with an attached garage and a circular driveway. Shrubbery appeared immaculate, even having been denuded of all leafage by the change of seasons.

There were two oak trees in the front yard, and a few surviving Autumn leaves still clung to them. But the dying lawn was spotless. Not a solitary fallen leaf was in evidence. This meant that the house employed a diligent gardener.

All appearance of outward respectability, however, was belied by the fact that two men patrolled the grounds, wearing heavy overcoats which failed to completely conceal the bulge of heavy automatics nestled in shoulder holsters.

Having parked just up the street, Ham fell to watching through a pair of binoculars, and spotted the pair.

"It appears that you are correct," the dapper lawyer murmured.

"About what?" wondered Long Tom.

"There are two men stationed before the Shine residence, and judging by their behavior, they are not there to rake fallen leaves."

Taking the binoculars from Ham's hands, Long Tom growled, "Let me see."

After adjusting the focusing screw, the pallid electrical wizard remarked, "They look like perfect targets for my magnetic gun."

Ham considered that. "Be my guest," he said at last.

"Drive by slowly," suggested Long Tom. "I'll hit them and then we can double back and take the place."

Getting the machine into gear, Ham observed, "If that weapon is as silent as you say, they will not suspect a thing."

The sedan nosed away from the curbing, and tooled past the quiet house.

Cranking down the window on his side, Long Tom unlatched the safety lever, and pointed the distorted barrel in the direction of one of the men. He squeezed the trigger once.

Nothing seemed to happen in the immediate vicinity of the weapon. It was entirely silent in operation. The sound made by the missile escaping the barrel was negligible.

The end result was that the man's hat flew off.

The guard looked momentarily startled, and gave out a yelp. The other guard came trotting up and started wondering loudly what the hell was going on?

Redirecting the barrel, Long Tom potted the second thug in one shoulder.

The man did not react in the typical way of a gunshot victim. For the slug did not strike him with any great velocity. Instead, he suddenly grabbed at his shoulder as if stung by a bee.

It was the hatless guard's turn to demand what was happening.

He received a reply in the form of a silent hypodermic bullet, which caught him on the back of his hand. A vein was punctured. Blood spurted.

Now he gave out a cry of alarm, but almost immediately collapsed in a heap beside the other, who also fell to the ground.

"It worked!" crowed Long Tom. "Now let's charge the place!"

Ham killed the engine, coasted to the curb, and they popped out of the angled machine.

Streaking up the circular driveway, they came to the spot where the two hoodlums had fallen. Ham demanded of Long Tom, "Why did you shoot his hat off first?"

"It was an accident," retorted Long Tom. "This thing has no recoil, and I'm used to compensating for the kick of a super-machine pistol."

"Help me drag them out of sight," said Ham.

Together, they pulled the pair into some shrubbery and left them there.

"Break a window next?" suggested Long Tom.

"I have a better idea," returned Ham firmly. "We will simply ring the doorbell."

Stepping up to the entryway, the dapper lawyer touched the push-button with the tip of his elegant cane. A satisfactory buzzing sound was heard.

When the front door opened, what passed for a butler showed his stern face. The man was not exactly dressed in traditional butler attire, but he had the demeanor of a manservant.

His voice, however, was coarse. "What do youse guys want?"

To Long Tom's surprise, Ham Brooks proffered a business card, saying, "Theodore Marley Brooks, Esquire. I am an attorney of some note. I have been retained by Mr. Shine about his legal complications."

It was such an audacious approach that the manservant accepted the card and said, "If that's the case, step right in, gents."

The fellow shifted to one side while Ham and Long Tom entered, the latter holding the magnetic gun carefully behind his back.

As the supposed butler was closing the door, Long Tom turned, shot him in the back, high up just between the shoulder blades. The bullets stuck out of his coat after impaling the flesh beneath.

Ham caught the stupefied one before he made too much noise in falling, then dragged him over to one side.

"I am becoming a believer in your magnetic gun," commented Ham tartly.

Grinning, Long Tom led the way, deeper into the dwelling.

A murmur of voices could be heard, and Ham Brooks immediately recognized the gruff tones of gang lord Joe Shine. Canvassing the first floor, they discovered the sounds were coming from behind closed doors.

The portals were of the type that slid apart, indicating a drawing room or den of some kind lay beyond.

Creeping up to the closed panels, Ham and Long Tom laid ears flat against the carved wood and listened carefully.

Behind the door, the rough voice of Joe Shine was saying, "I don't know how much hot water I'm in, but it will be your job to throw ice cubes into the pot. Cool everything down. Understand?"

An educated voice was saying in round tones, "Of course, Mr. Shine. I understand perfectly. You have kept your hands as clean as possible. This affair may be a small concern."

"Well, it will be a big concern if any of my boys start wagging their tongues to get out of jail."

"Your men are loyal. They also understand that, even behind bars, they are not safe from your reach."

Joe Shine laughed nastily. "You got that right. So many of my old mob have been locked up, I could hold a reunion in Joliet Prison. But that ain't my worry right now. Doc Savage and his boys are what's troubling me. If they testify against me, my goose is cooked."

"As your attorney, I can do little about Doc Savage prior to trial."

"You fixed the judge. Can't you fix anything related to Doc Savage?"

"I am afraid I cannot. I doubt that the President of the United States could fix Doc Savage. The man is practically a law unto himself."

Joe Shine's voice became low and strange. "That's what's worrying me. When Doc and his boys rounded us all up, they stored us in a plane over at the airport. It didn't look to me like they were planning on turnin' us over to the cops."

"What do you think they had planned?" returned Shine's attorney.

"I don't know. But from coast to coast, guys like me have run up against Doc Savage and vanished off the face of the earth. What do you make of that?"

The attorney was a long time in answering. Evidently, he was giving the matter considerable thought.

"Doc Savage has a reputation for avoiding the infliction of physical harm, not to mention death. It is out of the question that he intended to do away with you when your men were in his toils."

"What if that rep is just a front?" snapped Shine. "What if that's what his press agent puts out, but behind the scenes he's happy to knock off guys like me?"

"It does not follow. The Doc Savage reputation is sterling. Impeccable. No, Savage had something else in mind for you."

After absorbing this exchange, Long Tom whispered to Ham Brooks, "These two birds are getting awful close to the truth."

"Doc said nothing about taking this counsel," mused Ham, "but it appears that he is not exactly on the up and up either."

Long Tom lifted his strange magnetic gun, and used his thumb to switch the safety latch into the off position.

"On the count of three, we barge in," he whispered.

Ham Brooks unsheathed his sword-cane blade. "You take Joe Shine; allow me to dispose of this traitor to the bar."

"Deal," said Long Tom. They braced themselves.

While they were doing that, Joe Shine was saying, "That's funny."

"What is, Mr. Shine?" wondered the attorney.

"I got a funny ringin' in my ears all of a sudden."

"Now that you mention it, so do I. Whatever could it be?"

"Maybe it's these new cigars I got. The smoke smells a little funny, doesn't it?"

"Now that you mention it—"

The attorney's voice trailed off strangely.

Joe Shine was saying, "I roll these babies myself. I got the makings in a glass jar. Yeah, I got some foul leaves...."

Joe Shine's voice, too, trailed off. The lawyer did not respond.

THE SMELL of cigar smoke had not penetrated through the closed doors, but now Ham Brooks' delicate nostrils began sniffing, and he thought he detected some slight aroma of tobacco. It had a charcoal quality.

Long Tom was about to throw the door open when the white-faced barrister seized him and hissed, "No! Not now!"

"Why the heck not?"

"You were not in New York when Ned Gamble was felled while smoking a cigarette. It may be dangerous to enter."

Long Tom's high forehead puckered like the hide on a chicken that was being plucked.

Ham reached into his coat and pulled out a small gas mask, while signaling for Long Tom to do the same.

Hastily, the puny electrical wizard followed suit. Soon, he was wearing his protective mask.

No further conversation had penetrated the door, so they did not wait any longer.

Ham threw open the doors, which slid into wall recesses, and they stepped ahead.

The drawing room was wreathed in a grayish tobacco haze; their eyes fell upon Joe Shine seated behind a fumed oak desk.

Off to one side was the man they took to be Shine's lawyer lounged in an upholstered chair.

Neither man was moving.

Ham marched straight up to the attorney, looked him over through the smoke that was making his eyes smart, and remarked, "Jove!"

Long Tom had already reached the desk, and was pointing the magnetic gun at the center of Joe Shine's shirt front.

The crime czar was slumped in the wooden swivel chair, his cigar in his lap, his mouth hanging open, his hollowed eyes rolled up in his head.

Long Tom bleated, "He looks dead."

Ham had placed one hand over the other fellow's shirt front, feeling for a heartbeat. Finding none, he picked up the man's wrist and searched for a pulse.

"Dead!" Even muffled by the gas mask, his voice sounded horrible.

Both men noticed the smoldering cigars. They had already burned down to nubs. Stamping feet crushed the remains to powder.

Long Tom blurted, "What do we do now? No point in bundling them off to the college."

Ham was very quick-witted. He thought fast. Almost no time elapsed between that question and his reply.

"If Dr. Rockwell's process is sound, these two men may yet be saved. We must reach Doc Savage at once."

Prudently, they retreated to another part of the room, found the telephone, and asked the operator to be connected to Mercy General Hospital. An administrative functionary soon came on the line.

"This is Ham Brooks. I have an urgent message for Doc Savage, who is visiting your hospital. Inform him that Joe Shine and his attorney have succumbed to the strange brain-petrifying power. If action is undertaken swiftly, they yet may be saved."

The hospital operator promised to convey the message.

Long Tom and Ham Brooks returned to the den, where they threw open all windows in an attempt to clear out the tobacco smoke which was so strangely redolent of charcoal.

Joe Shine had four small boxes resting on the desk in front of him. In three of the boxes was black, ominous looking tobacco. In the fourth box was tobacco leaves suitable for wrappers. These last were as green as frog skins.

There were no cigars, however. Evidently, the deceased mobster rolled his own smokes.

Long Tom and Ham evacuated the dwelling to get as far away from the pernicious cigar smoke as humanly possible.

Chapter XXXVI

THE GORGON WARNS

AN AMBULANCE WAS dispatched from Mercy General Hospital to Joe Shine's suburban residence.

At the same time, the Superintendent of Police sent a Black Maria wagon with the intention of taking the bodies to the morgue.

The two vehicles arrived at approximately the same time, but the attendants were prevented from entering by Ham Brooks and Long Tom Roberts, who declared that the place was too dangerous for entry.

Doc Savage and Monk Mayfair arrived in a taxicab only seconds behind the ambulance, and the bronze man stepped into the middle of the argument, settling it with his imposing presence and backed by the letter from the Superintendent of Police of Chicago, which caused the morgue wagon attendants to back away, wearing glum expressions.

Ham explained to Doc Savage what had happened. The bronze man listened intently, and said, "I will go ahead and retrieve the bodies alone."

"I'll go with you," suggested Monk.

"Too dangerous," insisted the bronze man. "If I do not come out shortly, it will be your task to go in after me."

This made the face of Monk Mayfair grow slightly pale. It took a lot for him to lose his color. But the thought of Doc Savage succumbing to the brain-petrifying force did it.

Everyone remained well clear of the dwelling while Doc entered.

The ambulance internes and morgue attendants were greatly surprised to see the bronze giant emerge with one limp form slung under one arm and another thrown over his great shoulder.

Doc was wearing his gas mask. He watched as both bodies were shoved in the back of the ambulance, where the internes swiftly went to work on them.

Applying stethoscopes, they shook their heads in the negative. A pocket mirror held up to still nostrils produced no fog on the glass.

"Allow me," requested Doc, removing his gas mask.

The internes stepped out while the bronze man climbed in, and began examining the pair.

"No outward signs of life," he told the driver. "Take us to Mercy General at once."

The rear door was slammed shut and the ambulance took off, its raucous bell clanging.

The Black Maria fell in behind it, like a vulture following a dying animal. As a consolation, the occupants had taken possession of Joe Shine's still-sleeping bodyguards.

Monk, Ham and Long Tom piled into their sedan and took off in hot pursuit.

The three machines arrived at Mercy General's underground garage in short order, and the two apparent bodies were transferred to wheeled gurneys, then taken to separate examining rooms.

Dr. Warner Rockwell was waiting for them, unblinking eyes troubled.

Doc Savage informed him, "The men were found in a smoke-filled room, and we believe their cigars were laced with the calcifying chemical."

"You seem to think you know a lot about this," commented Rockwell.

Doc said nothing to that. Instead, he stated, "I would like to observe your attempt to revive these men."

"I am afraid that is out of the question, Dr. Savage. I am not yet ready to reveal my procedure to the world."

The bronze man appeared on the verge of objecting when Dr. Rockwell cut him off with the sharp chop of one upraised hand.

"Need I remind you that, just because I revived one man, does not mean I can repeat the process successfully. Furthermore, these men may have been subjected to a greater dose of whatever overcame them than was Malcolm McLean. I can make no promises as to the outcome. Only that I will try."

Eyes brittle, Doc Savage said, "Very well. We will await your report."

"Thank you," said Rockwell, following the gurney containing Joe Shine into the examining room, which was promptly shut.

Doc went to the room where the stricken attorney lay, waiting his turn.

With the permission of a police guard, Doc went through the man's pockets, removed his wallet and read the identification found therein.

"Gale Michaels," commented the guard. "He's a big-time mouthpiece in this town. Shine has been using him for years. He can get anybody off the hook. Or could. He doesn't look so active right now."

Doc Savage removed a scalpel from an inner pocket, and suggested to the police guard, "You might wish to turn around."

The cop laughed raucously. "I've been a Chicago cop for fifteen years now. I seen it all."

"As you wish," said Doc, inserting the scalpel into attorney Michaels' left nostril and producing an unpleasant scraping sound as of steel encountering stone.

Evidently, the police guard had not seen it all, as he had boasted. He grew a little green around the jowls, and excused himself hastily.

Doc Savage's examination was brief, but he was satisfied on one point: the attorney's brain had been calcified.

Pocketing the scalpel, he took an elevator to the lobby and rejoined Monk, Ham and Long Tom.

"Do you think Dr. Rockwell can pull off another miracle?" asked Ham.

"That remains to be seen," said Doc. "By all appearances, a poisoned cigar was back of this."

Long Tom offered, "Before he succumbed, Joe Shine claimed that he rolled his own cigars. That means the makings will be back at his house."

Doc said, "Long Tom, why don't you go back there and confiscate that tobacco. It will no doubt repay examination."

"I'll be back in a jiffy," said Long Tom, departing in haste.

Ham Brooks turned to hairy Monk and remarked, "Long Tom's magnetic gun impressed me greatly."

"Is that so?" growled Monk.

"Yes, that is so," nodded Ham. "He clipped the two body-guards with his hypodermic bullets, and they fell down faster than any man struck down by a mercy bullet that I ever witnessed."

"That could be," rumbled Monk. "But I've got bullets that nobody ain't ever seen yet. What they do to a man will make your eyes pop."

Ham gave his dark stick a supercilious twirl. "I will be very interested to see if you can outdo Long Tom in that department. But I think his magnetic gun is superlative in operation. I may take one up myself."

Listening to this exchange, Doc Savage broke in, remarking, "There is no telling how long Dr. Rockwell's process will take. Rather than wait, we might make good use of the time."

"What do you propose?" questioned Ham.

"A further investigation of the coal mine in Vermilion County might be in order."

"What do you expect to find up there?" wondered Ham.

"Last night, I spied a disturbance in the surface of a coal-slurry pond adjacent to the mine. What appeared to be a gray-faced body lay at the bottom. We might check to see if McLean is at his usual haunts, and then go up to the colliery."

Ham looked perplexed.

"I had intended to investigate the matter further, but the presence of dangerous gasses released in the wake of the mine collapse made that impractical, not to mention dangerous," explained Doc.

Ham fingered his chin. "Why did you not mention it at the time?"

"There was no need to alarm Miss Falcon, who is friendly with McLean."

"So you think the body is that of Malcolm McLean!"

Doc did not reply directly, saying only, "Miss Falcon insisted that McLean was a prisoner of the Grogan gang, yet no sign of him was found. The poisonous gasses have by now dissipated. It should be safe to investigate the pond."

They slipped out the back way in order to avoid the press, and only encountered one journalist. Interestingly enough, it was the one who first blew the whistle on them when they arrived at the Chicago airport more than twenty-four hours before, Jack Swangle by name. He wore a red press card in his hatband.

"Hey! Doc Savage! How about a morsel on the latest developments? Who do you think is gunning for Joe Shine?"

"Word travels fast," growled Monk.

The reporter grinned broadly. "Ain't you New York boys heard? Chicago is a beehive. Lots of bees buzz. Most of those buzzes ring telephones in this town. City editor's telephones, if you take my meaning."

"No comment," said Doc Savage sharply.

Leaving Swangle to Monk and Ham, Doc raised a great corded arm and hailed a taxicab.

The homely chemist got down on all fours behind the fellow, while Ham placed the blunt end of his black stick against the man's middle coat button.

"Now see here, my good fellow," Ham started to say. He gave the cane a sharp prod.

The unsuspecting journalist fell backward over Monk Mayfair's broad back and let out a squawk of surprise on his way to slamming the seat of his pants against hard pavement.

"You dandified diplomat!" Swangle gritted. "Why don't you beat it back to where you came from?"

Before the legman could rise, the dapper lawyer popped him in the forehead with his cane's heavy gold head, saying airily, "For that crack, I offer this ringing retort: Go peddle your papers."

The back of Swangle's head collided with concrete and he sprawled out like beached starfish, glassy-eyed and dazed.

Scrambling to his feet, Monk picked up the scribe's hat and dropped it over his face, then stepped on the hat on his way to join Doc Savage in the taxi.

The cab departed, the sound of its accelerating engine drowning out the reporter's shouted profanity.

"You were unnecessarily rough on that reporter," remarked Doc Savage.

The hairy chemist only grinned. Ham Brooks kept a straight face. There was no further upbraiding. Evidently, Doc Savage's disapproval did not run deep. He did not care for the press as a rule. The Fourth Estate was always digging into his background, trying to unearth his secrets. The bronze giant did not appreciate any of that. He preferred his privacy, for he had many enemies.

THEY called for Malcolm McLean at his home. After repeatedly pressing the doorbell and getting no response, Doc Savage picked the front door lock with ease.

The dwelling appeared to be empty, and a quick look around produced nothing of interest. The place showed no indication that anyone had been home in several days, but this impression was not conclusive in any way. McLean was a bachelor. The spotless appearance of the kitchen, combined with a sparse larder in the icebox, suggested that the owner took most of his meals outside his home.

"Bed is made," reported Monk. "No tellin' when it was slept in last."

Ham came up from a tour of the basement, noting, "You would not suspect the fellow was a chemist. There is no chemical apparatus anywhere."

To which Monk said, "Probably has a private set-up somewhere. Most guys don't do their experimentin' in their homes. Somethin' might blow up and wreck the joint."

Exiting, Doc said, "We will reclaim our speed plane at the airport."

On the way, they detoured to Joe Shine's residence and intercepted Long Tom, who was lugging a great glass humidor, in which there were a few fresh cigars and a great many black and green tobacco leaves.

Ham accepted this from the pallid electrical wizard. While Long Tom climbed into the machine, Monk grunted, "Some of this tobacco doesn't look like it's been properly cured."

"Time enough to concern ourselves with that later," said Doc.

LESS than an hour later, they were overflying the coal mine works, looking for a place to set their aircraft down.

Inasmuch as it was broad daylight, there was traffic. This presented a problem.

Doc Savage solved this dilemma by waiting for the traffic to thin, and putting the plane down on the same road upon which they had alighted the night before. This time, the bronze man kept the propellers turning and trundled the great plane into a grassy meadow that supported a sufficient number of trees to offer a modicum of shelter, but not enough to impede parking the aircraft.

All four men climbed out, and made their way to the colliery.

Bathed in sunshine, the place looked even more ramshackle than before. The unpainted board and batten sides of the coal-washing plant looked like something that had been abandoned by a race of giants.

Doc Savage first made a thorough search of the coal mine grounds, looking for any sign of an exit that might have been used to escape the cave-in. He found some signs of shafts that had been boarded up, but no indication that there was a usable way out of the mine other than the sealed main portal.

After that, the bronze giant led them to the impoundment, whose still surface looked scummy with a coating of pulverized coal dust that had been expelled from the mine collapse the previous evening.

Doc Savage approached the edge of the slurry pond. The former break in the surface had been obscured by the fresh fall of coal dust, but the bronze man found the spot he sought without difficulty. Quickly, he proceeded to divest himself of his street clothes, stripping off everything except the pair of black silk bathing trunks that he wore in lieu of underwear.

There was no splash as he entered the black water and sank beneath the dusty-looking surface. Doc was down a long time— an incredibly long time, searching for whatever lay in the foul water. He could hold his breath as long as a South Seas pearl diver, which is where he picked up the handy skill.

Finally, the bronze giant came up with the body of a man.

Monk's eyes bugged out. "Blazes!" he squeaked.

The others crowded closer, the better to see the corpse, but kept a respectful distance.

Doc lay this cadaver down, then scrutinized the features. They were gray. The body had not been there for very long. There were no outward signs of decomposition. But it had been weighted down with iron fragments stuffed into every available pocket.

Having satisfied the grim suspicion which had brought him to investigate, the bronze man now donned his clothing after carefully drying his hair on the lower end of his trouser leg. The foulness of the water had darkened it. Such dampness as remained might be readily mistaken for mere dew, for Doc's hair possessed the remarkable quality of shedding moisture in the manner of duck down.

Everyone gathered around to look at the dead man's face. It was gray. It was almost impossibly gray. Not the ashen gray of the pallor of death, but a leaden hue that they had seen only once before in their lives.

"Malcolm McLean," pronounced Long Tom Roberts.

"Undoubtedly," seconded Ham Brooks.

"The poor cuss," grunted Monk. "Imagine walkin' around all your days like an animated cadaver, and ended up lookin' even worse when your time came."

Doc Savage knelt and examined the body, but said nothing.

The face of the gray cadaver had been distorted by its immersion in water, much the way that a man's palm will shrivel up after he spends too long in a swimming pool. In this case, death made the condition permanent. Gullies and wrinkles marred his pinched features.

But in the general size and contours, it seemed to be the countenance of Malcolm McLean.

Doc Savage used one bronze hand to open first one, then the other eyelid, which revealed gray irises consistent with those of Malcolm McLean in life.

"Well, that's the end of him," said Long Tom without much sympathy. "I guess I'll never get to hand him a sock in return for the clobbering he gave me."

Doc Savage seemed on the verge of concluding his examination when the scalpel appeared in his metallic hand once more. This he inserted into the corpse's right nostril.

The bronze man's aides considered this simply an example of the methodical thoroughness with which the bronze man conducted his investigations. They were startled when the probing scalpel brought forth a gritty grating noise which set their teeth on edge.

"For cryin' out loud!" exploded Monk. "His brain got turned to stone!"

Coming erect, Doc Savage said, "This is an intriguing development."

Everyone looked expectantly at the bronze giant, but he offered no further comment. Nor did he bring up again the fact that he had seen a creature resembling the Medusa in the mine before its collapse.

Doc scrounged up some canvas from the coal-washing plant and used it to make a makeshift shroud for the body they had claimed from the impoundment. The bronze man carried this back to the waiting plane, and they were soon in the air with very little difficulty.

Once they were winging back to the Windy City, Monk Mayfair commented, "One thing's for sure. That Dr. Rockwell won't be able to revive *this* stiff. Malcolm McLean is as dead as Lazarus."

"Miss Falcon will be disturbed to learn of this development," mused Ham.

"Say nothing of this to Miss Falcon," Doc cautioned. "Until we identify the body with certainty, we do not wish to compromise our investigation."

Monk scratched his nubbin of a head. "Wait a minute! Ain't we all agreed that that stiff back there is McLean?"

"The body appears to be that of the man who was struck down by the brain-petrifying influence which attacked Malcolm McLean at the scientific exposition," stated Doc firmly. "But he does not appear to be McLean, although the resemblance is marked."

Various ejaculations of astonishment were wrung from the lips of Doc Savage's aides.

Long Tom wanted to know, "Is this the gray-faced one who was revived by Dr. Rockwell?"

"If it is," said the bronze man, "the revival appears to have been short-lived."

This remark threw the others into excited argument.

"This must mean that the real McLean is alive!" Ham exclaimed.

"Nothing of the sort," gritted Long Tom. "It means—"

Monk eyed the slender genius of the juice skeptically. "You don't know what it means. And neither do the rest of us! Admit it. It's got us all buffaloed."

Doc Savage volunteered nothing to this running commentary.

AN HOUR later, they were back in town and the newsboys were crying extra editions on many street corners.

"*Wuxtra!*" they howled. "Read all about it! Mystery avenger comes to Chicago! Declares war on underworld."

"What in the world is happening now?" snapped Ham.

Doc Savage pulled up to one corner and the dapper lawyer tossed a nickel out and received a fresh newspaper in return.

The scare heads were alarming.

UNKNOWN POWER DECLARES
WAR ON CHICAGO UNDERWORLD!

Letters were received at city newsrooms all over Chicago this morning. These letters were identical, investigation has shown. Text is as follows.

"For too long has the Windy City been a snake pit of vice and criminality. We hereby declare war on the Chicago underworld. It is in our power to Gorgonize the brains of men, and it is our will that the czars of the illicit rackets go to their graves without delay.

"Joe Shine was not the first. Nor will he be the last.

"Gorgones Vincit Omnia."
The letter was signed, *Medusa S. Euryale.*

The article continued:

Educated persons know that Medusa was the mythological figure of a snake-haired woman whose gaze was so horrible that mortal men were turned to stone.

Police have discovered an outline suggestive of the viper-headed monster at the home of the late Joe Shine, whom celebrated physician Warner Rockwell is at this very hour attempting to bring back from the netherworld.

It remains to be seen whether this can be done, or if Rockwell will fail. But at this hour it looks as if the doctor's practice is about to pick up in a major way.

Ham read all of this aloud, concluding with, "It appears that, contrary to our expectations, this Medusa plague is not winding down."

"So it would seem," stated Doc, pushing the machine back into traffic. "It may only now be getting underway in earnest."

Doc Savage's men all began asking questions at once, and the questions overlapped one another in such a way that none stood out.

This did not matter, for the bronze giant maintained a brittle silence as he drove in the direction of Mercy General Hospital, as was his custom when he did not wish to divulge his thought processes.

Chapter XXXVII

DEMONSTRATION

DR. WARNER ROCKWELL wore a glum mien when they found him at Mercy General Hospital. The craggy-featured physician had repaired to his private office.

This expression told them what they needed to know before the words came out of his mouth.

"I am afraid that my procedure did not accomplish anything in the case of the two men brought to me today," he said in a resigned voice. "The gangster known as Joseph Shine and his attorney have already been removed to the city morgue. There was nothing I could do. From what you describe, Savage, both victims were subjected to a greater concentration of the noxious fumes that resulted in the calcification of their brains than was Malcolm McLean."

Doc Savage regarded the dejected physician steadily.

"You suspected that might be the outcome," stated Doc without emotion.

Rockwell sighed heavily. "And I fear that I was correct."

"Are you now ready to reveal your process?"

Rockwell shook his head firmly, saying, "I am not. That was not a fair test of the process. I have proven that it works, but I must now prove that it will work on the other victims."

Monk growled, "As far as I can see, you ain't proved nothin'. No one's seen hide nor hair of Malcolm McLean since you released him."

"Why, I spoke with McLean just a few hours ago. He sounded hale and hearty. And grateful, I might add."

No one said anything to that.

Ham Brooks waved an extra edition of an afternoon newspaper and asked, "Have you seen the latest headlines?"

"I have not. I have been reviewing the events of the last two days."

The dapper lawyer tossed the newspaper on the desk, and suggested, "You might wish to read this."

Picking up the folded sheet, Dr. Rockwell absorbed the headline and began scanning the article beneath, outlining the campaign against crime threatened by the enigmatic Medusa S. Euryale.

The medical man seemed at a loss for words, then he murmured, "I may have my work cut out for me."

"No doubt," said Ham. "The only positive thing is that this Medusa seems to desire the eradication of Chicago's underworld."

Rockwell looked up and his unblinking eyes bored into them all unflinchingly.

"Be that as it may," he said heavily, "it is my bounden duty as a physician to attempt to revive any victim brought to me at this hospital. And I stand ready to do exactly that," he finished firmly.

"If this threat letter the papers received is genuine," suggested Doc, "the bodies may accumulate faster than you can deal with them."

"If it comes to that," assured Dr. Rockwell, "you may be certain that I will be sharing my procedure with you and other doctors so that we can manage the tidal wave of potential victims. But until that time, I must return to my studies. My process was something I stumbled upon, and now I must consider how to refine it in order to deal with more extreme cases than Malcolm McLean."

No one spoke for almost a minute. The ticking of the clock in the office was the only sound. Afternoon traffic outside the hospital window was an intermittent hum. The clanging of streetcars was raucous in the extreme. Not far away, a train rumbled along the elevated tracks, and the building shook a little in sympathy.

Dr. Rockwell seemed lost in his reverie, his face troubled. All through this, his eyes never appeared to blink. Not even once.

Suddenly, he looked up and inquired, "Is there anything else, gentlemen?"

"You might," requested Doc Savage, "ring up Malcolm McLean and ask if we might drop in on him."

"Of course. I will do that."

Picking up his desk telephone handset, Dr. Rockwell put in the call to the hospital switchboard and listened to the connection ring and ring.

Finally, he hung up, saying, "McLean does not answer. He may not wish to. No doubt he is being besieged by reporters. He may even have left the city."

"What makes you say that?"

"He had planned to give a lecture at the scientific exposition today but, after his ordeal, the presentation has been ruined."

Rockwell suddenly looked at his wristwatch and said, "Our mutual friend, Marvin Lucian Linden, is giving a talk in half an hour. I had been planning to attend. I don't know that I dare spare the time now."

Doc Savage said, "Perhaps we might all go over. It is always possible that McLean has changed his mind and is in attendance as well."

Rockwell seemed to give that considerable thought, and at last he said, "I believe some fresh air and diversion will do me some good. Yes, let us go over to the scientific exposition."

WHEN they entered the great auditorium, the crowds were as large as they had been the day before.

Seeing this, Monk grunted, "I guess havin' a guy keel over dead in the middle of everything didn't hurt attendance any."

Long Tom growled, "Some of these birds may be hoping to see a repeat performace."

Ham declined to comment, feeling it beneath his dignity. But his sharp eyes skated about the room, already in search of the missing Malcolm McLean.

Once more the ticket takers were sufficiently awestruck by Doc Savage that they passed him through without incident. Monk and Long Tom were also recognized, but Ham Brooks was stopped and asked if he held a ticket.

Flustered, the dapper attorney turned beet red and expostulated. "But I am with Doc Savage."

The ticket taker looked to the bronze man, who had already passed through the turnstile. Doc gave him a firm nod.

The ticket taker relented. "O.K., you can go in. As long as you're with Doc Savage."

"That is what I told you!" snapped Ham.

Monk took that opportunity to launch a dig, saying, "This soirée is for scientists, which you are not. Bein' merely an ambulance-chasing wart on the face of common humanity."

Ham lifted his sword cane as if to thrash the hairy chemist about the head, but he was distracted after Dr. Warner Rockwell stepped through the turnstile behind him.

Chicagoans began noticing him. This was remarkable. Doc Savage towered over everyone and all eyes would typically go to the giant man of bronze. But this did not happen.

Rockwell emerged from the turnstile. The crowd, which had begun to press in the direction of Doc Savage's men, shifted suddenly, and surged instead toward the steady-eyed physician.

"Dr. Rockwell!" a man said enthusiastically. "You are the hero of the hour!"

Another chimed in, saying, "That was incredible what you accomplished with that poor fellow, McLean."

Another asked, "When will you reveal your restorative process?"

Dr. Rockwell lifted pleading hands and said, "I am still working to refine the process by which I reanimated Malcolm McLean. I have yet to repeat the feat, so I must, in all modesty, decline to answer your questions. Rest assured, I am endeavoring to guarantee that if any others are struck down by this hideous power, their period of catalepsy will be brief and they will be restored to their families. Now, if you'll excuse me."

Rockwell moved forward, and joined up with Doc Savage and his men, his eyes as unblinking as opals.

"That was a nice speech," said Ham Brooks sincerely.

"Thank you," returned Rockwell crisply.

"You're getting to be as famous as Doc Savage," muttered Monk in a tone that was not necessarily complimentary. The homely chemist was extremely loyal to his bronze chief.

Rockwell said nothing to that, but took the lead, suggesting, "Please follow me. I will take you to Marvin Linden. We may be able to catch him before his speech."

Knowing that Linden was an electro-mechanical magician like himself, Long Tom asked, "What invention is he demonstrating today?"

"I do not wish to spoil the surprise," said Rockwell. "But I have seen it in operation, and it is a marvel."

Looking around, and seeing booth after booth of ultramodern scientific devices, Monk Mayfair said, "The whole joint is full of marvels. Linden will have to work some to beat them."

"This device of Linden's is a world beater," promised Rockwell, his unnervingly steady regard going to Long Tom for some reason.

That statement impressed those hearing it, and they followed Rockwell in a single file through the milling crowds until they came to the section given over to electrical and mechanical inventions.

At the far end auditorium, the stage was being readied, while Marvin Lucian Linden held forth at an exhibition booth, fussing with a device that he was endeavoring to remove from a wooden crate. A small crowbar lay to one side. Linden was carefully giving his invention a final going over until he was ready to make his demonstration.

As the electrical expert plucked excelsior off the complicated apparatus, Dr. Rockwell lifted his voice and said, "Marvin, Doc Savage and his men are here with me."

A startled expression roosted on the inventor's round features, but when he took in the sight of Doc Savage, his placid face became wreathed in pleased smiles, as his natural effusiveness came to the fore.

"Doc Savage! As I live and breathe! Have you come to observe my demonstration? I am flattered, if that is the case."

"We are very interested in your demonstration," Doc informed him, "but what concerns us here is the question of Malcolm McLean's present whereabouts."

"McLean! I have not seen him since the unfortunate events of the other day. But he is well, I take it?"

"He was healthy when he left the hospital last night," supplied Rockwell solemnly.

Linden evinced a short laugh, then assayed a rather lame jest. "Well, you say? But not in the pink? You wouldn't say *that*, now would you?"

Marvin Lucian Linden began tittering like a small child, amused by his own attempt at humor.

Eyes unblinking, Dr. Rockwell enjoined, "No, I would not call McLean in the pink. The poor man has not had a healthy complexion in a good many years."

Doc Savage interrupted, "It was our hope that McLean would put in an appearance, for he was not at his home earlier."

"I would like to congratulate him on his escape from death," said Linden more seriously. Turning to Dr. Rockwell, he added, "And I would also like to offer my heartiest congratulations to you, Warner, for having aided in his escape. Well done, sir. Well done indeed."

As Linden rattled along, Long Tom Roberts was watching him fiddle with the complicated apparatus from the packing crate.

When his eyes rested upon the thing, the puny electrical wizard's orbs narrowed and he snapped, "Let me see that!"

The vehemence of Long Tom's expostulation caused Linden to momentarily recoil, and his demeanor shifted entirely.

"See here! I must ask you not to take such a sharp tone with me. This is my device, and you may not touch it without my permission."

"I don't want to touch it. I want to know what it is."

"That," returned Linden in a better humor, "is a surprise that I am about to unveil."

There was a buzzing in the immediate vicinity and everyone noticed, including Long Tom.

"That is not a mechanical noise," he said suspiciously.

"Far be it for me to disabuse you of your opinion," said Linden, smiling mischievously. "But I will admit my device has not been turned on as yet."

Keeping a respectful distance, Long Tom shifted about while studying the contraption, suspicious eyes growing even narrower.

The mechanism had a homemade quality about it. A great deal of it consisted of electrical antennae. The thing positively bristled with steel quills.

It brought to mind a metallic porcupine built around a transformer.

"Is something wrong?" asked Doc Savage.

"If there is," Long Tom said querulously, "I'm going to wring someone's neck before the day is out."

Everyone looked at Long Tom quizzically.

"That buzzing," he said, as if it explained everything, "sounds like bees."

Marvin Lucian Linden's mischievous smile quirked slightly but did not become any less mischievous.

"All will be revealed to you shortly."

"It won't work," Long Tom said suddenly.

"I beg your pardon?" returned Marvin Lucian Linden. "Are you referring to me or my device?"

"It will not work," Long Tom repeated. "Except at short ranges."

Marvin Lucian Linden's mischievous smile did not know what to do with itself. It quirked, retreated, quirked anew.

"Assuming that we are speaking on the same subject," he said graciously, "this early model is not designed to work at any distance greater than the compactness the mechanism allows. It is my hope and expectation to increase its effective range, as I refine the mechanism."

"That's the rub," clucked Long Tom. "My own experiments haven't solved that problem."

Now Marvin Lucian Linden's smile collapsed totally. He became flustered. "Are you intimating that you have been working along the same lines as I?"

"I'm not intimating any such thing," snorted Long Tom. "I'm saying it straight out. You can't increase the range without building a completely different mechanism. The rays won't travel far enough with the lethal force necessary to accomplish the job."

Marvin Lucian Linden possessed a rather peaked complexion, but now it paled alarmingly.

His voice became cold, but there was a tremor in it when he spoke next.

"If you gentlemen will excuse me," he quavered. "I must ready my invention for its first public demonstration."

With that, he carefully placed the device back in the packing crate, set the wooden lid back in place, smothering the peculiar buzzing. Taking the thing under one arm, the wild-haired inventor walked in the direction of the auditorium stage.

After he had gone, Monk and Ham got in front of the slender electrical expert and demanded, "What gives?" This from Monk.

"I'll bet my hat," Long Tom gritted, "that's an insect eliminator modeled along identical lines to the device I've been working on these last few years."

"Your bug killer?" Monk said.

"No, my bug *aggravator*. So far I've only got it to work at short distances. It will kill insects that fly close to it, but it only chases away others. Once they wander into the area of its electrical field, the rays disturb them and they go flying off."

Ham commented dryly, "Rather sounds like it works to me."

"Sure, if you want to kill bugs that fly in through your windows. But if you need to clear a swamp of mosquitoes, or an infestation of cockroaches or other vermin, my insect killer is a bust."

"A qualified bust," corrected Ham.

Long Tom shook his head vehemently. "No. It's a dud. Until I get it working right, it's a bust. And it looks like that Marvin Lucian Linden has produced a similar one. I can tell by how its wired up. His contraption won't do anything more than mine."

"Perhaps we should observe the demonstration, gentlemen," suggested Dr. Rockwell patiently.

Doc Savage returned, saying, "It might be interesting, at that."

After a substantial introduction, Marvin Lucian Linden took the stage, placed his device on a plain deal table, and lifted a glass bottle containing nothing that could be clearly seen.

His demeanor was that of a professional illusionist, preparing to perform a trick. He had a showy manner about him, which was evident in his lavish hand gestures. His wild shock of crispy hair made his round head resemble a fantastic dandelion seed head.

"Ladies and gentlemen," Linden began, "in my right hand I hold up a glass jar containing several bees from a local apiary. These bees, as you can hear when I hold the microphone up to the jar, are hale and hearty despite being out of season."

Linden waved the bottle before the microphone stand, and the sound of bees buzzing about was magnified throughout the auditorium.

Linden's voice swelled. "This device on the table is one that will prove to be of great value to humanity. Farmers will sing its praises. Households will display one in every home. Larger versions, installed in tropical climates, will eradicate disease-carrying mosquitoes and other pestiferous enemies of mankind."

A buzz went racing around the gathered audience.

"I call this machine my Insecto-eradicato. Any six or even eight-legged creature flying or crawling into the zone created by its deadly rays will perish in a matter of seconds. Insects on the edge of the zone of influence will be driven away, and remain at a respectful distance as long as the exciter is operating."

Standing between Monk and Ham, who towered over him, Long Tom Roberts was growling under his breath. He sounded rather like a junkyard dog that had spotted a rival canine.

Ham whispered to Monk, "I have never before heard Long Tom make such sounds."

Monk nodded, saying, "His dander is up."

"My dander," growled Long Tom, "is fine and dandy."

"Then why are your hackles raised?"

Long Tom said nothing; he was studying the man on the stage.

Marvin Lucian Linden now unscrewed the lid of the bottle, whose top was screened with fine mesh wire, permitting the insects to breathe and their buzzing to be heard.

"I am now going to release these bees. Have no fear. They will not enter the crowd. Upon that you have my guarantee as a scientist."

Now the assembly began to shift and mutter, not quite certain what to expect.

"The reason I use bees instead of insects such as mosquitoes," explained Linden, "is because bees are large enough so that you may see them with the naked eye."

The lid came off. Linden set the jar down, and one by one the bees crawled up to the lip, poised briefly, and took wing.

In the bright lights it was possible to see them meander about. One was a plump bumblebee.

"You can see they are healthy. Now I will throw the switch."

Marvin Lucian Linden reached over and tripped a switch, and the device began humming distinctively.

Almost immediately, the bees began to swing and dive about, as if agitated.

Then one dropped straight down, and made a tiny tick on the wood floor of the auditorium stage. Another dive bombed the table, rebounded off it, and landed near its mate.

There were five bees in all, and every one of them quickly succumbed.

The buzzing was heard no more and the mechanism hum stopped.

"The principle of my Insecto-eradicato is complicated," said Marvin Lucian Linden, beaming happily. "Ultra-sonic waves are the key. As many of you know, ultra-sonic vibrations are used to sterilize milk by killing harmful microbes. My device is modulated to a frequency that affects insects alone. Only insects are harmed. Humans are not. This device is safe for all households, including those with children and pets."

Applause erupted here and there, and soon turned into a wave of noisy approval that washed over the audience.

Doc Savage and his men did not participate in that applause. For his part, Long Tom Roberts was red-faced.

"Did he beat you to the punch?" Monk demanded.

"Marvin Lucian Linden beat me to the same knockout punch I got every time I tried to make my invention work on a larger scale," grated Long Tom. "What he's got will work in a fair-sized room. That means you'll need one in every room of the house, if you're going to keep bugs out. But on the industrial scale, where the idea is to drive injurious pests away from crops, and mosquitoes out of fever swamps, the thing is practically useless."

Monk grunted, "Well, you warned 'im."

The audience began asking questions. Marvin Lucian Linden parried them expertly, highlighting the advantages of his invention, but also candidly acknowledging its shortcomings.

"This model is designed to clear an ordinary house of unwanted insects," he was saying. "Once I develop the industrial version, I predict that the Insecto-eradicato will be remembered as one of the great inventions of the Twentieth Century."

Came another round of applause, this one verging on the thunderous. Photographers in the audience began taking flashbulb pictures.

Just as the polite thunder of clapping hands died down, Marvin Lucian Linden packed up his device, and brought it off the stage.

A janitor came along and swept up the dead bees into a dustpan.

Linden soon returned to his booth, where he set up his gadget for all attendees to examine up close.

The inventor was immediately surrounded, and it was not possible to get close to him again.

Ham Brooks turned to Long Tom Roberts, asked, "Were you planning to demonstrate your own version at this affair?"

Long Tom shook his head vehemently. "And make a darn fool of myself?"

"What do you mean? Linden appears to have been well received."

"That's because he's promising an improved version. Until he produces one, that's all it is. A promise. You can't peddle promises."

"So what are you showing?"

Long Tom patted his coat, where he kept concealed the oversized magnetic gun.

"This honey here. I perfected it, so there's no question that it will do what I claim it will."

To which Monk Mayfair snorted, "I got my own ideas on that score."

Long Tom tugged at one ear in annoyance and said, "I have a feeling the best man is going to win that bet."

Monk jerked a thumb toward his barrel chest and said, "In which case, have your money ready. Because I'm takin' it."

"The only thing you're going to take," rejoined Long Tom sourly, "is a jump into the cold lake of disappointment."

"Says you?" grunted Monk.

"Says me," insisted Long Tom.

Ham Brooks suddenly looked around and noticed someone was missing.

"Where did Doc go?" he wondered aloud.

Everyone looked about, but there was no sign of the giant man of metal, although he should have towered over all others in the crowd.

Chapter XXXVIII

VEIL OF HORROR

HAD MONK, HAM and Long Tom been paying attention, they would have been both intrigued and baffled by Doc Savage's subsequent actions.

The bronze man had been observing the crowd gathering around the booth of Marvin Lucian Linden, and was quietly studying the faces thus arrayed.

One individual attracted the intent regard of Doc's golden gaze.

This fellow was rather nondescript in overall appearance. He was tall, but walked in a stooped manner. His face was thin and he had a wiry look about him. His clothing did not quite fit him, and had a slightly seedy air to it. He had all the outward appearance of a casual attendee of the exposition of science.

Doc Savage's eyes scrutinized the man's face, the dull brown hair and other outstanding aspects of his appearance.

Quietly, Doc Savage detached himself from the group of quarreling aides, and drifted in the direction of Marvin Lucian Linden's booth. As he moved through the crowd, his intent eyes never left the other man's form.

Although the bronze man's absence had not yet been detected by his aides, several passersby attempted to intercept him, seeking autographs.

Doc Savage had always avoided such autograph hounds, and managed to sidestep them while they fumbled for pens and pieces of paper on which they hoped for a personalized inscription.

In short order, Doc Savage was closing in on the nondescript fellow who had attracted his interest.

The man was attempting to catch the attention of Marvin Lucian Linden, who was busy explaining the inner workings of his Insecto-eradicato.

Linden happened to look up, spotted the bronze man approaching. Face brightening, he lifted a welcoming hand.

"Why, it's Doc Savage!" he exclaimed loudly.

All heads turned, including that of the nondescript man. When the latter's eyes fell upon the bronze giant, whose head topped all others, they narrowed in the extreme, and he immediately detached himself from the crowd.

Changing direction, Doc Savage fell in behind him. He did not want to make a scene; regrettably, the outcry of Marvin Lucian Linden had unfortunate results.

The name, Doc Savage, shouted over the buzz of the crowd, drew additional autograph seekers. The bronze man was soon surrounded, and the press of human bodies was such that, although he was able to deftly avoid the first few, the gathering throng soon obstructed his path.

"Excuse me," Doc Savage said in his remarkable voice. "Please let me through."

Many, of course, respected this polite request. But others did not. Fountain pens and notepads were thrust into his face, and Doc had to push them away, lest he lose sight of the individual who interested him so much.

It was a losing battle for a few minutes; finally, Doc Savage was forced to retreat and work around the group. The eager crowd flowed after him, but with such skill and economy did he move that the bronze man soon enough left them behind.

For his part, the nondescript fellow was making a beeline for an exit, but frequently threw an anxious glance behind him.

Every time that he did, his eyes came to rest upon Doc Savage, whose head towered above the sea of moving persons.

This was one of those times when Doc Savage regretted that he had been formed by nature to be such an outstanding specimen of humanity. His metallic color, combined with his great height and physical symmetry, made it impossible for him to blend into any group of ordinary people.

Thus, Doc Savage's efforts to follow the man unsuspected failed utterly.

Disappearing through the exit door, the man slammed it behind him; at that point Doc Savage broke into a sprint.

It was not practical to make a dash for the exit door in an unbroken manner, but shifting deftly, Doc did his best to weave in and out of the crowd. He finally reached the door, pushed through.

A set of stairs led up to the hotel's lobby, and Doc mounted them three at a time, and soon found himself in the lobby proper.

His flake-gold eyes swept the room, appraised and discarded numerous faces of hotel guests and casual loungers. It was the closing of an automatic door that drew him toward the elevator shaft.

Reaching the shaft, it proved too late to halt the departing car, whose operator was taking it up. Doc Savage watched as the indicator arrow climbed. It did not stop until it reached the sixth floor, whereupon the bronze man pressed the button that would recall the cage.

When the cage arrived, the door failed to open. Doc pressed the button, but received no response.

Employing his great strength, the bronze man inserted metallic fingers and found the edge of the door, pushing it back by main strength.

When the door rolled aside, the elevator operator fell out as if he had been leaning against the door.

Doc caught the fellow, who was attempting to articulate something.

"What is wrong?" Doc rapped out.

"Ringing, humming," the man mumbled. His eyes suddenly rolled up in his head, and he went lax in every limb.

Only then did the bronze man detect a strange burning smell emanating from the empty cage. It had a charcoal flavor. He immediately held his breath.

Retreating, Doc Savage pulled the elevator boy with him, gathered him up, and carried him into the lobby. He laid him on a couch, and felt of the man's wrist and throat as he quietly expired.

Swiftly, Doc Savage inserted a needle probe into one nostril, and was not greatly surprised when he encountered a gritty obstruction.

The hotel detective came bustling up, saying, "What's going on here?"

Doc Savage said, "This man has been felled by the affliction that calcifies human brains. Dr. Rockwell is attending the exhibition in the adjoining hall. Have him summoned at once. It may not be too late to save this man."

Without waiting, Doc Savage rushed to the elevator bank. Ripping off his coat, he used it to disperse the burning stink that was emanating from the elevator and, taking the precaution of donning his chemical filter mask, stepped aboard and sent the car climbing up to the sixth floor.

Doc Savage went immediately to the room occupied by Janet Falcon, knocked briskly, and the door fell open.

"What is it you want?" the woman asked, her green eyes rimmed in red. Obviously, she had been crying again.

"A suspicious man came to this floor. Did anyone knock on your door?"

One slim hand flew to her mouth. "Why no, no one did. Why would you think he would?"

Without replying, Doc Savage said, "It is necessary that I search the room."

Janet Falcon did not resist. Woodenly, she stepped aside and said, "You have the authority. I shan't get in your way."

Doc Savage moved through the small suite, examined every room, opened the closets, and even investigated the curtained shower stall. It was unmistakably clear that Janet Falcon was the only occupant.

"Thank you," Doc said. "Keep your door locked and do not open it for any stranger."

Then the bronze man exited the room, and was swiftly moving along the corridor, his ever-active eyes roving.

There are many ways to track a man through woods, deserts, and even along city streets. A hotel is another matter entirely. Doc Savage sniffed the air, seeking any sign of a man's cologne that might suggest a passerby of recent vintage.

But there was nothing. He knelt at different points, felt of the rug nap, and attempted to discern crushed fibers straightening after the passage of a person.

Twice, he found patches that were slightly warmer than the surrounding carpet as if someone had loitered at the spot, and the vague trail seemed to go in the direction of the fire stairs.

Moving to the fire door, Doc Savage eased it open, looked up and down, went up one flight, examined the hallway, returned and searched the floor beneath.

Despite all his efforts, the trail had gone cold.

Returning to the lobby, Doc arrived as Dr. Rockwell was being escorted in by a security guard, his face like stone, his eyes staring without blinking.

Doc Savage imparted, "My examination showed me that the man's brain has hardened. It happened in the last ten minutes."

Rockwell nodded grimly. "An ambulance has been called. There may yet be time to save this poor devil." Meeting Doc's steady gaze with his unnerving stare, he inquired, "How did you come upon this victim?"

Doc Savage hesitated only slightly. "I happened to spy an individual who appeared to be suspicious in the exhibition crowd. When I attempted to approach him, he fled to the hotel lobby in a nervous and guilty manner. He disappeared into an elevator; this is the elevator operator."

As a physician, Dr. Rockwell had seen many unpleasant sights, and his stolid features and unblinking eyes did not reflect a great deal of emotion. But looking at the stricken elevator operator, he lifted a hand and ran it through his thick hair, saying, "It baffles me how these poor people are being struck down."

"A burnt charcoal odor in the elevator cage indicates a combustible substance at work."

"He was killed to discourage your pursuit, no doubt."

"Evidently," said Doc.

Rockwell nodded heavily. "I take it you put no stock in the newspaper reports of a Medusa stalking the streets of Chicago?"

"None whatsoever," stated Doc, returning Rockwell's emotionless stare with one of his own.

"Are we supposed to believe that this poor elevator operator is a criminal of some sort?"

"That remains to be seen," replied Doc. "I must once again request to witness the procedure you intend to perform on this man."

Rockwell shook his heavy head slowly. "It is very tempting, for you may be able to assist me, but my present preference is to work alone. Nevertheless, I thank you for your offer."

Doc Savage said nothing for a long moment, then added, "The suspicious person may have circled back to the exhibition hall. I must continue my pursuit."

Rockwell had been staring at the deceased elevator operator and suddenly looked up. "What was so suspicious about him?"

"He rather reminded me of Malcolm McLean," replied Doc.

Rockwell gave vent to an unexpected laugh. "Rather reminded! I would think anyone whose appearance smacked of McLean's would stand out in any crowd."

"This fellow was notable for being nondescript in his general coloring. But he possessed McLean's height and gaunt features."

Rockwell cocked a thick eyebrow and asked, "I fail to follow your reasoning."

"Call it a hunch," said Doc.

This seemed to further befuddle Warner Rockwell, but by this time the clanging of the ambulance could be heard and he excused himself to meet the arriving attendants.

Doc Savage quietly departed the lobby, and was soon filtering through the exhibition crowd, making a circuit of the great auditorium hall, avoiding as much as possible persons who might wish to accost him for one reason or another. Finally, failing to accomplish anything constructive, he drifted back in the direction of his aides.

Monk and Ham were badgering Long Tom Roberts.

"Is it possible," Ham was asking, "that this insect exterminating device could have the ability to turn a man's brain into something hard?"

Long Tom seemed to take the suggestion rather personally. "Have you gone bughouse? Why would I build anything that could do that?"

Ham bridled, saying, "I am not referring to your device. But the one invented by Marvin Lucian Linden!"

Monk inserted, "I was kinda thinkin' along the same lines. It would take something really unusual to produce such a chemical reaction in a human brain. Maybe it could be done by special rays."

Rubbing the back of his neck, Long Tom said, "Hardly likely. In fact, it's flat-out impossible."

"You don't know that Linden's device is identical in the way it operates to yours, do you?" questioned Ham.

"No, but it's close. And what you're saying is ridiculous. The both of you. Cut it out."

Doc Savage was suddenly in their midst. Caught unawares, Monk all but jumped out of his hairy hide!

"Dang your spooky way of gettin' around!" he squeaked.

Ham asked, "Doc, what do you think of this? Perhaps Linden's device is causing all this trouble."

Instead of replying directly, Doc Savage asked, "What makes you suspect Marvin Lucian Linden?"

Both Monk and Ham were slightly taken aback, but Ham admitted, "We do not suspect him specifically. It is only that we seek a reasonable explanation for these mad occurrences."

"Linden's device would not produce these effects," said Doc. "Have you forgotten the cigarette smoke that felled Ned Gamble? Or the fatal gasses that emerged from the coal mine?"

Both men looked sheepish.

"They're just grasping at straws," said Long Tom heatedly. "Don't listen to them. They don't know what they're talking about, neither of them. I'm disgusted by everything that's happened today."

Changing the subject, Ham Brooks asked, "Have you seen any sign of Malcolm McLean in the vicinity?"

Once more, Doc Savage dodged the question and related the events of the last few minutes.

"I trailed a suspicious individual," the bronze man concluded. "He managed to elude me, but he does not seem to have returned to the exhibition hall."

Monk, Ham and Long Tom looked suitably impressed.

"What attracted your attention?" inquired Ham.

"The fellow," replied Doc, "bore a general resemblance to Malcolm McLean."

"*Ye-e-o-w!*" yelled Monk. "Do you think it was McLean?"

"It is impossible to be certain. I did not see the fellow clearly. But he appeared to have gone to Janet Falcon's floor only to double back, managing to throw me off the trail."

"Could it be a coincidence that he went to that floor?" Ham wondered.

"It is always prudent to be skeptical of coincidences," Doc Savage pointed out. "But Janet Falcon was not approached. If that was the man's intention, it was foiled."

Doc gave a specific description of the man and all four of them fanned out and canvassed the exhibition hall.

An hour later, they regrouped and were forced to admit that there was no sign of the mysterious individual anywhere in the great convocation.

"We keep hittin' dead ends!" complained Monk.

"This is one of the most baffling matters we have ever looked into," agreed Ham in spite of himself.

"Disgusting, I call it," said Long Tom. "It's just flat-out disgusting."

No one contradicted the pale electrical wizard.

"Well," Monk muttered, "the newspapers are gonna have a field day with this latest killin'."

Which caused Doc Savage to remark, "No doubt reporters will be descending upon the hotel at any minute, looking into different angles of the story. Best we make ourselves scarce. We do not want any further entanglements with the Chicago press."

They went in search of the service elevator, so they could return to their hotel suite undetected.

Chapter XXXIX

SUSPICIONS

ONCE THEY WERE again ensconced in Doc Savage's hotel suite, the bronze man sat down at the writing desk and took out a sheet of hotel stationery and a pencil.

Without explaining his actions, he began to sketch the individual he had observed slipping through the crowds of the great exposition.

The likeness was remarkable, and would have done credit to a police sketch artist. Inwardly, the bronze man felt it lacked a sense of personality, but it was a distinct and accurate likeness.

He passed this to the others, saying, "This is a rendering of the suspicious man."

Long Tom took it first, considered the drawing thoughtfully, and made a face.

"Reminds me of that sideshow freak, Malcolm McLean. But not exactly."

Monk and Ham studied it next. The homely chemist said, "Could be him at that."

Predictably, Ham said contrarily. "Or perhaps a relative."

Long Tom asked, "You say the man looked normal?"

Doc Savage nodded. "He was uncommonly pale, his hair was a dull brown, but the resemblance was marked, although not perfect."

Ham wondered, "There are too many men walking around looking like this one. It is an unpleasant thought."

Monk pointed out, "We still don't know for sure if McLean's livin'. No one's seen him."

Long Tom snapped his fingers. "That's right! We have only Dr. Rockwell's word that McLean made it."

"And the word of the hospital staff," reminded Doc. "They are unlikely to be mistaken in that regard. McLean's appearance is too distinct."

Ham unsheathed his cane, studied the blade and declared, "This may be the most maddening puzzle we've ever blundered into."

Doc Savage said, "Long Tom, have photostatic copies of this made and distributed to police stations. I will request of the Superintendent of Police that a dragnet be cast for this man."

"Sure," said the pale electrical wizard.

Doc turned to the others. "Monk, Ham, why don't you to go to McLean's residence. See if he has returned. If not, stand watch and wait until he does."

"Righto," said Ham. "What will you be doing in the meantime?"

"We have acquired scant clues in the course of our investigation," replied the bronze man steadily. "Without our complete chemical laboratory back east, we are somewhat handicapped."

"What about Janet Falcon?" wondered Monk. "The police don't know it yet, but she's the main suspect in the killing of Duke Grogan."

"Janet Falcon will have to keep," said Doc. "She is very much like a safe with a combination lock. If we continue working on her, perhaps the door will fully open and she will reveal her secrets."

Ham Brooks suddenly made an intrigued face. "She will need a competent attorney in any event."

"Perhaps you might offer Miss Falcon your services at the appropriate time," suggested Doc. "But for the moment, we will keep her under wraps."

With that, Doc Savage and his men went their separate ways.

NEWSPAPER extras were already on the streets and newsboys howled the headlines, which were in two-inch type.

"New Medusa Murder!" yelled one. *"Wuxtra!* Read all about it! Another victim struck down!"

They related the death of the unfortunate elevator operator at the Hotel Chicago, with plenty of sob-story stuff about the man's family and additional color concerning past efforts by Dr. Warner Rockwell to salvage such unfortunate victims.

Holding the open sheet high so as to help conceal his distinctive features, Doc Savage read this as he left the hotel, signaling the doorman that he did not require a taxicab.

Instead, the bronze giant climbed the covered stairs of an elevated train platform, rode a rattling train several blocks, and walked until he came to an imposing building—the Chicago Public Library. He entered through the Washington Street entrance.

The hour was growing late, but the library was still open— although it showed signs of being readied for closing.

Doc Savage presented himself at the main desk, and requested a courtesy card that would permit him to use the microfilm files.

"We are closing in ten minutes," the librarian told him, unimpressed by the bronze giant's Herculean stature.

"This may be important," said Doc quietly. "I am investigating the wave of murders in the city."

"In that event," the librarian hastily amended, "we may make an exception for you, Mr. Savage. Step this way."

Doc was led to a reading room, and from memory recited a certain date three years in the past, saying, "I would like all Chicago newspapers for that date."

The bound volumes were promptly produced and Doc Savage began to go through them one by one.

At the end of his perusal, he stood up, returned the boxed volumes to the librarian, saying simply, "Thank you. This was very helpful."

A guard had to let Doc out the front door, which had been locked during his study.

A cab conveyed the bronze giant to Mercy General Hospital next, where he inquired at the reception desk, "How is Dr. Rockwell progressing with the latest victim under his care?"

"He is still working," the receptionist told him.

Doc asked, "I understand from my reading that a Dr. Marsden treated the victims of the Ryerson Coal Mine disaster of a few years ago. Is this the same physician listed in your hospital directory?"

The receptionist was not sure, but consulted with the head nurse, who said, "Yes, our Dr. Marsden handled some of those patients. Although by the time he got to them, they were immediately pronounced dead. So they were not truly his patients."

"Where might Dr. Marsden be found?"

The head nurse consulted papers at her desk. "Try his office, on the fourth floor."

After thanking the women, Doc rode the elevator to the fourth floor, knocked at the door and stepped in without waiting for response.

Dr. Marsden shot out of his seat, and the expression on his long face alternated between flustered startlement and genuine admiration.

"Dr. Savage!" he cried out. "I heard that you were in town, but I did not imagine I would ever meet you."

Doc got right to the point, saying, "You were the physician on duty when the victims of the Ryerson coal mine disaster of 1931 arrived at the county hospital."

"However did you know that?" said Marsden, waving Doc to a seat.

Doc Savage remained standing, however. He addressed this point. "By consulting the Chicago newspapers for that year. You, among other physicians, were quoted in regard to the disaster."

Dr. Marsden shook his head sadly. "It was a terrible thing. There were no survivors."

"Were any of the victims autopsied?"

Dr. Marsden had to think about that a moment. Finally, he admitted, "I do not believe so. As you might imagine, coal-mining disasters happen from time to time, and once the bodies are removed, it is usually assumed that the dead expired as a result of inhalation of firedamp—as coal miners call poisonous gasses."

Doc nodded. "Did the bodies display any unusual charac-teristics?"

The medical man did not have to think about that. "No, I do not believe that they did."

"Were there signs of acute hypoxia?"

"No, no, none of that. The skin lacked any unusual discolor-ation. But you have to understand that, with over two hundred victims, the bodies were very quickly examined, then released to their next of kin. There was no question but that they were all deceased. Nor that they had been subjected to a poisonous atmosphere. So the state coroner did not dig too deeply. The mine was immediately closed, and has remained shut since that time."

Intrigued lights played in Doc Savage's flake-gold eyes for a moment. Dr. Marsden watched him, awaiting another ques-tion. But none came.

"You have answered all questions to my satisfaction," said Doc Savage. "Thank you for your time."

The bronze man turned to go and Dr. Marsden asked, "Do you think that they perished in an unusual way?"

"It is a certainty that their deaths were out of the ordinary," said Doc. "But nothing could have been done for them. Thank you again."

Exiting the office, Doc Savage returned to the lobby, where he was informed that Dr. Rockwell had finished his ministra-tions.

"The procedure did not go as expected," reported the head nurse sadly. "Dr. Rockwell was unable to revive the elevator operator."

Doc Savage took this news in silence.

"Did Rockwell give any explanation for his failure?"

The nurse shook her head, saying, "No, he did not. But he seemed very shaken. We all had very high hopes for his restorative process, whatever it is. Would you like to speak with him?"

"Not at this time," replied the bronze man. Without another word, he exited the hospital, hailing a taxi, which took him back to his hotel.

LONG TOM ROBERTS was waiting in the lobby for Doc Savage when the latter entered. His normally sour features were excited.

"Doc!" he said urgently. "I hung back, waiting for you. Monk and Ham just called in. They say someone is rattling around in Malcolm McLean's house."

"Did they observe the individual?"

The slender electrical expert shook his head. "No. I told them to hold their horses and not to barge in."

"That was prudent. We will go directly to McLean's residence and look into this."

At the garage, they claimed their rental sedan—Monk and Ham having taken a taxi—and were soon whipping through the city streets, dodging automobiles and streetcars.

As Doc drove, Long Tom said, "I happened to knock on Janet Falcon's door. She didn't answer. Thought I'd flash your sketch to see if she recognized the face. No soap."

Doc nodded. "We will interview her again once we have concluded our investigation of Malcolm McLean's whereabouts."

"Dig up anything new?"

Without taking his eyes off the road, Doc Savage said, "A great deal of this trouble seems to center on that closed coal mine down in Vermilion County."

"Maybe we should open it up and pull out those bodies."

Doc Savage said nothing. He drove with expert control, but the speed with which he whipped around corners and shot up Chicago's congested thoroughfares showed that the bronze man was anxious to reach the McLean residence.

When at last they pulled up, the rain had commenced again, and Monk and Ham stood huddled and unhappy under an oak tree.

The quiet neighborhood was fully enveloped in night.

Monk Mayfair said, "He's been there about twenty minutes. You can see him through the drawn shades, but I can't make out who the heck it is."

Ham added, "Whoever he is, the fellow has not been still since he arrived."

Doc said, "We will surround the house so he does not escape, if he is of that mind."

Monk and Ham unlimbered their supermachine pistols, while Long Tom brought out his clumsy-looking magnetic gun, which he had stuffed into his belt.

"Between Doc and the three of us," the puny electrical wizard said, "he hasn't a chance of escaping."

They set out. Long Tom stationed himself before the attached garage. Monk and Ham went around back.

Doc Savage drifted up to the front door, his hands empty. The bronze man habitually eschewed firearms, although he had invented the supermachine pistol. It was his personal philosophy that a man could easily become reliant on such a weapon, and consequently reduced to helplessness should he lose control of it. This opinion he did not extend to his men, who were perfectly free to use whatever weapons they chose, provided they produced no fatalities in the course of their activities.

Observing carefully, Doc Savage saw a figure flit before the drawn blinds of an upstairs window. For the inhabitant had moved on to the second floor. Nothing much could be seen of this person, except that he or she appeared very active—going from room to room, as if searching for something.

This would not seem to be the behavior of someone comfortable in his own home, so Doc approached the front door cautiously.

He rang the doorbell, and stepped back to watch the reaction.

A silhouette visible through a fully-drawn blind, the figure froze, appeared to hesitate, and then flitted furtively from view. It could be discerned that the head of the active individual was oversized in comparison with an ordinary human being.

Doc Savage closed the distance between himself and the door, put his shoulder to it, and drove the panel inward. Wood splintered and the lock broke free.

Flashing through the living room, Doc Savage located the staircase leading to the second floor and charged up the carpeted risers. For all his Herculean stature, the bronze giant made surprisingly little sound.

At the rear of the house, window glass shattered, and the bronze man knew that Monk and Ham were impatiently barging in through the back.

Reaching the second floor landing, Doc Savage whipped toward a front room, and demanded, "Come out of there!"

"Who is it?" quavered a voice.

The voice was one that Doc Savage recognized. He pitched to the door, and immediately seized a cowering figure.

"Oh! It's you! Imagine that! What a surprise!"

The look on Marvin Lucian Linden's round face was one of immense relief. His wild, frizzled hair quivered like myriad insect antennae.

"I—I thought that burglars were breaking in," Linden stammered. "It is a distinct relief to learn otherwise."

Doc demanded, "What is your business here, Linden?"

Marvin Lucian Linden pulled himself together, straightened his rather flowery tie and said, "Why, I could ask the same of you, Mr. Savage."

Monk and Ham charged up the stairs, followed by Long Tom, who had come through the front door, all bristling with assorted weaponry.

Doc Savage said, "We are seeking Malcolm McLean, who has not been seen since he was released from the hospital last night."

"And I am doing the very same thing. McLean is a close friend of mine. I had become concerned not hearing from him."

"How did you get in?" asked Doc.

From a pocket, Linden produced a key, saying, "I happen to have a house key. I am free to drop in at any time. You may ask Malcolm about that when he shows up."

Observing Monk and the others, Linden added, "You can lay down those weapons, gentlemen, for I am completely harmless, as you can see."

"I don't like the look of this," gritted Long Tom suspiciously.

"Yeah," growled Monk. "Something don't smell right."

"You appear to be searching the place," Doc Savage pointed out.

"Yes, I was. I admit it. I was looking for Malcolm. Or any sign of where he might have gone. He often leaves notes behind. Alas, I discovered none. No clue, nor any hint. It is almost as if he has not been restored to life, after all."

"That is the way it is beginning to appear," said Doc.

This simple declaration took a moment to sink in. When it did, Marvin Lucian Linden's voice sank into a sad whine. "You do not suspect Dr. Rockwell of tomfoolery, do you?"

Rather than reply directly, Doc said, "It is unusual for a physician to release a patient so quickly, and not entirely understandable that that patient should subsequently disappear."

"The reputation of Warner Rockwell is impeccable," Linden said stiffly. "I do not associate with him as much as McLean, but I do know him socially. Moreover, I am well aware of his background. He belongs to one of the finest families in Chicago.

His forebears have been esteemed medical men for at least three generations. Rockwell asserted that he cured Malcolm McLean. I, for one, am taking that to the bank—even if you choose not to do so."

Doc Savage said nothing, while Long Tom remarked sourly, "Everybody involved in this is starting to look suspicious to me."

Marvin Lucian Linden seemed to take that personally, for he frowned deeply, changing the contours of his normally pleasant features and remarked, "I take exception to that canard, sir."

"Take what you want," said Long Tom peevishly. "But everything about this deal is fishy."

Linden became thoughtful and he said, "I have an idea. Why don't we all make ourselves comfortable and await Malcolm's return? Night has come on and surely he will be seeking his own bed."

"If he is yet among the living," inserted Ham dubiously.

Linden turned several shades paler than normal. He distinctly trembled, which made his frightful hair quiver alarmingly. "Do not say that! Malcolm McLean is my closest friend. If anything unfortunate were to befall him—"

"Something did," reminded Doc Savage. "His living brain was apparently fossilized—at least temporarily."

Marvin Lucian Linden closed his eyes, and shuddered momentarily.

"Yes, I recall. I will never forget the stony aspect of his eyes as he laid there. It was a medical miracle that Malcolm was plucked from the jaws of death."

Long Tom made a skeptical noise in his throat, and looked around as if he were seeking a convenient cuspidor.

Then he spied something which caused his pale eyes to narrow. The room in which they all stood was the master bedroom. A partly open door led to an adjacent room. Something in the other room had caught Long Tom's eye.

Drifting to the door, he pushed it wide, and craned his head about.

"Better take a look at this," he called out.

Led by Doc Savage, the group followed the electrical genius into the other room, which proved to be an attic space built into one corner of the second floor. A cunningly-concealed door hung open.

The odd-shaped room was bare of furnishings, being a wedge with little floorspace. The three angular walls were a pale ivory. Or they had been.

For now the far wall screamed at them in a yellow-green hue they had seen before.

"Jove!" exclaimed Ham, pointing with his cane. "Medusas!"

Monk said thickly, "Looks like a nest of them!"

There were, in fact, three Medusa silhouettes imprinted on the opposite side. Overlapping one another, they formed a single broad shape. Only the snaky heads stood apart.

Marvin Lucian Linden stared at the wall, seemed not to understand the significance of the unlovely shapes parading along the otherwise-blank surface.

"I fail to fathom what upsets you gentlemen," he expounded. "It appears to me that Malcolm has unusual taste in decoration, but he is an unusual fellow."

"Do you not recognize the three Gorgons?" demanded Ham.

Linden squinted, then said, "Oh!" so abruptly his crispy hair shook like thin leaves in a wind. "I do not know what to say, gentlemen. Really and truly."

Doc asked, "How did you discover the secret room?"

Linden replied, "Oh, it was never a secret. It used to be McLean's experimental laboratory, until he moved it. I knew where the hidden catch is."

Doc said abruptly, "We have business elsewhere. If McLean returns, we would appreciate your notifying us through our hotel."

"Happy to do so," said Marvin Lucian Linden, in a relieved tone. "You can be certain that I will do exactly that. As a matter of fact, I may stay the night. McLean has a spare bedroom, and I am welcome to use that. I will stand sentinel until his return. Good night to you all, gentleman."

Doc Savage led his men out, and they reclaimed the sedan, which Doc put into motion. It was now steadily raining, and the monotonous drumming depressed their spirits.

"What do you make of those Medusa silhouettes?" asked Long Tom, who had not previously encountered the uncanny shadows.

"They are highly suggestive," admitted Doc.

"Yeah, but of what? That's what I want to know."

Monk said, "They mighta been planted there as a warning."

"But to whom?" countered Ham. "To McLean himself, or to anyone prowling about his residence?"

"Either theory is plausible," advised the bronze man, who offered no more insight.

"Bally dead end," complained Ham.

"It's startin' to look like Malcolm McLean did not make it after all," growled Monk. "And that can only mean one thing."

"Yeah," grated Long Tom. "Rockwell is pulling a fast one on the city."

They waited in vain for Doc Savage to confirm this theory, but the bronze man maintained a grim silence as he propelled the sedan through the city's rain-washed streets.

As was often the case, Doc Savage's mental workings were not immediately understandable to his men.

Chapter XL

BIG SPOTS STEPS IN

THE DEATH OF mobster Joe Shine proved to be headline news. It was electrifying.

By itself, the crime lord's expiration would have rocked the
city which, in Prohibition times, had all but celebrated its
gangland figures. But when police revealed that Shine's entire
mob had been captured by Doc Savage and turned over to the
city police, it was a cause for celebration.

News of the death of Shine's arch-rival, Duke Grogan, had
not yet reached print. At Doc Savage's suggestion, his body had
been removed from his Cicero hideout, and consigned to the
city morgue adorned by an anonymous toe tag proclaiming him
to be "John Doe."

But such was the underworld grapevine that rumor of Duke
Grogan's untimely passing raced around the city, transmitted
from barber shop to saloon to even less reputable establishments.

One such place was a pool hall known as Mulligan's, situated on North Clark Street, not three blocks from the garage
where the infamous Saint Valentine's Day massacre had taken
place.

There, in a back room, Big Spots Bender held forth. Big
Spots was a rare survival of the gangland rivalries of the 1920s,
and was a key figure in the infamous "taxi wars" of a decade
gone by. Competing taxi companies had locked horns over
lucrative cab stands in the Loop, with one faction encroaching
upon the supposed territory of the other—the inevitable result

being sporadic gunfire, leading to bloodshed. At its worst, the conflict erupted into a full-blown war for control of the city's numerous cab stands.

When the worst was over, several companies had gone out of business or fled the city. Those that remained flourished. Big Spots Bender had been a bare-knuckled enforcer for one of those companies, and had done well for himself, earning himself a flaming reputation undiminished by changing times.

He was still available to handle that kind of work, but these days Big Spots provided the torpedoes, instead of doing the dirty work himself.

When one of his gunmen barged into the office waving a late edition, Big Spots barked, "What's up, Spats? You look like someone gave you a hot foot in both brogans."

"Listen to this, Big Spots. A little birdie just told me that Duke Grogan is in the morgue."

"You don't say?"

"I do say. I got it straight from the morgue attendant. It's the McCoy."

Big Spots took a cigar out of his mouth and rolled it thoughtfully between thumb and trigger-calloused forefinger.

"They autopsy the Duke yet?" he asked carefully.

"Yeah, they did. Not that they needed to go to all the trouble. Duke took four slugs in the guts, but the one that finished him off went into his brain."

"His brain, huh?" grunted Big Spots. "Had it turned to stone?"

"Nothing like that, Big Spots. Duke got it the day before Joe Shine met his maker. It don't look like the two killings are connected to one another, but Shine's killing points to that Medusa what's got the whole town worked up."

Big Spots laughed crudely. "Do you see me getting worked up over anything?"

"That's not the point, Big Spots. The connection is something different. Something very serious."

Big Spots put his stogie back in his mouth and said, "I'm listening. Spread it out on the desk for me."

Spats pulled up a wooden chair, plunking his rangy frame onto it. "I don't have the story completely straight, but somehow Doc Savage is tangled up in what happened to Duke Grogan's gang."

"Gang? You told me Duke got put on the spot. You didn't say anything about his gang. You holding out on me, Spats?"

"No, Big Spots. I ain't. It's just that I don't have all the dope yet. But Duke is in the cooler for sure, and his boys ain't nowhere to be found."

Big Spots eyed the burning tip of his cigar. "Nowhere to be found, you say? Ain't that interesting? Yes, that's very interesting. You know what they say about Doc Savage?"

"Yeah, I do. Guys who pile into Doc Savage get run out of town."

"Run out of town, my left ear. They up and vanish. Like ghosts. Nobody ever hears from or of them again."

Spats grew fidgety as he asked, "Do you think Doc Savage blew into town to clean it up?"

"I don't figure that exactly. But that Medusa, or whoever she is, seems to have that bright idea in mind."

"Maybe we should lay low, huh? What do you say, Big Spots? Miami might be a good place to spend the coming winter."

Big Spots scowled. "What have you, gone balmy in the brain? Duke Grogan is chilling his corpse on a marble slab. Joe Shine is being fitted for his funeral suit and you want to go on vacation? This town is wide open now! Any gorilla can grab a bigger hunk than he has already."

"Is that what you're thinking, Big Spots? Taking over Chicago?"

A slow smile unveiled the mob enforcer's crooked teeth. "I was thinking that when I read about Joe Shine; now that I know Duke Grogan is out of the picture, there's a lot more room to move around in."

"I get you. But what about this Medusa what's declared war on wise guys like us?"

"Let the damn Medusa knock off the big fish. That works in our favor. Thins out the herd. Then we move in, big and bold as brass."

Spats made uneasy faces. "Shine and Grogan were the biggest fish in town. The rest of us are small fry by comparison. How do you know this Medusa won't come after us next?"

Big Spots leaned back in his chair and cocked his thumbs into his suspenders and puffed away at his cigar, staring at the still blades of his ceiling fan.

"Shine and Grogan liked to get their pictures in the paper. They wanted to make a big splash. Attracted a lot of attention, they did. People ate it up. That was their mistake. If you draw the spotlight, you're a big fat target. That's not how our outfit's been operating. You know that."

"Yeah, Big Spots. I know that. The limelight ain't part of our racket."

"No, it ain't. We're no starched-collar politicians. Strictly guns and muscle, that's our racket. But now we're moving up. We're going to start quiet and move careful-like. Over time, we'll grab off a piece of this and a hunk of that until we own a man-sized chunk of this town's graft and rackets."

Spats scratched behind one ear. "You're counting on the Medusa not noticing us? Is that right?"

"That's about the size of it. As for Doc Savage, he's out of New York City. He won't stay in Chicago any longer than he has to. Whatever his business is in this town, it'll blow over soon enough. Doc Savage won't be a problem for long." Big Spots chuckled to himself thoughtfully. "Hell, Doc Savage may not be a problem at all."

A brave grin crept over the underling's face. "Sure, Big Spots, sure. We'll ride out Doc Savage and lie low until this Medusa scare dies down. It'll all blow over eventually, and what's left will be ours."

"Like picking up a poker pot after you've gunned down the other players," chuckled Big Spots Bender.

Both men began laughing rather ghoulishly, perhaps reflecting on times in the past when they had done exactly that. For despite his high-sounding name, Big Spots Bender was small potatoes in the Chicago underworld. Long considered a comer, he had never risen to prominence, nor had he ever owned a section of town or controlled its rackets. A hired gun at the start, he was still nothing more than a manager of younger enforcers. His nickname was acquired because he liked to hit the night spots, but only the biggest and best of them.

Leaning forward, Big Spots slammed down the front legs of his chair and took his thumbs out of his stretched suspenders. His face was serious. Seeing this, Spats cocked a wary eye in his direction.

"I know that look, Big Spots. Do I get you right?"

"Yeah, you do, Spats. I'm thinking it won't hurt to lay low for a little bit. What say you and me knock off for the day? Go back to my place and relax. We won't take any vacation. We'll go on what the college professors call a sabbatical."

Spats had never before encountered the word. "What's that?"

"It's kinda like time off, for good behavior."

Having served jail time and received that same consideration, both men chuckled in unison.

Jumping to his feet, Big Spots barked, "Bring the car around, will you Spats?"

"Sure, boss. I'll do that little thing."

Spats, who served as both chauffeur and bodyguard to Big Spots Bender, went out and brought the criminal's sedan out of a nearby garage and parked in front of the pool hall, awaiting his employer's pleasure.

Soon, they were tooling through the city, and in short order they pulled up before the gangster's residence.

Outside, two vehicles were parked. One was a coal truck, and the coal deliveryman was busy pouring rattling lumps of anthracite down the chute into the cellar coal bin.

"Take a look at that, Big Spots."

Misunderstanding, Big Spot's eyes went to the other vehicle, a rather shabby coupe. A man was seated behind the wheel, perusing a newspaper.

"I recognize that bird. Jack Swangle. He's a legman for the *Tribunal*. Wonder what *he* wants?"

"Probably a few choice words, Big Spots."

"Well, he ain't going to get any. We're laying low. Keep your trap shut and let me do the talking."

Spats tugged at his boss' sleeve. "That snoop wasn't what I was wondering about, Big Spots. It's that coal truck."

Big Spot's eyes veered toward his property. "What's the matter? Guy's just delivering coal, ain't he?"

"Didn't you get a load in just a week or so back?"

"Yeah, I did. But it's been snowing, and then raining, and winter is coming on. You can't have too much coal, now can you?"

Spats shrugged. "I guess not. It's just that they usually don't make deliveries so close together."

"Well, forget about it. Here comes that long-nosed reporter. Let me handle this."

The scribe in question pushed his toothy smile through one car window and asked, "How's the boy, Big Spots? Seen the latest edition?"

Big Spots guffawed self-consciously. "You know I can't hardly read, Jack."

The reporter laughed carelessly. "Don't hand me that. You can read as well as the next bozo. What have you got to say about Joe Shine and what killed him?"

"Nothing. But don't quote that. I didn't know Shine, and I barely knew Grogan."

Jack Swangle's hungry features quivered with sudden interest. "Duke Grogan? What about him?"

A canny light came into Big Spot's eyes. "Ain't you heard?"

"Heard what?"

"Tell you what," said Big Spots. "I'm allergic to newspapermen. Leave me out of your story and I'll hand you a hot lead."

The reporter's face broke out in a big grin. "It's a deal. What's the scoop?"

Big Spots leaned close to the other and spoke in a conspiratorial whisper. "Duke Grogan was gunned down the other night. Nobody knows who done it. But he's plenty dead. They got the stiff down in the city morgue. If you get yourself a good photographer, I'll bet you could take a swell camera study of the guy."

Swangle whistled softly, his eyes a little strange. "First, Joe Shine and now Grogan! This is going to bust the Chicago underworld wide open."

"You want my opinion," Big Spots remarked, "I think things will be quiet for a little bit. Very quiet. Now if you excuse me, I'm going to take my ease."

Jack Swangle hopped into his coupe, and took off like a scared rabbit.

Turning to his bodyguard, Big Spots Bender said, "That's how you handle the press. You hand them a line, and they run with it. You want to stay healthy, Spats, keep your name out of the papers."

"Smart thinking, Big Spots."

"That's why I'm still walking around, and Joe Shine and Duke Grogan are on ice, waiting on their wakes."

"It will be a big week for the florists!" breathed Spats.

Laughing raucously, the two men entered the dwelling, where they made themselves drinks, and turned on the radio.

They had to wait until the coal man had finished filling the bin, and departed to finish his round of deliveries, before they got truly comfortable.

"Sounds like you got enough anthracite to last you all winter," remarked Spats.

"That suits me. I figure on staying home a lot. 'Til everything blows over, you understand."

The two criminals chuckled as they downed their drinks, neither one of them suspecting what lay in store.

"Put some of that fresh coal in the furnace, Spats," ordered Big Spots. "It's gonna be a chilly night."

HEADLINES the next morning read:

BIG SPOTS BENDER AND BODYGUARD FOUND DEAD

The article was riveting. It ran:

> Police this morning were called to the Canaryville home of Jerome "Big Spots" Bender, an underworld figure little known outside of Chicago.
>
> Several crows were discovered in the vicinity of the dwelling, having expired. This was noticed by neighbors, who, fearing a gas leak, called it to the attention of the Chicago police.
>
> When authorities arrived, they canvassed the neighborhood, knocking on doors. Failing to receive a response from the Bender residence, and noting the owner's vehicle parked at the curb, they took the liberty of forcing the door.
>
> Inside, they found Mr. Bender and an associate, known as Spats McGillicuddy. Both men were found dead sitting in easy chairs, the parlor radio operating. There were no signs of foul play nor any injuries observed by arriving ambulance attendants.
>
> It was, at first, suspected that the two died as a result of a faulty coal furnace, but the furnace was found to be in good working order and neither body displayed the telltale cherry-red skin coloring which accompanies carbon monoxide poisoning.
>
> The bodies were transported to Mercy General Hospital, where all efforts to revive them were met with failure.
>
> It was only discovered hours later that the brains of both victims had been inexplicably petrified—a condition linking

them to the queer fate of the late gang leader, Joe Shine.

By this time, Dr. Warner Rockwell was summoned, but quickly declared that the two men had been dead far too long for his reversing process to take effect.

"It is my determination that the victims died not long after sunset last night, and sat, deceased, in their easy chairs all night," pronounced Dr. Rockwell.

Alerted to this new finding, Chicago police went back to the Bender dwelling, where they discovered a note in the owner's mailbox, which had not been left by the postman, for it bore no address or stamp.

The contents of this note have not been released, but police have declared that these latest killings are definitely tied to the terrorizer calling him or herself Medusa.

Chapter XLI

QUEER COAL

DOC SAVAGE WAS conferring by telephone with the Superintendent of Police of Chicago when news of Big Spots Bender's demise reached the latter's ears.

The bronze man was explaining that some small progress in his investigation of the calcified-brain slayings had been made, when an orderly handed the Superintendent a teletype report.

"One moment, please," the official told Doc. There was a rustle of papers, and the Superintendent's voice came back on the line, charged with excitement.

"I was just handed a bulletin that Big Spots Bender and one of his bodyguards was found dead in their home this morning."

"I am not familiar with the name," admitted Doc.

"A small-time enforcer. Bender was an up-and-comer a while back, but has not been very active in recent years," the official reported. "This has all the markings of another petrified-brain case."

"I would like to examine the scene," requested Doc.

"You are more than welcome to," advised the Superintendent, providing an address and adding, "I will meet you there. We can finish our conference on the scene."

Hanging up, Doc Savage called in his aides, saying, "It appears that the Medusa has struck again. This time at the home of a gangster of seemingly little importance."

"Events are accelerating toward an unknown goal," Ham mused, polishing the head of his cane.

Monk grunted, "Somebody is sure cleanin' house. But why?" They exited the suite.

"Any word from that Linden?" asked Long Tom when they moved together through the corridor.

Doc shook his head. "No telephone call was received overnight. We will look into that later."

Soon, they were pulling up before the Bender residence, and Doc Savage's uncanny trilling was briefly audible when he spied a sprinkling of dead birds on the lawn.

The Superintendent had not yet arrived at the murder scene, but a police officer standing guard had evidently been alerted by radio to expect the bronze man's arrival, for he walked up briskly, saying, "If it wasn't for the fact that the corpses aren't red, the medical examiner says he would take this as carbon monoxide poisoning. We shut down the furnace anyway."

Doc asked, "Was the home heated by coal?"

"It was. Why do you ask?"

"It may be relevant," said Doc, moving toward the front door.

Behind the bronze giant, Monk, Ham and Long Tom walked along in single file. Monk muttered, "Coal is poppin' up all over this crazy business."

Inside, Doc found the detective in charge of the case, who remarked, "We haven't turned anything up of interest, Mr. Savage. The neighbors didn't notice anything unusual until daybreak, when all those dead birds turned up on the lawn."

"Were any other homes affected?" queried the bronze man.

The detective shook his head firmly. "Just this one. And both victims died in their parlor. Imagine that? A couple tough customers like Big Spots Bender and his bodyguard. Men of his ilk don't usually go out in easy chairs."

Monk bustled up, toting his portable chemical laboratory.

"Want I should take samples of the air and residue on the walls?" he asked Doc.

"If that is all right with the investigating detective," said Doc.

"Be my guest," said the plain-clothes sleuth. "But the air seems to have cleared out when we opened the windows."

Doc Savage's nostrils dilated as he sampled the air.

There was a faint charred smell, as of burnt charcoal. But nothing else out of the ordinary.

Monk got to work, the bronze man went from room to room. His flake-gold eyes seemed to miss nothing, but neither did he touch or disturb anything in the crime scene.

Turning to the police detective, Doc requested, "I would like to examine the coal furnace."

The detective seemed a little puzzled by his expression, but he led the bronze man into the cellar, which was nothing remarkable. Cobwebs clung to a cluster of rusting garden tools, indicating disuse.

The coal furnace was modern, a great black monster of a thing with several fat ducts reaching out of its top in the manner of an octopus, each duct feeding air to a separate room of the dwelling above through forced-air registers.

The feed door on the bulky furnace yawned open, and the bronze man trickled the beam of his spring-generator flashlight on the interior fire pit and saw the grayish lumps of combustible coal cooling down in the grate.

"We tossed water onto the coal bed," explained the detective, "to put out the fire."

"It might have been better if water had not been used on these coals," Doc remarked without emotion.

The detective shrugged. "We had to, in case it was generating poison gas."

Doc found the coal bin. It was a pen situated in a dim corner of the cellar which had been walled off with unpainted board. There was a simple door mounted on hinges. Doc opened this. The interior proved to be heaped high with coal. Not a single lump looked out of the ordinary.

Shutting the bin door, Doc found a dustpan and whisk broom and returned to the furnace. He collected samples of the burnt coal first. Kneeling, the bronze man then opened the ash pit door at the furnace's base and collected a sufficient sample of ashes which had sifted down. These he took upstairs to Monk Mayfair.

"Residue from the coal furnace," Doc informed Monk. "Place it in a container for later analysis."

"You think somebody put somethin' in the coal?" asked the homely chemist, taking the dust pan.

Doc nodded wordlessly.

The detective volunteered, "There's a reporter outside. He told a funny story about that."

Turning, Doc asked, "About what?"

"He swung by last night, purely to get a comment from Big Spots about this Medusa murder spree," related the detective. "And while he was talking to them, Spats made a comment that the driver delivering coal seemed to have come early."

"Early?"

"In the season, I mean. Seems Bender took a coal delivery just two weeks ago."

Doc Savage's trilling came, sounding like an avian air. The seemingly sourceless sound surrounded those assembled, owing to its uncanny ventriloquial nature.

Looking to the window, the detective remarked, "Sounds like the healthy birds are back."

Doc asked, "What concern delivered the coal?"

"I didn't ask him that. Didn't seem important. I thought it was funny because the reporter asked Big Spots about Joe Shine's passing, and hours later Big Spots is put on the spot. Kind of ironic, don't you think?"

The bronze man declined to reply. Instead, he moved into the kitchen, and looked around until he found a business card among others. This was a file of local establishments Big Spots Bender did business with. Among them was a card for a coal delivery company.

Going to the telephone, Doc Savage put in a call to the delivery company. He spoke for a few minutes, and then hung up, saying, "Thank you."

Addressing the detective, Doc said, "The coal concern did not make a delivery yesterday. The truck was a fake."

The detective tilted back his hat and whistled in mild astonishment. "That cinches it! The coal must've been phony, too. Big Spots was assassinated by a lump of coal. Won't that make for an interesting obituary?"

Doc pointed out, "It will make more interesting headlines if it gets out."

"What do you mean?"

Ham Brooks had been listening to all this and volunteered a response.

"What Doc Savage means is no one in this city is safe who burns coal in his furnace and has a criminal record."

"That takes in a lot of territory," the detective said, pulling at his lower lip. "A hell of a lot of territory."

"I would like to speak with that reporter," said Doc.

The detective laughed shortly. "I'm sure he would love to speak with you. In fact, most of the so-called journalists in this town would love to pelt you with a bunch of questions."

"What I have in mind," stated Doc Savage firmly, "is the opposite. I intend to press this reporter with several questions. What is his name?"

"Jack Swangle. He's with the *Tribunal.*"

Long Tom made a distasteful face, and said, "Wasn't that the wiseacre we ran into twice before?"

"The very same," said Ham suspiciously.

"Lead us to him," requested Doc.

ALL WENT outside, and moved toward a gaggle of reporters who were being held two houses away by the police, who did not wish their investigation interfered with.

As they walked to that group, the Superintendent of Chicago Police pulled up in his official car. He stepped out, and asked, "Have you learned anything new?"

Doc Savage said, "It appears that a full supply of coal was delivered last night and the combustion of one or more lumps released the deadly gas."

"Murder by coal!" gasped the Superintendent.

"Don't that beat all!" chimed in the detective, who added, "Everything Mr. Savage says fits the facts in the case. We've got to warn the populace to check their coal supply."

Doc said. "A reporter witnessed the coal being delivered. He may have seen the face of the deliveryman."

As a group, they all moved up the street, but as they were doing so, a low-slung touring car screeched up, slewed to a halt, and the door popped out.

Out stepped a man who looked gaunt in the extreme. His eyes were sunken, his cheeks hollow, and his lips were shreds of gristle from having been habitually chewed. He wore a wide-brimmed fedora pulled low over his head, but now he tipped it back to reveal haggard features.

From under his overcoat, he yanked out a Tommy gun, and addressed Doc Savage, who was walking in a group of police several yards distant.

"You're the mug behind all these crook killings!" he roared. "First you greased Duke Grogan and Joe Shine, now Big Spots is in the dead box. Well, damned if you're gonna get me. I'm gettin' you first. Take this, bronze guy! Take it and like it!"

The bronze man had been known in the past to dodge a bullet or two, but there were limits to even his seemingly superhuman skill and reflexes. Doc stood in a crowd, and the entire group was menaced by the impending bullet storm. Too, neighbors had gathered about, watching anxiously. He could not move without drawing lead in his direction and that lead would massacre those around him—many of them unprotected.

BEFORE the bronze man could move, Monk, Ham and Long Tom whipped out their assorted personal arsenals and opened up in unison.

A fusillade of mercy bullets and hypodermic slugs struck the fellow in arms, legs and elsewhere. His hat went flying.

These bullets were low caliber, so even their combined mass and energy did not knock him backward.

As such, the assassin managed to squeeze off a brief burst.

Pushing the nearest persons aside and out of harm's way, Doc Savage set himself to take the first blast in the chest.

The metallic giant was struck, forced backward. Astoundingly, he held his feet for a few seconds, then was forced to the ground, the punishing power of the stream of .45 caliber slugs proving greater than his muscular resistance.

At that point, the bluecoats had drawn their service revolvers and began blazing away.

The gunman wilted before he could squeeze off another burst. He had one foot on his running board and one elbow on the sill of the open door window. Thus it was that when he crumpled, he got hung up on the door, which fell further open, causing him to slide to the ground in a heap of worsted woolen coat and scuffed shoe leather. Crimson began dyeing his winter coat.

Jaw sagging alarmingly, Monk Mayfair turned to Doc Savage, his supermachine pistol still smoking. "Doc, Doc! Talk to me, will ya!"

The bronze man lay on his back, the glittering flake-gold of his eyes nearly still, as if they had been stunned in their incessant circular motion.

Doc took a deep breath, and levered himself to his feet—much to the astonishment of Monk and the others.

Doc took a few seconds to compose himself, but it was evident that his bulletproof vest had spared him from death, even if it had not been sufficient to keep him from being seriously bruised.

Long Tom said, "My hypodermic needle bullets sure did the trick."

Ham said, "On the contrary. I struck him with at least a dozen mercy bullets."

"What makes you think my dope didn't work first?" Long Tom snapped back.

"There is more anesthetic in a mercy slug than one of your needle bullets."

An argument seemed ready to ensue, when both men realized that Monk's own supermachine pistol had also been in operation.

Ham asked, "What sort of ammunition did you use, you slope-skulled gorilla?"

Monk shrugged carelessly, saying, "I was so busy shootin' I didn't stop to think." He detached the small ammunition drum from in front of the trigger guard, looked at the array of bullets rattling within, and said, "Dang! These are scintillator bullets."

Both Ham and Long Tom looked at him doubtfully.

Monk explained, "They're designed to frighten an enemy. Since they're basically a chemical explosion that's harmless."

"I did not see any such pyrotechnics," Ham remarked.

"They work better at night, I guess," mumbled Monk in a disappointed tone.

Long Tom waved a dismissive hand in the hairy chemist's direction, saying, "He's just an also-ran in this game. Those bullets didn't count."

The detective in charge interrupted. "None of your fancy ammunition counted in the end. Didn't you hear those Police Positives barking? They bit deep. This mug is a goner."

He was kneeling at the body of the machine gunner, and found on the back seat of his machine a folded newspaper. Harvesting it, he opened up the sheet, read the front page, and said, "Looks like 'Shivering' Ellis had shivered his last. Seems as if the tabloids got him all riled up."

The detective brought the newspaper over and passed it around. It was an extra. Fully half of the front page was headline. It read:

SUSPICION DOC SAVAGE
BEHIND MEDUSA MURDERS!

This left not much room for the story to go with the headline, and not very much story at that.

The article referenced the events in New York City the previous month in which numerous individuals had been killed by a mysterious pop-eyed malady. Suspicion had pointed in the direction of Doc Savage.* Although the bronze man had been exonerated, the article writer brought forth new suspicions with a leading question that was unsupported by any known facts:

> Has Doc Savage imported his war against crime to Chicago? And is there nothing he will stop at?

There followed a series of quotes given in response to reportorial questions by local notables, including amateur criminologists, college professors and others who might be counted on to give an opinion even if that opinion was not supported by facts.

The account also reported growing rumors—at presstime unconfirmed—that the infamous Duke Grogan and his gang had vanished from their usual haunts and were presumed deceased.

The Superintendent of Police read the article in his turn and burst out, "This is outrageous! There is not a shred of truth in this pile of malarkey."

"It is enough to create problems for the investigation," said Doc Savage.

"I'm going to have a talk with the editor of this rag," promised the police official. "All this will do is frighten Chicago blind. Aren't our citizens scared enough?"

---

* *The Annihilist*

During this exchange, Monk wondered, "Who was that bozo?"

The investigating detective offered, "That's Raymond 'Shivering' Ellis. A local torpedo. They call him 'Shivering' because he's a hophead. He's always got the shakes. Looks like that headline set him off. Oh well, another stiff for the Black Maria. No one's going to miss that piece of human wreckage."

Having composed himself, Doc Savage discovered that he needn't bother accosting the reporters gathered up the street; they were rushing in his direction.

Monk, Ham and Long Tom formed a cordon around the bronze giant to fend off the overeager scribes. But the trio could not fend off their shouted insistent questions.

"Savage, what do you know about the Medusa murders?"

"Are you the Medusa?"

"If you aren't, who is?"

"Why is it everywhere you go, criminals disappear mysteriously?"

This last question came uncomfortably close to one of the bronze man's deepest secrets, so he deflected it with a response.

"The investigation is continuing, but the master brain behind it has yet to be unearthed."

This brought another rash of questions, and Doc Savage suddenly strode forward, grabbed hold of the reporter named Jack Swangle, and took him aside.

"You witnessed the delivery of coal last night? Did you notice the features of the delivery man?"

"What does that have to do with the price of beer?" Swangle whined.

"Answer the question," said Doc firmly.

"A tall fella, kind of pale, wore a cap over his head. Not much about him stood out. I barely paid attention. I was too busy jawing with Big Spots."

"What did the truck legend say?"

"Vermilion Coal," replied the puzzled scribe.

That was the concern which regularly delivered to the Bender household. This meant that the person delivering the coal knew the routine of the house. The bronze man had noticed that the coal in the bin stood heaping full, indicating an excess of heating supply.

Extracting a sheet of paper from a pocket and unfolding it, Doc showed the reporter the sketch he had made of the mystery man who resembled Malcolm McLean, asking, "Is this the man in question?"

Swangle said instantly, "Yeah, that's the fella."

Doc Savage released the fellow, saying, "Thank you."

Returning to the police official, he imparted, "My men and I will be going now. We will keep you apprised of any progress in our investigation."

The Superintendent nodded gratefully. "And we will do the same. Don't you worry about these scare headlines. You have our full confidence."

"Thank you," said Doc, climbing behind the wheel of the sedan.

They had not driven far when Ham Brooks burst forth with an opinion.

"Everything so far has pointed to Malcolm McLean. His family history in coal mines, his friendship with Janet Falcon, not to mention the fact that he is a chemist prone to doing strange experiments. Yet indications are that McLean is no more."

"I never trusted that gray-faced ghoul," added Long Tom.

For a change, Monk Mayfair was the voice of reason, possibly because by habit he was disinclined to agree with Ham Brooks.

"I say we don't jump to any conclusions until all the facts are in."

"How much more evidence do you need?" demanded Ham.

Monk's pig eyes narrowed. His brain worked fast.

"Motive. We need a motive."

"Motive? Why it's—"

The elegant attorney fell silent. His jaw snapped shut—a certain indication that he was stumped. Producing a silken handkerchief, he fell to polishing the rich ebony sheen of his cane.

"What *is* the motive?" grumbled Long Tom. "It sure beats me to work one out."

Doc drove on, offering no comment, his bronze mask of a face resolute.

Chapter XLII

THREE GORGONS?

HAM BROOKS, MONK MAYFAIR and Long Tom Roberts were still arguing over the mystery of the Medusa murders when they entered Doc Savage's hotel suite.

Long Tom was complaining querulously, "Maybe there isn't a motive. Maybe McLean was just crazy in the head. Going through life looking like a walking cadaver might do that to a man."

"Makes sense," Monk said, taking out his portable chemical laboratory and setting it up on a table.

"Nonsense!" sniffed Ham. "All criminal activities require motives. This one is too sophisticated to be merely the work of an insane person. McLean, if he was the Medusa, must have a hidden motivation."

"None of it makes sense," complained Long Tom. "The victims have ranged from Ned Gamble to assorted hoodlums and other riffraff. How does it all tie in?"

Doc Savage was silent as he moved about the room; he was searching for signs that the suite had been invaded again. After a single turn around the suite, he concluded that it had remained unmolested.

Joining Monk, the bronze man began working with the portable chemical laboratory, saying, "First, we will examine the burnt coal and ashes scooped from Big Spots Bender's furnace, then the smoky residue on his walls. Finally, we will test the tobacco leaves Long Tom collected at Joe Shine's residence."

They settled down to work. Since Ham and Long Tom were not versed in chemical matters, they took their argument into the adjoining room. It had not been an argument at the start, but the fussy lawyer managed to turn it into one.

"I have just realized that Malcolm McLean cannot possibly be the culprit," Ham snapped.

"That was your opinion at the start!" returned Long Tom peevishly.

"McLean could not have struck down the elevator boy, for he was already dead. Doc found his body in the impoundment at the coal mine. For I am now convinced that the gray cadaver was he."

"Then who delivered the bad coal?" Long Tom retorted.

Ham twirled his elegant stick while he considered the question.

"There appear to be two identical or nearly identical Malcolm McLeans. Perhaps he has a twin brother."

"Aw, you've been watching too many murder mystery movies. That gag doesn't happen in real life."

In the other room, test tubes clinked and chemicals bubbled and sizzled as Doc and Monk subjected the various items of evidence to a succession of scientific tests.

The apish chemist could be heard muttering, "Tough break we don't have your full laboratory set-up here, Doc. We'd get to the bottom of this much quicker."

"We will have to work with what we have," advised Doc. "We are not so severely handicapped that we cannot find answers."

They continued working while Long Tom and Ham batted theories back-and-forth as if playing tennis at high speed.

"Perhaps," Ham Brooks was saying, "Duke Grogan was the Medusa."

"You know that can't be!" Long Tom said harshly. "Grogan was killed by Janet Falcon, we think. The killings continued long after that."

"Perhaps after Duke's death, one of his surviving gang, or some other party, continued carrying on his reign of terror in his stead."

Long Tom threw up his hands. "What's the motive? There's got to be a motive. It's not money. Nobody is demanding ransom or tribute. It seems to be terror."

Ham was silent for a pause. "Doc revealed that he saw a creature resembling Medusa in the coal mine before it collapsed. Perhaps there really is a surviving Gorgon. Were there not three Gorgons? Only Medusa was slain. Perhaps one of the others survived into the modern day. It sounds far-fetched, but what if such a creature had been discovered in the coal mine and brought under control by criminals?"

That suggestion seemed to flummox the slender electrical expert. He was momentarily stunned into silence.

Finally, he growled, "Medusa is a fairy tale. That's out. Try floating another one. I'll shoot it down with my magnetic gun."

From the other room, Doc Savage's voice resounded.

"Consider the possibility that there is more than one master brain."

It was unusual for the bronze man to broach a theory too far in advance of his ability to prove it, so all parties gathered in the room where Doc and Monk were toiling.

Monk was grumbling aloud, "These clinkers don't seem to be much more than ordinary burnt coal, although I'm gettin' some peculiar reactions from the reagents."

"What does that mean, you hairy ape?" Ham demanded.

"It means," Monk admitted, "there's something funny about these ashes, but I can't tell exactly what it is. The same with the smoke residue I took off the walls. It wasn't carbon monoxide that killed Big Spots and his bodyguard, but I'll be daggone if I know what it was, chemically speaking."

Ham addressed Doc Savage. "What do you mean by saying there might be more than one master brain?"

"You will remember that the voice of the Medusa kept speaking in the royal 'we.' And that the message left by the body of Malcolm McLean read: '*Gorgones omnia vincit*'— Gorgons conquer all.'"

"This would not be the first time an egotistical master criminal employed the majestic plural," Ham pointed out.

"True enough," admitted Doc. "But recall the signature on the letter sent to the Chicago newspapers. Medusa S. Euryale. The name comprised those of all three of the Gorgon sisters. This suggests a triumvirate."

Monk grunted, "That's smart thinkin'. I hadn't thought of that."

Long Tom fell into a fresh argument. "Let's see," he said, "if there were three gorgons, Malcolm McLean is one, Duke Grogan is another, but who's the third member of this terror trust?"

"Janet Falcon!" Ham exploded. "She has yet to tell the complete story of why she sent Ned Gamble to New York."

Long Tom made a rude snorting noise. "Why would she send for help from Doc Savage if she was part of the plot?"

"Because she sent her fiancé deliberately to his death. She is a murderess. There is no escaping that conclusion."

Everyone looked to Doc Savage for confirmation of that theory.

Instead, the bronze man continued working on the tobacco leaves taken from the Joe Shine residence. The green leaves had been used to roll home-made cigars, and it was Doc Savage's working theory that doctored tobacco had killed both Shine and his attorney, Gale Michaels, as it had Ned Gamble in New York.

Doc said, "It will be difficult to tell if these leaves have been treated with any dangerous substance without burning them. If we do, we will subject ourselves to the deadly fumes."

Long Tom suggested, "We can wear gas masks."

Monk Mayfair let out a braying laugh and said, "If we wear gas masks, what is that gonna tell us? We only know if the smoke is dangerous if someone's brain turns to stone. Maybe you want to volunteer to be the guinea pig."

"That's not funny!" snapped Long Tom.

Bright sunlight was streaming through the hotel windows as they worked. The rain of the previous day had given way to a glorious afternoon. Dust motes danced in the solar rays, and it felt warm despite the season. A steam radiator hissed and knocked, adding a pleasant humidity.

While Doc Savage was examining the green tobacco leaves, a voice was suddenly heard in the room, hissing, venomous.

"Doc Savage! It has become too hot for you in Chicago! It is time to leave town, lest you be arrested for the slaughter of the city's criminal element."

"Blazes!" blurted out Monk, bullet head swiveling around, seeking the source of the sound. "There's that blamed Medusa voice again!"

Ham Brooks unsheathed his sword cane, and attacked the drapes, plucking them aside, stabbing them, checking closets, looking under the bed. The smallest of them all, Long Tom Roberts, crawled under the bed, seeking the source of the disembodied voice.

Doc Savage began acting strangely. Moving about the room, he swept his great hands about, as if attempting to capture the sunbeams streaming in through the window.

"This is your final warning!" the voice of the Medusa resounded. *"Go at—"*

The uncanny voice broke up into an unintelligible garbling which only added to its mystery. Doc froze, moved his hands quickly, clutching at empty air.

It looked for all the world as if the bronze giant had somehow captured the weird, disembodied voice in mid-sentence, for it was heard no more.

Attention elsewhere, his men failed to notice this. They left off their searching, satisfied that no present mortal had uttered those words.

Doc Savage went to the window, and searched the rooftops across the street, as he had done in New York City. His flake-gold eyes were ranging the rooftops and the windows of the buildings across the busy avenue.

Seemingly discovering nothing, he turned his back and said, "Long Tom, go to Miss Falcon's room and bring her here. It is time that she made a full confession."

"Confession!" blurted Ham.

"Ham, I want you to call the patent office in Washington, District of Columbia, and look into any recent patents filed by Malcolm McLean and Marvin Lucian Linden."

Ham's dark eyes glowed with keen interest. "Do you suspect Linden in this conspiracy?"

Doc only said, "We have too many suspects to overlook possibilities. Of the parties involved, only McLean and Linden are capable of patenting inventions of their own."

"I'll get right on it," snapped Ham, retreating into the adjoining room.

As Long Tom exited the hotel suite, Doc and Monk finished their chemical work, and the expression on the hairy chemist's anthropoid features was one of utter disappointment.

"Goose eggs!" he grunted. "That's all we collected for our pains. Goose eggs."

Doc Savage nodded slightly. He began putting away the accumulated evidence for possible later study. A trace of disappointment showed on his metallic features, also a vague air of worry.

Long Tom Roberts was not gone long. When he returned, he was alone, and the look on his thin features was white and shocked.

"Doc! Better come quick!"

Monk grumbled, "Don't tell me Janet Falcon got kidnapped again."

Long Tom said breathlessly, "She got away from us all right. But not in the way you think. Hurry!"

Chapter XLIII

THE DEATH NOTE

LONG TOM ROBERTS had left the door of Janet Falcon's hotel room slightly ajar. Doc Savage rushed to it, flung the door open, stepped in and then his trilling commenced keening.

The sound of it was unexpectedly harsh, wild. As it sank in register, it became doleful and disappointed.

When the bronze man entered the room, it was with a marked deference, as if he were entering a church or cemetery.

Crowding behind them, Monk and Ham stuck curious heads in, not knowing what to expect.

What they beheld stayed with them forever.

The others saw the shadow of the woman before they noticed the mortal form casting it.

The shadow was weird in that it floated in midair. Their eyes veered to its source, became fixed. The first thing they noticed was Janet Falcon's feet. She wore only one shoe; the other had fallen to the carpet beneath her bare toes.

That told them that they need not look any higher.

Long Tom said it first: "She hanged herself."

It was true, for the dead woman hung suspended from the ceiling fixture. She had used one of her own stockings. Her forlorn form twisted slightly, impelled by the rush of air created by their arrival.

The chair on which she had stood in her last minutes had tipped over, knocked aside by her flailing out during the final moments of mortal existence.

Righting it, Doc Savage stepped up, removed a clasp knife from his vest and cut the woman down, catching her with one cabled arm.

Laying the body on the divan, the bronze man sliced away the hose wound around her neck, felt of her wrist and throat, but failed to detect a pulse. A pocket mirror was held to her pale, parted lips. No condensation from respiration was produced.

Congested purple features combined with the coolness of the woman's flesh told that medical intervention would avail no one in this case. Most unnerving of all were Janet Falcon's eyes. Even in death, they had remained open. The blood vessels in the whites of her eyes had turned blood red due to hemorrhage. The contrast with her emerald irises made for a stare that was ghastly.

Closing them with his fingertips, Doc Savage went in search of a sheet to cover the body.

As his observant eyes swept about the room, Ham noticed the envelope on the night table. It was addressed: *To Whomever It Concerns.*

Snapping this up, he opened the envelope, read the short note contained within.

"She left a suicide note," Ham announced. "It says simply 'I cannot live with what I have done.'"

Long Tom mumbled, "So she admitted her guilt."

Ham murmured, "This note is signed 'Medusa.'"

This statement seemed to hit Monk Mayfair hardest. "Guilty! Who woulda believed it?"

Doc Savage had by now returned with a fresh sheet. As he prepared to cover the cooling form, he rearranged her head on the divan. One hand brushed the longish hair at the back of the dead woman's head, and encountered something unexpected.

When his hand came away, it was holding a small automatic pistol. A .22 caliber make.

"Where did *that* come from?" Ham wondered.

"Evidently, Miss Falcon was in the habit of carrying this weapon for protection," supplied Doc. "It appears to have been gathered up in her hair, and held in place by rubber bands and bobby pins."

Jacking back the slide caused a bullet to pop up. Doc caught it. Removing the magazine, he saw that it held only one additional bullet, although there was room for seven cartridges.

"Five shots have been fired recently," he revealed.

Long Tom shouted, "Want to bet those bullets will match the slugs in Duke Grogan's corpse!"

There were no takers.

Pocketing the pistol, Doc gave the room a quick going over with his active orbs. They alighted on one window shade, which was the wrong color.

Reaching up, Doc pulled this down, revealing for all to see one of the unpleasantly serpentine silhouettes that had previously been found at many but not all of the petrified-brain slayings.

"Jove!" Ham exclaimed. "That is the shade stolen from our hotel suite."

"Unquestionably," said Doc Savage, taking down the thing and studying the image. "It is the identical silhouette."

"Janet Falcon is the Medusa," said Ham in a husky voice. "How is this possible?"

"It is not," said Doc Savage. "This is a ruse. The blind is a clumsy plant, calculated to make it appear that Miss Falcon was the author of all these mysterious slayings."

"Are you suggesting she didn't commit suicide?" wondered Ham.

"Tomorrow is Ned Gamble's funeral," reminded Doc Savage. "It is entirely possible that Miss Falcon, overcome by guilt over her fiancé's demise, might have succumbed to grief and committed this deed of self-destruction. But it was not Janet Falcon who hung that blind in such a way as to cause whoever found her body to pull it down and discover the Medusa silhouette. This is designed to throw us off the track."

"So we're back to the beginning?" Long Tom muttered.

Doc nodded. "We will inform the police and the coroner's office of our discovery; they can handle the details. We have our work cut out for us."

The bronze giant and his assistants filed silently out of the death room, Doc closing the door behind him. They repaired to their suite of rooms, where the telephones got a busy workout.

AN HOUR later, Doc Savage was consulting with the coroner in the hotel corridor as the sheeted body of Janet Falcon was being removed from the hotel room, and taken down by the back stairs so as not to create a commotion which might upset guests.

"Sure looks like suicide," the coroner was saying.

"It may well prove to be so," said Doc Savage. "But do not jump to conclusions. This is a complicated case."

"You're telling me?" the medical examiner grunted. "Should I check her brain to see if it's turned into a rock?"

"I took the liberty of doing that for you. Miss Falcon's brain is normal. She is not a victim of the Medusa murderer."

"Good," grunted the medical examiner. "I wasn't looking forward to opening up her skull. Now I don't have to."

With that settled, the body was taken away and Doc Savage returned to his hotel suite.

There, Ham Brooks had fresh news.

"Both Malcolm McLean and Marvin Lucian Linden have recently secured patents, or have patents pending on new inventions."

"What are these inventions?" inquired Doc.

"Linden took out one for a device called a photophone."

Long Tom looked suddenly interested. "Photophone!"

"Yes, that is what it is called, but it does not seem to be a photographic device."

"That's because it's not," snapped Long Tom. "The first photophone was constructed by Alexander Graham Bell, inventor of the telephone. He believed it would replace the telephone and telegraph one day. Didn't work out, though."

"What exactly is a photophone?" demanded Ham, impatient for Long Tom to get to the point.

Doc Savage answered that. "A photophone is a device to transmit sound and voice in a wireless manner."

"Like radio?"

Doc Savage went to the window where light was streaming through the glass and said, "No, the means of transmission is modulated light, not electricity, acting upon a special mirror, which in turn reflects the light to the receiver."

It hit them then.

"That creepy voice!" howled Monk. "It seemed to be coming out of nowhere. But every time we heard it, bright sunlight was streamin' in through a window."

Doc nodded. "No doubt. The window glass served as a receiver. The voice of the speaker was coming from a not-considerable distance, possibly only a few hundred feet. Someone setting up a photophone transmitter on a rooftop or in the room of a nearby building could transmit his voice across a busy street in a focused manner, provided weather conditions were favorable."

Long Tom—who might be expected to know of such things—inserted, "Atmospheric interference was the main reason the photophone never caught on. But this gimmick is a clever new wrinkle, as far as the receiving apparatus goes. A parabolic mirror set with selenium cells was the original method. Replacing that with ordinary window glass means that anyone operating this new-type photophone doesn't have to install a receiver anywhere. He can point it at just about any window and be heard clear as day."

"So who was transmitting the voice we heard earlier?" wondered Ham.

"It was not Janet Falcon," Doc Savage pointed out. "She had been dead for several hours. In New York, the voice we heard in that hotel room could only have been Duke Grogan, secretly operating a photophone. I suspected as much then, but it was not possible to cross the street in time to intercept the speaker, since his face was entirely unknown at that time."

"That means Marvin Lucian Linden is the culprit behind this?" Long Tom said slowly.

"I am not yet done making my report," Ham interjected. "Malcolm McLean had also patented an interesting gimmick. Its application is not clear to me, except perhaps as a trick valuable to professional magicians, but it was an arrangement by which one could treat any flat surface, such as a wall, with an invisible chemical which could only be revealed by the ignition of photographic flash powder, which activates its true colors. This could be applied with something as simple as a child's water gun, employing a paper form cut into the desired shape or outline."

Doc Savage lifted the blind with the Medusa silhouette imprinted on it and said, "No doubt that is how the threatening silhouettes were produced in New York and here in Chicago. In each case, it was not an ordinary flash powder but the combustion of the deadly matter that generates the vapors which, when inhaled, calcifies the human brain."

Ham mused, "Such a complicated set-up requires advance planning and no witnesses, which explains why the man felled at the scientific exposition was found with that Latin warning inscription, and not another green silhouette."

"Recall the trio of Medusa silhouettes found at Malcolm McLean's attic," reminded the bronze man. "One of those exactly matched the pose imprinted in Ned Gamble's hotel hallway, while another was identical to the one which discolored the corridor marble at our headquarters."

Ham snapped two fingers sharply. "No doubt the application of the transparent chemical solution was facilitated by use of a cardboard form shaped to resemble a serpentine figure."

Monk grunted, "This is startin' to add up to somethin' interestin'...."

"All except who the three Gorgons are," grumbled Long Tom.

The hairy chemist counted off his fingers, "Malcolm McLean is one. Marvin Lucian Linden is the other, and maybe Duke Grogan was the third."

"He *had* to be the third!" Ham insisted. "He was the first suspect in this entire maddening chain of murders."

Monk's grin became fierce. "It's time to round up Marvin Lucian Linden, since Malcolm McLean was probably the one who died in that cave-in." He looked to Doc Savage, saying, "Ain't that right, Doc?"

The bronze giant surprised them all when he remarked, "We have not as yet assembled all the facts in this case."

"In that case," said Monk, "let's start assemblin' Marvin Lucian Linden, and maybe take him apart while we're doin' that. He has a lot to answer for."

FINDING the missing electrical inventor did not prove to be as simple a task as Doc Savage and his men had supposed.

The bronze man made a phone call to the Superintendent of Chicago Police and asked that a prowl car be dispatched to the home of Malcolm McLean, in the hope that Marvin Lucian Linden was still camped out there.

It took less than a dozen minutes for the police official to call back and report that, "Linden is not at the McLean residence. Nor is his automobile. I have dispatched a radio car to his own residence, and will have a report shortly. You might wish to keep the line open."

"Thank you," said Doc.

That report was not long in coming, for the police official's voice was soon back on the wire, saying, "The Linden residence appears to be empty. There is no sign of the man. Why is it you believe he is culpable in the wave of criminal slayings?"

"This is merely a suspicion," clarified Doc. "Proof must come from Linden's own lips."

"Well, we have the dragnet out for him. Have you any other thoughts as to his whereabouts?"

"It is possible that Linden is attending the scientific exposition. But I thought it best to check on those residences before seeking him there."

"Do you think he will bolt?"

"Marvin Lucian Linden does not know he is a suspect. It is doubtful that he will run. We should know shortly," added Doc, hanging up.

Addressing the others, the bronze man said, "Marvin Lucian Linden most likely returned to the exposition. We will take him there."

"Now you're talkin'!" barked Monk. "That's what I wanted to do in the first place."

"Linden cannot cause any great mischief at the exposition, but should he be at large in the city, it is imperative to have him taken into custody as soon as possible."

As they rode the elevator down, Long Tom remarked, "It would have been as easy as pie for Linden to slip out of the exposition, set up his photophone gimmick across the street, make his threat, and repair back to the exhibition booth. No one would be the wiser."

"In which case," supplied Ham, "we will catch him red-handed with the invention."

Mayfair blew on his rusty knuckles. "I'm hopin' he puts up a fight."

"Endeavor to take Linden without any violence," asserted Doc Savage. "We need his complete story in all its ramifications.

There is a great deal that needs to be divulged about this case yet."

They stepped off the elevator into the lobby. There, they were immediately greeted by a great press of reporters clamoring to speak with Doc Savage.

One waved the late edition extra and yelled, "Savage! What have you got to say about this?"

Monk reached out a long, hairy arm, snagged the paper and pulled it to his nose.

The headline read:

JANET FALCON A SUICIDE
WINDY CITY WEIRD STRIKES AGAIN

The article was sensational in the extreme, and consisted of many questions and accusations without any supporting evidence.

Prudently, the police had withheld from the press the precise details of the woman's suicide note, except to leak the incriminating signature, *Medusa*.

Ham read over Monk's burly shoulder, and exclaimed, "Doc! They are accusing you of being complicit in Janet Falcon's death. The Superintendent of Police has confirmed that she was in your personal custody, and that she is connected to Myer Sim and Ned Gamble, the first victims of the petrified brain murderer."

"What do you say, Savage?" snarled one reporter. "Are you behind these killings? If so, what's your motivation? Crooks are dropping like flies, but so are upright Chicagoans. What is going on? What are you *really* doing in Chicago?"

Shouted questions were hurled with such violence that Doc Savage elected to retreat to the elevator, his men falling back with him.

The elevator operator took them up two floors, let them out and Doc Savage's men considered their options.

"We can shoot down to the garage and make our way from there," suggested Monk.

The bronze man shook his head in the negative. "No doubt the exhibition hall is swarming with reporters, seeking to interview me. It has been reported that I have been in attendance for two days running."

"How the heck are we gonna nab Marvin Lucian Linden then?" howled Monk.

"You better go on ahead," suggested Doc. "Use the garage elevator. I will follow in a few minutes."

"We'll get swarmed," Long Tom complained.

"Avoid answering their questions, but keep them occupied. I have a plan."

With that, Doc Savage sought the fire stairs and the upper floors.

Monk and Long Tom looked at one another, shrugged almost in unison as Monk growled, "Well, let's face the music. Give Doc time to pull whatever hare out of his hat he's gonna pull."

"Doc doesn't wear hats as a rule," Long Tom groused.

"It was just a figure of speech," said Monk, pressing the elevator button. "Why are you so touchy all of a sudden?"

"I've been touchy ever since I got conked on the noggin by Malcolm McLean," complained Long Tom. "Until I get to clobber someone back, I'm going to stay that way."

Of all Doc Savage's men, the puny electrical wizard's temper was the most violent. He did not look like much, but in a fight he was a wildcat with lightning fists. Monk suspected that tinkering with electricity all his life had somehow speeded up his reflexes, because his left hook could not be seen coming and his right cross was usually just a few inches behind the left. This made for a terrific combination. Many men who tangled with Long Tom Roberts in a fight never knew what hit them.

Sure enough, when they reached the garage they were immediately accosted by a mob of reporters. The seemingly ubiquitous Jack Swangle stood among them.

"No comment, gentlemen," Ham said superciliously.

"Stand aside," growled Monk. "We're comin' through."

"Where is Doc Savage?" Jack Swangle demanded.

"Looking into your sordid past," snapped Long Tom.

"What have you got to say about the suicide of Janet Falcon?" asked another.

"No comment, I say!" Ham repeated, exposing his glittering blade, which caused the push of reporters to retreat in alarm.

Waving the blade before him like a fencer, the dapper attorney cut through the shrinking representatives of the Fourth Estate, and they pushed their way toward the exhibition hall, the reporters falling in a respectful distance behind them.

Making their way to the exhibition booth of the electrical inventor, they found it was unmanned.

Long Tom entered the booth, fell to rummaging around. There were several crates and boxes there, and he opened each one until he suddenly exclaimed, "Jackpot!"

Standing up, he slammed a peculiar device onto the booth table. It consisted of a pair of flexible mirrors in part, one for capturing sunlight and reflecting it upon the other, which functioned as a combination diaphragm-transmitter.

"What is that?" said Ham.

"Ten bucks says it's a photophone," piped Monk.

"It's a newfangled photophone," confirmed Long Tom. "This proves it. Marvin Lucian Linden is one of the Gorgons. Now we just have to run him to earth."

"I say we fan out," insisted Ham. "No doubt he is circulating among the throng."

They went their separate ways, hands not straying far from the openings in their coats so they could yank out their assorted weaponry in a hurry.

Chapter XLIV

THE RESURRECTED

A T THE SAME time that Doc Savage's men were working their way through the exhibition crowd in search of Marvin Lucian Linden, the eccentric inventor himself was making his way toward one of the exit doors.

Linden's genial face was flushed, and there was a sheen of sweat on his forehead and cheeks. A sick, hunted light danced in his too-round orbs.

The inventor showed none of his usual politeness as he wended his way between attendees, occasionally elbowing one aside, and nearly knocking others over. Linden was manifestly a man in a hurry, but either he did not wish to show that, or the surging crowd prevented him from breaking into a mad dash.

Yet Marvin Lucian Linden looked for all the world like a fellow who was trying to run away from something or someone he feared.

As he worked around knots of individuals, the inventor ducked behind a vehicle that resembled a cross between a sedan and a small tank. Instead of front wheels, it was fitted with steerable skis mounted beneath the radiator grille. Three sets of rear wheels were joined together by a caterpillar tractor tread arrangement so that they could operate in tandem. Mounds of white confetti were sprinkled about the contraption to simulate snow.

By all appearances, it was designed to operate in snowy environments through a combination of traction offered by the caterpillar treads, turning via steerable skis mounted forward.

A banner over the preposterous vehicle proclaimed:

SNOW SEDAN

Marvin Lucian Linden circled around this display, hovering there for a bit. His eyes, still sunken and hunted, peered about.

Shortly, a nondescript individual pushed into view. He was painfully thin, rather tall, and very colorless in appearance. Only his brown hair offered any distinction. It was a little too brown, like the fur of a mink.

This fellow was evidently hunting for someone, for he lifted his head, craned his neck about and seemed in search of a particular individual. His eyes, combined with the grim set of his features, marked him as a man of determination.

Seeing this person, Marvin Lucian Linden ducked down. The ducking of course attracted attention, so furtive and out of place was it in the public gathering.

The man in charge of the Snow Sedan display inquired, "May I help you, sir? Are you lost?"

Marvin Lucian Linden made a hissing sound and attempted to wave the man away, which made his actions even more suspicious.

"See here, I will thank you to step away from the Snow Sedan. You may not enter it."

As if that was some form of reverse invitation, Marvin Lucian Linden reached out to take hold of the ordinary car-door lever. Unlocking it, he slipped inside, ducking out of sight.

Now the flustered display manager became truly upset. "You come out of there at once! Do you hear?"

No doubt Marvin Lucian Linden had heard, but he merely hunkered even lower.

This incipient altercation caught the attention of the trailing man, who swiftly changed direction and drifted up to the display area. This was a raised island, rather like those in dealer show-rooms where new automobiles are put on display.

The thin man stepped onto this island and said, "Come out of there, Linden. Step out right now and face the funeral music!" His voice was terrible, twisted with some inner emotion that sounded like hot metal on the verge of its melting point.

"Call the police!" shouted Marvin Lucian Linden. "That madman wants to murder me."

This caught the nervous display manager quite by surprise. But he took the outcry seriously. He looked around, seeking one of the gray-uniformed security guards who were circulating around the exhibition, helping to keep order and incidentally prowling for pickpockets who unfortunately infest assemblies such as this one.

While he was looking away, the pale man stepped into the so-called Snow Sedan and fell upon Marvin Lucian Linden, cowering on the floorboards.

Seeing his face, Linden emitted a frightened screech, and that screech turned into a terrible series of screams.

"Stop! Stop! Oh, someone help me. Murder, murder!"

It was pathetic, the way Marvin Lucian Linden called out, sounding like a character in an old silent melodrama. He was being murdered. There was no question about it.

The crowd, attracted by these cries, could see a maddened figure lifting and plunging downward one arm over and over again. The sounds of a blade going into Marvin Lucian Linden's unprotected chest were grisly and distinct.

Five times that blade rose and fell and, with each reappearance, it was more crimson with gore than it had been before. Droplets of blood splashed, becoming scarlet tears running down the windscreen's interior.

As it happened, Long Tom Roberts was near the scene. Hearing this altercation, he smashed his way through the crowd, stepping on toes and using his sharp elbows to nudge blocking bodies aside.

When he did finally make his way to the Snow Sedan, the assailant had fled into the throng. The door to the Snow Sedan hung open. Gawkers were staring into the blood-splattered interior, their eyes weird with mesmerized horror.

"What's going on?" Long Tom yelled out.

A woman moaned, "A man was stabbed before our very eyes. He's inside that contraption."

Long Tom stepped up onto the dais, pointing his magnetic gun ahead of him.

Inside, Marvin Lucian Linden lay in a welter of gore.

He was not yet dead, but the numerous stab wounds which had perforated his heaving chest made breathing a painful ordeal.

His mouth open, Linden tried speak. "Murder, murder," he moaned.

"Who did this?" Long Tom demanded.

"Oh, woe is me," Linden moaned. He seemed only dimly aware of his surroundings, for his eyes held a light that was fast fading.

"Speak up!" Long Tom said hotly. "Who stabbed you?"

"It was the Medusa, damn him. The Medusa murdered me."

With that, Marvin Lucian Linden gave out a creaky sigh and expired. It was as if his heaving chest were a punctured balloon that had leaked out its last reserve of air.

Shucking off his coat, Long Tom Roberts threw it over the dead man's face and turned to the nervous crowd, demanding, "Did anybody see who did this?"

A patron sputtered, "Yes, yes. The pale, thin man. He took off in that direction."

Long Tom followed the stabbing finger. It pointed toward an illuminated sign that said: EXIT.

He took off in that direction and saw, many yards ahead, an individual fitting that description. He was traveling fast.

Attracted by the noise, the crowd was moving in Long Tom's direction, and the slight electrical wizard knew he would have difficulty bulling his way through the incipient stampede.

Leaping up onto a display table, he aimed his magnetic gun in the direction of the fleeing slayer. Lining up the sights carefully, Long Tom depressed the trigger, but nothing seemed to happen.

Yet far ahead, people began dropping. Screams rang out. Panic ensued, swiftly turned into pandemonium. Long Tom ceased fire immediately.

"Aw, damn this thing!" he complained.

"I will take that, Long Tom," a voice said distinctly at his side.

Wheeling, Long Tom found himself facing a broad-shouldered individual with extremely blonde hair and wonderfully blue eyes. He was well-dressed, but not otherwise known to him.

"Who the heck are you?" he demanded.

"Doc Savage," said the disguised bronze man.

Long Tom blinked, seemed stupefied. It dawned on him that the new arrival possessed generally the same stature as Doc Savage. It was evident that the Man of Bronze had disguised himself for the purposes of reconnoitering the exhibition hall without being harassed by reporters or stopped by autograph seekers.

Handing over the weapon, Long Tom said dolefully, "I'm still not used to firing a gun that has no kick. It looks like I dropped a lot of passersby, but I don't know about the killer."

Doc accepted the weapon, stepped onto the table, surveyed the crowd. The bronze man was in hopes of spying the fleeing slayer, if in fact he had not succumbed to the spray of hypodermic bullets unleashed by Long Tom Roberts.

But it was impossible to ascertain who had succumbed, so Doc Savage stepped down, handed Long Tom back his weapon, and invited, "Follow me."

Doc led the way, pushing through the crowd, and soon they were joined by Monk and Ham, who had their supermachine pistols out.

Four exhibition attendees had fallen as a result of Long Tom's hypodermic bullets. They were not otherwise harmed, but among them was no sign of the tall, pale killer who had wielded the fatal knife.

Doc said to the crowd. "Did anyone see a tall and too-pale individual flee the scene?"

"What did he look like?" asked one person.

Long Tom told them, "I didn't get a good look at him."

From an inside pocket, Doc Savage produced the police sketch that the bronze man had earlier made of the person who resembled Malcolm McLean.

Showing this to the crowd, Doc said, "This is the man we seek."

One person recognized the image. "He went through that exit door over there."

"Thank you," said Doc, departing in that direction, followed by his men.

The exit door led to a hotel corridor in the kitchen area, but there was no sign of the individual.

"Drat!" Ham snapped. "He could have gone in any number of directions."

"Why don't we split up and conduct a search?" suggested Long Tom. "I'll take the street."

"No need," said Doc Savage. "I have a good idea where he went."

Everyone looked at the bronze chief in somewhat stupefied surprise.

"I don't see any kinda trail," mumbled Monk.

"There is no discernible trail," said Doc. "His goal is purely psychological."

The bronze man's aides looked wholly dumfounded. But they followed him to the nearest elevator bank, where Doc showed the police sketch to the elevator starter, adding, "The individual we seek will be very bloody."

"He just went up," said the starter. "When the cage comes back down, the operator can tell us which floor."

"Never mind," said Doc. "It could only be the sixth. We will go there."

The starter summoned another cage, and they rode this up to the sixth floor, Ham holstering his supermachine pistol in order to take his sword cane blade out of the concealing barrel.

"No doubt the assailant is seeking us in our hotel room," he said firmly.

"We will get the drop on him there."

"He's in for a hot time," said Long Tom, checking his reloaded magnetic gun.

Grinning, Monk added, "I've got some red hots in my superfirer drum that will make him dance a hot jig."

When they stepped off the elevator, the bronze man led them, not to their hotel suite, but down the hallway to the room formerly occupied by the late Janet Falcon.

Their astonishment mounted when the bronze man said, "Remain here. I will enter alone."

"But Doc," Monk pointed out. "He's got a knife and probably a gun. Let Long Tom and me fill the place with slugs. You can rush in after we drop him."

"This may not be the confrontation you imagine," said Doc Savage quietly. "Remain outside until you are summoned."

Stepping up to the hotel room door, the bronze man tested the knob and found the panel was not locked.

Slowly and carefully, he eased the door open, just enough to admit his great frame, and silently slipped within, closing the door behind him with the faintest click.

Ham, Monk and Long Tom all swapped bewildered glances and crowded close to the shut panel as they listened intently.

Only Monk offered any opinion. "What does Doc know that we don't?" he mumbled.

Once inside, Doc Savage paused.

Lights were on and someone was rattling around in the wash room.

Doc Savage went to a closet, and slipped inside in order to observe undetected.

After a bit, the person stepped back into the room, looking somewhat worried.

It was the tall, pale individual with the mink-brown hair Doc Savage had seen earlier and for whom the police were searching based on the bronze man's sketch.

The man wore a nondescript suit that was splattered with blood. His hands showed indications of a fresh washing—no doubt done in the adjacent wash room—so they were clean, but not yet fully dry.

The man took a pointless turn around the room. He appeared greatly agitated, and uncertain what to do with himself. Low moans of emotional agony were coming from deep inside him.

It was clear that the person was having difficulties managing his feelings, so he paced, making aimless circles. He was utterly unaware that he was under observation.

"McLean," a voice said quietly, "you appear to be upset."

The pale man all but jumped out of his skin. His anguished eyes grew round. Seeing no one, he attempted to bolt, lunging for the door.

Suddenly, a human wall blocked his escape. Or so it seemed. For the fellow rebounded off the obstruction that was suddenly standing before the exit door.

Doc resumed speaking. "Your skin has been coated with a preparation designed to give it a pale but lifelike appearance, and your hair, which you had dyed brown, is already beginning to grow out, showing the original gray. But your deception has been discovered."

"What—what are you doing in here?" the man addressed as McLean stammered.

"Merely observing you," replied the bronze man.

"Who are you?" he quavered.

"My voice should tell you that."

Shock was replaced with comprehension. "You're Doc Savage!"

"And you are Malcolm McLean."

There was no point in denying it. "Yes," said the tall, pale man. "I am McLean, come to pay my respects to Janet Falcon. For I have read the newspaper accounts of her murder."

McLean's voice was dull and dead-sounding. All the life appeared to have been drained out of him. He had lost his fire.

"Why did you slay Marvin Lucian Linden just now?" asked the bronze man without emotion.

"Haven't you figured it out?" sneered McLean, reaching into his coat pocket.

One of Doc's hands flashed out, seized the man by the wrist, forcefully brought out the hand from the pocket as if the other had lost all power over his arm.

Clutched in thin fingers was a simple package of cigarettes.

"I need to smoke," he said, and his hands were trembling so much with emotion that the bronze man was convinced, despite his suspicions.

Shaking out a group of slim paper tubes, McLean carefully selected one and placed it between dry lips.

With normal skin tones and youthful brown hair, Malcolm McLean did not look so much like a walking corpse as before. But neither did he appear healthy. The preparation he used to normalize his skin tones lent his cadaverous frame an unhealthy pallor. The result was a distinct improvement, but still not one appealing in a human being.

In his own peculiar way, he rivaled Long Tom Roberts so far as unhealthy appearance went.

Fishing into another pocket for a cigarette lighter, McLean snapped the flint wheel and applied a leaping yellow flame to the cigarette. Thoughtfully, he began smoking.

Since he was taking his time with speech, Doc Savage prompted, "You were in love with Miss Falcon, were you not?"

"I was," admitted McLean. "But it was a hopeless love. I could never divulge it. Not with my condition, which repelled women. But also because she had a fiancé, Ned Gamble, with whom she was very much in love."

"You suspect Marvin Lucian Linden of having slain Miss Falcon?" prompted Doc.

McLean nodded. "Linden is the Medusa who has been terrorizing the city," said McLean. "There is no doubt about it. I appear to have done the city a favor."

Doc studied the man with his animated eyes, saying, "Why would Linden wish Miss Falcon dead?"

"Is it not obvious from the newspaper reports? He forged that suicide note signed Medusa in order to frame her. That was all. He wanted to throw suspicion on an innocent woman. So Linden overpowered her, hanged her, and trusted in the press doing the rest."

"That is a reasonable theory," said Doc Savage. "But you seem to have overlooked something."

Malcolm McLean took a long draw on his cigarette, and blew wispy smoke into the air.

"And what is that?"

"That Miss Falcon may have indeed committed suicide over the untimely death of her fiancé."

Malcolm McLean blinked rapidly, and a cigarette in his hands hung poised in the air.

"That does not explain the incriminating suicide note," he said flatly.

"Consider the possibility that Miss Falcon committed suicide, and her intended killer subsequently discovered that she was already deceased. So the killer went ahead and planted clues suggesting culpability in the so-called Medusa murders, since it would serve his purposes."

"I don't believe it! I don't think Janet would ever do away with herself!"

Doc said firmly, "Janet Falcon was distraught over the death of her fiancé. She consequently blamed herself for sending him to New York to his death."

"That was not her fault!" snapped McLean. "That is the fault of the killer or killers!"

Doc nodded. "Precisely. The killer or killers are indirectly responsible for Miss Falcon's suicide."

This assertion seem to strike Malcolm McLean forcefully. So forcefully that he dropped his cigarette and took a backward step. He appeared momentarily incapable of speech.

Stepping on the smoking butt, the ashen chemist ground this into the carpet, fished out the cigarette pack and very carefully selected a replacement.

Lighting this, McLean resumed smoking even more furiously than before.

"This is a shock!" he said thinly. "I hardly know what to say."

"A confession would be in order. For I entertained the suspicion that the weird Medusa who was caught in the coal mine cave-in was none other than yourself."

Malcolm McLean declined to reply.

Doc continued, "There is reason to believe, however, that there was not one Gorgon, but three. Legend speaks of three Gorgon sisters. It follows therefore that there must be three modern editions of those Gorgons. You are but one. Inasmuch as you are complicit in the numerous Medusa slayings, the death of Janet Falcon lies at your feet as equally as it does those of your confederates."

"You think you have everything figured out?" McLean sneered nastily. "Don't you?"

"Not everything," admitted the bronze man. "But you might fill in the gaps."

A crafty look came into Malcolm McLean's disguised eyes. "I imagine I have very little choice in the matter. Perhaps you can figure out why I slew Linden."

"Because you believed he was the one who planted the incriminating suicide note, and therefore was directly responsible for Miss Falcon's apparent murder."

"In which you say I was mistaken."

"Mistaken," countered Doc Savage, "but not entirely so. For if Marvin Lucian Linden was one of the three Gorgons, Miss Falcon's tragic fate rests on his guilty conscience, as well as yours."

Malcolm McLean's gristle-like lips writhed. He started laughing unexpectedly. An explosively ghoulish giggle erupted from deep within. It was entirely a nervous reaction, and not an expression of mirth or hilarity.

The laugh was terrible to hear, and Doc Savage for a moment suspected that the man's mind had snapped.

Suddenly, there was an odor in the room that was different than the aromatic smell of burnt tobacco. It possessed the disagreeable stink of charcoal.

McLean evidently smelled this, yet he took a long drag on his cigarette, and suddenly blew a great cloud of smoke in Doc Savage's direction.

Sealing his lips, clamping his nostrils shut with thumb and forefinger, the bronze man abruptly backpedaled. The door was behind him, and Doc got it open and slipped through before the cloud of smoke could reach him.

Outside, Doc rapped out, "Gas masks everyone!"

Monk, Ham and Long Tom reached into their coats and drew out their masks, donning them hastily.

Still holding his breath, the bronze man urged the trio down the corridor, and once they got clear, they listened.

Even through the closed door, the thud of a falling body came distinctly.

As a precaution, Doc Savage had drawn on his own gas mask, which consisted of a cuplike chemical filter covering mouth and nostrils.

Striding back to Janet Falcon's room, the bronze giant used his coat to fan the smoky air around the closed door before he entered.

He shut the door behind him and was inside only a few minutes.

After he reappeared, Doc again sealed the door and rejoined his men, removing his chemical filter mask thoughtfully.

"Malcolm McLean is no more," he told them. "The realization of the extent of his crimes in all of their ramifications caused him to resort to smoking a cigarette that was impregnated with the charcoal substance that calcifies human brains."

"Daggone!" Monk exploded.

Ham mused, "That means there remains but one Gorgon left!"

"But which one is he?" wondered Long Tom.

"The answer to that question," said Doc Savage, "might or might not be found in the collapsed coal mine."

"Well," exclaimed Monk, "what're we waitin' on? Let's mosey!"

"Not just yet," said Doc. "It may be that Dr. Rockwell can restore Malcolm McLean to life. If possible, it is worth taking the time to do so. The body of the Medusa in the coal mine is going nowhere. It can wait."

Chapter XLV

ENVY

IN ORDER TO save precious time, Doc Savage carried the lifeless form of Malcolm McLean down to the hotel lobby while Ham Brooks summoned an ambulance from Mercy General Hospital by telephone. Monk and Long Tom accompanied the bronze giant.

Once they stepped into the lobby, the front-desk clerk spotted Monk and Ham, then noted Doc Savage who, while still in disguise, towered over his aides.

There were reporters loitering outside on the sidewalk, evidently herded there by combined efforts of the hotel detective and the doorman.

Monk grunted, "Want me to run them off, Doc?"

"It may be that they will not recognize me."

This exchange caused the hotel clerk to step up and inquire, "Are you Doc Savage?"

Doc nodded. The clerk looked slightly perplexed, but maintained his professional aplomb.

"A message was left for you at the desk," said the clerk, offering an envelope marked with the hotel crest. "The bellhop brought it down earlier in the day, at the request of the guest in Room 612."

Doc laid down the body of Malcolm McLean on a chair and examined the envelope. It was addressed to Doc Savage. He opened it.

It was a letter, covering six sheets of hotel stationery. The bronze giant read this rapidly, and before he had turned to the second page, his trilling piped up, low and intrigued at first, but growing in crescendo, expressing a kind of satisfied wonderment.

"What is it?" asked Long Tom.

Strange storms played in the bronze man's flake-gold eyes, denoting uncommon emotions. "Janet Falcon wrote this. We suspected that the suicide note found with her body was not genuine, but here is proof. This is the actual note. The handwriting is different. It is a full account of what she knew."

"What does it say?" asked Monk.

"It is quite involved, but does not tell the complete story. We still have work to do before we wrap up this affair."

Then the ambulance pulled up, bell clanging, and Doc Savage folded the missive and pocketed it.

Gathering up the body of Malcolm McLean, he instructed Monk, "Go to the airport and prepare our plane for departure. Do not wait for me. Go directly to the coal mine. See if you can open it up. I will join you as soon as possible."

"Gotcha," said Monk. "Long Tom and I will get the job done."

"Wait for Ham," reminded Doc.

The bronze man shouldered out into the street, and his stature caught the attention of the Chicago reporters loitering outside in hopes of snagging a story.

The great height of Doc Savage impressed them, but his blond hair and ruddy features did not. They failed to recognize him.

"Who is that?" one demanded, pointing a pencil at the body in Doc's arms.

"Another suicide," said the bronze man in a voice not his own.

"Is that so? What's his name?

Ambulance attendants had rushed out and yanked open the back door for Doc to place the body within.

"Take us to the hospital at once," Doc ordered, climbing into the back with the body of Malcolm McLean.

The rear door was shut, the internes reclaimed their seats and the ambulance tore off, rocking on the corner turn.

The reporters next set their sights on Monk and Long Tom, whom they readily recognized.

"Do you mutts have anything to do with what just happened here?" accosted one. It was the *Tribunal's* nosy legman, Jack Swangle.

"What's it to you?" challenged Long Tom.

"It's a story and we want it."

"Well, you just missed your scoop." Long Tom jerked a rude thumb in the direction of the departed ambulance. "That was Malcolm McLean. He ended his own life."

"The bird that Dr. Rockwell revived?"

"The very same," said Ham Brooks, who had joined them. "And if you're smart, you will file that story."

"What did Doc Savage have to do with this? An awful lot of people are committing suicide around him."

"You'll have to ask Doc Savage," clipped Ham. "We must be going."

The three Doc Savage aides went off in search of their rental sedan, while the reporters raced to public telephones to file their copy.

"A whole swarm of reporters are gonna show up at the hospital," grunted Monk.

"Doc will handle them all right," said Long Tom. "Let's get going."

DURING the noisy ride, the bronze man had not paid much attention to the body, but instead finished reading Janet Falcon's letter, which he had once again pocketed. Once he felt it safe to do so, Doc removed the blue-optical shells that concealed his remarkable flake-gold eyes, for he did not want any confusion arising about his identity once he arrived at Mercy General Hospital.

Dr. Rockwell was waiting in the emergency room when the ambulance pulled in. He paced in an agitated manner while orderlies set up a wheeled gurney to convey the body of Malcolm McLean inside.

Doc Savage's impassive features were without outward expression when he addressed the waiting physician in his unmistakably vibrant voice.

"Malcolm McLean has once again succumbed to the brain-calcifying influence," Doc told him.

The look that crossed Rockwell's face was one of stunned astonishment. He appeared disinclined to believe the words striking his ears. His professional demeanor quickly returned, however.

"I cannot accept what I am hearing," he said thickly.

"It was suicide, brought on by guilt connected to the suicide of Janet Falcon, for whom he cared very deeply," replied the bronze man.

The body was being wheeled in now, and Rockwell's unblinking eyes sought the face of the dead man.

"I scarcely recognize him."

"McLean was in disguise, the better to go about his nefarious work."

"Nefarious?"

"Malcolm McLean was the so-called Medusa, or should I say, one of the Gorgons who have been terrorizing Chicago. Evidently, he had a falling out with another conspirator, Marvin Lucian Linden."

All normal color drained from Rockwell's craggy features until they resembled cold marble. "Linden!"

Doc nodded as they walked along on either side of the moving gurney.

"McLean stabbed Linden to death at the exposition, apparently blaming him in part for the death of Janet Falcon. I found McLean in her hotel room, overcome by grief. Upon questioning, he dosed himself with a cigarette that was laced with the unknown combustible substance which, when inhaled, reduced human brain tissue to the consistency of stone."

"He confessed?"

"Fully," admitted the bronze man. "There are still more pieces of the puzzle that need to be assembled, however."

"Did he say who the third Gorgon was?"

"I did not mention that there was a third Gorgon," countered Doc.

Dr. Rockwell's staring eyes met Doc Savage's aureate gaze and locked. They were unflinching in their steady regard.

"You said that there were two, and I know my classical mythology. The Greeks told of three Gorgon sisters. The terrorist who is sending threat letters to the newspapers employed all three names. Was Janet Falcon the third?"

"She was not," returned Doc. "There is reason to suspect that the third Gorgon perished two days ago in the collapse of the Ryerson Coal Mine in Vermilion County."

Warner Rockwell said nothing to this. An examination room came into view, and he told the orderlies, "Place the body on the examining table. I will join you directly."

Addressing Doc Savage, he said, "I revived Malcolm McLean once, perhaps I can do it again. Of course, if what you say is true, I am merely reviving him so that the state can execute the misguided wretch at a future date."

"Justice must be served," said Doc Savage, "no matter how harshly it is meted out."

If Dr. Rockwell had been a blinking man, he might have blinked at that. Something like a nervous twitch touched his composed features as he commented, "That does not sound like you, Savage, for you are considered a great humanitarian."

"Justice may be tempered with mercy, but it must retain the essential qualities of justice," stated Doc firmly.

"Well spoken. Have you any suspicion as to who this third Gorgon must be?"

Instead of replying, Doc Savage stated, "It is always preferable to deal in certainties, not suspicions. Once I reach Vermilion County, all may be revealed. Except, perhaps, for the motive, which remains murky."

Deep frown lines etched Dr. Rockwell's craggy features. "I do not wish to speak ill of the dead, but perhaps I might volunteer some useful information."

"Go ahead," invited Doc.

"I have known both McLean and Linden for a good many years. My opinion of them is very high. Nonetheless, they were subject to professional jealousy. Neither fellow felt he had advanced in his chosen career as rapidly as expected. Some of this envy, I am sorry to inform you, was centered upon yourself."

A flickering troubled Doc Savage's golden eyes, and one knowing the bronze man well might suspect that this reflected a recognition of certain facts.

Rockwell explained, "Marvin Lucian Linden's envy was centered much more on your associate, Long Tom Roberts, than upon yourself, but it may be a case of guilt by association. As for Malcolm McLean, he was envious of anyone who possessed more fame and accomplishment than he had attained. Sorry to say that, as bright as he appeared, McLean was more of a dabbler than an accomplished chemist."

"As motivations, what you suggest sounds rather thin."

"Perhaps, but I am not offering certainties, merely suspicions. Now you must excuse me, for I have work to do."

"As have I," said the bronze man.

As he turned to go, Dr. Rockwell paused. An ironic warp touched his mature features.

"I have suspected you, Savage, of doubting my ability to raise Malcolm McLean from the dead. But now that you have delivered him to me, once more deceased, I imagine you have greater confidence in my abilities."

"You are very clever, Dr. Rockwell," said Doc Savage expressionlessly.

"A compliment from the great Doc Savage," murmured Rockwell. "I shall cherish it always. Wish me luck."

"Better to marshal our respective skills in order to win the day," advised Doc Savage.

The door closed, and the bronze giant departed rapidly.

There was a commotion in the main lobby. Doc Savage was not surprised to see it packed with milling Chicago reporters, among them the dogged Jack Swangle, clamoring for news of Malcolm McLean, the man who had been brought back to life only to perish once more under identical circumstances.

Seeing this, the bronze man slipped out the side door, worked his way around to the back, and hailed a passing taxi.

"Where to, High-pockets?" asked the cabbie once Doc sank into the back seat, causing the taxicab springs to groan in complaint.

"Airport," directed Doc. His flake-gold eyes were speculative.

Chapter XLVI

FLASH!

MONK MAYFAIR LANDED the big speed plane in the vicinity of the Ryerson Coal Mine just as dusk was falling.

Switching off the engines, he sprang out of the control bucket, and went barreling down to the rear of the plane, where he began excavating ammunition cases. He worked with a kind of mad abandon which caused Ham Brooks to flounder about and Long Tom Roberts to demand, "What's eating you?"

"That coal mine entrance is probably sealed by a ton of rocks, and we don't have any dynamite. I'm puttin' together some of my special bullets to take care of that."

Alarm rode the puny electrical wizard's thin features.

"If you're thinking of blowing that entrance wide open with explosives," he warned, "better think again. There's no telling how much poison gas may be trapped inside."

"I got bullets for that, too!" chortled the apish chemist.

Ham fingered his dark cane and asked, "What manner of ammunition would be proof against poison gas?"

"You'll see!"

To which Long Tom growled, "If it's all the same to you, I'm bringing along a fresh gas mask. I suggest everybody do the same."

Heavy-duty gas masks were excavated and passed around. Monk lugged a heavy metal case crammed with assorted ammunition drums to the cabin door.

"One of us oughta wait behind in case Doc radios in," he suggested.

There were no volunteers. Monk made thinking faces and said, "Come to think of it, it might be smart to let a little more dust settle before we go to pokin' around. No point in attractin' any attention from the local cops."

That was a sensible suggestion, although neither Ham nor Long Tom cared to give Monk any credit. Instead, the dapper lawyer went to the radio and took a seat at the cubicle.

"Doc Savage is likely to have chartered a plane by now. I will see if I can raise him."

Several minutes of trying produced nothing other than noisy static fry and silent frustration.

"Deuced nuisance," Ham frowned. Fiddling with the dials, he tuned in to a commercial radio station until he found a news report.

Evidently, he came into the middle of something interesting, because a news announcer was trying to contain his excitement.

"Authorities are being tight-lipped. Here is what we know at this hour. Malcolm McLean, noted Chicago chemist, who was previously struck down by the mysterious Medusa menacing the Windy City, has again been felled. All attempts by the famed Doctor Warner Rockwell of Mercy Hospital to revive him a second time have failed miserably. Efforts to learn more from the physician have been met with silence."

"I didn't think they were going to pull him back from the grave a second time," commented Long Tom.

To which Ham Brooks added, "I, for one, was not convinced it was accomplished the first time."

The excitable announcer was saying, *"The Chicago medical examiner has released a statement confirming that a waterlogged body discovered in the last forty-eight hours, which bore a resemblance to Malcolm McLean, was in fact not the chemist himself. Authorities have identified him as Doane McLean, a cousin of the now twice-deceased chemist. Police remain mum on the circumstances of this discovery, except to say that the dead man had not drowned."*

Monk drove a hairy fist into the opposite palm and yelled, "So that's who that gray corpse was!"

Long Tom mumbled, "This is getting weirder by the hour."

"Quiet," Ham admonished. "There is more coming."

"The Superintendent of Chicago Police has announced that no less than the famous Doc Savage is now being sought in connection with the death of Malcolm McLean. For it appears that McLean's body was discovered by the Man of Bronze himself. This marks the second victim to die mysteriously while in Doc Savage's custody. The police official maintains that Doc Savage is not at this time a suspect in the Medusa slayings, but is only wanted for questioning as a material witness."

Ham barked, "That means he *is* a suspect. This is not going in a good direction."

"It also means that Doc took it on the lam," added Monk. "No tellin' when he'll show up now."

Ham offered, "If Doc Savage is smart, he will not try to hire a plane, but instead drive south. Do not forget that he is still in disguise, which will help him avoid capture."

They stood around a few moments while considering their next move.

As they were doing so, the announcer came on with another bulletin. It was shocking in the extreme.

"This just in! Flash! Dr. Warner Rockwell, prominent Chicago physician, was discovered in his office late this afternoon, barely breathing. Upon examination by his fellow doctors, it was discovered that his eyeballs showed outward signs of petrification. The famed medico is being examined at this hour, but hope is not held out for his survival, inasmuch as the only doctor who has so far revived any victim of the mystery Medusa is Rockwell himself."

"That means the danged Medusa is still at large!" Monk howled.

"But who could it be?" wondered Long Tom.

Ham Brooks rubbed his chin thoughtfully and said, "I completely fail to see any motivation for all of this macabre madness. These killings now appear to be the work of an insane person, not someone with a definite goal in mind."

Monk said, "Doc said a lot of it was explained by Janet Falcon's last letter. Maybe he can figure it out."

Ham seized the dial, and set the plane radio to the wavelength they used for private communications. Picking up the microphone, he chanted, "Ham Brooks calling Doc Savage. Ham Brooks calling Doc Savage. Come in, Doc Savage."

Again, only static sizzled through the loudspeaker.

After several futile minutes of this, it was decided to investigate the coal mine.

"Doc knows where we are," piped up Monk. "If he's on his way, we should have this joint cracked open by the time he gets here."

With that, the three men disembarked from the speed plane, locking the cabin door behind them.

Trudging through the woods, their feet made mushy sounds in Fall leaves soaked by the rains that had not entirely departed the state. They soon put the aircraft behind them. The tilted roof of the coal-washing plant peeped over the tree tops.

None of the group heard the radio loudspeaker when it commenced reproducing the distinctive tones of Doc Savage's voice.

"Calling Monk. Doc Savage calling Monk."

There was a static-laden pause, and the voice resumed speaking once more.

"If you can hear my voice, proceed with extreme caution into the coal mine. If my calculations are correct, the true author of these hideous slayings may be en route to the place. Await my arrival."

The static resumed, and the voice of Doc Savage was heard no more.

Chapter XLVII

THE GLARING GARGOYLE

EMPLOYING THEIR INEXHAUSTIBLE spring-generator flashlights to pick the way forward, Monk Mayfair, Ham Brooks and Long Tom Roberts filtered between stands of leafless trees, and crossed the seldom-used roadway to the old abandoned coal mine.

"Spooky joint," grunted Monk.

No one contradicted him.

A quarter moon was coming up in the sky. This added to the illumination, throwing stark shadows in the lee of the great coal-washing plant. A single broken window pane in the lop-sided structure was reminiscent of a square eye reflecting cold moonlight with a baleful but blank opacity.

They walked around the dirty waters of the slurry impoundment, where only two nights before a body had been fished out by Doc Savage.

This sight caused Ham to remark, "Taken in its entirety, this has been a maddening affair. Dead men are brought back to life, discovered to be dead after all, then coming to life again, only to perish once more."

Long Tom barked, "Shut up! Such crazy talk is making my head hurt. We have work to do."

Purpling in the moonlight, Ham firmly clamped his wide, mobile mouth shut. His legal mind was struggling with the complexities of the case, but now was not the time for such cogitations. They had to penetrate the mine, if they could.

Coming upon the entrance set in the brow of a hillock, they directed their blindingly-white flash beams inside. The ingenious torches could be manipulated by an adjustable ring set around the lens so that they sprayed fanning illumination, or the light could be tightened to the diameter of a string, proportionally increasing the brilliance and penetration of the slender cobweb of light.

Ham widened his beam while Long Tom collapsed his to a thread. Taking care not to step inside, they directed their varied rays about, seeking to discern how obstructed the tunnel might be.

The mouth was not obstructed at all, so they entered cautiously, feeling their way in, stepping carefully. Monk toted his case of ammunition drums which rattled with every step.

Presently, they ran into a formidable blockage of boulders and stony, dirt-choked debris. Scrutinizing this, Long Tom complained, "This will take all night to dig out."

"We ain't got all night," growled Monk. "Everybody clear out of this dump. I'll handle this."

"What are you going to do, you fool ape?" demanded Ham, a trace of concern flavoring his cultured tones.

"Don't worry none. I'm not about to get myself in a jam. I'll be with you in two shakes."

Everyone retreated, and Monk called back, "Better put on your gas masks. Afterdamp fumes could be tough."

Afterdamp was the name given to poisonous carbon monoxide gases often present in old mines after methane explosions, which are known as firedamp.

They did this, Monk included.

Voice muffled, the apish chemist fished out from his pockets a number of the small hand grenades of the type Doc and his men sometimes carried. These could be actuated through a timer.

Monk warned, "Get clear around to the other side of the bluff. I'm gonna pitch some of these babies in. When they let go, that should clear the tunnel."

"What if it collapses the entire mine?" demanded Ham.

"We'll cross that timber when we come to it," said Monk, setting the timers.

There was no dissuading the homely chemist. He was intent upon destruction. Ham and Long Tom retreated around the corner while Monk wound up like a baseball pitcher, and let fly three times.

Grabbing up his ammunition case, Monk followed the others around to shelter.

The timers had been set to let go only seconds apart, and this they did.

The noise produced was a species of muffled thunder, and the ground shook alarmingly. Ham stuck his manicured fingers into his ears to protect the eardrums. Quickly, Long Tom and Monk copied that precaution.

Out of the mouth of the mine came a violent upheaval of smoking dust and expelled gases.

Monk next did a strange thing. Clutching a supermachine pistol, he rushed around to the mine's fulminating mouth, and fired wildly into the onrush of smoke.

The mechanical bawling sounded like a small, ineffectual thing after the great triple detonation. It moaned on until the drum ran empty. Whereupon Monk slipped a second drum into the feed jaws and resumed firing.

When he returned, his twinkling eyes were amused. "That oughta do the trick."

Ham eyed him dubiously, asked, "What trick, you miscreant?"

Monk's grin could not be seen through his protective mask, but it could be heard in his squeaky voice.

"Them slugs are loaded with anhydrous calcium chloride. It's a dryin' agent, sometimes used to disperse fogs. It should dry up a lotta that afterdamp and make it harmless."

Long Tom demanded, "Are you sure about that?"

The apish chemist shrugged sloping shoulders. "Naw. But it was worth a try. I developed those bullets for times when we might run into mustard gas or stuff like that. I haven't had time to test it out to see if it exactly works the way it should."

Monk was slapping another drum of bullets into the receiver, and barked, "Come on, brothers. Let's explore!"

They moved cautiously, knowing that the explosion likely weakened the mine at the place of the detonation, prepared any moment to beat a hasty retreat if supporting timbers or rock ceiling showed themselves to be unsafe.

Spring-generator flashlights sprayed illumination haphazardly as they worked over tumbles of broken rock and scree, but surprisingly little in the way of dusty air or afterdamp.

Long Tom grumbled, "Sure wish Renny was on this trip. He could tell us how dangerous this place is now."

"Plenty dangerous," admitted Monk. "But we gotta get to the bottom of this. Doc said he saw someone who looked like old Medusa in this works before it blew up. I'm itchin' to see who that was."

"As long as it is not the actual Medusa," breathed Ham. "You all remember the legend. Her gaze was so horrible that men froze into literal stone statues."

Both Monk and Long Tom snorted at the notion. It was plain that they did not put any stock into such a creature—despite all they had encountered over the last few days.

It was a difficult winding path they trod through bent and twisted rail and cross ties over which the hopper cars had once run. They paused every few steps to shine lights on the ceiling and trickle them over the ancient timbers. They detected nothing especially alarming. So they pressed forward.

When at last they came to the great ballroom-sized gallery where the diggings had ceased, they were impressed by the size of the area. A locomotive and caboose could fit with room to spare, were it not for the piles of debris that had come loose in the aftermath of the recent explosion. Several of the supporting pillars of unmined coal had collapsed, making the ceiling a dangerous weight over their heads.

They advanced with caution. The air was dusty, but likely breathable for short invervals. They soon came to a scorched wall that gleamed blackly of anthracite.

Monk grunted, "Looks like this is where they stopped diggin' after that mine accident a few years back."

Ham nodded. "No doubt this is the area where Doc found Duke Grogan's men excavating. Let us see what they were doing."

Long Tom found the spot first; it was an exposed seam of coal.

Studying this, Monk said to Ham, "Lemme see that overgrown pig sticker of yours."

Ham made a disagreeable face. He was reluctant to let his prized sword cane out of his hands, much less place it into his rival's hirsute paws. After some hesitation, he withdrew the blade, and presented it to Monk.

"Be careful with that, you clumsy oaf," he warned.

Monk took the blade, and used it to poke at the seam of coal, which gleamed darkly under their flashlight beams.

"Bituminous coal," he pronounced. "That means it's the soft stuff good for makin' coke for heatin' home furnaces and the like."

Switching his flashlight around, the apish chemist came to a scarred portion where there had been recent cutting and digging, into which a hole had been gouged. It was not very great in size, but what was found there was not the black of coal, but a greenish-gray mineral that proved harder than the surrounding coal.

"This ain't coal," he mumbled.

Ham and Long Tom drew closer, fingering the outcropping.

"I don't recognize this stuff," murmured Long Tom, bathing the seam in his flash glow.

"Nor do I," said Ham, who was not qualified to comment either way.

Monk found a discarded pick ax, cut off a chunk, took it in hand, and tried squeezing it between thumb and forefinger. It was a mineral, much harder than bituminous coal.

"Whatever the stuff is," he squeaked, "it's hard as anthracite."

"I wonder if Johnny would be familiar with it?" asked Long Tom.

"Search me," grunted Monk. "He's a whiz at geology, but that don't mean he knows every rock and mineral there is."

Johnny was William Harper Littlejohn, the other missing member of Doc Savage's band of adventurers. A noted archeologist and geologist, Johnny was at present temporarily occupying the natural science research chair—a position he once held regularly—at a renowned college due to the illness of a colleague.

At that moment, Ham Brooks' questing flashlight fell upon something not far away.

"What is that?" he said aloud.

Monk and Long Tom directed their flash rays and illuminated the object of interest.

It was a body. Redirecting their lights revealed other bodies. These were partially buried by loose rock that had fallen from the shattered ceiling.

Not squeamish in the least, Monk Mayfair pushed the others aside and ambled over to investigate.

There were four bodies in all, and the hairy chemist used his big feet to kick rock clutter aside, exposing faces that were blackened by coal dust, but also discolored by putrefaction.

"This here looks like Patches Cordovan," decided Monk. "He's one of Duke Grogan's boys. So's the rest of these mugs."

Joining him, Ham nodded somberly. "According to Doc, some of the Grogan gang were caught in the mine collapse. Therefore, we can rule those men out. None could have been responsible for the most recent series of Medusa murders."

Long Tom nodded. "Not one of the Grogan gang has shown their face in the last day or so. This kind of proves they're all out of the picture."

Monk said, "Well, if these stiffs are still here, then the Medusa that Doc saw must be around somewhere. Let's go find that body, and see what's what."

The three men separated, their flashlight beams ranging high and low. They concentrated on the ground around their feet, and the litter of rock and bituminous coal bits that had naturally accumulated over the years.

Ten minutes of cautious searching led to an unavoidable conclusion. Ham Brooks voiced it.

"There is no body present—other than the ones we have already discovered."

"Maybe one of them was the Medusa, tricked up in a masquerade costume," suggested Long Tom.

They went back to the remains of the Grogan gang, carefully looked them over for any sign of a damaged or discarded disguise.

"Nothin'," Monk decided at last.

Ham declared, "Nonsense! Doc Savage saw the Medusa standing here, so the body must be around somewhere." He redirected his flashlight up to the great vaulted ceiling as if expecting to find it there. There was nothing. Not even roosting bats.

"Bodies do not evaporate," suggested Long Tom. "We're just not looking in the right places."

The pallid electrical wizard, being smaller in stature than the other two, started rooting around in the dim corners of the rock chamber.

He soon found a flat stone that seemed out of place. Kneeling, he bathed it in electric light, then called out, "Found something interesting."

The others rushed up just in time to see the puny electrical expert muscle the flat stone aside, disclosing a vertical shaft that led deeper into the earth.

"Secret tunnel," rumbled Monk. "Maybe the dang Medusa escaped that way."

"Exactly what I was thinking," murmured Long Tom, directing his flashlight downward. The beam disclosed a rickety wooden ladder, and the fact that the shaft was only about a dozen feet deep before going off in a horizontal direction.

"We should investigate it," suggested Ham.

"You first," prodded Monk.

Ham looked uneasy, and said, "Long Tom is the smallest. He would do the best job of mimicking a mole."

The slender electrical wizard seemed on the point of objecting, realized reluctantly that this was the truth, and said, "Hold my light. I'm going down."

Swinging downward, Long Tom got his feet on the wooden rungs and his fists around the upper rungs. He climbed down like an agile monkey. Soon, his feet touched wood. A plank had been laid for walking purposes.

"Drop it down," he called up.

Monk released the flashlight. Long Tom caught it, began moving along the horizontal passage, and was soon out of view, only the rustle and clatter of feet stepping from plank to plank and the fading backglow of his flashlight indicated his progress.

Monk and Ham waited with more than a trace of nervousness about them. It was an unpleasant thing to find oneself so deep within the earth—and Long Tom had plunged even deeper. No telling what he would discover, nor how safe the passage might prove to be.

No little time passed when suddenly, they heard a hollow yell.

"Damn you, get back! *Back, I say!*"

Long Tom's voice! It sounded higher and more fear-stricken than they had ever heard it before.

"Don't come any closer!" the electrical wizard yelled.

Came a low, venomous hissing, remindful of vipers arguing, followed by the racket of feet running, echoing hollowly, coming closer.

Ham called down, "Long Tom! What is going on?"

Monk was getting ready to jump down into the pit, when the flash glow swelled, and Long Tom Roberts was scrambling up the wooden ladder, the visible portions of his masked face paler than they had ever seen.

Monk reached down a comically long arm, grabbed Long Tom by one forearm and yanked him up, setting him on his feet.

In the electrical wizard's right hand was his magnetic gun. He had drawn it.

"It's the Medusa," he said breathlessly. "It was stalking along the tunnel. Came right at me!"

"Well, why didn't you shoot it?" Ham screeched.

"I did!" Long Tom yelled. "I emptied every bullet I had into her. She just kept on coming, face terrible. Her eyes were as green as a lizard's."

For the briefest of moments, Monk and Ham stared at Long Tom, wondering if the puny electrical genius was playing some kind of practical joke on their frayed nerves.

The gas mask he wore prevented his face from being clearly seen. But the abject fear in his tone was unmistakable. Long Tom was speaking the truth.

Ham went to the shaft, and spiked his flash beam down, listening carefully.

Measured footsteps could be heard below. Something was approaching. No question of that.

"It's coming this way!" he hissed.

"I'll believe it when I see it!" grunted Monk, picking up a heavy stone.

The hairy chemist waited; they all hovered over the hole, looking down into the pit-eye.

Then the apparition stepped into view.

Under the glare of three flashlights, it was a hideous sight.

The cranium was a nest of snakes, vipers writhing and twitching with hideous life. The tangled head tilted back, and lizard eyes stared upward. The marble-white face of the thing was fixed, ugly beyond comprehension.

From its warped lips, a violent hissing escaped.

"Lookit!" Monk squawled.

"No, *look away!*" Ham screeched. "Don't let her gaze petrify you!"

It was a preposterous warning, but under the circumstances—deep in the bowels of the earth—it rang true. All three of Doc Savage's men felt their marrow grow cold in their bones.

Only Monk reacted in that instant. He dropped his stone. It struck the nest of twining serpents and the creature staggered, hissing angrily.

"Did you see that?" Ham yelled out. "That hair is alive! It's real!"

Monk Mayfair yanked out his supermachine pistol, and unleashed a blazing burst at the frightful form.

The creature staggered slightly, swept around, its long pale garment swishing like a skirt under the rain of bullets.

From its crown, writhing serpent heads flew away as they were clipped by the slugs.

"What are you shooting?" Long Tom demanded. "It's hardly hurting her at all."

"Blamed if I know!" Monk yelled. "Let me try another drum."

Long Tom barked to Ham, "Help me push this lid back on. We'll stand on it."

They did exactly that. The entire weight of their bodies pressed down on the makeshift trapdoor, while Monk scrambled to get a fresh ammunition drum.

When he returned, the simian chemist was panting with exertion, and perhaps a mixture of atavistic terror. Monk's tiny eyes were very wide.

"Step aside!" he snarled. "I'm gonna blast that thing."

Long Tom and Ham Brooks were only too happy to comply. For something was pushing up from below, straining and shaking the flat rock lid vigorously. Each man leapt to one side.

Monk charged in, bent down, jerked up the lid, and opened fire.

The bawl of the supermachine pistol was long and loud. But the effects it produced were like nothing the others had ever before seen.

It was as if skyrockets had exploded in the shaft. They had to shut their eyelids to protect their sight. Even Monk threw one hairy beam of an arm across his tiny orbs.

When the supermachine pistol ran silent, and the last of the brass cartridges had ceased to ring and clink on the stony floor, they dared to look.

The mouth of the vertical shaft was deserted. Frantically, they looked about to see if the Gorgon had stepped out and was loose among them. Flash rays showed only shifting, grotesque shadows.

Monk stepped up to the yawning pit mouth, and speared his flash beam downward. It disclosed only litter. Nothing more.

There was a clatter of retreating footsteps discernible.

"I chased it off," Monk cried exultantly.

Long Tom asked, "What was in those slugs?"

"Scintillator bullets. They work a lot better in the dark. I figgered if that thing was going to stare us into stone statues, I'd better blind her first. Looks like it worked. Medusa turned tail and run off, and we haven't been turned to stone, have we?"

No one disagreed with the hairy chemist. It was the truth.

Ham Brooks was waving his sword cane around in high dudgeon. He looked as if he wanted to either fight or flee, but could not make up his mind which course to undertake.

"We appear to have chased it away," he panted. "But what do we do now? Pursue the Medusa?"

Long Tom eyed Monk. "Got any more explosive grenades?"

Monk turned his pockets inside out and said, "Fresh out of eggs."

That left them standing where they stood before, not sure which plan of action would be wisest.

"Sure wish Doc Savage was here," muttered Monk uneasily. "He'd know what to do."

Ham suddenly asserted himself, saying, "I know what I wish to do. I intend to vacate this infernal mine. There is no telling what will happen next."

It sounded like a good plan, so they moved in a mass toward the main tunnel, giving their spring-generator flashlights frequent windings to keep the juice flowing to the incandescent bulbs.

As they trudged along, Long Tom lamented, "My hypodermic bullets didn't even faze the thing. She charged at me like she was going to sink her fangs into my throat."

Monk said, "At least some of my trick bullets did some good."

"Sure," said Long Tom sourly. "But how much good? Medusa got away. Maybe she can't see, but she's probably around this maze somewhere."

"All the more reason to depart these dank confines," reminded Ham.

They picked up their pace, motivated by a desire to see open sky and breathe fresh air once again, for their gas masks were running low on oxygen supply.

So when the unexpected rumble commenced, they were already traveling fast.

The rumble started as a low feeling in the ground, but very quickly, they were having trouble keeping up their pace, for the ground beneath their feet quaked and quivered.

"Run for it!" Monk yelled. "Sounds like this place is gettin' ready to let go!"

So they ran. They whipped around corners, tripped over railroad ties, but before they could see daylight, ahead of them the ceiling tumbled down.

The noise was sickening in its utter finality. Coal dust rolled their way like the breath of some foul subterranean beast.

Undeterred, they kept moving. Rounding the final corner, their hearts sank. The way was blocked. In truth, they were not greatly surprised, merely disheartened.

"Trapped like rodents!" Long Tom complained.

"Nonsense!" contradicted Ham. "There remains the escape shaft behind us."

They started backing up, but Monk grabbed the others, warning, "Hold on! Maybe that's what the Medusa wants. Maybe she's layin' an ambush in that shaft, waitin' for us to walk into her trap."

Ham demanded, "Do you know another way out of this pit, you miserable mistake of nature?"

"You know I don't," raged Monk. "But I don't feel like walkin' into another dang trap tonight."

"This is no time for your monkey-minded arguments," Ham snapped, striking him with his cane. "If we don't find our way out of here very soon, we will run out of air."

The imminent expiration of their air supply ended all argument.

So they turned, and began retreating further into the mine, deeper into danger.

Chapter XLVIII

SECRET TUNNEL

DOC SAVAGE DROVE south from the city of Chicago through the deepening night.

The bronze man was well aware that a police bulletin had been issued for his apprehension. He was under no illusion that this was a routine matter. The mounting deaths in Chicago's criminal underworld, combined with the fatalities associated with his investigation, and fueled by sensationalistic newspaper speculation, had forced the hand of the Superintendent of Police.

Doc Savage would be brought in for questioning, but there was more to it than that. Public sentiment had turned against the bronze man. He would be held as a material witness, he realized, but also as a test, to see if the killings stopped while he was incarcerated.

Doc had no intention of allowing that to happen. He learned the truth at the Chicago municipal airport, when he attempted to rent an airplane, and saw that the police had congregated around the hangar in which he had kept his speed plane.

The bronze man maintained a comfortable distance, but he was a skilled lip reader. Observing the conversing bluecoats, he quickly gleaned the truth of the situation.

Monk had left the rental sedan parked in an out-of-the-way spot. Doc claimed it without being seen. Departing the airport discreetly, the bronze man headed south. His restored disguise helped him to evade capture, but he could not be certain that his rental machine was not known to the authorities.

The bronze giant drove at an efficient but cautious pace, lest he be pulled over. This cost him valuable time, but he counted on his aides to proceed without him.

As he drove, the bronze man fished around the commercial radio frequencies, and learned of Dr. Rockwell's failure to revive the twice-deceased Malcolm McLean. Evidently, the physician had given up almost immediately.

Nothing disturbed his impassive expression as the bronze man listened.

The announcer was saying, "*Hope has dimmed that a scientific savior had been found. The administrators at Mercy General Hospital have gone into seclusion, refusing all comment. Rumors of Dr. Warner Rockwell's death abound, but remain unconfirmed at this hour. Authorities remain tight-lipped in their search for the notorious Doc Savage, a so-called crusader for justice who had been given a free hand to investigate the Medusa Murders by the Chicago Police Department.*"

Doc pulled over at a roadside filling station, and purchased an extra edition. While the attendant was filling his tank with gasoline, he gleaned more details of the situation in Chicago.

Newspapermen were describing a tangled web of deceit in which Doc Savage had arrived in Chicago to simultaneously wage war on the Chicago underworld and cement his growing reputation as a righter of wrongs.

Certain facts had surfaced, for which the Fourth Estate could not account. The murder of Myer Sim, the theft of his snorkel automobile and the suicide of Janet Falcon, did not fit into the overall picture. This did not dissuade editorial writers from putting forth wild assertions that made for engrossing reading, but lacked persuasive logic.

"The motivation for all this mad carnival of murder, remains to be discovered," admitted one columnist.

None of the reporters seemed to have concluded that more than one wicked brain stood behind what they had dubbed the Medusa Murders. Nor did the police put forth any specific criminological theory, other than to insist that Doc Savage was wanted for questioning only.

Driving on, the bronze giant kept the dash radio tuned into a Chicago station that was issuing frequent news bulletins. One brought his eerie trilling back to life.

"This just in!" broke in the announcer. *"Reports that Dr. Warner Rockwell has himself succumbed to the brain-petrifying doom have been denied by the directors of Mercy General Hospital. It seems that an overeager reporter working for a tabloid known for reporting rumors as facts started the story. The sheet in question has withdrawn the story and legman Jack Swangle has been summarily discharged. But Dr. Rockwell has yet to surface, and the story refuses to die."*

By the time he approached Vermilion County, Illinois, Doc Savage had successfully eluded all police notice. But it had cost him valuable time.

Coming up to the old abandoned coal mine, the bronze giant pulled over and brought from the floorboards a portable short-wave radio transmitter-receiver. He had placed the set in the sedan upon renting it, and had used the transmitter upon departing the airport to warn his aides, but received no reply.

The set was still warmed up. Doc lifted the microphone and began speaking.

"Doc Savage calling Monk Mayfair. Doc Savage calling Monk. Come in, Monk." He paused, then continued, "If you can hear my voice, proceed with extreme caution into the coal mine. If my calculations are correct, the true author of these hideous slayings may be en route to the place. Await my arrival."

There was no response of any type. Doc did not try again. He assumed by now his men would have invaded the coal mine and were searching assiduously.

Engaging the automobile, Doc completed the journey, and soon found his speed plane behind a shelter break of trees, in a spot identical to the one in which they had previously parked.

Seated in the darkness, the bronze man took stock of his surroundings. All seemed quiet. Satisfied on that score, he began divesting himself of his disguise, removing the blue optical shells that had concealed his flake-gold orbs last. When this was accomplished, Doc did something to his eyes and nose that could not be discerned in the darkness of the automobile interior. Next, he went through the pockets of his handy gadget vest, as if taking inventory. Certain items he replaced, others he stored about his person for convenience. It was impossible to tell very much about these things, or their purpose, but they soon vanished from view.

Exiting his vehicle, the bronze man checked the plane, discovered it to be securely locked, and moved in the direction of the looming coal works.

The quarter moon furnished greater illumination than it had two nights previously. Thus the bronze man spotted the coupe that was parked in a turn-off from the main highway.

Gliding to the dark machine, Doc examined it carefully. It was a moderately expensive make of automobile, but it was unoccupied. The license tag number meant nothing to him. But the presence of the vehicle told of someone visiting the colliery who was not one of his aides.

The vehicle was securely locked. In the back seat rested a black valise, but nothing else to indicate who owned the machine. Coming to rest upon the valise, Doc Savage's eerie orbs did not register any flicker of surprise. Indeed, they looked cold and opaque in the moonlight, as if the gold flakes had been transmuted to silver by some arcane alchemy.

As a precaution, the bronze giant let the air out of one of the tires, using a clasp knife to puncture the inner tube. This precaution might or might not prove useful, but it was an example of the bronze man's foresightedness. Doc left little to chance.

Doc Savage drifted from shadow to shadow, keeping to the shadow-drenched side of the great coal-washing plant, slipping into it, but not employing his spring-generator flashlight, lest he betray his prowling presence.

The bronze giant gave a great deal of attention to the ground, seeking footprints and other telltale signs of recent visitors.

The distinctive tracks of Monk, Ham and Long Tom were plain to read. There was another set of footprints, which led away from the coupe, but took a meandering path. Doc studied these and, if one could conceivably read the bronze man's mind, he would have learned that Doc had deduced from the size and depth of the prints the owner's approximate size and weight.

He seemed on the point of following these unfamiliar footprints when his acute nostrils began twitching slightly. They had picked up an odor.

Doc traced this smell, and his progress paralleled the tracks left by his men to the mouth of the coal mine. He paused to listen, and heard no sound. The air smelled of freshly disturbed coal dust, which brought the briefest flickers of concern to the bronze giant's chilly eyes. For this was the scent that had aroused his concern.

Gliding into the yawning maw, he moved along the tunnel until he felt it prudent to turn on his flashlight, which illuminated the way.

Fifty yards in, Doc discovered the blockage of rough stone and broken timber. The atmosphere was choked with particles of disturbed coal. The bronze man quickly realized that there had been a calamity.

Lifting his voice, he called out, "Monk! Ham! Long Tom! Can you hear me?"

His voice echoed hollowly, but no response penetrated the plug of broken rock.

Doc Savage removed his coat, revealing his many-pocketed gadget vest, rolled up his sleeves and attacked the plug with his bare hands, after first setting his spring-generator flashlight on a slab of stone to illuminate the work.

The muscular strength of Doc Savage was prodigious. Few witnessed exactly how powerful his muscles could be. There were no witnesses now. Had there been any such observers, their jaws would have sagged comically, and their eyes protruded like finger-squeezed grapes.

Doc Savage wrapped his corded arms around a great boulder, pulled it back, flung it aside. The boulder probably weighed two hundred pounds. But Doc Savage handled it as though it fell short of fifty.

Metallic fingers dug in, yanked out smaller stones, pitching them backward. Doc was forced to pause and wind the spring-generator flashlight several times, which hampered his progress significantly.

The bronze colossus' strength seemed to be inexhaustible. Rocks flew. Boulders were yanked out of cavities, timbers hoisted free. It soon looked as if Doc Savage was poised to single-handedly break through.

A trickle of dirt and coal dust came down from the vaulted ceiling to spill onto one broad shoulder.

With flashing speed, Doc swept up the flashlight, gave it a twist, and examined the source of the leakage.

It was well that he did so. For high above, fissures showed, and from one crevice poured grit and dirt in a lazy but alarming trickle.

Came a kind of threatening rumble. Doc stepped back with alacrity.

He swept his flashlight about, examining the situation.

A stout timber, half buried in debris, showed a distinct bowing in its middle. Before his eyes, thick hairs of splinters were slowly popping free.

Doc moved to this weakening support, put his back to it, seeking to arrest its imminent collapse. As he leaned backward, he could feel bristling wood splinters bite into his back. The weight of the ceiling was slowly and inexorably buckling the ancient timber.

His broad back to the thing, the bronze giant moved his great hands around, searching for a means to avert disaster.

But this particular disaster proved beyond his power.

Doc sensed the approach of the breaking point before it happened. Whipping to one side, he scooped up his flashlight and sprinted for the entrance, knowing that it was the only recourse left to him.

The ceiling gave away. A giant coughing came next, expelling an ugly breath clogged with gas and grit. Doc Savage was out of the mine before the cloud of dust chased him into open air.

The final collapse consisted of a splintering, grinding, gnashing of timber and stone. It went on for perhaps half a minute, and was followed by the trickling of dirt and a clatter of settling stones.

Doc Savage donned a heavy-duty gas mask that had been stuffed in a coat pocket, gave the spring-generator flashlight fresh juice, and attempted to penetrate the mine.

When he reached the plug, it was more choked with debris than before. All his efforts had been for naught.

Once again, he lifted his voice in a great crashing cry. "Monk! Ham! Long Tom! Answer me!"

Doc tried several times, but received no encouragement that his associates still lived.

Reluctantly, the bronze giant picked his way back out to open air, and began a careful reconnoiter of the dismal old coal works. On his previous visits, he had sought other ways in and out, but had discovered none. Before, he had been pressed for time, but now the urgency of locating another means of egress consumed him.

During the course of his investigation, Doc Savage again picked up the trail of the meandering footprints that originated from the parked coupe.

Having no better trail to follow, Doc followed the licking light of his flashlight as they illuminated the earth-ridged impressions which swept around to the north side of the prominence forming the mine.

The area was messy with colluvium—a mixture of stony debris and sediment deposited by rainwash and what a geologist would call downslope creep. The tracks began to peter out. They came to a stop abruptly. Here the silty sheetwash gave way to rock and stone clutter, some of this rather flat.

Nothing stood out, so Doc knelt and searched for any indication of where the owner of the footprints might have vanished to.

Doc Savage was a fund of varied knowledge. Geology was but one of the studies he had mastered. He recognized the stones as the type that were common to this part of Illinois. But one of the flat stones was a segment of shale that the bronze man knew to be out of place. It seemed unremarkable except for its flatness.

His questing flashlight disclosed nothing out of the ordinary, but when Doc reached down, he discovered that the shale plate lifted up easily.

Below was a cavity large enough for a man, which showed indications of having been entered. The sides of the hole were ordinary soil, and some of this had sifted down, and in the middle of the mound, at the bottom, was a nearly perfect footprint.

It matched the print he had followed to this point.

Doc Savage squeezed his massive frame down the hole, dropping several feet, landing on the dirt pile, and directing his flashlight all about.

He found himself in a kind of natural tunnel, but there were signs of shoring—though not of the type involving heavy timber. Planks had been laid along the floor, end to end, to form a makeshift walkway. This passage was not a typical drift carved out to follow a coal ore seam, but a hidden entrance.

There was room enough for one man to walk single file, although Doc Savage's broad shoulders had difficulty avoiding the sides of the wall.

Illuminating the way ahead with his torch, Doc moved with great stealth, preferring to keep his presence unknown to any who might be lurking up ahead in the shadow-clotted darkness.

Where the occasional footprint was illuminated, it showed a lack of heel, indicating the the person passing this way did not wear a modern shoe.

Chapter XLIX

ENTOMBED!

MONK MAYFAIR, HAM BROOKS, and Long Tom
Roberts made their cautious way back into the forbidding
depths of the ancient coal mine. They crept carefully, for every
misstep dislodged rocky detritus, creating ghoulishly unnerving
echoes rebounding off the unsafe passage walls.

Long Tom had removed from a pocket his extra ram's horn
ammunition clip containing hypodermic needles. He was fitting
this into the clumsy-looking magnetic gun, which in its most
recent use had utterly failed him.

Eyeing this operation in his flashlight wash, Monk muttered,
"What good's that trick pistol gonna do you?"

Long Tom said sourly, "Maybe I can hit the thing in the
eyes."

"Good thinkin'!" admitted Monk. Turning to Ham, he asked,
"What kinda ammunition are you packin'?"

"Mercy bullets," whispered Ham. "That's all. And you?"

"I hadda leave my ammunition case back at the coal seam,
but I got an extra drum in my pocket. I'm just not sure what it
is, though."

Monk had holstered his supermachine pistol in order to
wield his flashlight, at the same time fishing around in his
pocket for the ammunition drum.

He paused, took his flashlight between his strong teeth,
withdrew the weapon and inserted the canister, locking it tight
with the lug nuts.

"Aren't you going to check on the ammunition?" demanded Ham, tight-voiced.

The homely chemist shrugged carelessly. "What's the point? It's all I got. It'll be a mighty big surprise if I have to uncork this thing."

They continued moving, Long Tom taking the lead. He seemed determined to demonstrate that his magnetic gun could finish off the prowling Medusa haunting the old coal works.

They stepped carefully, trying to avoid making any betraying sounds. Shifting shadows crawled along the crumbling walls, and a cold dread seized at their vitals, for they knew they were walking into the very den of their awful adversary.

Monk was muttering, "Do you suppose there really is a Medusa? One that lived in this mine?"

"Rubbish!" snapped Ham, contradicting his former opinion.

"Whatever it is," Long Tom admitted, "it doesn't act human."

They crept along, flashlight beams waving about like questing feelers of light.

It was perfectly natural that they would pay more attention to the passage ahead than what lay at their feet, and so it was that Long Tom, shoving ahead in the lead, failed to pay sufficient attention to where he stepped. As a consequence, he put one foot atop a board that was one of a group that lay athwart a drainage pit, which had escaped their notice before.

The board slipped, clattered, and before he knew it, Long Tom went tumbling down, his flash beam spinning madly.

"Long Tom!" howled Monk. He rushed up, drove his torch ray downward, and saw the puny electrical wizard sprawled in a litter of planking and mining debris at the pit bottom.

Long Tom's flashlight had fallen in such a way that it illuminated his stunned features. He looked up with an expression of dull incomprehension in his eyes.

Ham joined Monk, spiked his beam down as well and bleated, "Stunned!"

"At least he's not out cold!" grumbled Monk. "Hold my flashlight, shyster. I'm gonna need a lot of light. I'm climbin' down after him."

Without waiting for a response, Monk dropped from sight, grabbing hold of the crumbling rim of the pit with his hairy paws, held himself suspended for a few moments, and then let go.

The simian chemist landed next to the prostrate electrical wizard, scooped up his flashlight, and gave Long Tom a violent shaking with his other paw.

"Snap out of it, you clumsy runt!" Monk growled. "This ain't no time to fall down on the job."

Low moans escaped Long Tom's lips, and his eyes had a glazed look.

Seeing that the electrical expert was for the moment not himself, Monk gathered him up, threw his slender form over and across one burly shoulder, and began scrambling up the shaft, using the irregularities and rocky outcroppings to make his way back up.

Standing guard alone at the lip, Ham Brooks' anxious eyes naturally followed what transpired below in the pit eye.

No audible sound signaled the approach of the Medusa.

The dapper lawyer suddenly directed his gaze upward, sensed something, then heard the rhythmic rustling of a long garment. His flashlight jumped toward the stealthy sounds.

The beam was set wide, and it happened to fall upon the head of the thing. Ghastly apparition! The face was like a mask of unearthly flesh, thick and cold as marble. All around the hideous features varicolored serpents jerked and twisted, jaws distended.

But it was the eyes of the creature that made Ham Brooks emit a startled shriek. He later denied he had done any such thing. But in that awful instant, the horrid gaze of the Gorgon struck him with full force.

The thing recoiled from the brilliant beam, and in that moment of reaction, Ham lifted his supermachine pistol and depressed the trigger.

The compact superfirer commenced jittering, pouring smoking cartridges out of its fast-shuttling receiver. The marvelous mechanism was reduced to a busy blur. The roar, so reminiscent of a bullfiddle violin string being plucked and vibrating for long moments afterward, filled the entire tunnel passage like a moaning ghost.

The tattered gray garment that sheathed the two-legged apparition twitched and plucked madly, and the thing staggered back under the force of multiple mercy bullets striking it, dashing themselves apart, and releasing the potent chemical.

A hissing came from the lips of the gargoyle.

It held its hands at its side. These members resembled scale-covered snakeskin, angry fists squeezing spasmodically. Only in the bullet-stung twisting of the vipers surmounting its hideous head did the monster show that it was bothered by the slugs pummeling its chest.

Monk's voice cried out. "What's goin' on up there?"

"The Gorgon!" Ham yelled. "I just shot at it."

"Did you get it?" Monk yelled up.

"Yes, yes," Ham said. Then a pause. "No, it's still coming on."

"Dang it! Shoot at it again."

Ham did. But the ammunition drum had already been largely expended. A short hooting erupted from the supermachine pistol. A brief glimpse of sparks snapped from the weapon's spiked snout, but these were only tracer bullets mixed in with the mercies.

The Medusa did not even flinch this time. It only hissed. The hissing was loud and angry, and it could not be immediately understood if these ugly noises came from the open maw of the thing, or from its crown of fierce vipers, whose slit eyes gleamed in the strong light.

By this time, Monk had scrambled out of the pit. He lay Long Tom down as quickly and gently as he could, then spun about and unlimbered his supermachine pistol with the speed of an old-time Western gunfighter.

On the point of firing, Monk snarled, "Take this, you bug-eyed harpy!"

Eyes going wide, Ham howled, "Monk, wait! What if those are explosive bullets! You could kill us all!"

Monk hesitated, and before he could decide, the Medusa suddenly turned in a swirl of ragged skirts, and fled into the deeper passages of the mine.

In an amazed voice, Ham gasped, "It understood us. It understood what explosives are!"

Monk growled, "That means it's afraid. Good, let's hunt it down."

Ham demanded, "With what? You've only got one drum of ammunition and you don't even know what's in it."

"You still got your sword cane with you?"

The dapper elegant lawyer did. It was tucked under one arm. He holstered his pistol—which was now useless anyway—and drew the blade. Examining its needle-like tip, he saw that there was a brown substance coating the uppermost metal.

"I have enough anesthetic on the point of my blade to put an elephant to sleep," he declared. "But my mercy bullets didn't even bring the Medusa down. I am not certain this will be of much help."

Monk was down on one knee, slapping Long Tom boisterously about the face saying, "Wake up, Long Tom. We can't leave you behind in the shape you're in."

The dazed electrical wizard seemed to come around slowly. The glazed look in his pale eyes started to go away.

"What happened?" he blurted.

"Ham shot the Medusa with a full drum of mercies."

"Did it go down?"

"No," admitted Ham diffidently, "but it ran away. Under the circumstances, I am grateful."

Long Tom picked himself up, and Monk provided some long-armed assistance.

Looking about, the pallid electrical expert remarked, "In that case, I don't feel so bad about my magnetic gun."

"Never mind that!" snapped Ham. "We must run this creature to earth."

They advanced once more, moving rapidly, flashlights painting the crumbling tunnel walls, which were black with coal dust and grime, breathing in a controlled manner, for they full well understood that the supply of oxygen in their gas masks was rapidly diminishing.

Chapter L

THE DECAPITATED

DOC SAVAGE HAD traversed the tunnel leading into the bowels of the mine for more than fifteen minutes without encountering anything other than the occasional centipede flowing along on its multiple legs. The dank passage appeared to be without end.

After a short period, Doc extinguished his flashlight and extracted from his gadget vest a pair of goggles. Simple in construction, the lenses were designed to enable one to perceive otherwise-unseeable infra-red rays.

He disassembled the forward part of his flashlight, unscrewed the tiny bulb, and inserted another taken from a compartment back of the flashlight barrel. After he swapped bulbs, Doc thumbed the flashlight on. An observer would have sworn that no light issued forth.

The infra-rays were sufficient for the bronze giant to see through his special goggles, and he resumed his underground trek, guided by this eerie light that shed no shadows, for it could not be seen with the unaided eye.

So it was that the Medusa, feeling its way along the shaft up ahead, did not suspect the Herculean obstacle in its path that was Doc Savage, mighty Man of Bronze, until it blindly blundered into view.

Seen in the infra-red light, the living Gorgon was a garish and unreal apparition. Several of its hair serpents hung limp. A few were missing. This only added to the objectionable nature of the monster. Most of her snaky locks squirmed like earthworms in a bait can.

There was insufficient room for the bronze man to step aside, even if he had a mind to do so. While it was tempting to let the creature pass and follow it, and perhaps overcome it by seizing it by the throat from behind and exerting spinal pressure on its neck nerves, the narrow passage made that an impossibility.

So Doc Savage planted his feet, lifted terrible hands, and waited. The sway-skirted Medusa ran smack into him. It was rather like hitting a brick wall.

Hissing venomously, the human monster rebounded, slammed back onto its spine. The air came out of its lungs in a gusty rush.

Doc Savage leapt ahead, fell upon the grotesque thing. Seizing the throat by main strength, he lifted high, bringing the unlovely form entirely off the ground so that its sandaled feet kicked the air like a condemned man in the throes of being hanged.

The bronze man intoned, "It is over."

"Savage!" hissed the other, recognizing the metallic voice. And began kicking, but it was like kicking a stone. Doc Savage, who in repose sometimes looked uncannily like a statue of metal and not a human being formed of flesh and blood, was unmoved by the flailing feet.

The bronze man retained one grip on the thing's pulsing throat, shifted the other hand to the neck of the flowing robe it wore. With a violent tearing motion, the bronze man removed the upper part of the garment, revealing what appeared to be scales of iridescent serpent skin.

For Doc had seen the perforations on the chest of the Medusa; mixed in with them were the mashed blobs of mercy bullets which had penetrated the cloth, only to flatten harmlessly against protective scale.

"My men tried to bring you down, but failed," said Doc firmly. "Where are they?"

"Dead!" shrieked the Medusa. "Their living brains have been turned to inert matter. And now, that doom is yours!"

"This whole affair," stated Doc Savage, unmoved, "has been a build-up, a mass of trickery and intrigue. There is no such being as Medusa."

"Lies!" Scaly fingers reached into the garment, slipped to one side, and brought out an object. This was pitched wildly. It struck the ceiling.

The surviving serpents surmounting the Gorgon's skull suddenly fell still, and there came a glare of greenish light, followed by an eruption of oily smoke.

Doc Savage suddenly released the thing, retreating backward down the tunnel. He understood the awful significance of the green flare and the resulting vapor. The Gorgon's deadly glare!

Doc's retreat was not complete or utter. He got back as far as he could, reached into his vest, and brought out something that looked like an oversized marble. Had someone studied the thing, they would have found it consisted of two hollow compartments, each filled with a separate chemical solution.

The bronze giant flung the thing ahead of him. The thin-walled glass shell shattered, and the two chemicals combined in a violent reaction.

A hissing, sputtering resulted, illuminating the long passage.

As the Medusa stood poised, one hand about its injured throat, the other pointed long-nailed fingers in Doc Savage's direction.

"The doom of petrification is your fate! You cannot resist it."

Doc Savage advanced, walked boldly and unafraid through the roiling oily smoke, his dark-goggled eyes reflecting the sputtering light.

The Medusa was shaking its fist, saying. "Die, die, die—why won't you die?"

Doc had sealed his lips, and he was breathing through his nostrils in a normal fashion. If any smoke entered those nostrils, it seemed to have no outward effect.

Then, the bronze giant's lips parted slightly. From deep within him emerged the eerie trilling that was so evocative of faraway climes. This time, however, the tuneless melody sounded angry, vengeful, as if a swarm of ethereal bees had been roused to wrath. The trillation swelled in volume and barely-repressed rage.

The exhalation of breath which accompanied the phenomenon stirred the smoky cloud as it gathered around Doc Savage. It eddied, spreading out.

A serpentine tendril was drawn into one bronze nostril, to disappear like a vaporous serpent sliding into its burrow.

Suddenly, Doc raised one metallic hand, then the other lifted. The bronze giant acted for all the world like a man who had been caught by surprise.

Cabled hands going to his ears as if to block an unpleasant sound, Doc Savage seemed to stagger on his feet.

The Medusa crept forward cautiously, stepping around the spluttering magnesium eruption, lizard-green eyes alight.

"See! See!" hissed out the terrible voice. "You succumb! You are not impervious to my glare after all...."

Doc held himself rigid, as if fighting off a terrible influence he could not see.

Without warning, bronze fingers shifted from his ears, tore loose the goggles, exposing the metallic giant's natural eyes.

FASCINATED, the Gorgon saw the orbs of Doc Savage boring ahead, staring sightlessly, no longer twin flake-gold pools that were perpetually animated, but stony and opaque.

"What!" the Medusa exploded. "Impossible!" It seemed shocked that its power had not yet brought the bronze man low. Or possibly the sight of those stony orbs caused the hissing outburst.

The Medusa hesitated, apparently afraid to approach the fixed statue that was the Man of Bronze.

A commotion came from behind it. The bizarre figure turned, realizing Doc Savage's men were not far off.

Reaching into its garment, it drew another object, pitched it directly at Doc.

The bronze man shook off his fearful rigidity then. He threw himself to one side, simultaneously catching the thrown object and flung it over his shoulder. It flew quite a distance before rebounding off a bend in the tunnel, and vanished in a flare of sickly green light.

Picking up long skirts, the weird figure vaulted the bronze man's dodging form, seeking escape. It ran in the direction of the dying flare.

Doc Savage's powerful voice lifted in a crash of warning.

"Stop! If you flee in that direction, your destruction will be certain!"

"Medusa does not fear her own breath!" the weird voice hissed. Whipping around a turn in the passage, the thing vanished, ragged skirts swirling.

Almost immediately, Doc Savage shook off his seeming paralysis. Reclaiming his goggles, the bronze man raced toward his men, and called ahead, his infra-red flashlight once more in hand.

"Danger! Turn back!"

Monk's voice rolled anxiously down the tunnel. "Doc?"

"Go back! The vapor that causes brain-calcification is loose in this tunnel."

"What about you?"

"Chemical cartridge filters in my nostrils. Run!"

The commotion of men turning around quickly followed, and Doc Savage raced after that sound.

He soon came to the vertical shaft, and the wooden ladder, which he climbed, there being light there.

Monk, Ham, and Long Tom were hovering around the mouth of the pit when Doc Savage's head appeared. The bronze man climbed out with some difficulty, owing to the tight confines of the shaft.

"Seal this lid," Doc said flatly.

This was done, and they stood around, looking at one another.

Stripping off his goggles, Doc exposed stony orbs. They looked weird in the combined light of his men's flash rays.

"Doc!" cried out Ham. "Your eyes are—"

"Merely eye shells contrived to resemble stone," explained the bronze man, pocketing them. Doc often employed colored lenses to disguise his distinctive flake-gold eyes. These had been painted to mimic rock.

"What gives?" muttered Monk.

"It had been my plan to fool the Medusa into thinking that it had worked its magic upon me," Doc stated, "and so lure him into my grasp. Regrettably, your approach foiled that ruse. When a second gas bomb was thrown in my direction, I could not be certain that my chemically-treated nostril filters would continue to preserve my life and took appropriate steps. Regrettably, our foe has fled."

"I shot the thing," moaned Ham. "It wouldn't go down."

Long Tom added, "My needle bullets didn't even affect it."

"Chain mail armor beneath the cloth garment," explained Doc.

"Oh," said Ham and Long Tom in unison.

"That explains it," snorted Monk. "The harridan didn't seem human."

"The Medusa is human enough," advised Doc. "How is your oxygen supply?"

"Low and getting lower by the minute," admitted Ham. "And the way out is blocked. With that insidious brain-petrifying gas filling the escape tunnel, we are in a predicament."

"What about your ammunition?" asked the bronze man.

"I'm the only one with any left," said Monk. "I've got one drum, but I'm not even sure what's in it."

"This might," suggested Doc, "be the correct time to discover."

Monk yanked free the drum, examined it and grunted, "Looks like a mixture."

"Mixture of what?" asked the bronze man.

"Charlie horse rounds, scintillators, rock-salt slugs, probably some other stuff, like drying-agent bullets."

"Can you isolate the latter?"

"Sure, every slug has a different color dye on it for easy identification."

From a pocket, Doc Savage removed a heavy-duty gas mask, and said, "Each of you take turns with this while Monk works."

No one accepted the offered protection. Long Tom said, "I can still breathe. We better save that thing for when things get really tight."

Doc held onto the mask as Monk emptied out the assortment of bullets, and reloaded the drum with only drying-agent slugs.

"About twenty of these," the hairy chemist muttered.

"Let us hope it is sufficient for the job at hand," said Doc, taking the supermachine pistol.

Seizing the lid, he dropped down the ladder, rushed along the tunnel until he encountered the oily smoke. At this juncture, Doc donned his gas mask for extra protection, and opened up with the superfiring pistol, which shuttled and blared briefly, discharging its rounds.

The results were remarkable. The roiling oily smoke seemed to collapse in on itself, swiftly neutralized by the drying agent.

Doc called back, "It should be safe now. Follow me." The bronze man did not wait for his friends, but plunged ahead, bringing his infra-red flashlight to bear, the goggles which had been pushed up onto his forehead now back in place.

DOC SAVAGE raced perhaps one hundred yards when he encountered the obstructing form lying in the narrow tunnel.

It was the Medusa. The human monster had fallen on its face, and several of the colorful serpent locks had broken off. They were still. There was no blood.

Doc approached with caution, knelt, and carefully picked up one of the severed serpents.

This proved to be fashioned from segments of vulcanized rubber, and enameled in livid greens and reds. Feeling the ophidian thing, he discovered it was jointed. Giving it a shake caused the sinuous length to move in a lifelike fashion. But it had never been alive.

Doc was rolling the body over when Monk, Ham and Long Tom arrived, their flashlights blazing.

His goggles coming off now that they were no longer necessary, Doc Savage said, "As I feared would happen, the Medusa fell victim to his own deadly device."

To the astonishment of his men, Doc Savage wrenched at the hideous head of the thing. The scaly mass came away, showing it to be an artificial contrivance consisting of multiple jointed serpent heads affixed to an oversized mask that covered the entire cranium.

The face beneath was human. The craggy features were familiar to them all. They were still in death, and eyes that had stared unnervingly in life now glared glassily in death. As they watched, the dead man's eyes seemed to be retreating into his skull.

Ham was the first to speak the master brain's name. "Rockwell!"

Doc Savage was examining the helmet of the monstrosity that was fashioned to form the frozen-featured face of the Medusa of legend.

"What happened to him?" burst out Monk. "He was alive just a few minutes ago."

Doc Savage explained, "In exiting the mine, Dr. Rockwell encountered me in the tunnel, and attempted to inflict his petrifying smoke, not realizing I was wearing chemical nostril filters designed to prevent deadly vapors from infiltrating my sinus passages and thus my brain. Hearing that you men were approaching, and knowing what might transpire if you blundered into the cloud, I pretended to be stricken so that he would not turn on you, but flee past instead.

The bronze man regarded the dead man without expression. "It appears that in his haste to depart, Rockwell tripped and broke the protective mask that was designed to shield him from the combustible substance that produced the petrifying effect. He succumbed before he could climb back to his feet."

Monk suddenly looked peculiar. "Earlier, I dropped a rock on his skull. It mighta weakened the shell."

"Conceivably," said Doc. "I came upon an automobile parked a little ways off. No doubt it was Rockwell's machine, for it contained a doctor's valise. I disabled the coupe to prevent his escape, for it would have been preferable to take Rockwell alive and hear his story from his own lips."

"It was self-defense," Monk said quickly, knowing the bronze man's preference for capturing foes alive.

"No blame belongs to you, Monk," Doc told him. "Warner Rockwell was the cause of his own destruction."

"But Rockwell of all people?" Ham said wonderingly. "What possible motive could he harbor for all the slayings?"

"A motive as ancient as the legend of the Medusa herself," intoned Doc.

Everyone looked at him questioningly.

"Envy," said the bronze man. "Common green-eyed jealousy."

Doc passed the broken helmet to Monk, and he and Long Tom pored over it. The thing was ingeniously contrived, boasting vents for breathing that could be sealed by hand in order to make it temporarily airtight in order to block harmful fumes from penetrating. One of those vents had been jarred loose.

There were other features of interest.

"The snakes are pneumatic," Long Tom said. "I don't see how they operated, but somehow he forced air into them so that they squirmed as if alive."

Doc was back beside the body and pulled back one of the long white sleeves, revealing a rubber tube that ended in a bulb resting in the palm of the dead man's hand, which was covered by a scaled glove.

He explained, "A rubber bladder held in each hand. When squeezed forcibly, they produced sufficient air to pump the serpents so they seemed to writhe with sinuous life."

Monk grunted, "How about that? Rockwell turned out to be the third Gorgon."

"And you, you clumsy ape, turned into a modern Perseus," grumbled Long Tom.

Monk looked momentarily blank.

Doc explained, "Perseus was the Greek hero who slew the Gorgon Medusa by cutting off her head with a sword, rendering her forever harmless."

Ham groaned. "And Monk decapitated this modern monster by dumb luck—which is the only kind he ever has."

The homely chemist grinned his widest. "Guess this wraps everything up, don't it?"

Doc Savage stood up. His flake-gold eyes were bleak. "All except for the explanations."

Chapter LI

THE BRAIN BEHIND ALL

EXPLANATIONS HAD TO wait until Doc Savage formally surrendered himself to the Chicago City Police.

This was done after the bronze man landed his speed plane at the municipal airport. By this time, morning had chased away the darkness of night.

A contingent of police officials were waiting for him there, having been alerted by short-wave radio of the bronze man's impending arrival. As Doc Savage's attorney, Ham performed that duty, making all arrangements.

The Superintendent of Police personally did the honors. Doc Savage was not handcuffed, but he and his men were allowed to follow a convoy of official police vehicles. A curtained hearse took the body of Dr. Warner Rockwell to the morgue.

Doc Savage remained tight-lipped during the ride to police headquarters.

Doc was escorted to the Superintendent's private office, but he was neither fingerprinted nor formally arraigned. His men joined him there.

The Superintendent began the proceedings by declaring, "Based on what your attorney told me by radio, I am going to defer the decision on the disposition of your case, pending your full explanation."

Doc nodded. From an inner pocket, he removed the envelope containing Janet Falcon's final written testimony.

"This letter," he imparted, "tells Miss Falcon's side of the story. It is, as far as can be ascertained, entirely truthful. For reasons of her own, she had not always been so. Furthermore, there were many things she did not know."

The police official accepted the letter, and began reading silently. Behind him, the skies had clouded up and a light snow was falling. As he perused the pages, the flurry turned to sleet, which began pelting insistently at his window pane.

When the Superintendent was done, he said slowly, "According to this, the entire fantastic chain of events had its start in the Ryerson Coal Mine explosion down in Vermilion County a few years back."

Doc said, "Many perished, but none were fully autopsied. The actual cause of death was not discovered until mineralogist Ned Gamble, working with chemist Malcolm McLean, decided to open up the workings, to see if it could be restarted. During the course of that investigation, they discovered a hitherto-unknown form of amorphous carbon which was similar to coal in that it was highly combustible. Unlike coal, however, its fumes produced a peculiar effect upon the human brain when inhaled, essentially calcifying it upon contact. After performing tests on live animals, they dubbed the substance Gorgonite, inspired by the mythological sisters reputed to turn men to stone."

"This is fantastic!"

"Certainly," chimed in Ham Brooks. "But the fact that a brain-petrifying substance exists is not."

"No, it is not," the official said heavily. "Please continue."

Doc went on. "The two soon realized that the mine could never be reopened safely and began considering how to exploit the seam of Gorgonite. However, commercial applications of the strange substance did not present themselves. The pair went first to the inventor, Myer Sim who, while willing, was no great help. Sim, however, was friendly with both Marvin Lucian Linden and Dr. Warner Rockwell, who were separately consulted.

"While the original trio of conspirators—Rockwell, McLean and Linden—all knew one another, they had something in common they had previously not recognized. For one reason or another, all three were jealous of myself or one of my assistants. Linden, for example, had been working on an insect exterminator operating upon ultra-sonic principles similar to one pursued by my aide, Long Tom Roberts. Linden feared Long Tom would perfect his device before Linden's own could be finished. Dr. Rockwell had already discovered that a brain surgery technique he had been exploring had been achieved by myself. Malcolm McLean, although a chemist, suffered from an inferiority complex because he had never made a name for himself."

"Jealousy was the motive!" sputtered the Superintendent of Police.

Doc nodded. "When I last spoke with him, Dr. Rockwell put envy forward as an explanation for the actions of the other conspirators," stated Doc Savage firmly. "What he did not realize at the time was that I suspected him of being equally complicit."

"On what basis?"

"Initially, on his claim that he had restored Malcolm McLean to life after his brain had been calcified by the purported Medusa. When McLean's cousin Doane was stricken, Rockwell was the one who pronounced him dead, taking custody of the corpse, which he falsely certified was McLean. Furthermore, Doane McLean evinced symptoms no other victim of the Medusa had shown either before or since."

"What was that?"

"In addition to his brain having been petrified, his eyeballs had also taken on a stony aspect. This was a clever artifice designed to allay any suspicions that Malcolm McLean had, in truth, not been struck down by the mysterious force. The eye lenses were simply oyster shells ground down and fitted so that when the body was found, there would be no question that

Malcolm McLean was the victim. The reasons for this were clever: Rockwell needed to conceal something that might have given his subterfuge away. While the cousins both possessed gray eyes, their irises were not absolutely identical. In fact, the human eye is as individual as fingerprints—a fact that may prove useful to forensic science in the future."

The Superintendent of Police absorbed this explanation with a troubled brow. He did not offer further comment, so the bronze man went on with his narrative.

"Going back to the beginning," said Doc, "the conspirators planned a calculated reign of terror designed to elevate their status. At that point, only two were invited into the terror trust masquerading as a living Gorgon. Those were Dr. Warner Rockwell, the master brain, and Malcolm McLean. They initially approached Myer Sim, who turned them down flat. Sim confided in Ned Gamble, who became concerned that once Rockwell's grand scene was set into motion, Gamble himself would be implicated through his involvement with Malcolm McLean in the discovery of Gorgonite."

The police official tapped the letter on his desk, saying, "According to Miss Falcon, she was the one who sent her fiancé to New York."

"Although she knew about the discovery of Gorgonite and its terrible properties, Janet Falcon was unaware that the growing conspiracy focused on attempting to outdo the work of my associates and myself, but she had read of my work aiding those in trouble and, since Gamble was reticent to go to the authorities, he seized upon his fiancée's suggestion, and agreed that I should be immediately apprised. Gamble also feared for Myer Sim's life, since he was the only outsider with direct knowledge of the plot.

"By this point, Rockwell had already worked out his plan of action. McLean the chemist had invented a photosensitive process that allowed them to imprint the silhouette of the Medusa on the scenes of the killings, a process, incidentally, that had led to his unpleasant skin condition, since it involved experimenting with nitrate of silver. Marvin Lucian Linden had perfected a version of the photophone that could be used to transmit the Gorgon's voice to add to the atmosphere of impending horror, as well as becoming a terror device to warn off any threats."

The Superintendent rubbed the nape of his neck. "I see. Sim was slain to silence him, as was Gamble. But why was Janet Falcon spared?"

"Through a fluke," explained Doc. "McLean had developed an infatuation with Miss Falcon, and did not wish harm to come to her. Also, it was not definitely known to the conspirators if Myer Sim had confided in the woman in her capacity as his private secretary."

"But why did Miss Falcon hold back the truth?"

Ham Brooks answered that one. "In the beginning, because she received death threats if she talked. Later in the affair, she feared being charged with Duke Grogan's killing. She was a very frightened and confused young woman."

The police official cleared his throat. "Not so frightened that she couldn't gun down Grogan when she had the opportunity. But she needn't have worried. It was self-defense. So where does Duke Grogan fit into this?"

Doc replied to that. "Dr. Rockwell knew that if he were to institute a wave of brain-calcifying deaths, and then step forward as the one man in the world who could bring the victims back to life, he might need a scapegoat at some future point. Allying himself secretly with Duke Grogan but concealing his identity by masquerading as the Medusa figure, he enticed Grogan to slay Ned Gamble before the latter could divulge the truth. In that, Grogan succeeded and, after attempting to scare us off, returned to Chicago."

"So was Grogan one of the original Gorgons, or not?"

Doc shook his head. "Grogan was Rockwell's agent during the New York phase of the affair. He was armed with Gorgonite grenades and the means by which to imprint the frightful Medusa silhouettes at will, as well as a photophone apparatus to project his voice in warning. All of this was to build up an atmosphere of horror. This is conjecture, but it is likely that Dr. Rockwell plucked Duke Grogan out of the Chicago underworld because of the similarity of his last name to the Gorgons of legend. This would make it easier, when the time came, for the Medusa slayings to be pinned on Grogan and his gang."

"Which backfired when Janet Falcon shot Grogan down," suggested the official.

Strange lights played in Doc Savage's aureate orbs. "No one—least of all Warner Rockwell—could have anticipated that Miss Falcon would take the slaying of her fiancé so hard. She took to carrying a small-caliber automatic tied up in her hair for her personal safety and, when she fell into Grogan's clutches, she shot him down at her earliest opportunity."

The Superintendent slapped his palms on his desktop. "I might as well tell you that our ballistics boys confirmed that the bullets taken out of Duke Grogan's body match the gun discovered with Miss Falcon's body. So that part of it ties up in a nice neat bow."

Doc Savage continued, "It is not necessary to recount in detail the fact that Miss Falcon's suicide triggered Malcolm McLean's turning against Marvin Lucian Linden and then ending his own life when he realized that he had inadvertently brought about the chain of circumstances that led to the death of the woman he cared for very deeply." Doc's unusually vibrant voice grew dark. "I had hoped to coerce a confession out of McLean by convincing him of his responsibility for her death. I should have foreseen that he had become so distraught that he might also take his own life."

Ham Brooks broke in, saying, "I would like to state for the record that my client is not materially nor morally responsible for Malcolm McLean's unfortunate and unpreventable suicide. The man was criminally deranged."

"No one has suggested otherwise," returned the police official hastily. "What about that submarine car that was stolen from the exposition?"

"In plotting the reign of terror," Doc Savage related, "the three conspirators knew that they would need to cover their tracks. They had learned that Myer Sim had invented an amphibious machine that they believed might prove valuable as an escape vehicle should one of them need to disappear by water after doing evil. Malcolm McLean inveigled his cousin Doane to take his place at the exposition while McLean himself stole the vehicle. This had been arranged in advance so that McLean would not only have an alibi, which might normally be sufficient, but he would also become the first prominent Chicago victim of the Medusa, thereby ensuring that no criminal suspicion would attach itself to him."

"So how did this cousin come to be dumped at the coal mine impoundment, where you discovered his body?"

"The cousin was a pawn in a grisly game. Before Malcolm McLean abandoned the amphibious car after it became mired in the river mud, the decision had been made to do away with the cousin, lest he divulge the truth under police questioning. The body of the cousin was spirited out of Mercy Hospital and McLean took his place in order to make it appear that Dr. Rockwell had restored him to life. No doubt the Grogan gang transported the deceased dupe to the coal-slurry impoundment for secret disposal.

"It was McLean who was disguised as the Medusa when I first laid eyes on him in the abandoned coal mine three nights ago. In the aftermath of the collapse, McLean was able to escape via a hidden tunnel that allowed him to come and go at will in order to extract Gorgonite as needed. Apparently, this ingenious regalia had been used by each of the conspirators in turn whenever they were issuing orders to the Grogan gang."

The Superintendent interrupted with an objection. "I refuse to believe that a smooth operator like Duke Grogan would fall for such an preposterous disguise."

"It is doubtful that Grogan ever did," admitted Doc. "The cousin's corpse was left in the impoundment water on the theory it would never be discovered. But it was discovered. All credit for the identification of this body goes to the Chicago Police, who did the necessary work involved, and who learned that Doane had worked with McLean during the period the latter accidentally poisoned both men through careless experimenting with silver."

The Superintendent made an approving mouth. "You say that all this time McLean was moving about the city in disguise?"

Doc nodded. "This was done because the newspapers were eager to interview him, and he had work to do. Work that he wished to execute clandestinely, inasmuch as the Grogan gang were no more. There is little doubt that McLean was the one who delivered the coal containing a sample of the deadly Gorgonite to the home of Big Spots Bender. Doubtless McLean also planted the tobacco leaves that were laced with the lethal stuff that led to the deaths of Joe Shine and his attorney. This, incidentally, was part of Rockwell's devil's bargain with Duke Grogan.

"In return for the gangster's help, Rockwell promised to do away with his chief rival, Joe Shine, thereby paving the way for Grogan's eventual dominance of the Chicago underworld. Ironically, Grogan's unexpected death did not deter Malcolm McLean from going ahead and eliminating Shine, for it fit into their revised scheme to topple gangland crime figures as a ruse to point the finger of suspicion in my direction."

The Superintendent of Police gave a slight shudder as he reflected upon the number of corpses who had been discovered with their brains turned to stone.

"These malefactors may have been up to no good," he vouchsafed, "but they sure cleaned up the city's underworld. I'll give them that. The one thing I don't get is how Dr. Rockwell thought he could fool the city since he was only able to resurrect one dead man?"

"No doubt Rockwell planned to pretend to do the same with others, probably Marvin Lucian Linden, but my investigation caused him to panic. We may never learn who some of the original victims were going to be, but Rockwell and his cohorts found it prudent to kill off members of the Chicago underworld instead, as a kind of smokescreen against their true motives."

In his best lawyerly tone, Ham Brooks inserted, "This, of course, led to the development that caused suspicion to fall upon Doc Savage, who had only weeks ago been exonerated in the deaths of numerous members of the New York underworld."

The official shook his head in disbelief. "Damned clever, that Rockwell. He had us going, too."

"The scientific exposition, where so many men of science were gathered," said Doc, "must also have played a central part in the scheme. All the participants intended to show off their latest inventions. Since Rockwell slew Myer Sim, and thus set the stage for McLean to make off with his snorkel car, perhaps others would have succumbed to a similar fate, their inventions stolen from them, and the credit for those inventions reassigned to one of the conspirators. We may never know for certain, since events distracted the conspirators from their original plan. Doubtless the snorkel car would have one day resurfaced as the purported invention of Marvin Lucian Linden."

The Superintendent of Police began dry-washing his features. "Even after you explain it," he said slowly, "it's enough to make a man's head spin clear off his shoulders."

Monk Mayfair grunted, "That's about how I feel about it, too."

"Add me to that list," murmured Long Tom sourly.

Ham Brooks suddenly stood up and declared, "I take it that my client, having made these truthful representations to you, is now free to go."

The Superintendent of Police said, "I don't know how much of this can be proved in court, and I don't know how the hell we're going to explain this tangled mess to the army of reporters that are clamoring for your head, but Doc Savage, you have my parole and my admiration. Yes, you are free to go. No charges will be brought against you. The matter appears to be settled, except for burying the dead and ensuring the city that the terror trust of the three Gorgons has been shattered and broken."

DOC SAVAGE came to his feet and handshakes were offered all around. As a parting gesture, the official provided Doc Savage with a police escort to slip him out the back way, safely huddled in the rear of a windowless Black Maria.

The police machine took them directly to the airport, where Doc Savage reclaimed his speed plane. He and his men quickly got the great aircraft going.

"No sense in stickin' around this burg," said Monk. "We don't have to deal with pesky reporters' questions this way."

Long Tom said, "I never did get to demonstrate my magnetic gun at the exposition."

"You need to get some of the bugs worked out first," suggested Monk.

"Is that a dig?" snapped Long Tom. "First, that Marvin Lucian Linden steals my insect eliminator idea, and now you're making bug jokes."

Monk's grin collapsed, for he actually feared the ire of the puny electrical expert. When Long Tom got riled up, he would sometimes stay that way for days. The apish chemist had no interest in a prolonged disagreement. Long Tom could sock like nobody's business.

Ham Brooks inserted, "It seems to me that neither of you men proved your point. Long Tom's needle bullets did not faze the Medusa, but neither did Monk's ridiculous ammunition."

"Who are you calling ridiculous?" roared Monk, happy to change the subject and pick a fresh but familiar fight.

"I was referring to your absurd bullets, but you can take that label and paste it on your own forehead if you wish."

"My scintillator bullets made that Medusa retreat, and the drying agent ammunition sure came in handy, didn't it?"

"If any of those pellets had felled the enemy, you might be able to whistle a different tune," said Ham in a lofty tone. "I, for one, am not impressed."

The speed plane had turned out onto the tarmac at this point, and Doc Savage was blooping the motors as he lined up in preparation for take-off. The bronze man was anxious to leave Chicago and put behind him the bloody events of recent days. He was acutely aware, having been apprised by the Superintendent of Police, that the funerals of Ned Gamble and Janet Falcon were to be held later in the day. The distressing fact that the couple had sought the bronze man's assistance, only to perish in the course of his investigation, weighed heavily on Doc Savage's mind.

Soon the aircraft was bumping along, its tail lifted, and the yammering motors were clawing for altitude.

When Doc got the aircraft leveled off and pointed in an easterly direction, he said, "It does not appear that Long Tom's magnetic gun is yet suitable for our purposes."

Long Tom's face fell. "I'm going to keep working on it," he said tightly.

"As for Monk's ammunition," continued Doc, "some may have their uses. Possibly we can perfect even better versions for practical use, but for the foreseeable future, mercy bullets remain our best weapon for capturing criminals alive."

Monk made a face. He did not always agree with Doc Savage's policy of not taking human life, but a thought struck him.

"We kinda fell down on the capturing them alive part, didn't we? For a while there we had a whole pile of crooks to ship off to our crime college."

Ham nodded soberly, saying, "Once the Chicago Police took custody of Joe Shine's mob, we could hardly have laid claim to them."

Doc said, "This eventuality could not be helped. Given how matters worked out, it is unfortunate that so many perished, two by their own hand. We must endeavor to forget these tragic events, there being no present remedy for envy—or death, for that matter."

That seemed to be the last word, for the cabin fell silent and remained that way for much of the long trip back to New York City. Although many who had died could be said to have deserved it, several did not and the fact that they could not have saved Ned Gamble, who had come to their doorstep for assistance, nor his fiancée, Janet Falcon, was an unpleasant reminder that no matter how skilled they were, there were circumstances that were beyond their power to control.

It was a lesson they intended to carry into their future endeavors.

About the Author
LESTER DENT

LESTER DENT COULD be variously described as a westerner or a midwesterner, having been born in Missouri and raised in Wyoming and Oklahoma. A world traveler, he also lived in New York City, Miami, Florida and Paris, France, during his remarkable life, which ended where it began, in La Plata, Missouri, in 1959 at the relatively young age of 54.

He traveled to virtually every state in the union, which in his day consisted of just 48 contiguous states. Unquestionably, Lester visited Chicago more than once, since it was a stop on the old Santa Fe Railroad line he sometimes took to travel from his beloved La Plata home to the Street & Smith magazine editorial offices in New York City.

Although Lester set his Doc Savage novels all over the world, for some obscure reason he never saw the city of Chicago as a suitable locale for a major Doc exploit. Back in the 1940s, Lester was asked to lecture at the Chicago chapter of the Mystery Writers of America. Arriving late, he walked into the auditorium where a featured speaker was holding forth in his absence. When members of the audience noticed Dent, they stood up and burst into spontaneous applause, whereupon the speaker halted his talk, remarking, "I turn the podium over to the man you obviously came to hear." It was one of the highlights of the Missouri writer's life.

During the conference, Lester agreed to participate in a law-enforcement demonstration on how to defeat an armed assailant. Brandishing a .38-caliber revolver, the writer slipped around hotel corners until a Chicago police detective pounced, grabbing his arm and twisting it, deftly disarming Dent. A press photographer captured every step of the demonstration, and the dramatic shots subsequently appeared in newspapers and magazines nationwide.

Dent started writing pulp fiction in the late 1920s, when the Prohibition era was at its lawless bottom. Some of his earliest stories featured the classic underworld figures which remain semi-romantic well into the 21st Century. Only a few years along in Lester's writing career, those classic gangster figures became passé. But they live on in the popular culture, in pulp fiction and in this present novel, which was built from one of Lester Dent's unpublished gangster stories.

About the Author

WILL MURRAY

WILL MURRAY IS the author of more than 60 novels, including nearly 20 posthumous Doc Savage collaborations with Lester Dent under the name Kenneth Robeson, as well as 40 entries in the long-running Destroyer series. He has pitted the Man of Bronze against King Kong in *Skull Island* and teamed him up with The Shadow in *The Sinister Shadow*. His first Tarzan novel is titled *Return to Pal-ul-don*. His second is the forthcoming *King Kong vs. Tarzan*, a project first envisioned by film producer Merian C. Cooper back in 1935. Other Murray novels star Nick Fury, Agent of S.H.I.E.L.D., Mack Bolan and the Martians of the Mars Attacks! franchise.

For various anthologies, Murray has written the adventures of such classic characters as Superman, Batman, Wonder Woman, Spider-Man, Ant-Man, The Hulk, The Spider, The Avenger, The Green Hornet, Sherlock Holmes, Cthulhu, Herbert West, Honey West, The Secret 6, Sky Captain and Lee Falk's immortal Ghost Who Walks, The Phantom. He also contributed to the Planet of the Apes franchise and co-created Squirrel Girl for Marvel Comics.

Murray's non-fiction works include *The Duende History of The Shadow Magazine*, *The Assassin's Handbook*, AKA *Inside*

Sinanju, Wordslingers: An Epitaph for the Western and *Forever After: An Inspirational Story*. He has contributed to numerous encyclopedias and other reference works ranging from *The Dictionary of Literary Biography* to *Comics Through Time*.

For National Public Radio, he adapted *The Thousand-Headed Man* for *The Adventures of Doc Savage* dramatic series.

Will Murray grew up in and around Boston, and visited Chicago but once. That was to rush from O'Hare Airport to Union Station in order to catch an Amtrak Superchief train bound for La Plata, Missouri, home of Mrs. Lester Dent.

About the Artist
JOE DeVITO

JOE DeVITO WAS born on March 16, 1957, in New York City. He graduated with honors from Parsons School of Design in 1981 and continued his study of oil painting at the city's famed Art Students League.

Over the years, DeVito has painted many of the most recognizable Pop Culture and Pulp icons, including King Kong, Tarzan, Doc Savage, The Shadow, Superman, Batman, Wonder Woman, Spider-Man, *Mad* magazine's Alfred E. Neuman and various characters from World of Warcraft. Throughout, his illustrations have displayed an accent toward dinosaurs, Action Adventure, SF and Fantasy. He has illustrated hundreds of book and magazine covers, painted several notable posters and trading cards for the major comic book and gaming houses, and created concept and character design for the film and television industries.

In 3-D, DeVito sculpted the official 100th Anniversary statue of Tarzan of the Apes for the Edgar Rice Burroughs Estate, The Cooper Kong for the Merian C. Cooper Estate, Superman, Wonder Woman and Batman for Chronicle Books' Masterpiece Editions, several other notable Pop and Pulp characters, including a Doc Savage statue executed for Graphitti Designs, based on DeVito's own cover to Will Murray's *Python Isle*. Additional sculpting work ranges from scientifically accurate dino-

485

saurs, a multitude of collectibles for the Bradford Exchange in a variety of genres, to larger-than-life statues and the award trophy for the influential art annual *SPECTRUM*.

An avid writer, Joe is the creator of Skull Island and The Primordials. He is also the co-author (with Brad Strickland) of two novels, which DeVito illustrated as well. The first, *KONG: King of Skull Island* (DH Press), was published in 2004. The second book, Merian C. Cooper's *KING KONG*, was published by St. Martin's Griffin, in 2005. He has also contributed many essays and articles to such collected works as *Kong Unbound: The Cultural Impact, Pop-Mythos, and Scientific Plausibility of a Cinematic Legend* and "Do Android Artists Paint In Oils When They Dream?" in *Pixel or Paint: The Digital Divide-In Illustration Art*.

Of his *Glare of the Gorgon* painting, Joe notes:

> This image proved to be quite interesting in that it is the first close-up of Doc Savage I have painted for a front cover, and because of the concept itself, which is both symbolic and literal. At first, we entertained the idea of Doc standing against either a black or white background with the shadow of the Medusa falling over him. But that concept posed many problems, least of which was how to make the silhouette read properly and how to make it synch with the lighting on the classic Steve Holland pose we selected to work from.
>
> I had always liked the idea of a somewhat graphic image. It solved the issues of how to make a realistic shadow work with either the black or white backdrops. That iconic Day-Glo poster of Jimi Hendrix with the wild hair silhouetted against the green flames on a fuchsia background from the 1960s immediately popped into my head. For those of you who had one of those ubiquitous black lights that caused everything to turn blue in their room—and made the Day-Glo colors wildly fluoresce—you know exactly what I am referring to. That Hendrix poster was *the* poster for that particular visual experience.
>
> I could not get the image of using the outline of the Medusa's snake-haired head as a graphic backdrop for Doc out of

my mind. I chose a simple black background to echo that first *Man of Bronze* James Bama painting, since this pose is from that vintage photo shoot (which, coincidentally, I believe occurred around the same time that Jimi Hendrix poster came out). I also thought black was far better than white in conveying the desired mood. This approach worked well overall, but when the image was reduced, the green glow I put in Doc's eye was not obvious enough to tie the image together and tell the story. The composition needed more. So after some discussion it was decided to add the Gorgon's hand, and show Doc's shirt slowly turning to stone to clearly get the point across. Suddenly, the image took on an unusual synthesis of the reality of Doc Savage, scaly hand and the stone shirt, with the symbolic halo of writhing green snakes behind Doc's head. Combined, this made for a powerfully graphic, traditional yet uniquely satisfying Doc Savage cover.

Everything had come full circle. When finally discovered by the viewer, this gives the original hook—the glow in the eye—exponentially more power: Now that Doc's gaze has been caught, and his shirt has begun the transformation, can he resist, or will the Man of Bronze become one more victim of the Glare of the Gorgon?

I may have stated this before—if so, forgive me—but is this stuff fun or what?

www.jdevito.com
www.kongskullisland.com
FB: Joe DeVito-DeVito Artworks

About the Patron

DAVE SMITH

LIKE MOST ADOLES-CENT boys of the 1960s, Dave Smith was into comic books. Even before the 1966 *Batman* TV show aired, Dave had already filled his young mind with reruns of the old George Reeves *Superman* TV show. He began reading comics in the late 1950s and has been on the hunt ever since. He lived only a few blocks from downtown Anaheim and would ride his bike to his favorite drugstore selling the latest comics. Then in the late '60s, he stumbled upon Doc Savage and the awesome James Bama art that initially attracted him to the Bantam reprint books. Dave remembers starting with *The Man of Bronze* (you have to start with #1, don't you?) which engrained the origin story deep in his psyche. He still recalls reading *Brand of the Werewolf* and *Resurrection Day* early on. The paperbacks' copyright dates led him to discover the actual pulp magazines from which they originated.

Dave remembers the day when a used bookstore opened up in downtown Anaheim. He peered into the front window for the first time and saw on a pegboard display some old comic books. These weren't just old, they were really old, like from when his dad was young—titles such as *Superman* #14 (January,

1942), *Green Hornet* #23 (March, 1945), *America's Best* #14
(June, 1945) and many others. This new bookstore was The
Book Sail and would be a life-changing place for this young
boy. Dave started hanging around and learned all he could from
the owner, who taught him about not just old comics, but pulp
magazines and rare books. The first pulp magazines he ever saw
were a run of *Amazing Stories* back to #1. Eventually, he was
hired in 1969 to work for the store at age 14.

Dave also remembers his first hunt for a *Doc Savage* pulp
magazine. He had heard about this one particular story called
Up From Earth's Center where Doc goes to Hell... well, maybe.
That sounded intriguing to him and he started searching for
that issue. Dave eventually discovered an outstanding copy at
a comic book convention in Anaheim, CA. In retrospect, it's
interesting that the first *Doc Savage* pulp he ever bought turned
out to be the final issue of the run.

Dave learned all he could about the history of comics and
pulps, as well as all the characters and authors who started out
in the pulps. He educated himself about the various artists and
why some were more desirable than others. He also absorbed
the traditions of being a book dealer and made many connec-
tions. He learned the art of negotiation, buying wholesale, and
how to meet the needs of customers. He enjoyed speaking with
collectors and helping them find what they were looking for.
Sounds simple, right? Finding those last few pulps to finish a
collection for a customer is not easy, but it's one of the more
satisfying parts of the job for Dave. Finding scarce and rare
items for people has become a very important part of the business even to this day and it's almost as much a thrill as filling
in holes in his own collection.

Dave worked for The Book Sail on and off from 1969 to
1978, then opened his own comics store in Garden Grove, CA,
in 1979. Fantasy Illustrated went from a 500 square foot store-
front a mile and a half south of Disneyland to an 800 square
foot unit, allowing him to create a pulp section. Dave remembers one of his first big buys was a beautiful run of early *Docs*.

He kept the really high grade *Red Skull* because of the striking cover and he still has that pulp to this day. Alas, most of the rest of the run was sold to pay bills and living expenses. Ah! The bitter world of being a collector-dealer.

In 1992, Denver-based Mile High Comics wanted a piece of the Disneyland area comic book action and approached Dave about buying his store. A deal was struck that allowed Dave to keep certain items in the store, including the pulp section. He then helped manage their Anaheim Mega-Store of more than 10,000 square feet of comics and pop culture items. After his 18 month contract was up, Dave moved to Seattle in late 1994 and purchased Rocket Comics while keeping the Fantasy Illustrated name for his mail order business.

Over the years, Dave has published 30 mail order catalogues in the Comic, Pulp and Paperback fields, publishing his last one in 1999. That was about the time he switched to selling on eBay as the source of most of his mail order business. That last catalogue Dave recalls fondly as the one that introduced the Yakima Pulp Pedigree collection to many pulp collectors.

A while later, he met his future wife, Kelli. She was an attorney becoming burned out as a public defender. She wanted to get into another area of law, but didn't quite know how to go about starting her own office. Since Dave knew how to run a business and had been self-employed most of his adult life, they worked out a plan to open up their own law office. Dave went back to college and earned an advanced Paralegal certificate. A month after his 2005 graduation, they opened a law office. Today Dave works part time as a paralegal and office manager but the rest of the time buys and sells for Fantasy Illustrated. But it's clear Dave doesn't look at it as work. When you're passionate about something, it really isn't work, is it?

Currently, Dave spends a copious amount of his time buying and selling pulp magazines. In his spare time, he is a writer on the subject of pulps and also sharing what he has learned in the decades of running his own businesses. He has written for *Blood 'N' Thunder* and also publishes his own fanzine: "Dave's Clubhouse" for PEAPS (Pulp Era Amateur Press Society). After decades of collecting, dealing and chasing down all kinds of pulps both for himself and his customers, Dave now owns two complete sets of the *Doc Savage* pulps: a personal set he has been working on and upgrading for decades and one for sale or trade. What a great life!

www.fantasyillustrated.net

WORDSLINGERS

AN EPITAPH FOR THE WESTERN

WILL MURRAY

Will Murray's Wordslingers is not only the first in-depth history of the Western pulps, it's one of the best and most important books on the pulps ever written, perfectly capturing the era, the magazines, and the writers, editors, and agents who helped fill their pages. Pulp fans will be fascinated by the rich background provided by hundreds of quotes from the people involved in producing the Western pulps, while writers will benefit from the discussions of characterization and storytelling that prove to be both universal and timeless.

—*James Reasoner*

$29.95 softcover
$39.95 hardcover
$8.99 ebook

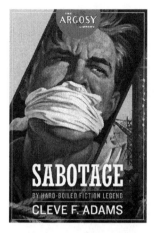

SABOTAGE
BY HARD-BOILED FICTION LEGEND
CLEVE F. ADAMS

CHAMPION OF LOST CAUSES
MAX BRAND

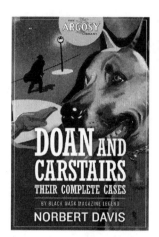

DOAN AND CARSTAIRS
THEIR COMPLETE CASES
BY BLACK MASK MAGAZINE LEGEND
NORBERT DAVIS

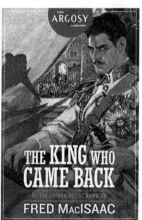

THE KING WHO CAME BACK
BY THE AUTHOR OF THE RAMBLER
FRED MacISAAC

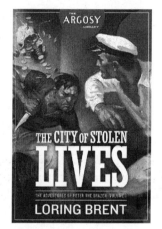

THE CITY OF STOLEN LIVES
THE ADVENTURES OF PETER THE BRAZEN, VOLUME 1
LORING BRENT

THE RADIO GUN-RUNNERS
BY SCIENCE FICTION LEGEND
RALPH MILNE FARLEY

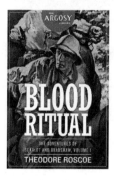

BLOOD RITUAL
THE ADVENTURES OF SCARLET AND BRADSHAW, VOLUME 1
THEODORE ROSCOE

THE SCARLET BLADE
THE RAKEHELLY ADVENTURES OF CLEVE AND D'ENTREVILLE, VOLUME 1
MURRAY R. MONTGOMERY

SEMI DUAL
THE COMPLETE CABALISTIC CASES OF
THE OCCULT DETECTOR, VOLUME 2: 1912–13
J.U. GIESY AND JUNIUS B. SMITH

SOUTH OF FIFTY-THREE
BY THE AUTHOR OF THE TORCH
JACK BECHDOLT

the

ARGOSY

library

™

SERIES 2 INCLUDES:

* BRAND * BRENT * ADAMS *
* MacISAAC * ROSCOE *
* GIESY & SMITH *
* BECHDOLDT *
* MONTGOMERY *
* FARLEY *
* DAVIS *

THE BEST FICTION
FROM THE FRANK
A. MUNSEY LINE

THE ALL-NEW *WILD* ADVENTURES OF
DOC SAVAGE

Doc Savage:
The Desert Demons

Doc Savage:
Horror in Gold

Doc Savage:
The Infernal Buddha

Doc Savage:
The Forgotten Realm

Doc Savage:
Death's Dark Domain

Doc Savage:
Skull Island

DOC SAVAGE

LIMITED EDITION FINE ART PRINTS!

WWW.JDEVITO.COM

83948095R00284

Made in the USA
San Bernardino, CA
01 August 2018